Saving Lord Whitton's Daughter

WHAT PEOPLE ARE SAYING ABOUT
SAVING LORD WHITTON'S DAUGHTER

As a rule I avoid romance novels because of their formulaic, predictable plots. This book is anything but. With a delicious, tingly, unpredictable love affair and suspenseful mystery, *Saving Lord Whitton's Daughter* surpasses the genre as much more than a mere romance novel.
—Tamara Hart Heiner, author— the *Perilous* series and others

Susan weaves a beautiful story with characters so real, so full of life and love, you feel as if you are right there in the Regency era. The breathtaking, raw attraction between Bethany and Lord Locke, mixed with the threat of danger and the dark mystery of the past, creates a page-turner sure to keep you up into the late hours of the night. I highly recommend this book!
—Jessica Cole—Reader

Loved it. Beautifully written and engaging from the very start. Loved the spunk of Lady Bethany. This isn't your typical love story, so I loved it even more. I didn't want to put this amazing adventure down.
—Cindy M. Hogan—Best Selling Author—The *Watched Trilogy*, the *Christy Spy Novels*, the *Code of Silence* Series, and others.

If you like romance novels, you will love *Saving Lord Whitton's Daughter.* I loved the author's use of words. They are so descriptive and they fit the era written about in the book. I had a hard time putting it down to fix dinner or even to go to bed.
—Lynne Dawson—Reader

"The author has woven this thrilling historical novel with all my favorite elements: intrigue, mystery, danger, and of course, heart-stopping romance."
—Rebecca Rode—Author of the *Numbers Game* Saga and others.

"Wow. Loved it. Just the kind of Regency Romance I like."
—Pam Mason—Reader

Saving Lord Whitton's Daughter

A Regency Romance Novel

Susan Tietjen

Sunbright Press

Crescent City, CA

Susan Tietjen/ Sunbright Press
Crescent City, CA

Publisher's Note: This is a work of fiction. Names, characters, places, and incidents are a product of the author's imagination. Locales and public names are sometimes used for atmospheric purposes. Any resemblance to actual people, living or dead, or to businesses, companies, events, institutions, or locales is completely coincidental.

Saving Lord Whitton's Daughter/Susan Tietjen. -- 1st ed.

ISBN 978-0-9904892-1-4

LCCN: 2016907314

This book is first dedicated to my mother, who was ever the believer in my father and in true love.

Second, it is dedicated to those who believe in protecting the defenseless, and in risking everything they have and are for those they love.

Susan

"'Tis better to have loved and lost than never to have loved at all."

Alfred Lord Tennyson

CHAPTER 1

The Whitton Country Estate, Kent County, England
June 12, 1814

The day was far too beautiful to be one of the worst in Lady Bethany Montgomery's life, but it seemed destiny had sealed her fate. Her riding boots felt leaden as she forced herself up the front steps to the manor and through the open doorway.

Over her shoulder, Bethany took one last glance at extraordinarily clear, blue skies and the lush meadowlands of her late father's Kent estate. With no male heirs, Whitton now belonged to her mother and would pass to Bethany if anything was left to inherit, although she had little faith in the prospect, especially after this morning's ordeal. Then the butler closed the door behind her, cutting her off from escape.

"Lady Whitton awaits you in the study, my lady," the butler said, his seamed face as close to expressive as she'd ever seen it. Sad, he was. And for good reason.

His demeanor meant the few servants remaining at Whitton knew what had happened that morning. They also knew the scolding she was about to receive—and what it would mean to all of them.

"Thank you, Mr. Drew." She relinquished her quirt, riding hat and gloves to the man. "Lady Camille is due here in a quarter of an hour. Please make her comfortable in the morning room when she arrives."

Mr. Drew gave a half-nod, but he avoided her gaze, suggesting her mother, Lady Katherine, had given him instructions that would override her request. She sighed, wanting to believe matters couldn't get any worse than they already were.

Steeling her nerves for the inevitable, she strode down the hallway to the study's door.

Before she could grasp the knob, the door flew open. She stepped back, surprised to see her twin cousins staring back at her. Neither of the young men's identical sets of gray eyes or handsome faces was lit by their usual devil-may-care grins. Without a word, Lord Matthew pushed his way into the hall, herding her ahead of him, a finger to his lips. Mr. Nicolas, his younger brother by a mere seven minutes, pulled the door shut behind them and together the threesome stepped lightly to the other end of the hall, where they could talk.

"You heard what happened, I suppose?" she whispered.

"We were here when Scarbreigh returned to the manor," Lord Matthew replied.

Bethany winced. "I'm so sorry. I didn't deal with him well, but—"

"No you didn't," Mr. Nicolas interjected. "Refusing marriage is one thing, Lady Bethany. Punching the Marquess of Scarbreigh in the nose is quite another."

Reddening in embarrassment, she said, "But he … he tried to kiss me. I realize he meant no ill will. We all grew up with Scarbreigh and love him dearly. But he's impetuous to a fault, and he caught me by surprise. You know that that never bodes well for me. And … and you know why." She searched their countenances for some scrap of compassion.

They at least sighed their concession.

"And I recognize our esteemed Kirkwood Bannister often presumes too much," Mr. Nicolas acknowledged. "Perhaps he deserved it. But his offer was sincere, you know, and would have saved you and your mother from ruin."

Bethany made an unladylike face. "Certainly it would. I couldn't have hoped for better. His friendship. His financial standing. His title. He even offered to allow me to maintain possession of the Whitton estate. But you and Lady Camille understand why I feel the way I do about marriage. Let Mum think I avoid the *beau monde* because I'm determined to find love and have failed at it. I care deeply about the estate's financial affairs, but under the circumstances I've no right to marry, even if I could bear the demands of a husband—and I couldn't. It would be unfair to both of us and a nightmare for me." &

Lord Matthew said, "Hmmm. But Scarbreigh is Scarbreigh. He's an old, treasured friend. He'd not only never hurt you, but if he understood the circumstances, he'd probably be most compassionate about it. Perhaps if you'd let us explain it to him—"

"No!" Bethany hissed. "You promised not to discuss it with anyone. If word ever got out—" She paused, the very thought leaving her winded. "Besides, I cannot love Scarbreigh. Not *that* way. He's too much like a brother."

She caught the quick look that passed between her cousins and her fences went up. Were they just testing her resolve? Did they not want her to marry Scarbreigh after all?

Mr. Nicolas said, "We're most sympathetic, Bethany, but what about Aunt Katherine? Your mother will suffer the consequences of your decision, too."

"I understand that all too well," she murmured. And prayed daily that things weren't as dire as she feared.

2

Mr. Nicolas shrugged. "In truth, we're not in favor of Scarbreigh's suit. Just wanted to make sure you've no regrets about refusing him. Lady Camille agrees with us. Scarbreigh really isn't suitable for you."

Bethany harrumphed at this statement. "Your sister wants the Marquess of Scarbreigh for herself. Has for a long time, if you hadn't noticed. And she's welcome to him if you want my opinion."

Mr. Matthew sighed. "Right. Well, then we're off, Lady Bethany. We'll catch Lady Camille on the way, take her home with us and leave you to talk to Lady Katherine. I appreciate your reservations and until now have supported them. But please be advised Mr. Bradbury left your mother not ten minutes ago. He didn't come here with either good news or *alone*. I—we—must warn you serious things are afoot and hope you'll consider some advice."

Bethany swallowed her anxiety. The estate's solicitor rarely brought good tidings.

Lord Matthew rested a gentle hand on her shoulder. "I love that you've endured the trials you've had without losing your faith, Lady Bethany. It proves that you know you can trust in the Almighty. That he won't fail you. So please open your mind to what Aunt Katherine has to tell you. It's important. It won't be easy, but some good might come of it, if you allow it. Send for us if you need us."

Then they left her in the shadowy hall that had once been decorated with precious trappings, paintings, and sconces. The majority were gone now, sold off to pay the estate's expenses. Naught but a miracle could replace them.

Gathering her courage, Bethany returned to the study, twisted the doorknob and stepped inside. That courage wilted, however, when she set eyes on her fair-haired mother. Pacing the room, the Dowager Lady Whitton's usually lovely Grecian features were drawn into unbecoming lines of worry. At the sound of Bethany's entrance she came up short, pale blue eyes widening.

"Lady Bethany!" she intoned, hastening to collect Bethany's hands in her own. "Thank you for coming from the stables so quickly. We haven't much time to talk."

Bethany followed her mother to the sofa and sat beside her, apprehension constricting her chest.

"Well," the dowager countess said, straightening her skirts nervously. "I heard what happened this morning, and I must say, my dear, that you do find extraordinary ways to discourage suitors."

Had Lady Camille said such a thing, Bethany would have laughed, but the worry lines and exhaustion on her mother's face meant she'd intended no jest.

3

"I'm sorry, Mum. Lord Scarbreigh admitted he asked your permission for my hand yesterday. If you'd forewarned me I'd have told you it wouldn't work. I—I'm simply not, well, attracted to him. He's far too impetuous, and a gossipmonger, and he's more like an annoying brother than were my own brothers."

Lady Katherine winced at such candidness. Forcing her fingers to stop pinching her skirts, she sighed. "I understand. I love the boy, but I've always imagined you needed a stronger hand."

"Well, I don't want a schoolmaster for a husband, either, Mum."

"I understand that, too, daughter. You've never tolerated restraint well. Lord Whitton was unduly lax with you, and look what good it's done us. Yet despite your unconventional ways, you've received two offers of marriage in the two months since we stepped out of mourning—three if you count today. All three gentlemen were rich enough to set our circumstances right for the rest of our lives. You, however, took none of them seriously. And don't recount their many flaws, please. I'm tired of hearing them. There are no perfect people in the world."

"That doesn't justify wedding someone entirely inappropriate. You and father—"

"Undertook an arranged marriage like most in our class."

"But you loved him," Bethany said, beginning to feel desperate. She'd run out of excuses and none of them mattered except the truth, to which her mother wasn't privy.

"I'd hardly seen your father before the offer came. Neither of us wanted the marriage."

"But you—"

"Were fortunate, but we also determined to make the best of it. I adored your father, and he'd have laid down his life for me. Nevertheless, we grew to love each other, Beth. Which takes time and patience."

"And risk. What if it hadn't worked?"

"As I stated, we were committed to make the best of it. And so must you."

Bethany felt her cheeks pale at the realization of what she meant. It was one thing to imagine the end of one's freedom. It was something else to look it in the face.

"I've tried, Mum, I really have. I just need more time—"

"*Time?* There is none. Are you determined not to face the truth? I told you in February that Whitton's reserves had grown dangerously low. In case you've forgotten, it's the twelfth day of June. If you'd wanted the prerogative to say yea or nay regarding whom you married, you should have taken it more seriously long ago."

More seriously? She'd taken all of the proposals more seriously than offers of death. And still she couldn't force herself to accept any of them.

Lady Katherine sighed and came to her feet, and despite the warmth of the day, Bethany felt icy dread spread from her cheeks to the rest of her frame. Shuddering, she looked towards the fireplace, presently empty, as had been most of the fireplaces all winter and into spring. This room, one of the smallest on the ground floor, was easiest to keep comfortable and, unable to provide wood for most of the other chambers, they'd spent the bulk of their days here. That thought, and the despair on her mother's face, made Bethany again swallow hard.

"Mr. Bradbury delivered the gravest of news today, my darling. Two weeks ago and again last week he warned me that our funds are near exhaustion. As of today, he has recommended letting everyone but the most necessary servants go—"

Bethany's jaw dropped. "You can't," she declared. "We can't manage an entire estate without help."

Lady Katherine stared at Bethany as if she were daft. "I wasn't finished with what I was telling you. We cannot manage it at all. Whitton is set to go up for auction this weekend—"

"No! It mustn't!"

"Unless...."

The word hung in the air, a momentary reprieve laced with barbs. Bethany blinked back the tears stinging her eyes.

"Unless what?" she dared ask.

"Mr. Bradbury arrived with a gentleman this morning, one who was disappointed to hear Lord Scarbreigh had requested permission to address you first. In all honesty, I told him I expected exactly what happened and encouraged his patience."

Shock overwhelmed Bethany. Hot, miasmic, it rose from her toes to her throat, choking her. "You've accepted this man's offer, haven't you? How could you? Especially when you'd already consented to Scarbreigh's proposal."

"I hadn't. I told Scarbreigh he was welcome to try but expected you'd refuse him. And if you must know, he reported the entire incident in detail, with a kerchief pressed to his bloodied nostril."

"Oh, Mum." Bethany bowed her head in embarrassment. "He tried to kiss me against my will. I—I overreacted, but it was inappropriate of him."

Lady Katherine laughed dryly. "I hardly think telling you he cares for you and will provide well for you all the days of your life, then offering you a kiss qualifies as forced affection. You had a chaperone with you; Jason would have intervened if he'd seen a problem. Still, it's over. We

5

can't change it. I've accepted the offer presented this morning, and you'll have no choice. Unless you wish us both turned out."

"Why can Lord Hannaford not take over the estate? My uncle's a good man, a kind one, and surely your sister doesn't wish us to starve."

"We've discussed this before." Lady Katherine's cheeks reddened in mild anger. "Your father's fortune—and therefore his capacity for debt—have always been greater than my brother-in-law's. Lord Hannaford would need to sell Whitton, too, along with your beloved horses, to pay those debts. My sister would give us a place in Hannaford's Dower House, if it came to it, but with her health so poor, we cannot place that burden on Lord Glen's shoulders."

Bethany spun around, throwing caution to the wind. "Why can't you remarry, Mum? You're a beautiful woman. You're fond of the pomp of the nobility—"

"Stop." Lady Katherine's order, quiet but terse, left Bethany gaping. She gripped Bethany's hands tight. "Choices do not exist without consequences. You must marry now, while Whitton's properties, even as entailed as they are, offer us some small advantage. Once it's gone, that advantage is lost. I understand you and your spirit, Bethany. That's why I'm giving you the last word in this, but not until you've met this gentleman. I'm barely acquainted with him, but the twins are his good friends, and Mr. Bradbury says he's one of the most respected, sought-after bachelors in England. He's also remained one of the least available. He prefers his country estates, as you prefer ours, and makes only rare appearances at London's soirées.

"Meet him. Hear his offer. Judge him for yourself. But please remember that while I'll give you the very thing other English parents would not give, the right to accept or reject him, should you refuse, we'll lose our home by week's end."

It felt as if her lifeblood had suddenly drained out of her. Whitton would be gone? Along with her precious horses? She couldn't let that happen. But how could she go through with this?

"Who is he?" she heard herself say.

"Lord Marcus Ashburn, the Earl of Locke. He has three estates here in Kent alone, and who knows how many others. His favored estate is Moorewood, just a few hours' drive northeast of Whitton."

The Earl of Locke? Bethany recoiled. His name sounded as forbidding as Newgate Prison.

"What sort of man is he?"

"I've little acquaintance with him, although Mr. Bradbury and the twins speak highly of him. It seems your brothers knew him as well.

Having the opportunity to meet him while you were engaged in bloodying Lord Scarbreigh's nose, I must say that he's at the very least impressive."

"Impressive? Does that mean he's as old as dust and as big as a barn?"

Lady Katherine pressed her lips together in annoyance. "No, dear. He's quite—" She paused. "I'll say no more. You'll meet him for yourself."

Bethany shrank inside. "When?"

"Now."

"Now? What do you mean now?"

"I mean he's waiting in the morning room and wants audience with you immediately. He has an appointment at noon and insisted I not even bother with sending you upstairs to wash up and change clothes. Mr. Drew has refreshments for us, and we mustn't keep the earl waiting any longer."

The countess scrutinized Bethany, sighing in exasperation. "Here, let me at least brush the dust off the hem of your riding habit."

Bethany had to bite her tongue. Bits of dust gathered from riding was a terrible thing? What would this Lord Locke think of her in a tunic and men's breeches? She'd spent most of her growing-up years sneaking off in them; it was easier to ride that way. She'd fought with her mother more than once over that and over other conventions she thought absurd. When to smile, when to avoid laughter. The use of titles even among family members, and proper clothing for a multitude of occasions. She didn't mind, for instance, wearing gloves for riding and at formal affairs, but fashion did not dictate that she wear them in her own home and she disliked her mother requiring it. She smiled at the irony that her mother hadn't time to force her into them now. But as for this Lord Locke, he ought to be glad Bethany at least had on one of her best riding habits.

Part of Bethany wanted the man to dislike her, so that he'd leave her alone, but panic seized her at the realization that if he declined, Whitton—and her horses—would go to auction in six days' time.

"Your hair is as independent as its owner," Lady Katherine muttered, pulling the combs from curls the same dark brown as Lord Whitton's had been. The countess's fingers tugged painfully at the tangles and pinned those curls into place, pinched Bethany's cheeks to heighten their color and grabbed her shoulders to remind her to square them.

"It will have to do," she muttered. "Now come. Meet your intended."

Bethany imagined a funeral dirge accompanying them to the entryway and the wide, double doors that guarded the morning room. Mr. Drew stood there, his expression wooden. He opened the doors and announced them to the occupant standing at the empty fireplace with his back to them.

The gentleman turned round to greet Lady Whitton when she approached, and bowed over her offered hand. Then his gaze shifted towards Bethany, who stood barely inside the room, as motionless and stiff as Mr. Drew.

That gaze, a rich, dark blue, pulled Bethany's feet loose from the floor and lured her to him. Bethany had never seen such irresistible eyes. The earl stood a good head taller than her, his bearing relaxed but dignified. Near-black hair, a firm jaw, a straight, slender nose. Her bold inspection of him seemed to amuse him, his handsome smile framed by deep dimples—bookend parentheses—on either side of a full, engaging mouth.

Bethany heard her mother say, "I'm sorry we've kept you waiting, my lord. Lady Bethany had no idea you were here, of course."

"I don't mind, Lady Whitton," the man replied in a rich baritone, those eyes twinkling. Then he added, "It's not every day a man chooses a bride, and if she's the right woman, she's worth waiting for."

Bethany paused at this baffling declaration, her heart flipping thrice in her chest. The man was gorgeous; he was engaging; he was far too kind. Which made her mind up for her, of course. She could not risk her heart with this man. No matter what, she could not marry him.

CHAPTER 2

When the dowager countess introduced them, Bethany told herself not to accept Lord Locke's hand, but she couldn't help it. As she couldn't help the way his kiss on her fingertips sent tingles racing up her arm to her chest. As she couldn't withhold the gracious curtsy that came automatically, her gaze fastened to his.

Those eyes skimmed over her, taking in her wardrobe and her figure. She blushed, not because his appraisal offended her, but because, despite her best efforts, she wanted him to like what he saw. In truth, he did it subtly and with honest appreciation. He couldn't, she imagined, be as impressed with her as she was with him. How could a man of his distinction even consider a girl like her? Despite wearing less than an earl's courtly finery, he was magnificent, from his starched white shirt and lavish neck cloth to his broad-shouldered brown riding jacket, from his ivory riding breeches that hugged well-muscled thighs, to his shining hessians. In short, he was grace and dignity itself.

"Thank you for meeting with me on such short notice, Lady Bethany," the earl said, leading her to the balcony table, already set with tea and scones. "I hold your family in high regard and am pleased that you're willing to contemplate my offer."

Bethany took the seat he held for her, convinced he surely knew little about her or he wouldn't consider marrying her. "You flatter me, my lord," she murmured. "I apologize for knowing nothing about you or your family."

Her mother shot her an irritated look, but Locke flashed another heart-melting smile, one that Bethany struggled to steel herself against. She'd learned young that attractive men were every bit as capable as less attractive ones of hiding black hearts, especially men with riches and power.

With a nod from Lady Katherine, Bethany poured their glasses of tea while Mr. Drew delivered the scones and jam to their plates. Lady Katherine dismissed the butler, leaving Bethany grateful for her mother's light chatter in the midst of tinkling crystal, silver, and china as they ate.

"I knew your brothers, Lady Bethany," Lord Locke said after finishing his scone and taking a sip of his drink. "You were lucky to have them. I'm an only child."

Bethany swallowed hard at the mention of her brothers. At eight years Bethany's senior, if Lord Christian were alive today he'd have recently enjoyed his twenty-seventh birthday. And Mr. Collin? He'd have turned twenty-four next month, just a year younger than Lord Matthew and Mr. Nicolas.

"I've upset you."

Bethany was sure her cheeks had paled. "No. I'm just—"

"Sad. I apologize for the painful reminder. It's been better than a year now, hasn't it."

It wasn't a question, merely a point of reference.

"Fourteen months," she murmured. Only a year ago April.

"And a most unfortunate set of circumstances."

Bethany still couldn't fathom the improbability of a mere two days separating Mr. Collin's demise in Portugal and the random carriage accident in Belgium that took the lives of her father and oldest brother. She could understand Mr. Collin's death. As a younger son, he'd chosen in 1812 to take up his commission and go to war against the French. As an officer and a gentleman he should have been kept well out of harm's way, but he'd perished in an unexpected skirmish in early April of last year.

Lord Whitton and Lord Christian's loss, however, was different. Lord Christian had fallen in love with one Lady Elizabeth Leclercq, the daughter of an English noblewoman and Lord Leclercq, a Belgian viscount. After more than a year's resistance to the match, the viscount had finally invited Lord Christian and her father to his home in Bruges, in late March of last year, to consider an arrangement. Mr. Collin seemed safe enough in Portugal and the risk to Lord Whitton and his heir negligible.

Notifications of their deaths had changed Bethany's life forever.

Lord Locke examined her with care. "You miss them greatly."

"Yes, of course. I adored my father. Mr. Collin was my co-conspirator in adventure, but Lord Christian was a second father to me. I suppose because he was so much older."

The earl allowed himself to look amused. "Oh dear, I think that doesn't bode well for me. He and I were of the same age. Does that trouble you, my lady?"

"At least you're not doddering, like Sir Bixley."

"Lady Bethany!" Lady Katherine hissed.

"Baron Bixley?" The earl queried, fighting a grin.

"Yes," Bethany replied. "He's eighty if not a hundred, and he was sure that I wouldn't hesitate to welcome his suit because I'd taken no one else's."

"I presume you refused him." He sipped casually at his tea, his eyes sparkling with amusement.

"Obviously, my lord."

"Obviously. Well, I'm glad you don't find me doddering."

"On the contrary. You're quite ... well, attractive." Even Bethany couldn't believe she'd dared say it and wasn't surprised when Lady Katherine mewed "Good heavens," pulled her fan from the cuff of her sleeve and applied it liberally.

Lord Locke chuckled. "I've heard you can be rather plain spoken."

"Not always. And I don't mean to offend people. I simply see nothing wrong with telling the truth."

"It's a flattering truth," he replied. Then his smile faded and he glanced at his empty plate. "I knew your father as well as I knew your brothers. Lord Whitton was one of the finest men I've ever met. And I believe you're aware I'm also friends with Lord Matthew and Mr. Nicholas. Lord Christian introduced me to all of them while we attended Eton.

"I believe you and I have at least one thing in common, my lady. You share my reservations regarding London society. Your brothers and the twins made attending to my duties as close to enjoyable as is possible."

Lady Katherine lowered her fan and narrowed her eyes at him. "My sons mentioned you upon occasion. If I remember correctly, the Incomparables hold you in the highest regard. In fact, if I may risk being bold as well, the sole criticism I've ever heard is that, similar to my daughter, you've avoided marriage as if it might poison you."

Lord Locke pressed his serviette to his lips before laughing quietly. Clearing his throat, he collected himself and offered a polite nod. "As, indeed, I've always thought it could. Bachelorhood has suited me well. I've a great deal of responsibility, little time, and no patience with the machinations of the *beau monde*. I also consider it unfair to inflict a woman with the discomforts of extended travel, but I'd feel guilty for leaving her behind as frequently or for as long as I must when I visit the Continent. "

"Particularly there," Lady Katherine said. "There's still danger over there and significant rumblings about Napoleon and his scheming to escape Elba. Do you take it seriously?"

The earl paused a moment before answering, "I'm of the opinion we'd be foolish not to."

"Hmmm. I agree." The countess nodded.

Bethany scrutinized Lord Locke, her mind racing from one consideration to another. Her mother recognized him, knew at least something of him, and he'd been good friends with her father, brothers and cousins. How could she have never met him? Or had she?

As if sensing her thoughts, Locke said, "It's been a while since we last met, Lady Bethany. At Almack's, a year ago April, in fact."

Bethany froze at mention of that night.

"Last year?" Lady Katherine interjected, frowning. "I can't remember you there, although it was an absolute crush that night. Lady Eva Camerfield—the Countess of Hannaford—is my sister, you know. She's troubled with ill health and not up to London's rigors. The twins' sister, Lady Camille, came with Lady Bethany and me that night. I confess the crowd made it difficult to keep my eye on them."

"I'm acquainted with Lady Hannaford's unfortunate indispositions," Lord Locke said, his gaze still fastened on Bethany. "But I've seen little of Lady Camille since she was small and doubt she would remember me."

Bethany's pulse began to race. "I don't, either," she said.

"The visit that night was brief, my lady. I wouldn't expect you to recall it. A friend of yours, Lady Jessica Trent, introduced us. Then a group of young ladies dragged me off to play a game of piquet. If I'd spent more time with you, perhaps danced with you, you might have remembered me, but alas, I did not."

At mention of Lady Jessica, the night in question suddenly unfolded in Bethany's mind, sending apprehension racing over her. She'd done everything she could to not remember anything about that evening; it was no wonder she had no recollection of the earl, until now. Lord Locke was even more devastatingly handsome today than he was then. Lady Jessica was head-over-heels in love with him, despite her disappointment that the man was so *old*. Bethany had laughed at Lady Jessica's opinion. They were eighteen at the time, and Bethany was approached by more than one gentleman twice Lord Locke's age. In comparison Locke didn't seem at all old.

The minute Lady Jessica introduced the earl, Bethany realized she'd never met a gentleman to whom she was more attracted. She also disregarded him as a suitor almost immediately. Besides not showing her any particular favor, he was old enough she didn't believe he'd take *her* seriously. Beyond that, she couldn't imagine a man of the Earl of Locke's caliber remaining unattached without good reason. Was he penniless? A determined bachelor with less than honorable connections to the opposite gender? Did he perhaps not care for women? Bethany hadn't given that thought more than a second's pause. There was something about him that suggested he was merely resistant to feminine wiles.

Lady Jessica's family knew the earl's, and the girl quickly reassured her that Lord Locke was not only well-heeled, he was no hell-rake, either.

Fascinated but sure he was out of reach, Bethany simply dismissed him from her mind.

"It's been long since we met, my lord. Why now?"

Lord Locke regarded her a moment and then to Lady Whitton said, "I hope you won't consider it forward of *me*, my lady, but I'd like to speak with Lady Bethany in private. Marriage is a complicated affair, as you know, and I'd prefer to hear her, uh, unhampered feelings before we proceed."

"Oh." Lady Katherine straightened, her gaze darting back and forth between them. "Oh, well, certainly. Would you care to walk in the gardens? I'll send our housekeeper, Hetty, to chaperone."

"Excellent," the earl replied, rising to his full height and offering Bethany his hand.

Bethany's breath nearly deserted her again as he pulled her to her feet, her heart hammering in her chest. Everything that had seemed perfectly normal that morning abruptly felt threatening, even Mr. Drew making his silent appearance to let them outside. How Lord Locke found the way to the gardens she had no idea, yet they were suddenly walking through them. Hetty trailed the couple, a distant shadow draped in servant's attire.

"The gardens are lovely," the earl remarked, what seemed eons of silence later. "Patterned after those of Capability Brown."

"They are," Bethany managed to reply. Her father had gone through half a dozen gardeners before he'd found Seamus, a man who understood the work of England's most respected garden architect. "I've been told they're outdated, but I love them."

"As do I. I'll leave them this way, if you want."

She shot him a frown. "Why would you do that? For me, I mean?"

His grin turned her knees weak. Charming dimples. Twinkling eyes. So gorgeous. She dared not let them persuade her. She still couldn't see her way to marrying this man, despite the consequences of refusing him.

"As part of the marriage contract, you understand Lord Whitton's estate shall become mine. I want it put to rights, and I've no opposition to making my wife happy with how it's done."

Bethany didn't know what to say. He wanted to make her happy? Why? He didn't even know her. She'd love the gardens restored to their original glory, but she'd have to accept the man's proposal for that to happen. Her mind told her she had no choice; she refused to surrender.

"Your cousins gave me sound advice which I plan to heed," he said. "I agree that you're very like your father. Charmingly candid. I liked that about Lord Whitton. He was a wonderful friend, more than I told your mother, and a mentor to me, my lady. And Lord Christian and Mr. Collin were, truly, my dearest friends. Please trust me when I tell you their deaths devastated me."

The sadness on his face told her that he meant it. The thought made her sad for him, too.

"It's a pity to see Lord Whitton's estate failing. Mr. Bradbury explained that following your father's death some of his investments went sour because of the war, which no one could have predicted. His Lordship would be overwrought if he knew the hardship it's caused you and your mother. I owe him recompense for kindnesses he showed me over the years, but the best I can do is to assume the care of what he cherished far more than his country. His home and his family." He gave her a small grin. "Unfortunately, while I can purchase Whitton, I cannot buy you or Lady Whitton. That would not be at all proper."

Bethany smiled at his light jest, but marriage seemed an excessive way to "repay" a man who was dead.

"Please take a seat, my dear?" The earl pointed towards a bench huddled within an ornate arbor. It was one of Bethany's favorite places to meditate. She went to sit, but as he handed her onto the bench, the cuff of his jacket caught on a link of the charm bracelet that encircled her right wrist.

She gasped. "Oh, dear, please don't break it."

"Here, let me help," he said, extricating it for her and sending warm tingles flashing through her at his touch. "Lovely piece," he commented, pausing to appreciate it.

"Thank you," Bethany said, admiring it with reverence. "My father gave it to me. Every charm has a personal message written on it. This one reminds me to sit tall in the saddle. That one tells me to settle for nothing but the best."

"You must treasure it." He stroked the bracelet into place, and it disconcerted her that that hand persisted in tingling even when he let it go—and that she liked it. She wished she'd worn her gloves after all.

"I do. It's the last gift he'll ever give me. I rarely wear it and certainly not when I ride. I donned it for church this morning before learning I had to meet with Lord Scarbreigh instead. I overlooked it when I changed clothes. Sometimes I hate its reminder that Father and my brothers are gone; at others, I'm terrified I'll lose it."

"Life is full of uncertainties, is it not? They're harder still when you've no say concerning them, like death. Unlike marriage, over which we may have some choices."

Bethany frowned at the suggestion, puzzled by the concern written on his elegant features. Was he worried that she'd spurn him? What an odd notion. He didn't know her, after all, and beyond the livestock and the land itself, he'd inherit little from Lord Whitton's estates beyond debt and hungry mouths to feed.

The earl sighed and shifted on the bench. "I've a tale to share that is rather involved, Lady Bethany. Your mother wouldn't approve, but for the sake of brevity I shall speak as straightforward as you'll allow me. And some of it, including what I can offer you and what I cannot, must remain between us."

Curiosity mingled with apprehension. "Certainly, my lord. I'd prefer not mincing around and am not given to repeating what others say." Of course, she didn't actually care what this man told her since she would allow it no bearing on her decision. Truthfully he most likely deserved more than she could ever give him, and she couldn't bear the thought of how her "secret" would offend him if he knew. She must at least remain as aloof from him as possible, even if she couldn't refuse his offer.

"Excellent. Then in short, you must undo the work of a thief, play the part of a mediator, refurbish a home that has grown embarrassingly outdated, and undertake the daunting task of becoming a wife solely for the sake of appearances."

Bethany blinked at him, this much brevity rendering her completely baffled. "A thief, my lord?"

The earl nodded. "I employ stewards at each of my properties to manage the daily details. Unfortunately Moorewood's steward of four years absconded with some of the manor's costliest trimmings and an impressive amount of furnishings, equipment and supplies."

"He just up and stole them?"

"Yes. And the scoundrel also lined his pockets with money from the estate's funds, first by fleecing my tenants and then purloining the funds from necessary repairs he left undone."

"How reprehensible!"

"Indeed. It lost me the trust of my tenants. To restore it, you'll have the support of Moorewood's servants and also the counsel of my solicitor with significant decisions. The tenants need someone to hear and quickly resolve their complaints, and ongoing reassurance that I did not condone Geoffrey Matheson's fraud."

Bethany's eyes widened in disbelief. "And you consider me capable of mending fences with your tenants and winning their loyalty? I'm not quite twenty years old, my lord, and I've no idea how to run an estate."

"You shan't run it, at least not in entirety; simply make peace with people ill-used. I have faith in you or I wouldn't be here. Keep in mind my relationship with your father and brothers, and also the twins. I know their opinion of your self-assuredness in matters that often lie in a man's domain. Your tenacity at facing green colts one day and attending a formal ball the next. Your defense of Whitton's tenants where needed. And as to the renovations, your mother can advise you, and likewise Lady Camille, if you wish. Her brothers say she has a natural flair with decorating. No, I have no qualms regarding your ability to transform my ancestral estate into the home of your dreams."

For a moment Bethany entertained visions of leaking roofs, cracked stone walls, and crumbling floors, crawling with bugs and rats. Then Whitton's manor flashed through her mind, merely wanting tender care, and she felt pleasure at the notion of achieving such a lofty goal with the Earl of Locke's home.

"I'm convinced you'd enjoy the project," Locke murmured, watching her closely. "I'm equally convinced you'll love the estate. On another subject we are of like mind, I believe. Many admired Lord Whitton's stud. He bred some of the finest horses in England. I look forward to assimilating Whitton's animals into my own breeding program and carrying on his work at Moorewood. I understand you've a great passion for horses, too, and that your father gave you a number of them."

"Gave them to me?" she bridled. "Father made me work hard for them, schooling me to ride better than most gentlemen, and then teaching me how to train them, too."

The earl chuckled in amusement. "I confess I heard him speak highly of you, Lady Bethany. I paid little attention to it then. You weren't more than a schoolgirl and my best friends' little sister. Lord Matthew and Mr. Nicolas, however, claim you're quite gifted."

Her cousins weren't ones for flattery, and the compliment warmed Bethany's cheeks.

"Your animals are beyond welcome at Moorewood, and if you're anywhere near as talented as I've heard, you're welcome to my horses as well."

Flattery became shock. Did he mean it? But there was still the matter of becoming his wife. Bethany's stomach twisted in fear at the full ramifications of it. Again his keen gaze seemed to dissect her thoughts.

"Perhaps your thorniest undertaking would be providing the appearance of a wife. As I professed earlier, I am a confirmed bachelor and a private man. I truly travel a great deal and have thus avoided the encumbrances of a wife. Unfortunately the longer I remain unattached, the more pressure the *beau monde* applies. I'm sick of being chased by desperate females, which shall not end until I marry."

"Which means you'll give them what they want. You will marry."

He chuckled and nodded. "But to whom I choose. And most women would expect everything attendant with marriage, which is where our arrangement must differ." His smile faded and he drew his pocket watch from his waistcoat and examined it fixedly. "Ah, our time draws short." He replaced the watch and met her eyes again. "This would likely offend Lady Whitton. If you feel likewise, then I understand, and I'll withdraw the proposal in entirety."

Bethany nodded with caution.

"I understand you, too, have preferred not to marry. Your reasons are yours and I reassure you that I respect them. As for me, I firmly believe a father should assist in raising his children, and if he cannot, he shouldn't have them. I'm fond of children, but I'm gone too much, and for that reason, I don't want them. I've a female cousin with three fine boys, and the oldest knows he's in line to inherit if something happened to me—and you. This is a simple contractual arrangement, Lady Bethany. Should you marry me, you must serve as a wife in name only."

"My lord?" Had she heard him rightly?

"It's imperative you agree, however, to do all you can to convince the *ton* we're happily matched. It will put an end to the gossip I utterly detest and the schemers who hound me. In return, you'll have everything I've offered you. Support for your mother. Repair for Whitton. A home at Moorewood. More horses than you can manage. And the comforts and distinction of being my countess all the days of your life."

The proposition rendered Bethany speechless, the realities of it leaving her feeling torn. First, came the most incredible sense of relief at knowing the earl wouldn't force her into his bed. Then, in a momentary flash of insight, she not only grasped the barrenness of the life she had considered her lot for the last fourteen months, she also recognized the thread of hope that had somehow buried itself deep inside her. That perhaps she would one day have what most women wanted. Could she truly stand a *lifetime* of never becoming a mother? Never know what it was like to love or to be loved by a man?

Never know how it would feel to be loved by this man?

She'd barely given these thoughts wings, wondering how she dared entertain them, when horrible images sprang into her mind, an evil darkness that twisted her stomach into knots. Panic surged through her. She snapped her eyes shut to stave off the recollections and the terror that came with them, the recognition that a man had the power to offer a woman great pleasure or terrible grief. She was grateful she did not remember some of that evil and hoped she never would. I can't ever give a man an heir, she scolded herself. Not if his touch always terrifies me this way. Not if it means Lord Locke would discover the truth about me.

Locke's brows furrowed slightly when she met his gaze again but he did not press her. She forced her heart and respirations to calm. The people in her life, those she loved and trusted most, apparently had faith in this man. Stubbornness reminded her that she'd determined from the first sight of him not to marry him. But such a peculiar arrangement would allow her to keep her secret to herself. She couldn't hope for better, not with only days left to losing Whitton. The pieces came together, and she suddenly found herself convinced enough to take the risk.

Cautiously she said, "I—I do think we'd work well together."

His inviting mouth curled with humor. "Then all that's left are the formalities," he replied. "Shall I go down on bended knee?"

Bethany pressed her eyes shut and swallowed hard. "I would die of mortification."

"As would my tailor," he responded, making her laugh. "Very well, then. Lady Bethany Montgomery, daughter of the late John Montgomery, Earl of Whitton, will you do me the honor of accepting my hand in marriage?"

"Oh, my," Bethany murmured. "I never imagined it would be like this."

"Have you reconsidered? I don't mind kneeling."

"No. No, of course not. I mean it's quite, well, overwhelming. But I ... I accept."

Lord Locke's visage brightened with pleasure. "I'm delighted, Lady Bethany. I do not think you'll be disappointed. Now, shall we visit your esteemed mother and give her the good news?"

CHAPTER 3

Bethany was moved by her mother's reaction when she and Lord Locke returned to announce the outcome of their discussion—minus the intimate details, of course. Hope shone brightly in Lady Katherine's pale blue eyes, along with the tears of relief she fought to control.

Obviously pressed for time, Lord Locke asked Mr. Drew to send for his horse straightaway, but while he waited, he assured Lady Katherine that she could not only keep Whitton's remaining servants, she could rehire any that had been dismissed over the last year if she wished.

"I've rooms at the White Hart Inn in Maidstone and plan to meet with your solicitor there this afternoon, to apprise him of the engagement and to make arrangements for the funds for your immediate needs. He will then meet with us here tomorrow morning to finalize the contract. Ten o'clock, if you will."

Lady Katherine's hands fluttered in nervousness. "My lord, you needn't live in leased quarters. We've ample room, and if you'd consider relocating here, it would make the arrangements more convenient."

"I would dislike being a burden," he replied. "I'll plan visits as needed."

Mr. Drew announced the arrival of Locke's horse, and Bethany and her mother trailed the earl onto the front porch. Considering his determination, Bethany couldn't help wondering if Locke had more than one reason for hurrying off. She had no doubt her mother would love the privilege of having the Earl of Locke as her guest, and Bethany thought it wise to become acquainted with him, but perhaps he did not feel the same.

"My lord, forgive me," she said. "We obviously haven't the luxuries to which you're likely accustomed, but we've never shirked our friends and visitors, despite our lessened circumstances. I cannot imagine any inn in Maidstone, of which there are few, could prove more comfortable." She paused but before Locke could reply added, "Considering one of your goals in our marriage is to keep the *beau monde* at arm's length, wouldn't spending time with me help foster the idea that our relationship is amicable?"

Bethany could see her mother disapproved of her outburst. One did not speak to a *non-pareil* this way; but she felt justified when Lord Locke's neck reddened just above his collar and he shifted in discomfort.

"I do sincerely apologize, Ladies. I meant no offense. You make a good point, Lady Bethany. I truly do not wish to burden you, but I can certainly offset any inconvenience I might cause. I will transfer here tomorrow."

His dark blue eyes reflected his sincerity as he added, "I'd already arranged to have foodstuffs and goods sent to you tonight anyway, if Lady Bethany accepted my offer, but I'll be bringing my carriage and horses, my driver and my valet, which will increase the strain on your provisions. To compensate, I will have more than I'd planned sent tonight and regularly thereafter until you again have a full larder."

"We are honored, my lord," Lady Katherine said.

Jason, the gangly old stable master who'd cared for Whitton's horses since before Christian was born, met the threesome in the manor's front drive, holding the head of a magnificent dun stallion. The animal grumbled a greeting and nibbled at Lord Locke's offered hand, closing his eyes when the earl scratched his throat latch. The beast might as well have been a statue he stood so perfectly still and well-mannered while Lord Locke climbed into the saddle. Bethany felt herself falling in love with the animal more surely than she thought she could ever fall for a man. Especially as puzzling a man as this one.

Lord Locke patted the stallion's shoulder. "You like him."

"He's dazzling," Bethany admitted.

"Bred and raised at Moorewood. Don't know of a more faithful servant, not even among the human variety. My father named the poor fellow Polyphemus. I call him Polly."

"Hello, Polly," Bethany mewed, letting the stallion sniff her hand and then her cheek. She so dearly loved the spicy scent of a horse's hide, almost a dusty cinnamon smell, and was sure no more elegant creature graced the earth. "You are a gorgeous lad," she said, and when the stallion grumbled at her and nodded his head, she laughed and patted his sleek shoulder. "I'm glad you agree."

Lord Locke gave Bethany a wry smile as he gathered the four reins from the animal's Pelham bit between his fingers. After setting them precisely, he nodded goodbye and touched a leg to the horse's side. Instantly Polly wheeled around and leaped into a rocking horse canter down the drive towards Maidstone.

"He is, at the least, impressive, is he not?" Lady Katherine said, squeezing Bethany's hand.

"At least." Bethany smiled, watching horse and rider go, admiring the man but unsure she was supposed to like him. Remembering the horse farm he described at Moorewood, however, she could at least console herself with the thought that if the other horses the earl owned were even half as good as Polly, she would be in heaven.

* * *

Marcus Ashburn enjoyed the feel of Polly's collected gait, along with the warm breeze and the sea-green meadow's splendor. Whitton's lands and livestock were excellent, despite the estate's insolvency.

Lord Matthew and Mr. Nicolas would be beyond ecstatic when they met with him later this afternoon to discuss his success with Lady Bethany.

His smile vanished, however, when he ruminated deeper about the future Lady Locke. He'd visited Whitton many times over the years, almost always when Lady Whitton was in London and Lady Bethany either off riding horses or climbing trees. He barely remembered the girl from their meeting at Almack's last year, and although she was extraordinarily beautiful then, she'd seemed too young to take seriously. He might never have met her again if not for the twins.

Lord Matthew and Mr. Nicolas had come to him several weeks ago in a panic. It had shocked him to learn of Whitton's financial ruin, but not nearly so much as their having uncovered a credible threat to Lady Bethany's life. They'd begged for help with protecting her, a more difficult request than he could have imagined. Besides needing to keep her unaware of the diplomatic connections Lord Whitton and Lord Christian had entertained, she must be spared the obligations of a typical arranged marriage. Short of explaining why, Lord Matthew alluded to her inordinately independent nature, while Mr. Nicolas hinted she had difficulty trusting men.

The three of them had tossed more than one idea about but none that worked. Then Mr. Nicolas pointed out that Lady Bethany shunned marriage as much as he did, and what if Locke could take her under his wing? Offer her a marriage in name only?

The proposal took root and was about to become a reality. A marriage of convenience. A woman who wanted as little from him as he would from her. It would leave him as free to focus on his duty to the Crown—a commitment that had consumed his life for a decade—as it left no room for romance, which he'd avoided as if his life depended on it, as indeed, it did. With no strings attached, and when this menace was eliminated, he could easily let Lady Bethany go, especially if she changed her mind and wanted more of him than he could give.

Or so he had thought. If only he hadn't found the lady nearly irresistible, far more exceptional than the twins had warned him. She bore the Montgomery stamp: dark brown hair, the most fascinating emerald green eyes, finely sculpted features. He'd wanted to stare at her heart-shaped face, her small nose, and lips that were much too quick to smile. Luscious lips that deserved to be kissed.

He recoiled from the unbidden pleasure the idea planted inside him, the realization that his defenses might have met their match. The reason he'd wanted to escape her and her mother as quickly as possible. The longer he looked at Lady Bethany, the more he wanted to touch her.

No, that would never do. He needed to keep her at arm's length. Thankfully, he'd be far away from her most of the time, carrying on unhampered, intent on the affairs of the Realm.

And with his heart safely out of reach.

* * *

"I cannot believe it!" Lady Camille Camerfield cried, hurrying into the entry and throwing her arms around Bethany in a rare display of emotion.

"Camille!" Bethany said, daring to use her only girl cousin and dearest friend's Christian name despite it being frowned upon. This was, after all, an auspicious day. "I barely sent my note," she said, setting Lady Camille away from her. "I swear Jason headed for Hannaford not thirty minutes ago. You must have ridden like the wind, but where is your horse?"

Lady Camille grabbed Bethany's hands, excitement sparkling in her gray eyes, her fair curls bouncing.

"I left home before Jason did. I couldn't wait. I tied Cooper in a stall where Jason can find him when he arrives. Beth, I'm stunned at your rejecting Lord Scarbreigh this morning and an hour later becoming engaged to the Earl of Locke. I want to hear every detail."

Bethany made a face. "It's ludicrous, is it not? I cannot believe it, either. I assume your brothers are following you. Hetty is putting together a hasty luncheon for us."

"Please don't ask me to wait for them to hear what happened."

"Of course not. I cannot wait that long to tell you." She began the story as they headed towards the privacy of the rear veranda. "It's not what you'd think, Cam," she said with caution. "Certainly no fairytale. We each have situations the other can remedy, and that's the sum of it."

Lady Camille's enthusiasm dampened as the truth came forth, of Whitton's dire financial circumstances and Bethany agreeing to live the life of a nun while married to a man with the face of an angel. Bethany insisted it was a relief he didn't want her. Otherwise, it would be wrong to marry him. She desired neither pity nor censure; she just hoped to do as Locke had asked and to live a good life. Ultimately, she would become Lady Locke, and Whitton would be saved.

The twins arrived in much higher spirits than when they'd left Whitton earlier, joining the women in the dining room. The straight-laced surface they showed to the world—a majority of the time—was cast aside when they greeted Bethany so jovially they made her blush.

"You'll make an adorable couple," Lord Matthew said, his face alight with mischief. "Lord Locke loves to ride and to dance, dear cousin, and he's almost as good as you."

"Oh, stop, Matthew," Bethany muttered. "There's more to life than riding and dancing, and I'm no more than an average dancer. I met this Lord Locke once a long time ago and barely remember it. He must have a screw loose somewhere to do this. I just hope neither of us lives to regret it."

Mr. Nicolas laughed. "Not likely, Love. You're meant for each other." Then he turned his back to the group, wrapped his arms around himself, and made kissing sounds that had Lord Matthew laughing. Lady Camille and Bethany begged him to quit, and Lady Whitton sighed in exasperation.

"You're odious, Nicolas," Lady Camille insisted, fighting a grin.

"You're next, Cam," Mr. Nicolas insisted. "Now that Scarbreigh's finished making a fool of himself with our favorite cousin—"

"Your only cousin."

Mr. Nicolas waved Bethany's comment aside. "He might open his eyes and realize what a wonderful match he'd bring off with you."

"We'll not have that discussion again," Lady Camille said, her smile drooping. "Lord Scarbreigh isn't interested and I won't force what isn't right."

"What's your opinion, Aunt Katherine?" Lord Matthew asked. "Wouldn't Scarbreigh and Camille do well together?"

"Oh, no. I've done as much matchmaking as I want today. Come sit down and enjoy our meal. Lady Camille, you know Lady Bethany cares little about fashion, so it will be our duty to get her ready for the wedding."

Mr. Nicolas moaned and Lord Matthew insisted, "I'd rather muck out stalls and braid horsetails than plan a wedding. In fact, I believe my brother and I must undertake a drive to Maidstone. Soon as we've cleaned our plates. What do you think, Mr. Nicolas?"

Mr. Nicolas stared upward towards the ceiling as if consulting an oracle. "By Jove, you're right, Lord Matthew. Why, look! There! I picture me and you escorting Marc, excuse me, *Lord Locke*, to the Fisherman's

Arms for a toast and an insightful discussion on the extraordinary care he'll take of our cousin or else find himself drawn and quartered."

"After we've given him forty lashes."

"And keel-hauled him to boot." They crowed with laughter.

Bethany fought with laughter of her own. She loved her rowdy cousins but they could do it a bit brown. Neither of them entertained any greater interest in marriage than Bethany's brothers or Lord Locke supposedly had—until now—and planning a wedding wouldn't excite them one bit. Indulging in whatever bachelor endeavors would amuse Lord Locke until the wedding day arrived would be far more to their liking.

Glaring at her brothers, Lady Camille said to Bethany, "You didn't mention a wedding date, dear."

Bethany blinked at the sudden realization. "Oh. We didn't discuss it, other than that he mentioned soon."

Lady Katherine conceded he'd not told her, either.

"I'd guess right away," Lord Matthew replied, following a sip of his tea. "I do believe he's headed for the Continent soon and will want it done beforehand."

"Oh, dear. Well, we'll ask him tomorrow," the countess suggested. "This morning, before he met with Bethany, Lord Locke told me he wanted the ceremony kept simple but fine enough to please Lady Bethany. Either way, it will still take time to put it together."

Mr. Nicolas harrumphed and cleared his palate before saying, "Which means we might as well don sack cloth and ashes. Bethany would rather die than put on airs, or lavish attire."

"That's not true," Bethany complained, even if it were true, to some degree. "I love wearing beautiful clothes, but only when I feel like it."

The twins howled and slapped their legs, and Lord Matthew said, "Which is almost never."

"Would you rather exchange vows in a riding habit or a tunic and leggings?" chimed in Mr. Nicolas.

"I'd rather the two of you found something else to do and left us alone," she replied.

"My sympathies exactly," Lady Camille added, and Lady Katherine cleared her throat.

The men applied broad grins, dabbed their mouths with their serviettes, and rose to offer chaste kisses to the three women's upturned cheeks.

Mr. Nicolas said, "Thanks for allowing us to stay the night, Aunt Katherine. Means we can be on hand in the morning to harry the groom."

"And you'll do that harrying with at least some modicum of decorum," Bethany's mother insisted, "or I'll send you home."

"Yes, my lady," he replied, daring winks at his sister and Bethany.

"Tally-ho!" Lord Matthew cried, throwing an arm round Mr. Nicolas's neck and dragging him from the room backwards.

"Were they really born that obstreperous?" Bethany asked Lady Camille.

"I have no idea. They were five years old when I was born."

"They were scalawags at first breath," Lady Katherine grumbled. "I was eternally grateful to have such staid sons in Lord Christian and Mr. Collin."

"And then you got me," Bethany said, knowing her mother had always considered her a trial.

"You, my dear," the countess said, "have an independent streak that challenges decorum, but you're not given to mischief nor prankishness. Now, shall we put our heads together for the wedding?"

"I look forward to it," Lady Camille oozed, giggling when Bethany sighed in dismay.

* * *

Despite herself, Bethany couldn't help watching the road from her second story bedchamber the next morning, anticipating Lord Locke's arrival. A night's sleep had done nothing to erase her memory of his devastating, dark blue eyes and dimpled smile, and she hated admitting she could hardly wait to see him again.

Embracing Lady Camille's advice, she wore her mint-green chiffon day dress, one that supposedly complimented her eyes. In lieu of Lady Whitton's and Bethany's personal maids, dismissed a while ago, Lady Camille dressed Bethany's hair, drawing its mass on top of Bethany's head, while letting a single, curled lovelock fall over her left shoulder nearly to her waist.

Lady Camille squealed the moment she glimpsed a crested coach, drawn by a team of four-in-hand, coming towards them, the two men atop it dressed in the finest livery. Lord Locke's dun was tethered behind the carriage, while the Earl himself leaned slightly out of the window, gazing up at the two women.

"Oh, heavens, Bethany. I remember him! He's ... he's magnificent! Regal, like a king."

"Why don't you marry him, then?" Bethany muttered, starting to wonder if she could go through with this. Not because Lord Locke wasn't as handsome as she remembered him. It was because he was toe-curling and eye-dazzling, and, yes, magnificent, and she couldn't imagine becoming his wife.

"He didn't offer for me. I would if he had."

Bethany barked laughter. "Oh, I must collect myself. I cannot be laughing like a hyena in 'His Majesty's' presence."

"If it were me, I'd simply melt at his feet."

"Come along, cousin. Let me introduce you before you dissolve into a puddle."

The twins already waited in the yard, Jason on hand to help with the horses and carriage, when the women joined them. The perfectly matched team of dapple-grays drawing the splendid coach had Bethany awed. They pranced into the yard, as if they knew they were beautiful.

Lord Matthew greeted the coachman—named Seaworth—and Mr. Treadwell, the earl's valet. Seaworth was a grizzled, unkempt sort, despite his fine clothing, while the valet was a tall, thin, stately man of inestimable years. Both were briefly but properly polite.

Seaworth leaped atop the carriage to remove the earl's baggage, while the twins greeted Lord Locke with an exchange of exuberant backslaps and handshakes. Then the earl sobered and approached Bethany.

Today he wore a jacket of dark-blue superfine and beige trousers, and his hessians shone even beyond yesterday's brightness. She almost rued wearing her gloves today when he removed his right kidskin and took her gloved fingers in hand. A gentleman did not kiss a glove, although he did bow over it, and butterflies buzzing in her belly signified her disappointment.

It took her a second to gather her wits sufficient to introduce Lady Camille. It then required several more to shrug off a mild pique at her flaxen-haired cousin's natural grace at greeting men—and Locke's earnest response to her charms.

Bethany was uncertain what to say when he returned his gaze to her, but then he nodded toward his team and said, "There's nothing quite like quality horseflesh, is there?"

"No, my lord," she murmured, although she feared Lord Locke's handsome face certainly rivaled them.

Lady Katherine materialized, hurrying to meet the earl. "Mr. Drew will show your valet to your quarters, my lord. Lord Matthew, you haven't seen Mr. Bradbury yet, have you?"

"No, my lady. But I'm sure he'll arrive soon."

"Yes, of course. We'll have him join us in the sitting room, my lord."

They settled on the cluster of furnishings arranged around the unlit fireplace in the sitting room, and when every chair was taken except the one Lady Katherine had reserved for the solicitor, Bethany found herself sharing the small sofa with Lord Locke. Her heart fluttered strangely whenever his arm or knee bumped hers. She dared not look at him, fearful he'd realize how profoundly he disconcerted her.

Locke laid out his expectations quickly and succinctly. He had pressing matters overseas to attend to in the near future and wanted the wedding done beforehand. With his parents gone and few relatives or close friends nearby, he needed the ceremony small and quick.

Bethany had forever dreamed of only one thing for her wedding, a garden ceremony, and her eyes widened in surprise when Lord Locke requested precisely that.

Bethany could see Lady Katherine was disappointed. Her mother had always wanted her only daughter's nuptials to be first-rate, contrary to Bethany's preferences for something more modest.

The dowager countess pointed out one important matter. "You've said you want the wedding soon, my Lord, but we haven't discussed a date."

"Ah. Until this morning I couldn't have given you one." His gaze shifted to Bethany as he said, "Now it's imperative we address it. My meeting in Maidstone yesterday confirmed my need to leave Moorewood for the Continent in two weeks. To allow time for a brief wedding trip, we must set Thursday, the twenty-third day of June, as the date for the nuptials. I know it's short notice, only ten days from now, but, for your and your mother's sakes, Lady Bethany, we must be married before I depart."

The dowager countess's eyes flew wide, disapproval written all over her face. "But we must post banns, my lord, which requires at least three weeks; and my sister, Lady Hannaford, who isn't well, wouldn't be able to return from her physicians in Bath in time. We cannot possibly journey to London and have either the wardrobes or Lady Bethany's wedding dress done on such short notice, and what about inviting even a few guests? They need time to respond to our invitations."

Pulling her fan from its customary place up her sleeve, she applied it with vigor. For a moment Bethany wondered if her mother would revoke her consent for the marriage.

CHAPTER 4

"I regret the haste, my lady. Your solicitor made it plain, however, that Whitton needed funds immediately. I offered for Lady Bethany as quickly as I was able, but I cannot rearrange my business. If we don't accomplish the ceremony now, I won't likely be able to reconsider it until Christmastide. I would prefer the guest list short, and I'm sorry about Lady Hannaford, but I assume the delay would not do."

Bethany was aware of her mother's dismay, but Lord Matthew's brief exchange of looks with Mr. Nicolas raised the hairs on the back of her neck. The twins had a language of their own, and although she didn't always understand it, she did know they'd just communicated something they didn't want anyone else to know.

Was the earl's comment not entirely true? Was he hiding something? Was his journey to the mainland connected with her father's estate and his financial losses? Like most men, he wouldn't care to discuss financial details with Lady Katherine any more than was required, but what if he waited too long? Even such a *non-pareil* might not be able to pull Whitton back from the brink of complete ruin.

"Excuse me, my lord, but what will we do about posting the banns?" Bethany intervened, giving her mother time to calm.

"We won't. My personal solicitor left for London yesterday afternoon, to acquire a special license from the archbishop, and I've already contacted your vicar. He understands the gravity of the situation and is pledged to assist. Canterbury is closer to Whitton than London. I assume you've taken advantage of its shops in the past. I trust it will be an acceptable compromise for you now in acquiring your new wardrobe."

Lord Locke's answers almost felt rehearsed. As if he'd formulated a response to any objection either Bethany or her mother could present. Yet, knowing how dire their situation was, she, like her mother, realized they must comply, and leave the rest to Providence.

"It doesn't seem we have any choice, Mum," she said. "June the twenty-third or not at all."

A flicker of surprise at her abruptness wrinkled Locke's brow but passed quickly.

Locke then honored the cousins by inviting Lord Matthew to be his best man and Mr. Nicolas to stand for Lady Bethany, if she agreed—which she did, of course. The three men would take care of their own wardrobes, and the countess and Lady Camille would consult with Lady Bethany about her needs, both for the wedding ceremony and her trousseau.

Next, he turned to address Lady Camille. "I've an unusual request to make of you, Lady Camerfield. In my absence, I would like to invite you to join Lady Bethany, to keep her company, for as long as you both like. Perhaps you can arrive the evening before I'm to leave. I've an excellent staff at Moorewood, but they are strangers to her, and I don't want her lonely."

"I'd—I'd love to." Lady Camille's round-eyed gaze met Bethany's. "Does that suit you, Beth?"

"You need ask?" Bethany said, wanting to pinch herself. Beyond having a marriage that required nothing unpleasant of her, she could think of nothing else that would make the situation more bearable.

The pendulum clock near the doorway chimed 10:05 just as Mr. Bradbury arrived, puffing his apologies for his tardiness, caused by a fractious horse, as he scuttled his stout frame into the room. The Camerfields excused themselves to allow the solicitor to review the paperwork he'd drawn up.

"His Lordship has requested that I continue to manage Whitton's accounts, Lady Whitton," Mr. Bradbury said while he sorted through the sheets of papers. "He's examined my record-keeping and declared that I've managed adequately."

"Better than adequate, Bradbury," Lord Locke interjected. "You've kept this estate afloat despite extraordinary obstacles. I'm pleased you're willing to carry on."

Flustered, the solicitor wiped beads of perspiration from his brow. "You're very kind, my lord, and I'm grateful to remain."

As to the particulars of the estate, Bradbury addressed them in minute detail, rambling on and on, and growing bored, Bethany found her mind wandering to other things, especially Lord Locke's long legs stretched out alongside hers. His large but comely hands, now divested of their gloves, rested comfortably in his lap, his arms and shoulders clearly more muscular than the conventional nobleman's.

From under her lashes she caught a glimpse of the earl's striking profile, noting that his near-black hair was shorter than current trends dictated yet neatly arranged, and although he'd shaved that morning his beard was dark enough it still shaded his jawline and upper lip delightfully.

She had to force herself not to stare. He smelled delicious, of shaving lather and men's cologne and the faint muskiness of a man, and desires she'd never before experienced had her thinking thoughts about him that, under the circumstances, she had no right to entertain.

"I trust that pleases you, my dear?" Lord Locke said, resting those fascinating eyes on her.

Bethany gaped, not sure what to say. Someone had said something important while she'd been woolgathering.

"Your father bequeathed you the ownership of several horses, including a stallion named Raven?" the earl prompted.

"Oh. Yes."

He nodded his agreement. "I'll have those animals moved to Moorewood beforehand, so that they'll be at your disposal when you arrive."

Mr. Bradbury jotted a note to add to the others he'd already scribbled during their visit. After Lady Katherine and Bethany signed the contract, Locke added his own signature to the papers. Then Bradbury departed and Mr. Drew returned Lady Camille and the twins to their company.

"I have a request, if I might, Lady Whitton," Lord Locke said, rising. "I'd like to take a closer look at some of the grounds." His gaze took in the others. "And I'd enjoy having all of you ride with me."

Everyone accepted right off, the countess his designated guide.

* * *

Bethany still wasn't sure what to make of Lord Locke. On their ride he was most attentive to her mother and Lady Camille, and his camaraderie with the twins was enviable. With her, however, he kept his distance. Never impolite but as if he were uncomfortable in her presence. Truly, their conversations remained so superficial, Bethany had the distinct impression the man didn't want to know much about her.

Or perhaps he didn't want her to know much about him.

Preparations for the wedding took over, Bethany far too busy to further dissect her fiancé's conduct, but the more time she spent with Marcus Ashburn, the more certain she became that he presented a practiced face to her, the face of a consummate actor.

Oddly enough, in time she also became grateful for it. When he let his personable self show, he was far too amiable and definitely far too handsome. Without such suspicions, she had no doubt she could have fallen in love with the man in an instant, definitely not an option.

Thus, her reservations kept her emotions at bay, which also served to protect her from the consequences of trusting too blindly.

* * *

Bethany had no idea how she tolerated being rushed her through everything Lady Katherine deemed essential for the wedding. A major sticking point came when her mother sat down with her to go over their brief guest list: a few old friends to come from London, several neighbors summering at their country estates and the three Camerfield siblings were about the extent of it.

"I do have a special request," the countess said, her face pinched with dread. "I know you won't like it, and if you cannot abide it, I understand. I've another friend I wish to offer an invitation. Not only are her connections superior, you must also realize that she is the sort it would be unwise to insult by *not* inviting her."

"Then why can you not invite her?" Bethany asked, worried about the answer.

"Because the lady in question is the Dowager Lady Scarbreigh. Lord Scarbreigh's mother. To snub her would suggest that the *mishap* between you and the marquess was significant. She will not want his name besmirched."

Just hearing the marquess's name distressed Bethany. Still, this was only his mother. "If you feel it's necessary then of course she should come," she replied.

Lady Katherine sighed. "She's getting older, Beth. She rarely travels out of London these days. She's terrified of highwaymen or accidents along the way. She'll likely insist on bringing his lordship with her."

"Oh, Mum—"

"I understand you're embarrassed by what happened. But you cannot allow a misunderstanding to discount a friendship that has lasted most of your life. He did nothing wrong, after all. You just didn't appreciate it. I'm certain he's a forgiving man. If he's not, he'll not come. Perhaps if we send him a separate invitation, and you include an apology, it will set things to rights."

Bethany agreed with her mother on all counts but could hardly imagine doing any such thing. Not even for the sake of Scarbreigh's reputation, which she doubted she could sully. If Lady Camille's sweet face had not spirited its way into her thoughts, she wouldn't have considered it.

Her cousin had long admired the marquess, and Bethany truly believed that Scarbreigh was fond of Lady Camille. She was also convinced that in honor of her father and brothers, and to rescue Bethany and Lady Katherine from penury, he'd been trying to play the hero when he proposed to her. She really ought to feel more charitable toward him.

Besides, left to their own devices, Lady Camille and Scarbreigh might well make a match, and if they did, Bethany would have to learn to deal with the marquess's presence at all and sundry holidays, family gatherings and other pursuits anyway.

Swallowing her pride, she said a prayer, collected pen and ink and a most precious piece of paper and did exactly as her mother had asked.

* * *

If one believed the gossipmongers, the marriage of Lady Bethany Montgomery, Lord Whitton's daughter, to Lord Marcus Ashburn, the Earl of Locke—and other sundry titles—was to be hailed as one of the most unexpected events of the year. With so few invited, it also amused Bethany that it would forever remain a mystery to most of the *ton*.

The garden was exquisite—thanks to ten days' determined care from its reemployed gardeners. Bethany's dress was lovely despite its hasty creation, and the late-afternoon ceremony as brief and concise as Lord Locke had requested. Everyone played their parts without mishap, even the weather, which was comfortably warm and clear. Although Lady Katherine couldn't be dissuaded from encouraging their guests to remain for as long as they liked, at least there weren't very many of them and Bethany even liked some of them.

Among them were childhood friends, most already married, who offered sincere well-wishing, which made up for those who'd attended for less kindly reasons. Some came mostly to bear witness that Lord Whitton's "unsociable" daughter, the one who'd taken only one season in London and left it early last year, had truly captured one of the Uncatchables. She wouldn't have minded their prying if they'd kept their attitudes to themselves. Quite the contrary. If she didn't overhear snide remarks as she passed by them, she earned jealous glares and whispered slights.

"Is this why you temper your attention to Lord Scarbreigh?" Bethany asked Lady Camille at one point. "I fear I won't leave here in one piece."

Lady Camille stifled laughter with her lace kerchief. "Oh, heavens, it can't be that bad." Then she blinked when she saw the silent challenge Bethany threw her way. "Goodness, I had no idea. No, dear. I don't seek Lord Scarbreigh's attention because he's not interested in me. If he'd come today, I must confess I might not mind the use of my own claws to get close to him."

Bethany gasped. "Are you serious? I for one will never understand the sentiment." Then the truth of the matter saddened her. "I'm sorry for your sake that Scarbreigh and his esteemed mother didn't attend. The Dowager Lady Scarbreigh wrote that she wouldn't miss it."

Then she heard Mr. Drew announce someone in the distance and saw two people amble into the garden. Her heart plummeted to her toes.

"Oh, dear. Well, it seems I've spoken too soon. Beware, Cousin, the subjects of our discussion have made a late arrival."

"What?" Lady Camille stiffened.

"Lord Scarbreigh and his mother are making their rounds and shall soon be in our presence. Please take advantage of the sacrifice I made to get them here."

Lady Camille took a quick look over her shoulder then turned back, cheeks pinking. "Beth, that's beneath you."

Bethany couldn't help laughing. "It is, and I do apologize. Please make the best of it. I'm certain he's soft on you."

"I do not believe it…but you know I would welcome it if it were true. Are they close to us? Oh, Bethany, what shall I do?"

Bethany smiled. "Just be yourself, my dear. You're one of the most beautiful women here. And stay away from the punch. You know you cannot handle your spirits, and you'll want your head about you."

Bethany's brief nod had Lady Camille turning to observe their approaching guests, Scarbreigh trailing his mother at a good distance as guests hailed him.

"Lady Camille," the Dowager Countess mewed, bussing Lady Camille's cheeks and then turning to Bethany. The amused sparkle in her eye belied the elderly woman's slight, frail figure.

"Lady Locke. You have no idea the stir you've caused in London," she said, kissing her as well. "And you have no idea how disheartened I am to have missed the ceremony. Please accept my humblest apologies. Carriage horse threw a shoe and it took three hours to fix it. And lest any of these snarling cats, who look for the worst in all of us, dare to suggest this is not the truth, please remember I've known your family and loved your esteemed mother a good part of my life. I would never slight you."

"Thank you, my lady," Bethany replied, humbled by her unexpected kindness.

Still, her smile faded as Kirkwood Bannister, the man she'd known since childhood as Kirk, the Marquess of Scarbreigh, nodded and bowed his way past the other guests, his sky-blue eyes fastened to Lady Camille's soft gray ones. He was a tall man, slender in comparison to Lord Locke's powerful build but equally as handsome in his own right, his titian hair styled a-la-Brutus.

When he arrived and after removing his right-hand glove, he offered Bethany his hand and a bow in congratulations. "My humblest best wishes, my dear," he said in that winning voice that stole the ladies' hearts. "Becoming Lady Locke appears to suit you. You're not only lovely, you seem contented."

Bethany's cheeks warmed even more. "You're too kind, my lord, especially … under the circumstances."

A wry smile tweaked the corners of his mouth. "A bit of a spectacle, was it not?" He ran his fingers over the bridge of his nose. "Should have seen the bruises. At least you didn't break it." He glanced at Lady Camille and back at Bethany. "I appreciate your written apology, Lady Bethany. It meant a lot to both me and to Lady Scarbreigh. I ask for my own forgiveness. Had your esteemed mother informed me that Lord Locke was in the wings, I would never have approached you."

Bethany let out a soft breath that eased the tension inside her. "He wasn't, my lord. He arrived to address my mother shortly after you and I set out for our morning ride."

"Ah." Scarbreigh's brows rose high. "And was waiting for you when you returned?"

"Yes."

"That must have been awkward."

"Terribly. And my last hope for redeeming my father's estate." Perhaps she shouldn't have admitted such a thing, but it suggested the arrangement had been based on need, not on some quality in the earl that Scarbreigh lacked.

Scarbreigh glanced over her shoulder toward Lord Locke, surrounded by a few of their guests.

"He was one of the most Uncatchable of all the Uncatchables, you know. Quite a feather in your cap, my dear. Marc—er—*Locke* is an old school chum of mine, although I haven't seen much of him for the last year or so. Didn't matter that he and Lord Christian were older than the twins and Mr. Collin and I. They were always up to some diversion or another and taking us along with them."

Bethany could hardly imagine it. Lord Locke a young man, engaged in merriment? The idea amused her.

"But thankfully you survived it," she said.

His smile widened. "Quite well, actually."

"And now if you'd only settle down, find a wife and get an heir," interjected Lady Scarbreigh, dampening his humor. Then turning her sharp eyes on Bethany and, with a hint of disapproval, she said, "I was quite surprised by the haste of your marriage, my dear. Count me a relic, but it's most irregular, especially if one does not post banns."

Bethany blushed with embarrassment. Did the dowager think they were *forced* into marriage? Lady Katherine had feared far too many people would draw the same conclusion.

"My lord was kind enough to schedule the marriage before having to go to the Continent for business. Otherwise, we couldn't have done so until December."

The dowager's brows rose in understanding. "Not acceptable, considering your mother's financial affairs—but please don't tell her I was gauche enough to say so. Well, I'm assuming Lord Locke has at least planned a decent wedding trip for you. A voyage to France is certainly possible now, with the war ended. It's an important step in building a marriage, you know. Getting to know each other. I wish you the best."

Bethany worked hard to steady her smile. Let the nosey old woman think Bethany was going with Lord Locke to Europe. Let everyone think it. No one but Bethany and the family knew the truth, and her puzzling husband had asked them to keep the couple's destination to themselves for now. His excuse had been his concern for Bethany and Lady Camille, who would be at Moorewood without him. Thieves, highwaymen and kidnappers weren't uncommon in the country, after all.

She hadn't taken it seriously until now. Lady Scarbreigh had just given her more than one reason to keep the truth private.

"Well, my lord, my ladies," she said to the marquess, his mother, and Lady Camille. "Please make yourselves comfortable. I hope you'll have a pleasant visit. If you'll excuse me, I fear I must continue circulating among my guests."

"Of course, my dear," Lady Scarbreigh said, but she slanted a sly look toward her son.

Seemingly oblivious, the marquess offered his hand to Lady Camille, his blue eyes twinkling. When she took it, he placed an-air kiss above her fingers.

"Lady Camille. You are beyond lovely today. I would be the luckiest man in the world if you'd agree to walk with me."

Bethany was thunderstruck when Lady Scarbreigh's lips pursed into a self-satisfied smirk, her eyes bright with triumph. She had to press her own lips tight to avoid laughing out loud. To think, the old woman had not come to the wedding to congratulate an old friend's daughter so much as she had come to turn her spurned son's head in another direction.

It brightened Bethany's day immeasurably to realize that Lady Camille had another advocate in the war to win Lord Scarbreigh's heart. Now if only the new Lady Locke didn't dread having to meet with that small cluster of guests not far from the beverage table.

* * *

Locke watched the exchange between Lord Scarbreigh and Lady Bethany, surprised at how much he disliked like it.

He oughtn't to have any opinion about their relationship. He'd certainly never had any rivalry with Kirkwood Bannister in their lives. Until now, he'd wondered if the man would ever settle on any one female. He seemed to enjoy admiring all of them. Just knowing, however, that the friend of his salad days had offered to marry Lady Bethany annoyed him.

He had to remind himself that not only had the marquess's offer been refused, he had to deal with the embarrassment of being forced to the wedding by his domineering mother. Locke rather liked the Dowager Lady Scarbreigh; she accomplished things that few among the peerage could. He just couldn't imagine her hard-heartedness in making her son come here today.

Something moved in the corner of his eye and he turned to see Mr. Nicolas hurrying toward him, a hint of alarm on his face.

"Sorry for the interruption, my lord. We've a problem," he murmured. A quick jerk of his head had Locke following his lead out of the garden. The earl managed to do so while masking his concern with a bored look.

Once safely away from the gathering, Mr. Nicolas muttered as they headed toward Whitton's stable, "I promise the interruption was warranted."

"What's happened?"

"An attack on one of the horses."

"What?"

"Please see for yourself."

Locke was grateful the driveway to the stables had lamps to chase off the eerie shadows of falling night. Lord Matthew joined them halfway to the stable, and then they met Jason at the doors, a blood-stained rag in his hand.

"Didn't like disturbin' ya, m'lord," Jason said, his face drawn, "but I s'posed you'd wanna know right off."

He scurried bow-legged and stoop-shouldered to a stall near the back of the building, the others following. Locke's jaw tightened in anger when he entered the stall and saw the gaping wound and the look of misery in the poor beast's eyes.

"'Elped Lord Scarbreigh's coachman take care of 'is lordship's team and afterward thought I'd feed the 'orses a bit early. Got back 'ere and this is what I found. Couldn't 'ave 'appened long ago, but I can't see 'ow anyone coulda got in 'ere without one of us seein' 'im."

Blood oozed from the black gelding's neck in clotting rivulets and down his left foreleg, settling into a pool in the straw. Now that Lord Locke had seen the evidence, Jason pressed the cloth to the wound and murmured encouragement to the groaning horse.

"Found Shadow like ya see 'im, and then I turned and…." He nodded to the right, toward the wall near the door. "Saw that." A dagger was driven through an old rag into the wood. A note was scrawled on the rag, ink and blood mingling together and muddying some of the words.

Locke yanked the knife out and examined the message, his own blood turning cold upon surmising it was addressed to his bride.

Time you give us what we want. Do so, no harm to you. Don't, you die. Leave note nailed to willow tree on the lane before leaving today. Don't matter you're an earl's daughter. Will find you wherever you go.

"There's something else, Locke," Lord Matthew said. "Jason needed to clean Shadow's stall today. You know Shadow is Raven's half-brother and agree he looks a lot like the stallion. This was Raven's stall."

Locke's jaw tightened. "You think this knife was meant for Lady Bethany's stallion." That would have devastated his bride.

All three men shrugged but suspicion lurked in their eyes.

"Lady Bethany has to know," he muttered. "This was the last of her horses to be taken to Moorewood. Is it necessary to tell her about the note?"

"No," Mr. Nicolas responded, glancing at Lord Matthew. "I think it's best we don't."

Locke nodded. "Good. I'd as soon not o'rset her. She has enough to deal with under the circumstances."

"I also think you shouldn't wait too much longer to leave for Moorewood," said Lord Matthew.

"I agree. I'd like to avoid both the attention with our departure and the danger of traveling in full dark. Jason, do all you can to save Shadow."

"It's serious but he'll live, m'lord," the servant said.

Locke thanked him and then gave the twins a nod. They hurried with him from the stable into the yard.

"Guess we have our proof, Marc," Lord Matthew muttered, reaching for the note. He perused it and handed it to Mr. Nicolas who read it and shook his head in disgust.

"Not only proof that Lady Bethany is in danger," Mr. Nicholas said. "But also evidence concerning her conspirators."

Lord Matthew sighed. "Wonder if they realize it yet? An old rag ain't costly paper, and the ink is the shoddy type. Handwriting seems awkward enough to convince the reader that our thug is street variety."

"Yes," Locke concurred. "I'm guessing the author was using his left hand, trying to appear poorly educated, but his language is far from illiterate. Not a misspelled word in the bunch."

They all nodded their agreement.

"I'll find Bethany. Mr. Nicolas, please have Seaworth prepare my carriage and ferret out Mr. Treadwell, apprise him of the situation. Already had our luggage loaded in anticipation of our departure. Lord Matthew, gather Lady Camille and your aunt without any fanfare, bring them here for farewells."

* * *

Bethany managed to escape her guests by pretending to examine the flowers that edged one of the walkways leading through the garden. This path took a slight turn and hid her from prying eyes and allowed her a moment to relax.

"How are you holding up, my dear?"

Bethany's stomach fluttered when she abandoned the rose she'd bent to sniff and turned to set eyes on Lord Locke, strolling toward her from the outer edges of the garden. The man had been the perfect groom all afternoon, which meant he'd spent most if it with their guests. She did not pretend to understand convention and thought it absurd, but she supposed where arranged marriages were concerned it made some level of sense.

"Better than I expected but not without battle wounds."

"Oh?" His lifted brows made her smile drolly.

"The amount of venom packed into young women's frames defies understanding. It appears I've won more enemies than friends in accepting your proposal. No wonder you've given a wide berth to the *ton*."

He coughed soft laughter. "You've been a frightfully good sport, *Lady Locke*," he said with amused emphasis. "It would surprise you how many gentlemen here have lamented not being able to catch your eye."

"Truly? Please give me their names. I dare not believe it."

"I'd prefer my competition to remain anonymous. I wouldn't like it if my beautiful bride decided she'd made a mistake."

Bethany executed a quick double take, wondering if he would dislike competition—and truly considered her beautiful. Seeing her expression, the earl raised his brows in surprise.

"Yes, my lady, I think you're quite lovely," he said. "A man would have to be a fool not to see it. I wonder if you'd take a walk with me? Away from the crowd?"

She took his arm, relieved to leave the chatter behind them as they strolled through the garden. A flash of amusement gripped her at realizing they no longer needed a chaperone.

What a lovely evening she thought. Dusk was falling, and the lamps set along the walkways offered a cozy golden light. Already a glorious full moon smiled down upon them and the crickets serenaded nearby. She could have pretended all was well if only Lord Locke didn't look worried about something.

CHAPTER 5

Locke sighed. "I hate bearing bad tidings, my lady, but we've had trouble at the stables. Your gelding, Shadow, was ... injured." His countess's gasp made Locke grab her hands and squeeze them gently to keep her from flying off.

"What happened?"

"It appears an adversary of some sort was drawn to the estate." He then described the gelding's injuries, earning another cry of outrage. He hated having to lie to her, but he had no choice. "Perhaps a spurned admirer did it? Someone infuriated by not having the chance to grab Whitton at auction? Who knows what drives such a person."

"It's unbelievable," Lady Bethany insisted. "I want to see for myself."

Locke tightened his hold on her. "Please don't, my lady. Jason's putting some stitches to the wound now. 'Tis unsightly and there's nothing you can do to help. I think we should make our getaway instead, before it grows much darker."

Locke wasn't sure what to do with Lady Bethany's stillness or the tears gathering on her long, dark lashes. He sensed she wasn't the sort to cry easily, and it completely disarmed him.

Lord Matthew's advice drifted into his mind. "Lady Bethany's great fun, Locke. Treat her like a little sister. She'll love it."

But, try as he might, Locke harbored nothing even remotely akin to brotherly feelings towards this lovely young woman.

Without thinking, he took her into his arms and tried to comfort her. She felt small and soft and delicate, and smelled of honey-sweetened lemons. And, heaven help him, he enjoyed holding her against him.

Shock immobilized him when she wrenched herself from his arms.

"What's wrong—"

"Don't!" She hissed, gasping for breath, hands raised. "Please, don't—don't touch me," she demanded. But she seemed frightened—or perhaps embarrassed?—not angry.

"I'm so sorry. I was only trying to help—"

"I know, but I can't ... please, don't touch me." She spun away and buried her face in her hands and sobbed.

Locke stood there, at first feeling like a complete cad but not understanding why, and then remembering that Mr. Nicolas had said she didn't trust men.

"Lady Bethany! What's happened?" a familiar voice rang out.

Locke turned to find Lady Camille hurrying around a corner behind them, Lord Matthew trailing her. Locke was further confused when Lady Bethany squeezed Lady Camille's neck tight and Lady Camille squeezed back without censure for touching her.

In a torrent, Lady Bethany harshly whispered the whole tale, about the horse and how she'd reacted to Locke. Lady Camille's visage drooped in dismay, her eyes offering Locke pity rather than censure. Lord Matthew's gaze remained averted, his cheeks flushed.

"Lord Matthew told me about the horse, dear heart," Lady Camille said, hugging Lady Bethany again and then letting go. "I can't fathom it. You can't let your guests see you like this. I agree that this would be a fitting time for you and your groom to escape."

"As do I. What if one of our guests did it? Wouldn't that be horrid?"

Lady Camille's brow furrowed in disbelief. "I would think it would be hard to hide the evidence."

"Blood does damage kidskin gloves," Locke ventured. "Let's go, my lady. Lady Camille can follow us, and Lord Matthew will bring your mother to the stables for a brief private farewell.

He offered Lady Bethany his arm, hoping she'd take it. He needed to reassure her that all would be well and reassure himself he'd done nothing to her that she couldn't forgive. Theirs was hardly a traditional alliance, but his responsibility to safeguard her would evaporate if he couldn't safeguard their friendship.

Bethany's cheeks flushed to a more natural color. She wiped the tears from her cheeks, applied a feeble, apologetic smile to her lips and then, although hesitant, placed her hand on his arm.

* * *

The carriage waited for them, and in short order, all was ready for their parting. Before Lord Matthew delivered Lady Katherine, there was brief, muted discussion between Mr. Nicolas and Lady Camille regarding the gelding's senseless assault, but when Bethany's mother arrived, the scene dissolved into tears and anxious farewells.

Bethany rued having to leave Lady Katherine to learn about Shadow after their guests left but it would avoid scandal. Lady Camille lamented Bethany's departing so unexpectedly and that not being able to change her wedding dress meant it would surely be crushed on the trip. Bethany told her that she didn't care but she was eternally grateful Lady Camille would arrive on Sunday.

When the coach lurched forward, Bethany suddenly wished that she could undo all of this, heartbroken that Mr. Collin had died at war and that her father and Lord Christian had been killed in the accident, and that she was here today only because of their loss. She didn't want to be married. She just wanted to stay at Whitton and live here undisturbed. But then, remembering Shadow, she leaned against the coach's cushions and sighed away the sadness. How safe was she in a place where a man could, for no good reason, brutally stab a horse without being caught?

* * *

Lady Bethany's image was hardly more than a silhouette against the darkening sky, but Locke sensed her misgivings and rued not having permission to tell her why she was safer with him than anywhere else on earth. She must never learn the details surrounding his marriage proposal.

Fatigue plagued him, and he, too, reclined into the squabs. If he tried hard, maybe he could relax. Or at least find some way to mollify his anxiety over the duties that would pull him from Moorewood and from Lady Bethany almost immediately. He had no choice, because—besides doing all he could to complete the mission he'd headed for the last year on another matter—he was determined to help the twins hunt down her foes.

Less than three hours' drive separated Moorewood from Whitton, but he'd reserved lodgings for them at the Red Fox Inn for the night, not far down the road. It served three purposes. They could avoid traveling in the dark, it would discourage anyone who might follow them from Whitton, and colleagues waited for him at the inn who would make sure no one would trail them to Moorewood tomorrow. Let the world think he was taking his bride with him to the Continent.

He knew he'd made the right choice when he told Lady Bethany his plans regarding their night's stay at the inn and earned a wan but appreciative smile.

He was surprised to find that his reflection upon his wedding night dispirited him. The goodwife of the inn would expect the earl and his new countess to share his room, and his bed, and would prepare their quarters accordingly. Instead, the smaller chamber next door that he'd supposedly hired for Mr. Treadwell would belong to Lady Bethany, and Locke and Treadwell would occupy the one assigned as the wedding suite. One of the maids would attend Lady Bethany, but rather than preparing the new countess for her wedding night, in fact Locke's bride would sleep alone.

Locke had never dreamed he'd regret not being able to savor the pleasures of marriage. His duties for the Crown had consumed him for so many years he'd given thought to little else. Now he needed to push aside this beautiful woman's attraction and remind himself sternly that this was just a dangerous business transaction.

* * *

The next morning's full sunrise found Lord Locke's carriage crossing Kent's lush, rolling countryside, on a lane headed a tad northeast of Canterbury. Bethany's breath caught as they swept over a ridge and gazed down into a small valley whose loveliness far surpassed Whitton's. The road meandered between gray stone fences and patches of woodlands and meadows, numbers of farmsteads and rich farmland, and grazing cattle and sheep. In the distance, a narrow river was a mere sliver of shimmering azure in the midmorning sunshine.

"Moorewood encompasses everything you can see from horizon to horizon, and even more, further east," Locke was saying, his eyes following the curves of Bethany's face as he spoke, causing her to blush.

Disconcerted by his appraisal, she looked out the window, searching for landmarks to help acquaint her with this place. Her family had often traveled to Canterbury in her childhood and to the coast when they sailed from Ramsgate to the Continent, but she'd never taken this road before.

"Is that large brown spot your manor?" she asked, pointing at a small dot that, given the distance, was a substantial building.

"It is."

"It's absolutely grand," she said.

"On the outside, yes. As I said, you won't appreciate the inside." The earl sighed. "Whenever I contemplate Geoffrey Matheson, I want to pummel him for his gall. I hope that once you've restored the manor to its former beauty, you'll want to entertain your closest friends and family."

"As soon as you come home, of course."

"No, my lady. I've no idea how often or how long I'll visit. Behave as if you were the sole occupant. I understand you've no fondness for London's entertainments and won't mind avoiding it, and even if you did, I'd prefer you stayed close to Moorewood until I give you leave. The restoration should take at least the summer, and I want you to oversee it personally. When all's finished, enjoy your accomplishments."

Bethany struggled to assimilate what he'd just said. It still amazed her that he placed such confidence in her. Of course, she'd begun to realize she wasn't much more than a glorified employee, someone who filled a niche a servant couldn't because she was his wife, while she wasn't really his wife. The responsibility worried her, and more so the awareness of what might become a terribly lonely life.

Then she remembered her fortune in not marrying someone loathsome, like Lord Ansley, or ostentatious, like Lord Scarbreigh. Or a man who would force himself upon her, which would cause her untold amounts of grief. Looking around at the white fenced paddocks to which they'd now arrived, she saw an estate full of incredible horseflesh and reminded herself of the blessings of having all of this to enjoy.

When the carriage drew into the yard, a group of frisky colts in the yearling paddock cantered up to the fence to watch them. After the vehicle stopped, Mr. Treadwell brought the footstool for them and handed Bethany down, Locke following. Her gaze swept upward along the venerable, imposing Jacobean architecture of Moorewood Manor. Three stories high, its gray brick walls were draped in ivy and bordered with generous flowerbeds. Its many windows, fifty rectangular eyes, peered curiously down at her.

Bethany couldn't help the amazement on her face. It might be shabby on the inside, but the outside was enchanting.

Locke pointed toward the stables. "My head groomsman, Dimity, is on his way to take over the horses and carriage, and the stableboys will help Seaworth with our luggage. I've a few things to go over with them, so I'll have Mrs. Callen take you to your rooms."

A stocky man, with a shock of flaming red hair and a red beard streaked with gray, strode towards them. Behind him came four muscular men, not boys in even the broadest sense of the word, their expressions rather serious. They set about their duties as Lord Locke walked Bethany up the broad steps toward the front door where Mr. Treadwell waited for them. Just outside the threshold stood an older woman, a mop of gray hair poking out from under a mobcap. She dropped a proper curtsy when Lord Locke and Bethany approached her.

"Mrs. Callen, this is the new Lady Locke. Lady Bethany, Moorewood's housekeeper keeps the manor running smoothly at all times and will help you settle in." He turned back to Mrs. Callen. "I assume my lady's new abigail is ready to see to her needs."

"Yes, m'lord," Mrs. Callen replied.

"Excellent." His gaze returned to Bethany. "How are feeling, my lady?"

Puzzled, Bethany replied, "Quite well, my lord."

"Good enough to take a look at the stables and your horses?"

"Yes, of course," she said with enthusiasm. He responded with a wry smile.

"What about a ride? Would you care to see some of the estate?"

"I'd be enormously pleased."

"Despite riding in a cramped carriage for the last two hours?"

She smiled, seeing what he was about. Many ladies would beg a bath and a nap after such a ride. Not so for Bethany, who longed for the feel of her mount beneath her.

"Despite a carriage ride," she replied.

He nodded, his dark blue eyes sparkling with mirth. "We'll need time to change clothes. Shall I meet you in the entryway in an hour?"

Bethany agreed and he turned the women over to Mr. Treadwell, who opened the door to them.

Bethany's smile drooped when they entered the old manor. Its faded grandeur was far worse than Locke had described it.

"'Tis in deplorable condition," Mrs. Callen remarked, seeing her expression. As they headed up the stairs, she added, "I knew it at its finest, when m'lord's parents were alive and still cared to entertain. M'lord keeps the barest essential staff in the house. While he's here, Mr. Treadwell acts as both valet to his lordship and butler to the house. His lordship demands few comforts when he visits, but he loves a handsome garden and keeps his best breeding animals here and a full complement of servants on the grounds. We do the best we can, but, well, under the circumstances...."

"My lord told me about Mr. Matheson."

The housekeeper grumbled. "Devil take him. Kept the rooms locked, wouldn't let us clean, had no idea he was stealing late at night." Proof of her accusations surrounded them as they passed through the second floor landing. Bare spaces on the walls, cabinets devoid of ornamentation, empty corners that should be graced by handsome furniture.

"M'lord came home unexpected one night, caught the man with a wagonload of goods. You'd have thought someone set fire to m'lord's trousers he yelled thief so loud. Matheson dropped everything, run off, he did. Knew his lordship would lock him up in Newgate if he caught him, he did."

The story mortified Bethany. It was enough that worn carpets, faded paint, and outdated window hangings proved the house needed refurbishing, but its emptiness left it feeling desecrated.

Still, beneath these unpleasantries lay the architecture of a gorgeous mansion. Its lofty ceilings and the moulding around arched doorways were carved in a magnificent design, some of its walls paneled in the stoutest dark oak, and a broad chandelier of gold and crystal crowned the grand hallway. A gold handrail flanked the spiral staircase, which rose to a broad landing overlooking the hall below then continued onward to the next level. Small by some nobleman's standards, it still contained upwards of thirty chambers, twice Whitton's size.

"Here we are, my lady. T'was the late countess's bedchamber. Lord Locke kept the key to it, along with his own room and his study. I've the other set but never told Mr. Matheson, so he couldn't have stolen from either room had he dared. I've kept it clean these many years, but no one's changed anything since Lady Locke passed on."

Despite the outdated furnishings and trappings, Bethany felt as if she'd stepped into a palace. Print damask draperies hung at the windows and plush carpets graced the floor. A tall four-poster of maple drew her murmurs of appreciation, along with the fireplace of white marble. A small sofa sat before the hearth, promising a pleasant repose with a cup of tea and a good book on a cold night. A generous desk and chair spanned a portion of the distant wall, while the dressing room to her right, furnished with a wardrobe closet and a lavish dressing table that matched the bed, were generous enough that Bethany was sure she'd never fill them. She couldn't imagine wanting to.

A slender girl of fifteen, with auburn hair and winsome hazel eyes, stood just outside the dressing room, waiting. Mrs. Callen introduced Melissa, Bethany's new personal maid, to the new countess, then she pointed to the closed door on the wall that was shared with Lord Locke's room.

"That door connects your chambers to his lordship's; he keeps the key. There's a bell rope beside the bed should you require anything, day or not. Melissa," she added, "will help you change and settle in. May I get you some tea?"

"No thank you, Mrs. Callen. You've been very helpful, and I hope you'll share your impressions with me regarding the manor. You've intimate knowledge of it, and I've no doubt that together we can bring it right again."

"Yes, my lady." Mrs. Callen smiled with genuine pleasure. "Shall I leave you to Melissa?" She scurried off and the young abigail began to help Bethany out of her dusty travel dress. The girl seemed shy but eager, which Bethany liked instantly.

As the girl unfastened the multitude of buttons on her travel dress, Bethany's gaze drifted to the earl's adjoining door. Was it truly locked? The idea of not being able to prevent Locke's intrusion troubled her. Hopefully, he felt the same and would keep it locked, but she wondered if she'd offend him by asking for a bolt on her side of the door.

When Melissa finished helping Bethany into her riding habit and dressing her hair, Bethany proceeded downstairs and found Lord Locke waiting for her in the entry, hands clasped behind his back.

CHAPTER 6

Locke turned at the sound of Lady Bethany's footsteps on the stairs and felt a tightening in his chest at seeing her. He was torn between his duty, his worries about her, and the guilt that this necessary but unpleasant scheme had created—and the undeniable fact that everything about his bride nearly overwhelmed him. He was glad they'd have no more than three days together. He couldn't afford the temptation her charms presented. He wouldn't have volunteered to ride out with her now if he didn't need to familiarize her with the estate and both the people who would watch over her and those she would watch over in his absence.

Locke was masterful at reading other people. The rising color and the bashfulness on Lady Bethany's face meant he affected her more than she liked, too, which worried him even more.

Her dark hair, plaited and pinned, was topped by a small, unpretentious hat; the skirts of her sky-blue riding habit, lovely but sufficiently worn to testify of Whitton's financial strains, enfolded the long legs of a horsewoman; and, heaven help him, her fair and flawless skin and her shapely figure enticed him.

Mr. Treadwell materialized at the front door to open it for them. Locke cast him a meaningful look, one that reminded his man to intervene if Locke ever showed signs of falling prey to this woman's wiles.

Lady Bethany on his arm, Locke led her to the stables. "I'm glad you feel up to this, my lady. I haven't long to make you familiar with this place before I leave for London."

"On Monday morning," she verified.

His heart skipped a beat. Did he hear a hint of disappointment in her voice? "At an inhumanly early hour, actually. I'll bid you farewell Sunday night after supper. Thankfully Lady Camille shall arrive by then."

Lady Bethany cast him a grateful smile. "You're kind to invite her. We're as close in our own way, I think, as the twins, and have rarely been separated long. My twentieth birthday is the end of September and hers three weeks later, in October. Our only disharmonies are her infatuations with London and the *haute ton*."

"Then I'm surprised you can tolerate her," Locke responded, quirking a lopsided smile at her soft laughter. Then his thoughts drifted to her father and brothers, whom he still missed tremendously. "Such close friendships are rare. Treasure it, and her, as long as you can."

They paused for Lady Bethany to admire the several paddocks of horses that surrounded them. Her mares and geldings contentedly cropped grass in one of them, and Raven was housed in the stallion barn in a spacious stall connected to a private pasture.

Locke was nearly as proud of his stables as he was his horses, all three buildings airy and well-lighted, bearing markedly high ceilings and above them generous haylofts. In the stallion stable, the four brawny grooms were sorting equipment, cleaning and mending saddles, bridles and halters, and cleaning stalls, while Seaworth and Locke's red-headed stable master, Dimity, were engaged in polishing Moorewood's carriage.

Locke was unprepared for the besotted look in his countess's eyes as she passed horse after blooded horse in the stalls. If he'd ever wanted to put together a list of characteristics he'd want in a woman, he'd have placed sharing his appreciation for fine horseflesh near the top.

Troubling thought. What was he to do with this fascinating woman he'd sworn to protect but to keep at arm's length? Especially when, without warning, he ached to touch her.

"Raven," Lady Bethany called when her stallion whinnied to her, and it was he that she slipped her arms around and hugged. Raven grumbled and nodded his head, pushing his brow into her chest as if he were equally as joyous to see her. He stood still when she kissed his baby-soft muzzle and lovingly stroked the delicate skin above his nostrils.

"Were he a gentlemen, such a heavenly display of endearment would give him a heart attack," Locke commented, cocking a wry smile at her when she made a face at him.

"Were he a gentleman, he'd be the most perfect man on earth. He knows exactly how to treat a lady," she quipped.

"Oh, I'm wounded." Locke threw a hand to his chest. "The ignominy of being bested by a horse. Well, at least I'll provide you a pleasant outing, my dear. Perhaps that will offset my shortcomings."

"It would raise you to as close to perfection as is humanly possible."

Locke chuckled and then asked Dimity to ready their mounts. Because Polly needed rest from last night's trip, the stable master delivered Locke a gelding from the riding horse stable, a bay with a star on his forehead, a horse named Major. Seaworth tacked up Raven for Lady Bethany, cinching an ordinary saddle in place.

"You never used a sidesaddle at Whitton," Locke said as he boarded Major, "so I assumed you don't want one now."

"Sidesaddles should be burned," she grumbled, accepting Seaworth's lift onto Raven. "They're miserably uncomfortable and positively deadly.

I've ridden bareback—in breeches and barefoot even—more than I ever did in a sidesaddle."

Locke snorted laughter then cleared his throat in embarrassment. Such painful candidness could ruin her reputation—and reflect badly on him—but her sincerity amused him. "I concur as to sidesaddles' impracticality, my lady. However, I suggest you introduce the estate to your scandalous behaviors a bit at a time. That is, if you want anyone to take you seriously."

Lady Bethany laughed. "I promise, my lord, not to embarrass you too badly. At least for a while."

They set out on the same road that had delivered them to Moorewood, Lady Bethany seeming as caught up in the landscape as Locke was by her natural grace, her blue skirts draped across the coal black of the stallion's glistening hide.

She glanced at him, and then, having apparently sensed his appraisal, turned blushing cheeks away from him. "It's such a lovely day. Not a drop of rain in sight."

"Perfect for riding," Locke replied, forcing his gaze to the road in search of the intersecting path they'd soon take. "How are your bedchambers?"

"Palatial."

"You're too kind. The trappings are nearly prehistoric."

"Not at all. Your mother's tastes were exemplary. I don't want them changed, at least not right off. They make me feel ... elegant."

Locke fought not to tell her that she was a great deal more elegant than her surroundings could ever be. He oughtn't to even be considering such notions. "I hope you enjoy them, but if you change your mind, be aware that Mr. Gordon Davies, my solicitor, has set aside funds for the entire project, including your quarters."

"Thank you, my lord. But I have a fully appointed room. You mentioned many of the chambers are bare. They need the attention first."

Locke rolled his eyes. "Most noblewomen would demand all of it posthaste. I applaud your prudence, but please don't deprive yourself of your comforts. Alright, my dear, we've warmed the horses up enough to stretch their legs. Shall we have a good gallop?"

She nodded, her smile broadening, and with a touch of their heels, the animals sprang into action, sprinting along the road to a path that led to the right hand, eastward and up a small hillock. On the other side, the path meandered through light woods and across a stretch of meadow, scattered with feathery bracken, the last of June's flowers, and the lemony petals of the native gorse.

Major pulled at the bit, begging to challenge Raven, but Locke held him back, enjoying the sight of Lady Bethany leaning into her stallion, the wind tugging wisps of hair loose from under her hat and tossing her skirts along the animal's flanks. When they encountered a deep stream, she and her horse soared over it with grace.

The path narrowed to a trail, swinging onto another hillock and under the shade of overhanging trees. They drew up to let the horses breathe and to enjoy the landscape, a vista Locke never ceased to appreciate. He pointed out various landmarks, the division between his tenants' holdings, and what Bethany might expect those families to request from her.

"These are decent people, my lady. Despite our peers' insistence that compassion toward the impoverished is improper, I'm adamant regarding their treatment, and more greatly upset with Matheson's defection than I've let on. I deal fairly with my tenants, regardless of what others think."

"I understand, my lord. My father did the same. Too many work these poor souls to death for their own profit and take what they please from them without regard to the consequences. I'll do all I can to reassure them that Mr. Matheson betrayed you as much as he did them."

Locke had meant for the work with the estate and especially the manor to keep Lady Bethany so busy she'd not likely head off into more public places, but he sensed she wanted to please him. An uncomfortable thought. And a monumental task for such a young woman. Still, she was safe here. Or at least safer than at Whitton.

"I applaud your determination, my dear, but I can't predict how some of the tenants will react. Take one of the stablehands with you when you visit them, whether you're with Lady Camille or not. I want you safe."

"If you insist," she said.

"I do. I have records in my study we'll discuss later tonight. They'll familiarize you with Moorewood's holdings and my tenants' obligations. Tomorrow morning we'll look in on some of the those I've still not contacted since Matheson left, to explain the situation. Then next week my solicitor will visit you to discuss financial matters and your personal allowance."

She blinked in surprise, perhaps not expecting to be trusted with managing money. Not many noblewomen did.

They rode to the stream they'd jumped earlier to water the horses, and Lady Bethany sighed with pleasure, looking around her. "It's beautiful here. Beyond beautiful. It's breathtaking."

Locke chuckled. "Moorewood is my pride and joy. The manor is the smallest of my holdings but the land the richest."

"I love it." Smiling wistfully, she added, "I also can't imagine having anything grander than Moorewood Manor—or at least what it will become."

They let the horses walk to the stable to cool down and found the building empty when they arrived. The animals all now out to pasture, the servants had gone off to other pursuits. Locke offered Lady Bethany help dismounting, suspecting she didn't need it but unable to escape the temptation to act the gentleman while setting his hands to her small waist.

She swung her right leg over the saddle, kicked her left foot from the stirrup and let him support her as she slid towards the ground. When a ripping sound made her gasp, he stopped her progress.

"Oh no! My skirt. It's caught between the stirrup leather and the saddle and it's tearing."

"I'll hold you up," Locke said, raising her enough to tug it free.

She weighed almost nothing, but he was more than overwhelmed by the sweet lemony smell of her. When he at last lowered her to the ground, he found himself unable to let go, at least until she turned to face him.

Emerald eyes opened wide, Lady Bethany's cheeks flushed prettily. Was that wonderment on her features? He didn't see the slightest hint of fear in her. He felt her gaze admire him, drifting from his brows to his nose and arriving at last at his mouth. Her hands, so small and delicate against the firm muscles of his chest, gave no hint of the resistance she'd shown last night.

She stood perfectly still, obviously aware that his breath had faltered. Did she realize what she did to him? Had she any idea how much he wanted to kiss her? And then he saw it, the glimmer of desire in her eyes that battered at his resolve. He raised a hand to brush a stray hair from her cheek and her eyelids fluttered shut, a tremble sweeping over her. His resistance melted and he traced her jaw to her chin and lifted it, leaning towards the soft pillow of her lips, wanting more than anything to taste their sweetness.

A loud thud from the sound of leather and metal hitting the ground sent them flying apart.

"Oh, sorry, m'lord," one of the stablehands, said, not sounding at all sorry. The pile of bridles he'd dropped to the stable floor lay heaped at his booted feet. "Didn't see you there. Shall I unsaddle the horses fer ya?"

Locke blinked, feeling as if he'd just come out of a trance. "Yes, of course, Devon."

Lady Bethany's obvious confusion dismayed him, but there was no help for it. He couldn't believe what had just passed between them. He couldn't let it happen again. Not ever.

"I've some duties I cannot put off, my lady," he told her. "Please feel free to return to the house and see to your needs. Mrs. Ford will have dinner ready for us at noon. I'll join you then."

The hurt on Lady Bethany's face told him that he must have sounded painfully dismissive, which made him feel like an ogre. "Shall I walk you to the house? It won't take but a moment."

"That's quite alright, my lord," Lady Bethany murmured. "I don't want to inconvenience you." She spun around and hurried towards the manor, her habit's skirts swishing around her ankles.

"Sorry for the interruption, m'lord," Devon said, watching Lady Bethany for a moment and then meeting Locke's gaze. "Simply following your orders."

Locke shrugged, embarrassed. "Orders keep life on the straight and narrow, Devon, especially where the wiles of a woman are concerned. Fetch the others to Dimity's workroom upstairs, to review the plans again before I leave. I've only two days to be sure everything is in place."

"My lord, sir." Devon nodded, heading off to do as commanded.

Locke watched Lady Bethany's distant form as she approached the manor. He still could hardly rein in the emotions that his bride's lovely eyes and warm body had unexpectedly threaded under his skin and into his heart. No woman had ever breached the barriers he'd raised against them many long years ago, but he feared Lady Bethany had the power.

Locke knew the situation would have taken a new and irrevocable course had he given in to temptation. Many women of all ages had visited this place since his childhood, but not once in his life had he seen a woman, apart from his mother, who seemed to belong here. Yet the minute she'd set foot inside the manor's imposing entryway, Bethany Montgomery Ashburn had felt as natural to it as its very foundation. Locke was reassured she'd fit in, perhaps too well, and she'd always be here when he visited, like it or not. He'd never before pondered how it would feel to come home to someone to whom he was attracted. It had never dawned on him how dangerous that could prove. Perhaps enormously more dangerous in its own way than the perils of the quest that lay ahead of him in the outside world.

* * *

Bethany strode to the manor, torn between relief and fury. How dare a retainer speak to his master that way? As if he reproved the earl for touching his own wife! And Locke had let this servant *Devon* get away with it. Why would he do that?

Turbid thoughts and raw feelings flustered her. She disliked Devon for interrupting them and yet was just as grateful things hadn't gone any further. Would they have gone further? Would she have enjoyed it? What flashed between her and Lord Locke had caught her completely by surprise, but she had to concede she'd wanted him to kiss her. It terrified her to contemplate what could have happened had she not been able to bear it. But what if she had? What then?

Squelching these feelings, she welcomed Melissa's announcement that her bath was ready and, after Melissa helped her clean up in the manor's ornate but outmoded downstairs bathing room, don her light turquoise day dress and arrange her hair, she had the girl call for Mrs. Callen.

While they waited, Melissa appraised the rent on Bethany's habit. "Oh, m'lady, this is awful. Shall I burn it?"

"Good grief, no," Bethany replied. Besides loving the garment, she detested waste, a practicality she and Lady Katherine had argued about more than once. "I'm sure it's mendable."

"Oh, it is, but—"

"I've no aversion to wearing mended clothing, Melissa, especially riding clothes." She'd had to learn to tolerate it along with Whitton's reduced circumstances. "I can fix it if you can't," she added, the girl's eyes widening in surprise.

Mrs. Callen arrived, huffing like she'd run full tilt from the cellars.

"I hope you don't mind," Bethany said, "but I want to look over the manor. To get the renovations under way."

"Certainly, my lady. I'm at your service. Melissa, what have you there?"

Melissa handed Bethany's riding habit to the housekeeper, who clucked over the damaged hem. Melissa told her Lady Bethany's request and how she planned to repair it, and Mrs. Callen raised her brows in surprise but gave her encouragement.

"Well, Lady Locke, the easiest approach to seeing this place," the housekeeper said, fishing a large ring of keys from her apron pocket, "is to begin at the top and work our way down."

And so they did, Bethany soon realizing this vast project would require significantly more than a cursory appraisal to organize it. She'd need to make several trips, along with paper and pen for notes on her stratagem. She also had to allow inspiration to take its course. Now more than ever she wondered why anyone, especially her mother, considered her up to this task. She possessed a decent sense of color and design, and she knew a lovely room when she saw one; but matching fabrics and décor to existing architecture? Coordinating furnishings and trappings? Preparing more than thirty chambers for future guests? The endeavor overwhelmed her.

By the time they'd seen the guest rooms, the various parlors, the morning room, the sitting room, the dining room and kitchen, the spacious sitting areas on the landings of each floor, and the library, Bethany anxiously anticipated Lady Camille's arrival. No one had a keener mind for making a space stunning than her cousin, and Lady Camille loved the challenge. Beyond that, Lady Katherine was acquainted with the best decorators and designers in London, and would at this very moment be making plans for Whitton's resurrection. In the library, Bethany wrote a missive to her mother, asking who to hire for the project, sealed it and turned it over to Mrs. Callen to have it franked for delivery to Whitton.

Left to herself in the library's solitude, Bethany roamed its spaces. It was immense, and heavy with the scent of books, of paper, ink, and leather, a smell Bethany adored almost as much as that of horses. Browsing shelf after shelf and then standing back to scrutinize the catwalk and rolling ladder that reached the highest levels, she couldn't imagine someone reading so many books in a lifetime. She could choose between Chaucer and Lord Byron. Or Milton's *Paradise Lost* and Shakespeare's plays, or Jane Austen's works.

On the other hand, surveying a handful of the titles, she wouldn't want to read them all. Many still considered *The Monk*, by M. G. Lewis, and Daniel Defoe's *Roxana* vulgar. Why would Lord Locke have them in his possession? And she had no interest in the history of tanning hides or the foremost methods for indigo farming.

The library was in better condition than most of the manor, and although it, too, could use paint and new carpets and furniture, she would spend little time or funds here.

Tired from her travels and the anxiety of the last two weeks, Bethany carried a book to a chair by the window, grateful that Kent's early summer days were so pleasant. Sunlight filtered through the window between the aging but diaphanous draperies, casting a golden glow across the room.

Fatigue brought melancholy with it. She pushed aside the homesickness and convinced herself that she'd misinterpreted what happened at the stable. After all, she had no right to want Lord Locke to hold and kiss her, and the Earl of Locke had made it quite plain he wanted nothing from her. She needed to appreciate his generosity in giving her a position that would both entertain her and keep her out of his way, and protect that part of her that couldn't bear the test.

Again she sighed, opened the cover of *Pride and Prejudice* and let reading relieve her of her mental maundering.

CHAPTER 7

The noon meal felt awkward, with Bethany embarrassed and the earl withdrawn. He hurried to his upstairs study immediately after and left Bethany to entertain herself. Then, later that evening, Lord Locke sent Bethany a message that unexpected matters would make him late for supper. He appeared moments before she finished the last of her meal, begging her forgiveness but tired and distracted. When he cited a headache as a reason to put off their work with the estate's books until tomorrow, she suspected the Earl of Locke's true intent was to avoid her.

It was an odd, lonely end to Bethany's first full day of marriage, although she admitted that being in the company of the earl too much did not bode well. Heading for her room, heartfelt prayers, and a night's sleep seemed the appropriate conclusion.

Saturday morning dawned with a scattering of clouds and a hint of rain. Still, at the appointed hour Bethany donned her gray riding habit and joined Locke in riding out to meet with some of Moorewood's tenants. The earl's strained smile reminded Bethany that his time with her was most likely a trial of which he'd soon be glad to rid himself.

Polly and Raven, both meticulously trained for good behavior in the presence of another stallion, pranced their way from Moorewood's stable yard, the dew sparkling like emeralds and diamonds as they cantered over the fields.

Not knowing what to expect, Bethany felt on edge when they jogged into the farmyard of the first tenancy. The farmwife who met them did so with head bowed and hands clenched tight. Locke greeted the woman with deference, asking about her health and that of her family. One of her three children had been ill, she admitted, but otherwise they were good enough. Her husband was presently in the barn milking their half dozen goats.

"I'll fetch him, so's you can take what you want of the milk, m'lord," she said in resignation.

"I'm not here for milk, Mrs. Elway," Locke said. "I just need to speak with your husband."

Anxiety creased the woman's features and she bobbed a curtsy and hurried off to collect the man. When he came, wiry and thick-whiskered, he regarded them with mistrust.

"Morning, Elway," Locke said. "I bear important news." After explaining Matheson's schemes, he said, "When I lay hands on him, he'll rue the day he was born, but whether I do or not, I commit to setting everything straight as soon as I can with all of you. Should my efforts not suffice, I'll relieve you of your contract without penalty and help you find service elsewhere. I'd as soon you stay, but only if you're satisfied."

Elway's eyes widened in surprise and his gaze met Mrs. Elway's. To Bethany the farmwife seemed terrified, as if she expected her husband to insist on leaving the home—and farm—they'd occupied for nearly a decade.

Locke continued. "I regret that I won't remain in residence long enough to see everything rectified myself, but this, good people, is Lady Locke, my new wife and Countess. She will visit you again soon, to collect a thorough list of Matheson's offenses. For now, I want to address your most pressing concerns."

Pride held Elway's spine straight and his mouth shut, but his wife divulged a number of Matheson's abuses, including striking Elway when he tried to stop the steward from taking their chickens and rooster.

Bethany was horrified, but Locke's promise to replace both hens and cock on the morrow had surprise replacing the anger on the farmer's and his wife's faces and relief on Bethany's.

The visits throughout the morning mirrored this one. Some of the tenants became substantially more vocal, others remained sullen. All expressed pleasant surprise at Bethany's arrival, probably indicating their hope that as a married man, their master would better understand their needs.

At the last farm they visited, the wife, a comely younger woman, kindly offered to water them and their horses. While they quenched their thirst, Mrs. Hedley went for her husband.

Locke murmured that these people were his newest tenants and had no idea how Matheson had managed Moorewood before he turned corrupt.

"I doubt they can afford to leave," he said, "but I won't have disgruntled people on my property. Revenge comes in many forms. Hedley adores his wife and would do anything for her, so if you win her over, he'll follow suit."

Bethany looked at him askance, wondering exactly how she'd do that.

The cottage's crude front door squeaked open and a young girl ventured timidly onto the stoop. Bethany's heart went out to her, seeing her thin dress and bare, grimy feet. Her waist-length blond hair hung dirty and straggly, although her face was recently given a cursory wash.

"Hello," Bethany said, smiling when the girl tiptoed down the steps and came to stand close.

"You're pretty," the little one replied, giggling.

"That's very kind of you," Bethany replied, stooping to meet the girl's pale brown eyes. "What's your name?"

"Beebee," the girl replied.

"No, it's not" came a slightly older voice, and Bethany glanced up to see a second girl sidling onto the stoop.

"Hello," Bethany said. "What's your name? How old are you?"

"Laura. Be turnin' six in August. M' sister's name's Beatrice, but we call her Bea. She's almost four, calls herself Beebee. My brother Rob, he's but a babe. He's inside sleepin'."

"You're a fine family," Bethany said, seeing that the two girls were very pretty albeit uncomfortably lean. Had Mr. Matheson's underhandedness had something to do with this, too? "Do you like living at Moorewood?"

"'S'alright," Laura said. "Pretty enough, but Pa says we starve so's the lord's house is all fancy."

Bethany glanced at Locke, who came close to glowering. Then she asked Laura, "What is it that you need?"

The girl frowned thoughtfully then shrugged. "Pa says we'd have enough if it wasn't taken from us," she replied, leaning into the rickety handrail and easing down the steps. "Can't eat it if 'n we don't have it." The girl's eyes reflected her hunger and her already jaded soul.

"Well, today we hope to make sure your situation improves," she told the child. "Have you vegetables and fruit, and flour for bread? Oats and corn meal?"

Before Laura could answer, bustling footsteps heralded the arrival of the Hedleys, and Bethany stepped away from Bea. Mrs. Hedley's eyes rounded with a mother's worry, and Mr. Hedley's jaw set in irritation.

"Hedley," Locke said. "We must talk."

Hedley's gaze, stained with fearful skepticism, slid coldly over Bethany as Locke introduced the farmer to her and once again revealed the story of Matheson's offenses and escape. Hedley admitted they'd had difficulty and gave cautious account of their circumstances.

Locke said, "By sunrise tomorrow morning, I'll have half-bushels each of potatoes, carrots, onions and cabbage delivered to you, along with forty kilos of flour and twenty each of oats and corn meal. Are you short on tools, or did Matheson deny you the equipment you needed as well?"

A lengthy pause was followed by Hedley's bitter account of these things and more, the farmer pale with anger. "He ran his hands o'er my wife, said she was too pretty for the likes of me. Said he might give allowances to a man who'd be willin' to share. I raised a fist to him, and the men with him, they beat me. Knocked out a tooth, they did." He tugged his lip aside to show a gap between two back teeth.

Bethany gasped, hands to her mouth. She didn't like what she'd learned of Mr. Matheson thus far, but hearing this infuriated her.

"What other men?" Locke demanded. "Describe them, if you can. None of the other tenants has mentioned them, and I hired no one but Matheson to manage Moorewood."

Hedley gave thorough descriptions, but Locke conceded he didn't recognize them. Strangers they were—henchmen hired to do a vile man's vile work for him? No wonder the tenants were both so incensed and fearful. Repercussions for resistance had been violent.

"Your dress is shiny," Bea interjected, nearing Bethany. "Is it soft?"

"La, come away, girl!" Mrs. Hedley snapped, reaching for the child.

"It's alright, Mrs. Hedley," Bethany said. To the girl she added, "It is shiny, isn't it? I'll tell you a secret. I like it, but it's hot." The girl stroked the hem of the riding skirt that Bethany held out for her, her eyes wide with awe.

"You're hair's really long," Laura said, stealing past her mother and joining her sister. She dared rest a hand on the skirt's silk fabric, too, but snatched it back as if it burned her. "You've lots of curls and a pretty hat," she added.

"Thank you, Laura." Bethany self-consciously touched the lovelock she'd let Melissa leave free again today. "I think your hair is a lovely shade of blonde. I've always wanted blonde hair, but we have what we have, don't we? See your mother? She's a very pretty woman, and you'll both look a lot like her when you're young ladies." She tried to comfort herself with the realization that beyond good food, liberal use of soap—did they have any?—and water could do much for these children.

The girls giggled and batted their eyelashes bashfully, but Bethany sensed the exchange had touched Mrs. Hedley's heart and softened Mr. Hedley's scowl a fraction. She was glad to see a bit of hope in their eyes.

"I'll set the order for your provisions in motion as soon as we reach the manor," Locke said before they departed. "Remember, Lady Bethany will visit you again in the next few days to discover what else you need."

It wasn't the way a countess should behave, but Bethany couldn't help waving goodbye to the two grinning little girls as they set off.

* * *

"Thank you, Lady Bethany," Locke said, his bravado slipping once they'd left Hedley's place. "You handled all of that admirably. The situation's much worse than I imagined."

"I feel terrible for them. And for you." These people were servants, little elevated above the serfdom of centuries past or the slavery that infected many of the world's nations today. Nonetheless, she believed they were just as much children of the God she worshipped as was she. They hadn't deserved Matheson's mistreatment. No one did.

In contrast to the tenants, Bethany recognized the privilege her station provided her when she returned to the manor to don a clean day dress and take a wholesome lunch. Locke appeared pensive, and she knew he must still be pondering what they'd learned today. She at least hoped he wasn't overly worried about her managing everything in his absence. It was her responsibility to ease his burdens, not the other way around.

Locke escorted Bethany to his study after lunch and presented the records he'd put off showing her last night. As a door connected his bedchamber to Bethany's, so one on the other side connected it to his study. The desk, a monstrous thing, held a plethora of drawers, each of them locked. Bethany wondered what he hid there that was so important it needed locks.

The afternoon's work grew tedious, Bethany believing she was far from gifted in anything that involved money, inventory, or record-keeping. It reminded herself that she was far less a wife to this man than a glorified but less-than-ideal steward.

When they were finished, the earl handed her a key and said he'd lock the records in the desk drawer in the library when he departed, where she'd have easy access to them. They rose stiffly from their chairs, Bethany sighing in relief.

"You've been a champion," Locke praised her. "I'm not sure I sat that still or showed half your astuteness when my father turned these things over to me, and I'd been groomed for it my entire life. I had the feeling, and the reassurance of the twins, that you're capable, and I'm grateful I'm leaving Moorewood in good hands, my lady."

Bethany appreciated the compliments but disliked the reminder that Lord Matthew and Mr. Nicolas had discussed her with Marcus Ashburn. What else had they told him about her? What could she possibly get them to tell her about Lord Locke?

CHAPTER 8

After they finished supper that night, Locke folded his serviette and set it beside his plate. It was their last night together, and he couldn't make up his mind whether he was glad or regretful. Mostly, he'd racked his brain for something safe to do with Lady Bethany, rather than rudely abandoning her, as he'd done several times since her arrival.

"Your mother told me you play the piano," he managed at last. "Perhaps you wouldn't mind joining me in the downstairs gold parlor and playing for a while?"

Lady Bethany's emerald eyes widened in surprise. He sensed she truly wanted to use the exceptional instrument but perhaps not in front of him.

"I don't play all that well," she demurred. "And I need music."

He raised one corner of his mouth in amusement. "I've plenty of music. Believe it or not, I can play, but I haven't set my fingers to the ivories in at least a year." He signaled Mr. Treadwell, who came to pull her chair out for her. "Which means you'll be providing entertainment for both of us."

"You play?" she asked, bewildered.

"Yes. I know, not something to which a male peer of the realm should admit."

"The twins play. And I believe Scarbreigh does as well. My brothers wouldn't have been caught dead."

Locke chuckled. "My mother played well and I loved it, badgered her into teaching me. It's not something I make public, but I enjoy good music whoever plays it."

She sighed and took his offered arm.

* * *

Bethany's heart tried to pound itself through her breastbone. She could not have foreseen this. Play the piano for the Earl of Locke? Considering their awkward moments since arriving at Moorewood, she'd understood that Lord Locke had no obligation to entertain her and she'd had no expectations he would do so. It had never dawned on her that he might want her to entertain him.

She'd seen the exquisite pianoforte in the gold parlor during her tour of the manor. Mrs. Callen had told her Locke's father bought it for his mother right after they married. Bethany had longed to try her hand at it, but those hands were now shaking when she sat down to it. Amazingly, her dread at making mistakes fled the minute she heard the instrument's singular voice.

"Lovely," Locke said, sitting beside her on the bench. "You're quite good, my lady. Try these." He offered her several pieces of music from a covered box on a table beside the piano, each progressively harder than the last. His eyes sparkled when he handed her the last one.

Bethany tinkered with it until she got the feel for it. Despite her halting efforts, she loved the piece. "I've never heard it before. Who wrote it?"

Locke's dimples dug into his cheeks, giving him the look of a disconcerted schoolboy. "Actually, I did. I don't believe I play especially well, but my mother, who was well-accomplished, said I had a gift for composing. Play it again and let me join you."

Bethany found it easier the second time, of course. Locke set his fingers on the keys and played with her, two octaves above and sometimes in syncopation. It had her imagining faeries cavorting around a waterfall and made her giggle with glee.

"Oh, it's exquisite," she said when they'd finished. She slid to the edge of the bench and begged, "Play it for me, will you? I know the notes, but I'll never know the heart of it. Only you understand that."

Locke laughed and crowded her enough to reach the lower notes. He paused a moment, closed his eyes and began to play. Bethany's chest tightened at watching him. He brought out the pauses and the cascades, the thoughtful moments and the urgent ones. But beyond that, he loved what the piece meant to him. He saw the beauty inside his mind, the way an artist imagined a painting yet unpainted, and it made him … beautiful.

The last note was low and, when Locke reached for it and his shoulder bumped hers, Bethany gasped at losing her balance. His eyes flew open and he grabbed for her, shock on his face, but his awkward move sent them both tumbling backwards off the bench.

Bethany landed with her legs tangled in her skirts and the breath knocked out of her. Locke's face nearly crashed into hers and his elbow bruised her side, leaving her gasping in pain.

"Oh, heavens, Lady Bethany, I'm so sorry," Locke cried, scrambling to his knees and taking her hands in his. "Breathe, my dear, please. You're lips are blue."

Bethany gasped again and coughed, cringing at the ache in her back and side, but hurting too badly even to cry.

"Let me help you sit up."

She at least felt less like she'd suffocate when she did, although she fought dizziness and had to press her hand to her ribs to ease the pain.

"I hurt you, didn't I? Please forgive my clumsiness."

When he'd helped her to her feet, the ridiculousness of the situation sent her into a fit of giggles.

"Why are you laughing? I've made a fool of myself and near broken you in pieces. I don't see any humor in that."

His seriousness made her giggle that much harder.

"You looked completely engrossed," she told him. "And the music was lovely, and then you leaned over and I was falling, and you didn't yet realize it. Then I gasped and you reached for me but also lost your balance, and barreled down on top of me. And when you landed, your nose was so close to mine, all I saw was your right eye—you have exquisite eyes, you know—but with you that close and threatening to crush me, I had no opportunity to appreciate it, just that your eye was open so wide I thought it would pop out of your head."

She broke into laughter Lady Katherine would have considered unseemly and had to cover her mouth to quiet it. Then he chuckled, his dimples reappearing, and ran a hand through his hair, which had somehow become quite fetchingly mussed.

"I could have caused you serious harm. I'm still not seeing the humor."

"It was an accident," she insisted. "I should have moved to a chair; then it wouldn't have happened. I just wanted to watch. You play handsomely and make it look easier than it is."

Locke harrumphed and shook his head, nonplussed. "I cannot fathom what to do with you, Lady Bethany. I've never met a woman quite like you."

Bethany gave another unladylike snort and again had to cover her mouth. "I'm sorry. I don't imagine you have. I doubt very many of England's countesses are so uncouth. I promise I'll try my best not to shame you in public. Then you won't ever have to worry about what to do with me. But of course, you won't be around much, so I doubt you'll need to worry about it anyway."

Locke sobered and Bethany's amusement waned with it. Asked to name it, she'd have called his expression regretful. Why? Did she dare imagine he'd miss her? And why in heavens name should she want him to? She had no desire to come unraveled if the man changed his mind and decided to demand his marital rights of her. Best not to test the waters.

And yet, standing this close and breathing in the scent of him, her longing betrayed her. His shaving lather, the rousing male scent of him and the soft look on his handsome face drew her, making her want to lean into him, to touch him.

"It's fortuitous that I'm leaving," he said with amusement. "I fear I'm bad luck for you. First yesterday morning with tearing your hem, and now this. You'll probably wear bruises for days because of me. And your hair...." He took a step closer, dangerously closer. "Your pins have come lose. Shall I risk bayonetting your skull to put them back, or should I take them out?"

"Bayonetting does not sound appealing," Bethany insisted, trying not to laugh again. It hurt too much. "Please remove them. I'd hate to lose them."

Deftly his fingers pulled the pins from each curled lock, setting more and more of it free until it cascaded to her waist. "Law, it's beautiful. But I think I've created a worse mess of things. Shall I straighten it a bit?"

She nodded, warmed by the thought he liked her hair. His fingers threaded themselves through the curls, Bethany closing her eyes as shivers of pleasure swept over her. He took his time, stepping around and pulling it behind her shoulders and gently finger-combing it. What an amazing thing it was to enjoy a man's touch. How extraordinary to wish he'd never stop.

* * *

Lady Bethany smelled divine, again like sweet lemons and honey. Lemon Verbena? But sweeter. Would her lips taste like that? Her hair, thick and luxurious, draped her shoulders in a cascade of dark, shining tresses. Had he never befriended a woman, had he never known what it felt like to kiss one, he might have desired the experience for its own sake. But he'd had the pleasure of it, before he'd begun to realize kissing the right woman would mean far more than simply kissing someone because he could.

Duty had driven such boyhood fantasies from his mind, and discipline had protected him from it in the worst of situations. He wondered what it would take to force these unbidden desires from him now. He hadn't dreamed he could ever feel this way about Lady Bethany. Had the twins suspected it and, beyond its original purpose, suggested the arrangement to see if it would flourish? He wanted to curse them for it if it was true. They knew he stood in too much peril to let a woman into his personal life.

Then he caught her profile, with her eyes closed and her face dreamy, and his breath caught. No portrait, no sculpture could capture such beauty. She was devastating, with her hair free and pleasure pinking her cheeks. There was something warm and tender about her that could only be discerned face-to-face.

"Here you go, my dear," he said, his voice husky. He offered her the pins, and when her eyes fluttered open and settled on his, she opened her hand to him. He pressed the pins into the palm of that hand and closed her fingers around them, holding them in place for a lingering moment. He couldn't help it. He loved how soft her hands were, how small and dainty they felt between his own.

"Thank you," she said, making no effort to resist him, those emerald eyes wide and trusting.

A knock came at the parlor door, stilling the moment. Locke set Lady Bethany free, not wanting to but knowing he must. He called to Mr. Treadwell to enter, stepping away when his man delivered a tray of tea and sweet cakes.

"Mrs. Ford imagined you and Lady Locke would enjoy this, my lord," the man said, doing a double-take when he saw Lady Bethany's hair undone.

Locke's face reddened and he cleared his throat. "Excellent. Thank Mrs. Ford for me, will you? We experienced a small mishap. Lady Bethany fell off the piano bench and her, uh, her hair came loose. I'm sure she'd appreciate some refreshments to settle her nerves. Please set it down and feel free to retire."

Mr. Treadwell paused, glancing at Lady Bethany again. "I'll wait up, my lord. It's my duty. I'll be right outside the door if you require my services."

Locke stifled a grim smile as Mr. Treadwell departed. Curse his servants for obeying his orders so well. Bless them for being there. He didn't have to like their watch-care, but he needed it.

"Will you join me?" he asked, waving at the tray.

Lady Bethany paused and then took an anxious breath. "I ... I'm sorry, my lord, but I really should retire if I'm to rise early enough to ready myself for church tomorrow."

"Ah. Of course. And shall we take one more ride together, perchance after Lady Camille arrives tomorrow afternoon?"

Lady Bethany gave him a tight smile and a nod.

"Wonderful. Sleep well, my dear. I'll join you at breakfast."

Lady Bethany hurried to the door and gave it a quick tap. Mr. Treadwell opened it for her, surprise on his face at seeing her ready to leave so soon.

And then she'd gone, and Mr. Treadwell cast Locke a concerned frown before shutting the door behind him. Locke sat down and reached for a sweet cake, then returned it, wondering why he'd want to eat it. He'd spent half a lifetime of carefree moments in this room, some with friends, some with family or both. He'd often come alone to practice the piano or to pause and pray or meditate for a while, but he couldn't remember ever feeling so terribly lonely.

* * *

Why did Bethany want to cry? No matter how often she reviewed what Lord Locke told her the night he'd proposed to her; no matter how firmly she reminded herself that Marcus Ashburn wanted nothing to do with her; no matter how firmly she insisted she had nothing to offer the man, she couldn't deny her attraction to him. It was good that Providence seemed determined to keep them apart by placing Locke's servants between them. But why did she feel such miserable disappointment? Why did she ache to relive his stroking of her hair, or when he'd held her hand in his? What would it feel like to have her husband wrap her in his arms and kiss her?

She remained stoic while Melissa prepared her for bed and would have sent her away quickly if she hadn't noted that the girl seemed awkward with her duties. After teaching the abigail how she liked things done, she asked, "Melissa, where have you served as a lady's maid before?"

Melissa paused, at first startled and then uneasy. "Well, I-I haven't truly abigailed before, my lady, but Mrs. Callen once did, when she was a girl, and my aunt, she's a good friend of Mrs. Callen's, she is. Works for Lady Smithington, at the Smithington's estate to the south, has let me help there some, to learn the duties. Soon as his lordship announced his plans to marry, Mrs. Callen wrote for me, suggested I might work out, and began training me. I hope I can please you, my lady. I'd rather serve as a lady's maid than a housemaid."

Bethany understood Melissa's sentiments, even if the girl oughtn't to have admitted to her preferences. Either job was demanding, but there was an element of prestige—and higher wages—as a lady's maid.

"I hope Mrs. Callen hasn't pushed you too hard. You had little time to learn." Not likely more than a week or two of diligent instruction.

"Not so bad really. I've had six weeks. It's not near enough, I know, but I learn quick, and I promise I'll do whatever I need to, to please you, my lady."

Bethany did her best not to let her shock show. Dismissing the girl to the servants' quarters, she advised her that she wasn't one to rise during the night and wouldn't need the girl's services until the morrow.

Melissa bobbed a curtsy and wished her mistress good night, and Bethany locked the door behind her. Sinking to her bed, she buried her face in her pillows and tried to make sense of what her personal maid had just said.

Lord Locke had hired Melissa six weeks ago? He had to have begun making plans to marry Bethany even longer ago than that. He must have been incredibly sure of himself. Why didn't he propose sooner? Why wait until it was too late to post banns? Try as she might, she couldn't shake the feeling that there was something more to all of this than met the eye. The next time she saw the twins, she was determined to confront them. Surely they had some inkling of what this was all about.

Tears that made no sense dampened her pillow, but after what felt like a lifetime, they also calmed her troubled heart.

Prayers followed, silent, diligent prayers. Homesickness plagued her, and fear; loneliness loomed in front of her with no end in sight, even while she knew she'd agreed to it. Her husband was a handsome man, and even while she was as afraid of him as she was of all men, he not only puzzled her, he also enticed her. She prayed the Good Lord would set her free of such temporal cravings. She couldn't lose sight of the fact that in becoming the Earl of Locke's wife, she'd accepted a lifetime of celibacy. She had no right—and in fact every reason to not want—to betray that to which she'd consented. This she knew without question; and despite the temptations otherwise, with this she must learn to make peace.

* * *

Sunday morning's sunrise brought a new day's hope to Bethany. Church would lift her spirits, and later in the morning she planned to examine the manor in finer detail.

And this afternoon, Lady Camille would arrive.

Lord and Lady Locke, dressed in their Sunday best, boarded the carriage manned by servants dressed in Moorewood's finest livery. The brief ride brought them to the small chapel that served the estate and the surrounding villagers. It had nearly filled to capacity, the news having spread of the earl's return and his unexpected marriage.

Bethany found the vicar, Reverend James Munro, an eloquent speaker and a man of delightful character. He was the first to congratulate them after the service, followed by the crowd of curious townspeople. Bethany deduced that Lord Locke was liked, even if he wasn't in residence much, a thought that gave her at least some measure of reassurance.

Their midday meal awaited them when they returned, along with a missive from Lady Camille, announcing her arrival at around two-thirty that afternoon. Locke gave his regrets that he had more business at the stables to address, but he suggested they take her cousin on a ride before supper.

"I'm sure she'd love to see as much of Moorewood as she can tonight," Bethany replied.

"Splendid. I'll meet you in the entryway at half past four."

CHAPTER 9

A most unladylike squeal rent the air, and Mr. Treadwell stepped back from the door as Lady Camille and the new Lady Locke rushed into each other's arms. Bethany tried hard not to flinch from the bruises her cousin bumped. Falling off piano benches was definitely not the thing.

"Camille, you are an answer to prayers! How was the drive?"

"Not terribly disagreeable, despite the old carriage's cramped space."

"Excellent. Mrs. Callen has your quarters ready, and Melissa's available to abigail for you."

"I must change clothes and freshen up, but then I'm ready for whatever you like, Beth."

"A spot of tea and then a tour of the house. You won't believe the task I undertook when I accepted Locke's proposal. The house is ... well, come see for yourself."

Arm in arm they proceeded through the manor, chatting amiably. Lady Camille did her fair share of admiring the good and bemoaning the bad on the way to her room, while reporting that all was fine at Whitton and Aunt Katherine in transports over the plans for Whitton's manor.

Bethany's cousin gasped when she set eyes on both her bedchamber, opposite Bethany's quarters, and Bethany's. Matheson had stolen little from most of the rooms on this floor, probably because they were near Lord Locke's rooms. Even if not up-to-the-minute they were all lovely.

"Oh, this is extraordinary, Beth. Count yourself blessed to be here. Everyone's still prattling on about your marriage, you know. I've brought a missive from my parents, by the way, probably offering their regrets for not being able to attend the wedding and no doubt giving their felicitations for a happy life and a promise to visit as soon as Mum feels up to it."

Bethany was soon as exhausted by listening to her cousin's chattering as she was grateful for her companionship. Melissa made quick work of exchanging Lady Camille's travel dress for her day dress and then they sat down in Bethany's rooms to the tea Mr. Treadwell brought up for them. Bethany warned her cousin, however, that they had only a couple of hours to look over the house. After that, they'd don riding clothes and join Lord Locke for a ride.

"The estate is breathtaking," Lady Camille said. "I can hardly wait to see more. But I must admit the manor's renovation intrigues me more."

Bethany replied drolly, "Let me know how you feel after you've seen the whole of it."

Bethany bore her writing implements as they ambled through each chamber, knowing Lady Camille's immediate impressions were always the best and wanting to capture them right away.

"It's unbelievable," Lady Camille said, at last. "No doubt a great deal of work, never mind the expense, but this house must have been stunning in its youth."

"So I hear," Bethany said. "You must help me with it."

"As much as I can, considering I don't live here, of course."

"You could, if you wanted. You could act as my companion. You've no obligations to speak of at home, you'd have the time of your life, and you'd save me from death by loneliness."

Lady Camille searched Bethany's face, her brow puckering in concern. "It's none of my business, Love, but.... Have things turned out differently than you expected? I mean, between you and Lord Locke? I sense he's drawn to you, you know; and I dare say the same about you. You've had three days together, and I'd rather hoped...."

Bethany's cheeks flushed and she waved a dismissive hand. "No, Cam. We get along the way strangers do who've no commitment beyond convenience, but then—"

"What?" Lady Camille urged. "What happened?"

Bethany sighed. "We'll talk about it later. Let's change our clothes for riding. Lord Locke will soon come for us."

The earl was waiting for them in the entryway when they arrived, where he welcomed Lady Camille with sincerity and offered an arm to each of them as they headed to the stable.

Locke and Bethany again rode Polly and Raven, while Seaworth provided Lady Camille with a leggy bay gelding named Prince, promised to have wonderful gates. Bethany made mental note, however, that now that Lady Camille was here, they could concentrate on exercising the rest of her horses in the days ahead.

"Your estate is enviable, my lord," Lady Camille enthused. "The land's rockier and a bit hillier than at home, but it's amazingly fertile, and I swear I smell the sea. You were privileged to grow up here."

Locke smiled. "Wish I could spend most of my days here."

"At least when you do visit, you'll have Lady Bethany to keep you company," she said, twinkling.

Drat Lady Camille for her meddling, Bethany thought, flushing.

"Something to which I will look forward," Locke replied.

Bethany sighed, wondering what Marcus Ashburn meant by this comment. Aloof one minute. Endearing the next. She wondered whether she'd ever understand him. She wondered if she should even try.

When they returned home, Mrs. Ford served them a superb supper, and afterwards they strolled through the lovely grounds behind the manor. Beyond the lawns and flower beds stood a small woods and, a short distance behind that, Locke led them to a large pond and a stately pavilion. Bethany loved this private area and the benches that lined the inside of the building, offering an inviting, quiet place to visit.

They followed the walkway that hugged the serpentine shoreline, Lady Camille laughing at the ducks and geese that played in the water.

"This makes Moorewood even more exceptional," Bethany couldn't help saying to Locke as the path led them past handsome shrubbery, multitudes of flowers, and under the dangling branches of willow trees and clusters of alders, birches and maples.

His gaze latched onto hers. What he said next might have made her heart stand still if not for the sober look on his face. "I'm happy you like it. It almost seems as if it were made for you."

Bethany looked to her feet, uncertain how to respond. "I shall enjoy pretending it was."

With nightfall coming on, they retired at last to the gold parlor where Lady Camille exclaimed over the piano. An excellent pianist, she willingly entertained them, while Mr. Treadwell brought them a tray of cheese and wine.

Lady Camille appraised the bottle's label in surprise. "Chenin blanc, my lord. Has the ban against the French been lifted?"

"Not likely. It's from my wine cellar, dated from before my birth."

"Then it will be excellent," she said, taking the glass he poured for her. "Mmm. Tart and dry. Exactly the way I like it."

"Please don't like it too much," Bethany muttered, wincing at Lady Camille's sharp glance.

"Not now Lady Bethany."

"Better now than after it's too late."

"I did fine at your wedding."

"This wine is far stronger. It could have you foxed in a trice."

"Well at least it isn't flavored syrup, the way you like it."

Bethany couldn't help chuckling. Lady Camille was too charitable a person to know how to cut someone. "The joys of a good claret far outweigh it, the sweeter, the better." She paused to offer a wry smile to Locke. "This, however, is excellent, my lord."

"Glad you like it," he said, amused. "But when I return, we'll open an even older bottle of burgundy. I'm convinced you'll love it."

Were the man's eyes sparkling with mischief? It almost seemed as if he was flirting with her. Or pretending to? A part of her wished it were true while another knew how fortuitous it was that it was not. She dared not leave her heart out where it might get trampled—for surely it would.

She hadn't realized his gaze had mesmerized her until she pulled in a deep breath and broke the spell between them. Disconcerted, she turned to Lady Camille, who surveyed both of them curiously.

"Lord Locke writes music, Lady Camille. Can you imagine it? He let me play a piece last night. I couldn't do it justice, but I adored it." And fell off the bench after *he* played it, she thought. "If we ask nicely, perhaps he'll play it for us now."

"I'd love that, my lord. Will you?"

Locke gave a patient sigh and set aside his wine. Again he played, again with his eyes closed, and Bethany took note that Lady Camille appeared equally hypnotized by the man.

"Oh, you have to play whatever else you've written," Lady Camille said, clapping. "That was superb."

"I fear that was my best," he admitted, "and the only one I bothered to memorize. Unfortunately, I put my sheet music away years ago and can't remember where."

"How disappointing. Well, Lady Bethany, I'll need another invitation when your husband does find it. I can't wait to hear more."

"My sentiments exactly. Will you be gone long, my lord?" Bethany searched Locke's face for some clue. His mask slid into place, his expression unfathomable.

"Time is relative, my dear. What seems overlong to some may be but a moment to others."

Bethany looked away, as amused as she was vexed. Did he not know? Or did he not want her to know?

"Enjoy your wine, ladies," Locke said, finishing his drink. "I regret my bed calls to me. I'll be gone before the rooster crows. My lady?" He offered his hand and Bethany accepted it. "These last two weeks of our acquaintance have been lovely. Thank you for brightening them for me. I look forward to the changes you'll bring to Moorewood. Stay safe until I return."

He set those warm, moist lips of his to her fingers, and despite herself Bethany felt her knees weaken and giddiness sweep over her at his touch. Was it because she knew that this was all she could have of him that she wished it could be more? Or was there truly something special about the Earl of Locke? She couldn't answer either question, but when Locke walked away, she also couldn't help pressing those fingers to her lips.

"Oh, Beth," Lady Camille said, making Bethany tuck her hand behind her back to hide what she'd done.

Bethany met her cousin's gaze and cringed at the pity she saw there.

"What shall you do?" Lady Camille murmured. "I'm in love with him, and I haven't had to spend three days alone with him. I cannot imagine being his wife and never being able to share his bed."

"Lady Camille!" Bethany said, gasping. Her cheeks flamed and she turned her back on her cousin, lest Lady Camille see the tears that such a declaration had spawned. "I've never heard you speak so frankly before."

"Perhaps you're rubbing off on me."

"Most unlikely. Whatever possessed you?"

"Because I see the pain on your face, dear heart. After dealing with the misery from last year, it must torment you to have found someone to whom you could give your heart and have him so unavailable. It would eat me alive."

Bethany brushed aside her tears and composed herself before facing Lady Camille again. "Let's retire to my room. The staff is small, but I fear their ears are very large, and I'd love to talk."

"What's wrong?"

"I'm not sure. But I have a feeling the Earl of Locke isn't what he seems to be."

* * *

Ensconced in Bethany's quarters, they discussed her impressions of Locke since meeting him, what she believed was a near kiss at the stable, and last night's fall off the piano bench. Adding Melissa's being hired more than six weeks ago, and the tale grew even more unsettling.

"Something's not right," Lady Camille agreed, her eyes touched with worry. Then she shrugged, "But I have no idea what to do. In time, all may resolve itself, but clearly Lord Locke leaves in the morning, my dear, and he's given you an entire country home to explore, a manor to renovate, and enough horses I couldn't possibly count them in one day. You've enough to keep yourself busy without trying to solve mysteries, at least for now."

Bethany sighed and nodded. "You're right. Let's talk about something else, shall we?"

They did, but when they finally retired for the night, Bethany couldn't escape the truth. She was, despite his oddities, sad at Lord Locke's departing.

In mockery to her soul, rain pattered on the window panes, heaven weeping for Lord Locke in her stead.

* * *

Following breakfast, the women began the first of what would become a daily routine, in the midst of a most unseasonably warm, dry summer, for weeks to come. On days that provided sufficient sunshine, they planned to ride before breakfast, in the cooler hours, and again in the evening. On drizzly ones, like today, and every afternoon no matter the weather, they'd work on the plans for the manor.

A multitude of other pastimes also worked into the routine. Needlework or practicing the piano, reading in the garden, visiting around the pond or in the pavilion, playing games, or writing letters. And Bethany always had the dreaded estate's bookwork to address as well.

Bethany did not share Lady's Camille's love of writing in her diary, however. Her husband's activities puzzled her, but she refused to make note of them, believing there were some things that oughtn't to be committed to paper.

She pondered them, however, and the fact that Mr. Treadwell didn't accompany the earl on this trip. Why would Lord Locke not take his man with him? It made absolutely no sense, as well as the way Mr. Treadwell seemed to keep his eye on *her*.

Lady Katherine's return missive came to Bethany mid-morning on Tuesday, suggesting a certain Mr. Taylor-Ward to oversee Moorewood's renovation. Bethany sent for the man immediately. Then Locke's solicitor, Gordon Davies, arrived for his appointment but an hour later.

He again overwhelmed Bethany with both the obligations that would rest on her shoulders and the generous means her husband had left at her disposal to address them. Davies also reassured her that the goods and supplies promised to Moorewood's tenants had been delivered according to the earl's instructions, and if she was certain anyone needed more, she had only to inform him.

Mr. Taylor-Ward arrived on Thursday afternoon, a spindly gentleman with a thick mustache and narrow brows. He, in turn, sent outfitters, designers, and carpenters over the next several days to examine the job and make their bids for it.

Immersed in the work, time flew by. Four days without Lord Locke became six. Ten turned into a fortnight.

* * *

Mr. Treadwell cleared his throat to catch Bethany's attention at the breakfast table. "A missive just arrived for you, my lady," he said with kindness.

Bethany's heart tripped. A letter? Had Locke finally written? Correspondence was plentiful now with their residence, but she'd heard nothing from the earl.

Lord Locke's handwriting, however, did not grace the outside of it. Masking her disappointment, she perused the letter and told Lady Camille, "It's from Mum. I'd hoped she'd pay a visit, but she's as busy with Whitton as we are with Moorewood."

"Did she agree to a day in future?"

"No. On the other hand, your parents returned to Hannaford yesterday." The next few paragraphs furrowed her brow.

"What does that look mean?" Lady Camille asked.

"Your brothers have finished managing affairs of their own in London, saw your parents and then went to visit my mother yesterday. Presently, they're on their way to Moorewood to check on their sister. They fear I've done something nefarious with her."

"You have. You've driven me mad with decorating plans, riding two different horses a day since I arrived, taking me to visit Lord Locke's tenants often enough I can name them—"

"And took you swimming in the pond."

Lady Camille giggled. "It was hot."

"And you stretched out in the shade afterward with your skirts pulled above your knees and prayed none of the stablehands would catch you."

"I'll die if you repeat that to a soul."

"I know good blackmail when I see it."

She continued reading and, absorbing the final paragraph, felt her stomach dip with a touch of dread and then rise upward with hopefulness for Lady Camille.

"So when do the twins arrive?" Lady Camille asked.

"If my arithmetic hasn't grown inordinately rusty, I'd imagine within the hour."

"What? You don't sound enthused, Cousin. What aren't you telling me?"

Pushing her own dismay aside, Bethany smiled as she said, "Lord Scarbreigh retired from London and is on his way here with the twins. Your brothers tried to convince him it's a bit too soon after the wedding, but it appears he's determined to see *you*."

Lady Camille's eyes popped wide at the announcement and she sprang to her feet. "Oh, Beth, I want to choke you! Look how long we've wasted getting to the point of this discussion. I must fix myself. Send Melissa up for me, will you?" She all but flew from the room.

Bethany called after her. "Your Prussian-blue dress is far more fetching."

"And your green linen is significantly finer than that drab brown cotton," Lady Camille shot back at her. "It brings out your eyes." Then she was gone.

Bethany's smile faded. To herself she murmured, "But I'm not trying to catch a husband, cousin. I already have one."

CHAPTER 10

From the front steps, Bethany and Lady Camille watched as the Hannaford carriage rolled into the yard. The twins' and Lord Scarbreigh's valets disembarked from the top of the carriage to assist the occupants from the vehicle. Lord Matthew and Mr. Nicolas followed the Marquess of Scarbreigh, who went through the motions of brushing away dust that did not exist from his costly jacket, straightening his cravat and running his fingers through his far-too-perfect curls. When he'd finished, he swaggered towards them in a way she supposed was meant to impress them.

The man was, indeed, an arrogant cockerel. Of course, Lady Camille's flushed cheeks and sparkling eyes declared her determined admiration for him.

"Beautiful morning, ladies," Scarbreigh said, his countenance alight with mischief. "I vow you're the ones who've caused the sun to shine and the sparrows to sing."

"And I vow I'm about get ill," Mr. Nicolas remarked, passing Scarbreigh on the steps. "There ought to be a law against such eloquence before noon. Good morning, Sister." He placed a chaste kiss on Lady Camille's cheek. "Cousin." He did the same to Bethany. Then he gave quick instruction to the valets to consult with Mr. Treadwell regarding their luggage and accommodations.

"Eloquence raises a man from average to exceptional," Scarbreigh insisted. "Or would you prefer we all brayed like donkeys or barked like dogs?"

Lord Matthew, catching up to Scarbreigh, said, "Sometimes it's hard to tell the difference. Ease up, Kirk. We're in the country and you've no one nearby to amaze."

"Rubbish. I've two incredibly beguiling women to impress."

When he bowed over her hand, Bethany was glad to have donned her gloves before coming outside. It was as close to arm's length as she could keep the man.

Then he said, "Lady Locke, it appears Moorewood agrees with you even more than marriage. There's a glow about you I haven't seen in a long while."

Bethany wondered if she should be flattered or offended, but mostly she appreciated that Scarbreigh never held a grudge. Otherwise, she couldn't imagine having him as a guest. "Thank you, my lord."

"It wasn't a compliment. Just an observation. Either you bewitched Locke, or he's swept you off your feet, something I failed to accomplish."

"For which we shall both be eternally grateful, I'd wager." Bethany softened the remark by smiling sweetly.

"I suppose you're right."

"Of course I am. What brings you to Moorewood, my lord?" She meant the tone in her voice to remind him that a visit so soon after her marriage, by anyone unrelated, bordered on impropriety.

He sighed, his cheeks darkening, and cast a hand toward her cousin. "I was surprised to learn Lady Camille was here, but I also supposed that meant you were welcoming visitors. How else was I to call on her?

Bethany could not disagree with his reasoning. What would he do when he found Lord Locke *not* in residence? Unfortunately, seeing the rapture on Lady Camille's face, she couldn't deny him. The marquess turned to offer a courtly leg to her cousin and Lady Camille looked as if he'd given her diamonds.

"You're truly divine, Lady Camille," Scarbreigh murmured. "I pray I'll have the favor of your company today."

"I really am becoming ill," Mr. Nicolas insisted, making a face at Lord Matthew. "May we impose upon your hospitality, cousin?"

"Of course," Bethany replied. "Mr. Treadwell has tea for us in the morning room, one of the few rooms beyond a handful of bedchambers and the dining room with adequate furnishings for our comfort. I cannot tell you how wonderful it is to set eyes on familiar faces."

Mr. Nicolas wrinkled his brows in disbelief. "Even my ugly face? You've often said you wanted to punch it."

"No," she insisted, chuckling. "That was Lord Matthew. I still sometimes confuse the two of you, although he is uglier."

"Oh, that makes me feel loved," Lord Matthew intoned.

"How long will you stay?" she asked, choking back laughter.

"How long are we welcome?" Mr. Nicolas replied.

"Dear cousin, if you'd arrived only for the day, your driver and valets wouldn't be pulling baggage off the top of the coach."

Lord Matthew's grin broadened. "We'd appreciate a couple of nights, if you'll allow it."

"Tonight, absolutely. Beyond that depends upon how well you all behave."

Laughter spurred on the banter, the party moving to the cool of the morning room. Mr. Treadwell paused at the door, where the gentlemen began handing him their jackets, but before taking Lord Matthew's coat, he first rubbed his nose. Lord Matthew gave a most subtle nod and then handed over both his coat and an envelope.

"I've a note for Lord Locke. Will you see that he receives it?"

"Certainly, my lord," Mr. Treadwell said, leaving as quietly as a cat, the envelope balanced in his hand.

Bethany watched him go. Was it her imagination or had she caught a look of concern on Lord Matthew's face? One of reassurance on Mr. Treadwell's? It deepened her unease. She ought to confront her cousin about it. But how would she get him alone?

"Haven't visited in a while," Scarbreigh commented, confusion narrowing his eyes as he took stock of his surroundings. "What happened to this place?"

Mr. Nicolas explained Matheson's treachery and Scarbreigh grunted in shock.

"Confess I hadn't heard of it. Haven't seen much of Locke the last year or so and haven't visited here longer ago than that."

The twins egged Scarbreigh into imparting news from London which he did with relish. It included a list of scandals from all over Britain and the Continent, of fortunes lost and fortunes won, engagements and birth announcements, and whisperings of problems with those who were still devotees of Napoleon Bonaparte.

"Goodness, I feel as if I've lost touch with the entire world while staying here," Lady Camille mewed.

Bethany agreed. "Mayhap Locke will have tales to share when he returns," she said, but a sharp look from Lord Matthew startled her. Apparently they hadn't prepared Scarbreigh for Locke's absence as she'd assumed they would.

Again Bethany caught the barest exchange of expression between the twins, one that others would likely have missed, one with which she was too familiar. They were hiding something, particularly from Scarbreigh.

Lord Matthew drained his teacup and smiled. "He should return soon. He just had a few days' meetings of his own with very notable persons in London."

A few days? It had been two weeks. Or was her cousin prevaricating to help her save face?

"And what notable people might that be?" she couldn't help asking.

Mr. Nicolas's gray eyes twinkled with mischief. "I'm sure he'll enlighten us when he returns, if he's so inclined."

"You're impossible," Bethany grumbled. "One could get more information from a parrot."

"But we don't molt," Lord Matthew quipped, chuckling when Bethany pressed her eyes shut and breathed deep to muster patience.

Lord Scarbreigh cleared his throat. "I had no idea Locke wasn't in attendance, Lady Bethany. I declare I'm ... appalled. What in the world bore such import he'd desert his bride so soon after the wedding?"

Bethany cringed, but thankfully Lord Matthew intervened.

"Scarbreigh, you know as well as anyone, one cannot ignore a summons from the Prince Regent. As I said, perhaps he'll enlighten us when he comes in, but then again." He twitched a wry grin. "He may prefer discretion."

Scarbreigh rumbled his agreement. "Understood. Too many evils afoot in high places these days. Well, Lady Bethany, I understand you brought an entire herd of horses to Moorewood."

Glad for a change in conversation, Bethany was delighted to keep it there. When the twins finally came to their feet and announced they wanted to freshen up and make sure their valets had set their quarters to rights, the marquess followed suit.

"Please excuse me for a moment, Lady Camille," Bethany said after the men had headed upstairs. "I need to speak with Mr. Treadwell about the length of our guests' stay."

Bustling into the main hall, Bethany was nonplussed to find Mr. Treadwell missing from his normal post near the front. Perhaps he was helping the gentlemen's servants with the lords' belongings? But Moorewood's other servants, Mrs. Ford, Mrs. Callen, and the small handful of maids and footmen needed to know about their guests, too, so Bethany headed for the kitchen.

Today, Mrs. Ford and the kitchen maids were busy with what appeared to be more food than a dozen people could eat. Reassured that the entire staff knew about and was already preparing for their guests, Bethany nodded and left.

Nearing the dining room door, however, she paused, hearing voices on the other side. Brisk but hushed, the exchanges came and went. Bethany's pulse accelerated when she stepped closer to the door. Lord Matthew. Mr. Nicolas. And two other men's voices. Ah, Mr. Treadwell. Finally the fourth voice chimed in again and Bethany's heart lurched. Lord Locke! He was home!

She was so overwhelmed with the desire to rush into the hall she had to reign herself in. She wasn't supposed to care what the Earl of Locke did!

Caution brought her to the doorway to listen instead. It was wicked, but the tone of their voices made her want to discover what they were about.

If she'd hoped to learn much through a closed door, she was sorely disappointed. She did, however, catch that the twins were relieved to find Locke already home, and that Locke wasn't happy Scarbreigh had come with them.

Bethany couldn't resist pushing the door open a fraction, to hear better, to see more.

"Everyone likes Scarbreigh, but he's the world's worst busybody. We can't afford that right now."

"Couldn't help it, Locke," Lord Matthew insisted. "He wanted to address Lady Camille and nothing we said discouraged him."

"We simply need to be careful," Mr. Nicolas said. "Which we have to do around the women anyway."

Then followed references to Prince George, something about the English Channel, embargoes, and bootleggers being caught in the dead of night. It created more questions for Bethany than answers and raised the hairs on the back of her neck. She had no doubt to whom the men referred when they mentioned "The Corsican." But Bonaparte had given up his throne and been exiled to the island of Elba, near Tuscan Italy, just this April. He couldn't possibly escape.

"How successful was your *quest*?" Lord Matthew asked, his emphasis sounding cautious.

"Worth the risk," Locke replied. "We now have evidence that England has a band of traitors working with the French resistance. Mr. Treadwell gave me your note, Lord Matthew. It was enlightening. We'll discuss it all later."

Lord Locke questioned Mr. Treadwell, but the servant's hushed voice was muffled. Apparently satisfied with his man's reply, the earl thanked him, an oddly convivial exchange between master and servant.

"Tell me, has Treadwell erased the evidence of my exploits?" he asked the twins, touching his cravat.

Matthew replied, "Which ones? Acting the vagabond or getting trounced by a highwayman?"

Bethany's eyes flew wide. All of them laughed.

"How would you tell the difference?" Mr. Nicolas said. "At least I don't see any bruises."

"Yes, well, Mr. Treadwell's unrivaled in his ability to make me appear fresh as a daisy despite whatever I've put myself through."

"Thank you, my lord." The valet's twinkling eyes and half-cocked smile were as affable as the twins'.

"You're sure the two ladies didn't see me sneaking in early this morning?"

"Positive, my lord. Mrs. Callen said they were sound asleep."

The housekeeper had spied on them? Bethany let out a soft gasp and all four of the men jumped. She leaped back from the door and stood, fingers pressed to her lips, fearful what would happen next. After a long pause, the door swung open, Locke leaning into the room and pinning her with that remarkable gaze of his. At least he didn't appear angry.

"I'm—I'm sorry, my lord," she said. "I went to talk to Mrs. Ford and when I came to the door, I heard voices and took a peek to see who it was, and...."

The earl raised a brow to urge her on. When she didn't, that beguiling grin of his tugged at his dimples and curled her toes.

"Have we frightened you with our jesting and gossip? T'is the reason we gentlemen keep our conversations to ourselves. I promise you we're harmless. Please join us."

Reluctantly, Bethany followed him into the hall, where the others watched her intently.

"My arrival appears to be fortuitous, with Lord Matthew and Mr. Nicolas here," the earl said. "And I understand Scarbreigh joined them, which I'm sure Lady Camille will appreciate. It seems our old friend is truly sweet on your cousin."

"Yes. And she on him," Bethany agreed, wondering when Locke would question her about what she'd overheard.

"I came in quite early this morning, after riding most the night," Locke added. "Had an ... a, uh, spill on the road and landed in a mud puddle. I was grateful for Mr. Treadwell's help with cleaning up and getting to bed for a short nap. I swore him to secrecy. I'd wanted to surprise you, but I fear." He nodded at the twins. "I'm the one caught off guard. You say you spoke with Mrs. Ford?"

"Yes. And she seems perfectly capable of handling her own surprises," Bethany replied, feeling a bit miffed at being left out of the secret. She stared at Mr. Treadwell, who stood stone-faced and unflappable. Had Locke asked him not to tell her that his master was home? She doubted it was because Locke wanted to surprise her.

"She's a resourceful woman. I couldn't do without her. Dinner's usually simple, but I expect supper will dazzle us." Locke turned to Mr. Treadwell. "We'll need more refreshments in the sitting room. I'll join you there, boys. I need to speak with Lady Bethany alone for a moment, if you please."

Bethany's stomach twisted at the announcement. Locke's expression grew more serious when the twins journeyed to the morning room and Mr. Treadwell receded into the dining hall. Would he now censure her for eavesdropping? Drag the particulars out of her?

"How are you, Lady Bethany? You appear troubled." His gaze glided slowly over her face, as if admiring her.

She floundered for a moment, expecting neither his appraisal nor this question. She wanted to satisfy her own curiosity about the conversation regarding evidence of traitors and supporters of Napoleon Bonaparte, but if she brought it up, she feared he'd have more questions for her than she cared to answer.

"I'm alright," she tried to reassure both him and herself.

"Lord Matthew said Scarbreigh knows about my absence."

"Yes, and he clearly disapproved."

The earl made a face. "I'm sorry for the embarrassment, but I'm more worried about the consequences. Can't have the man nattering our business all over London. I'd truly hoped to return a bit sooner, to spend some time with you before you had any visitors."

Bethany's eyes narrowed in response. He'd wanted to surprise her? He'd wanted to spend time with her?

He took a step closer and lifted her hand, towering over her in a way that made her want to lean into him. The way he looked at her seemed far more intimate than it ought.

"I fear I need ask a favor."

Her unexpected pleasure at his attention dissipated. He'd offered his kindness to secure a favor?

Then he glanced upward, towards the stairs. "Lord Scarbreigh presents us a bit of a challenge. I've enjoyed his friendship for many years, but he's, well ... a man who could use a stitch through his lips."

Caught off-guard, Bethany couldn't resist snorting unladylike laughter. She could not disagree. "He gossips worse than a woman."

"Yes, indeed. If there were any gentleman in all of England I'd prefer not to know the facts of our *arrangement*, I have to avow it's him. I don't want you subjected to London's criticisms, and if some of the ton's less principled women learned the truth about our relationship, I'd lose the protection our marriage affords me. If you're up to it, I'd prefer we present an amicable face to the man while he's around."

"An amicable face?" Bethany drew her brows together. "What do you mean? Amorous?"

The earl executed a small bow in acknowledgement. "A bit of harmless flirtation, enough to convince him. If you don't mind."

She did. And she didn't. How amicable was amicable enough? Heavy footsteps at the top of the stairs announced Scarbreigh descending. She hardly had an instant to give Locke a slight nod before the marquess caught sight of them.

80

"Locke! You're home! And I'd barely concluded you'd gone off and abandoned Lady Bethany to my entertainments."

"Scarbreigh. What a surprise. Welcome, old friend."

The men shook hands, and then Locke slipped an arm around Bethany's waist and pulled her against him, something so on the edge of propriety it turned her cheeks hot. She ought to resist, but for the sake of their ruse, she leaned into him instead, acutely aware of his strength, his warmth, and the musky scent of his cologne. He turned his glittering eyes on her, the affection radiating from them almost convincing her that he was in love with her.

"My friend, you're welcome to Lady Camille," he told Scarbreigh. "But Lady Locke is mine."

Scarbreigh laughed and shrugged. "Have to admit I couldn't imagine what in the world could lure you from your brand new wife."

"Providing an ear for the Prince Regent's rantings? And that, dear Scarbreigh, is as boring as the vicar's sermon on repentance. Shall we join the others?"

"Well, if I'm not to learn anything more exciting I suppose we should."

The marquess strode towards the sitting room, but Locke held Bethany back. When Scarbreigh passed through the doorway, the earl gathered her hands in his again and Bethany felt, more than saw, Scarbreigh leaning out to watch them.

Grinning, Locke bent to press his smooth-shaven cheek to hers. His whisper tickled her ear and sent chills of delight racing down her spine. "I'm convinced we should give him a reason to spread the right sort of gossip."

Annoyed with Scarbreigh just enough to enjoy the subterfuge, and tantalized by the smoothness of Locke's skin against hers, she whispered her consent. She'd expected he'd simply cast her an adoring look and perhaps kiss her cheek, but when he pressed his soft, warm lips to hers, heat raced through her skin and pierced her heart and took her very breath away. Her knees nearly buckled, and the arms he wrapped around her were all that kept her on her feet.

* * *

Locke's skills at bottling up his emotions failed him. He'd done his best to put them aside while he was abroad, but as each day went by, he found himself worrying about his new wife, more and more eagerly anticipating seeing Lady Bethany again. It was the reason he'd met the twins here rather than in London, to see for himself she was safe. The reason the twins had lied to Scarbreigh, hiding the fact he'd been in Spain.

And now? Convincing Scarbreigh that their ruse was legitimate was important; the man could upset Locke's plans and his and Lady Bethany's scheme. But it had quickly metamorphosed into a good excuse for wresting a kiss from her.

He had not expected to enjoy it so much.

Now he needed to lean into her as much as she inclined towards him. What had he done? He'd worried at the fear and confusion on her face when she'd overheard what she shouldn't have, but there was no mistaking her pleasure at seeing him home. And now? She'd not only enjoyed that kiss every bit as much as he had, she wanted more. He could see it written in her eyes.

Her lips still lifted to his offered greater temptation than he could resist. He cupped the back of her head and drew her to him, savoring the sweetness of her mouth and the now-familiar scent of honey and lemon. For a split second he felt her resistance to being held tight, and then his kiss deepened and she melted into his arms.

The dining room door snapped open and the moment shattered. Locke pulled away, glancing first towards where Scarbreigh had been and then behind Lady Bethany at Mr. Treadwell, who bore a tray filled with pastries, empty glasses, and a pitcher of iced lemonade. The servant's eyes flew wide in surprise. Lady Bethany flushed red.

"Scarbreigh's gone, Lady Bethany," Locke said, studying Mr. Treadwell. "I'm confident we've made our point and need not fear. He'll be our witness in London should he care to spread gossip. Shall we join our guests before they consider us rude?"

Lady Bethany's face tightened, as if she'd been stung, and she shifted her gaze from him to Treadwell and back.

Locke caught the edge of rancor in her voice when she replied, "Of course, my lord. I'm sure our pretense is sufficient to convince all of England. Perhaps no further such displays will be necessary while Lord Scarbreigh is in residence."

Locke deflated at her comment. What a fool he was. He'd offended her—again—and taken far too great a risk with his heart. Catching Treadwell's look of dismay only magnified his own.

"You are my countess, Lady Bethany. There is no pretense in that," he said. "And I pray you'll find it to your benefit."

She cast Treadwell a resentful look, perhaps not liking that his servant seemed to disapprove of their kiss. She had no idea Locke had ordered the man to watch over and protect him from both Lady Bethany and himself.

"As you wish, my lord," she replied, taking his offered arm stiffly.

The twins fought with smug grins when they arrived, meaning Scarbreigh had tattled what he'd seen, but thankfully the marquess was flirting outrageously with Lady Camille and paid them little heed. Locke was glad. If the marquess found himself head-over-heels in love, he mightn't have time or thought for meddling in Locke's affairs.

He guided Lady Bethany to a chair beside his, amazed that having guests in this room made it feel more welcoming than it had in years. He wondered how different it would be when Lady Bethany completed the renovations. Most likely more like home, his own home, than ever before.

Yet, remembering Lady Bethany's kiss had his heart nose-diving towards his gut and he lectured himself not to let it happen again. His emotions mustn't override his head. Danger surrounded them, and Lady Bethany was at the center of it, and his mind had to remain clear if he wanted to protect her.

Suddenly grateful for his unexpected company, Locke realized they would keep him distanced from Lady Bethany, a terribly needful thing.

* * *

Moorewood's friends followed their midday meal with lawn games, where Locke fielded Scarbreigh's probing questions concerning Moorewood and Geoffrey Matheson and then enjoyed Lady Bethany's report of what she and Lady Camille had accomplished with his tenants during his absence.

"Encountered similar experiences at one of my own country estates," Scarbreigh mentioned at one point. "I admit my mother's approach did much. She visited the villages and towns, gathered donations for the tenants: clothing, shoes, material, needles and thread. 'Course, Mum has a soft heart for the destitute. I fear she'd bankrupt our entire estate to help them if I let her."

"I adore her compassion," Lady Camille noted, her voice soft with admiration. "None of us has a say over where we're born or what fortunes we'll have. If I were in poverty, I'd like to think people with sufficient for their needs would willingly offer help."

"A lofty ideal, I suppose," Scarbreigh replied, nodding.

Locke shared a dubious look with the twins. Scarbreigh, like most nobility, cared most of all for the profitability of his lands and his investments, even if it meant encumbering the poor. He wouldn't admit to such a thing, however, if it would alienate Lady Camille.

The day not only grew hot but oppressive, and when Lady Camille professed a headache, Locke took advantage of it to suggest they retire to their rooms and rest until supper. Lady Bethany seemed relieved, but the twins gave furtive acknowledgement as to his real intent.

They'd join him in his study in half an hour, where they'd talk in private.

CHAPTER 11

"I've eaten entirely too much," Lord Matthew moaned, pushing aside his supper plate and dropping his fork onto it.

"A meal worth gorging ourselves on," Scarbreigh said, watching Mr. Treadwell bearing a tray filled with plates of Madeira cake.

"Mrs. Ford is worth double whatever you're paying her," Bethany told Locke.

Lord Matthew said, "I'd forgotten my main reason for coming to Moorewood wasn't so much to see Locke—"

"As to sample whatever delectable collation Mrs. Ford would concoct," Mr. Nicolas finished for him.

"Offer her thrice what Lord Locke is paying her, Lord Matthew. Maybe she'll defect to Hannaford," Lady Camille intoned.

Bethany's smile curled to one side when Locke laughed.

"She's been as much a mother as a cook to me. I'm glad I'll never again taste the business end of her wooden spoon, but I'd dare any of you to bribe her away from me."

Mr. Treadwell appeared again, bearing an open bottle of wine to Locke. The earl glanced at the label and nodded, and the butler filled their glasses.

"Should have a toast," Scarbreigh remarked.

Locke's gaze turned to Bethany, his smile droll. "I had the same thought. My lady? It's not champagne, but I promised you a remarkably old, remarkably sweet burgundy. I hope you enjoy it. Friends?" He raised his glass. "First, to England. May she remain vigilant and may Bonaparte remain on Elba. Second, to Moorewood. May its resurrection bring my lady joy. And best of all, to Lady Bethany. May all your days be worth remembering, my lady, and filled with blooded horses and high fences."

"Hear, hear," said Lord Matthew.

The others cheered while Bethany's heart tightened in unexpected pleasure. She knew his words were meant to deceive Scarbreigh rather than endear him to her, but they did. As did the wine, which was far better than he'd boasted. She couldn't help breathe a sigh of pleasure.

"Delicious!" Mr. Nicolas said after emptying his glass, and the others agreed. "Well Locke, I, for one, would prefer to visit the pavilion than swelter in your study with a glass of port that couldn't possibly compare to this. Suspect it's a dozen degrees cooler by the pond."

Scarbreigh glanced at Lady Camille. "Wonder if Mrs. Ford has some bread crumbs for the ducks and geese."

"Oh, I do hope so." Lady Camille gulped her drink quickly and jumped to her feet, obviously delighted by the idea of joining the marquess in pampering the creatures.

Bethany's eyes widened in dismay at her cousin's quick disposal of the wine. Hopefully she wouldn't embarrass herself tonight. Lady Camille was truly a different creature when she unbridled her manners.

Bread crumbs secured and the walk to the pavilion accomplished, the group settled on the benches that lined the inside of the building.

"I especially love it here, Lord Locke," Lady Camille said, her cheeks flushed. "It's so peaceful and picture-perfect. I wish I had my oils with me."

"I'd forgotten you paint," Scarbreigh said. "Haven't seen your work in ages."

"Come by the house," Mr. Nicolas muttered. "She's virtually turned it into her private gallery."

"I must take up the invitation," Scarbreigh riposted. "Although you might want to consider conserving your supplies, my lady. Under the circumstances."

"What circumstances?" Lady Camille asked.

"You have been sheltered from the rumors, haven't you?" Scarbreigh said. "Relations with France have worsened again. Clashes on land and sea and more embargoes. Bourbon, silks, dyes, spices, paints and canvasses. The speculation about revolutionaries liberating Napoleon from Elba has the Empire on edge and forbidding most trade with the French. I, for one, don't understand it. Bonaparte's powerless."

Bethany felt blood leave her face at Scarbreigh's words. It was worse than what she'd overheard between Locke and the twins.

"I'm not convinced of that," Lord Matthew replied, head shaking. "King Louis has failed to win friends in France. Boney's supporters could take advantage of it, could trigger another revolt."

"Quibblers. A few diehard critics of government hardly make an uprising."

"Still, rebellion doesn't occur without it. We'll be caught napping if we're not careful."

"Mmm, I suppose." Scarbreigh vacillated. "Vigilance is certainly the wiser course. Heavens, Lady Bethany, you've gone pale. Is our conversation upsetting you?"

"We've barely ended a war. We don't need another one," she replied, thinking of her brother, killed in Portugal. Of her father and Lord Christian both dead as well, regardless of the reason.

"That we don't," Locke mumbled.

Bethany noted for the first time the lines of fatigue on her husband's face. They weren't just from lack of sleep; worry lie there as well. She had her doubts about Locke simply parleying with governmental bureaucrats or falling into mud puddles, with or without the help of a highwayman. She did not believe the twins' arrival at Moorewood was simply coincidental with the earl's return, either. Hadn't he admitted, among other things, that he'd collected evidence about traitors working with the French resistance?

"Look. A pair of swans," Scarbreigh commented, pointing towards an elegant duo landing in the pond's still waters.

"Oh, they're beautiful. I wonder if they'd like the bread," Lady Camille said, urging Scarbreigh to the pond's edge.

"I'd like to walk off dinner," Locke told Bethany. "Care to stroll around the pond with me?"

Bethany nodded and took the arm he offered her. Leaving Lady Camille and Scarbreigh busy with their birds and the twins to watch after them, they followed the walkway eastward, away from the manor.

She said, sighing, "How can you stand leaving all of this and for so long?"

Locke shrugged. "I grew up here. I suppose I take it a bit for granted, but there's no doubt Kent is the garden place of England. If I had fewer responsibilities, I truly would happily spend my life here."

"What sort of responsibilities trouble an earl?" She dared ask. His silence caused her to glance up, to wonder if she'd annoyed him.

Finally he answered, "The peerage is forever accountable to the crown, Lady Bethany. There's no end to the various committees, councils, and trusts required of us, never mind the demands of Parliament. The nobility compete with each other relentlessly, seeking acceptance in the eyes of our betters. It's tedious, even if all we want is to see our country improve."

"Are such obligations ever ... dangerous?"

Again came his silence and Bethany followed his gaze to the swans. The bread must be gone. The birds had drifted to the far side of the pond.

"I must take care," he said, "how I word my response, my lady. The machinations of governments and religions are the most dangerous of all schemes in the world, and when doubts creep in, other nations may conspire to use them as weapons. There are some who love King George and who refuse to accept that he'll never be himself again. His illness will eventually end his life. Our prince, in some people's opinion, won't ever be half the king his father was, but he is The Prince Regent."

"Such collusions could lead to war."

"Yes. You understand it from a personal viewpoint."

"My brother died fighting for everything in which we believe."

"You know the epitaph. There's no greater sacrifice than for a man to—"

"Lay down his life for a friend. Or his family. Or his country. My mind appreciates it, my heart resents it."

Locke nodded. "I understand. We invariably hope no one will ask us to give more than we're comfortable giving. I wish we didn't have to."

Bethany cast him a grave smile. He hadn't answered her questions directly, but what he'd said filled her with foreboding. The Earl of Locke had work to do, some that affected his own lands and wealth, some she supposed touched on things of greater importance. And she suspected more than ever that whatever it was that stood between the two of them would forever keep them apart.

* * *

The friends engaged in card games until bedtime, Lady Camille a little silly from the alcohol she'd drunk. Before they parted for the night, Locke suggested an early morning ride, to which Bethany agreed eagerly. Scarbreigh, however, grumbled over the insanity of engaging in activities until well after noon. It didn't surprise Bethany that Lady Camille declined, too; she'd want to entertain Scarbreigh. Equally predictable was the twins' refusal. They'd need to chaperone the marquess and their sister.

When the two women secreted themselves in Bethany's room, Lady Camille's grin blossomed. "This morning, when Scarbreigh joined me and the twins in the morning room, I saw him peek around the door frame into the hall. When he turned back, he announced that it appeared Lady Bethany had found her paladin. Mr. Nicolas asked him what he meant, and Scarbreigh pled guilty to having witnessed Lord Locke kissing you. I couldn't believe it. Was he right?"

Disturbed by the question, Bethany rang for Melissa, then settled at her dressing table and began unpinning her hair. It gave her an excuse to avoid looking her cousin in the eye and to reply with formality, "Lady Camille, Scarbreigh's a horrid busybody. I realize you care for him, but that's the truth of it. I must help safeguard our deception, and we agreed a harmless performance would protect us both from London's gossipmongers. The kiss meant nothing. It was merely a ploy. And if you tattle to Scarbreigh, I'll disown you."

Bethany caught her cousin's disappointment in the mirror over the table. She refused to admit that it reflected her own.

87

"You know the essence of my marriage, Cam. It will do me no good to expect more of it than it is. The world will conclude Lord and Lady Locke's amicable relationship will, sadly, never bear an heir. You and I will know there's a great deal more and significantly less to it than that, but it's no one else's concern."

"I won't accept it," Lady Camille said, lips turned down. "You get along frightfully well. I told you the way Locke looks at you no one could mistake for artifice. Not anymore than I could misunderstand the affection in your eyes when you gaze at him. How could you not hope for a love affair between you?"

Bethany's cheeks warmed. "Because he—we—don't want it. It's hard enough as things stand, Love. You can't expect the man to accept what took place last April, and I couldn't bear having him reject me because of it. Besides, Locke made it clear he wants no emotional entanglements, and considering he'll be away more than he's here and I've no desire to frequent London, I'll likely remain at Moorewood, mostly alone, for the rest of my life. Which, of course, means you need to visit often and bring your future children with you. Please don't fret for me, and please don't encourage me to want something I cannot have. I'll make life comfortable here. I promise. "

Lady Camille shook her head, her eyes shimmering with unshed tears. "But you could have so much better."

Bethany ignored the dampness that sprang into her own eyes—knowing what it meant. "No, I can't, dear. It's not my decision alone."

Melissa arrived to attend them then, ending the discussion and leaving a sadness in the air that Bethany also believed had no remedy.

* * *

Bethany scurried quietly downstairs to join Locke for toast and tea the next morning. Polly and Raven were saddled and waiting for them at the stable, and they were soon posting to Elway's holding. As taciturn as before, the farmer cast steely glances at them. Mrs. Elway, however, thanked his lordship for the chickens and praised Providence for making the hens fine layers.

"M'lady also sent us seed and salt and spices, and the children are eatin' well now, m'lord," Mrs. Elway informed him, eyeing her husband.

Elway managed a grunt and a nod. "Used the equipment and materials ya sent right off, fixed the roof. Floors ain't mud no more. Oldest boy was sick; Lady Locke sent a doctor. Grateful for the blankets, m'lady. 'ad none without 'oles in 'em ourselves."

"Shoes, too, Jim," Mrs. Elway added. "She brought shoes and clothes, and cloth to sew more, and scissors and needles and thread, yarn and knittin' needles. Broke one 'o my needles last year. I started makin' new socks and mittens right off to prepare for winter."

"Splendid," Locke said with sincerity, urging them to send word if they had further need. He and Lady Locke bid the couple farewell, visited the Cross and Garnett farms, and then aimed towards the Hedleys' place.

"You've done well, my dear," Locke said. "I'm pleased."

"I don't feel I've done near enough. I still can't imagine living as they do."

"I understand," Locke said. "I wouldn't wish privation on anyone. I'll do what I can for these people, my lady, but nevertheless, you must remain realistic. I can only do so much."

"Of course. I also believe most of them resent needing a handout. They want to manage their own lives. Those tenants whose families have lived here for generations say they always considered your family fair landlords. What Matheson did to them shocked them. It was evil, but it wasn't your fault. I'm convinced knowing the reason for it and having help to remedy it have done much to rectify things."

Mrs. Hedley was hanging wash when they arrived, her husband chopping firewood. Laura and Bea were tossing feed to the chickens, and Bethany caught site of a cradle in the shade near the clothesline and heard the babbling of a baby.

Hedley set aside his axe and stood silent but perhaps a bit less resentful while his wife offered her gratitude to both Lord and Lady Locke for the provisions. For Bethany, it was heartwarming to see the two girls in relatively clean dresses, hand-me-downs through the vicarage but in near-perfect condition. Already, the gauntness had left Laura's face, and Bea's hair shined with better health.

Locke commented as they rode homeward, "The work has been considerable, hasn't it?"

"Yes. Mountains of worries, actually, but it's been worth every minute. I'm truly enjoying it."

They loped partway across the meadow towards the manor then dropped to a walk for the final leg of the trip. Eventually they found the trail, lined with tall shade trees, which bordered the pastures and would return them to the front road.

Suddenly Raven shied. Bethany gasped and grabbed his neck to avoid falling. *Ffffft!* A sharp slapping sound followed by a *twang* made her head jerk towards a tree mere inches in front of her.

"Lady Bethany!" the earl cried. "Run!"

Bethany froze, shocked at seeing an arrow sunk deep into the trunk of the tree. Someone had shot an arrow at her!

"Lady Bethany! Now!" Locke slapped Raven's rump, driving the stallion away from the lane and diagonally across the meadow. At a pounding gallop, both riders leaned low over their stallions' necks.

The steady drum of the horses' hooves and their grunting breaths marked every step towards the safety of the manor. Polly leaped across a small stream and Raven followed, and then both hurtled over a low rock fence, flanks and necks soaked with sweat.

When they landed, Bethany jerked a look behind her shoulder, seized by fear at spotting three horsemen, dressed in black, standing beneath a sizeable ash tree. One had a bow in hand and an arrow knocked, gauging the distance.

"Raven, fly!" Bethany cried, kicking the stallion hard. Raven leaped forward, his ears pinned back, and they soared over a tall, wooden fence that separated the meadow from a paddock. Locke and Polly charged along a second behind her. Taking the outside fence at last, they landed on the main road.

They thundered into the stable yard, gasping for air. Locke shouted for Dimity, Seaworth and the stablehands, "To me! To me!"

Bethany nearly dived off Raven, rushing to check him for signs of injury. Then Locke was there, reaching for her and asking if she'd been harmed. The panic on his face had her heart racing even worse. Was she alright? Yes. But was Locke?

"Please tell me you're unharmed, my lord. Is Polly hurt? Did you see them?"

"Them? What do you mean them?"

"The men? Under the ash tree?" She described them, especially the one drawing his bow.

"No. I cannot believe I missed them." Locke sounded disgusted with himself. His fingers shook with anger where they gripped her arms.

"Are you sure you're alright?" she insisted. Sweat damped his hair to his brow and glistened on his cheeks, but she saw no injury.

"Polly and I are fine. Your Raven must have heard something, and just in the nick of time. I think he saved our lives, Lady Bethany. Seaworth, please escort Lady Locke to the house. Carter, Hugh, Josh, Devon, you know what to do. Find them. Whatever it takes, find them. And retrieve that arrow."

Nods and muttered oaths punctuated the air as the threesome ran off to saddle horses. Dimity, jaw set with anger, took Raven from Bethany and promised to see him well cooled and cared for, while Seaworth went to help Lord Locke with Polly.

Bethany hated the idea of being sequestered inside four walls. She wanted to stay near Locke and hear whatever the men found out.

90

Seaworth's warning look when he urged her towards the house, however, brooked no argument.

Mr. Treadwell opened the door to them, shocked at Seaworth's tale. When the stablehand departed, Mr. Treadwell locked the door behind him, his face drawn with concern.

"Have our guests risen yet, Mr. Treadwell?"

"Not that I'm aware, my lady."

"Thank you. I'll retire to my room. If they ask, tell them about the scare and that I wanted to lie down for a bit."

"Yes, my lady."

* * *

Bethany hurried upstairs, but upon reaching the second floor landing peeked over the balustrade to the entry hall. Mr. Treadwell stood rubbing his cheek, as if vacillating about something, and then headed off towards the kitchen, leaving her to take advantage of his absence. Tiptoeing back down, she hurried outside. She'd most likely reap Lord Locke's ire if he found out, but she couldn't remain isolated with such deviltry going on outside.

Jogging to the stable, Bethany peeked through one of the building's open rear windows and saw Dimity and Locke tacking up Major. Locke was preparing to join the hunt!

"How could this happen, Dimity?" Locke snapped, jerking the stirrup leather into place after tightening the horse's cinch.

"Wish I knew, m'lord. We've so many eyes watchin' this place Windsor Castle would envy it. Boys'll bring 'em in. We'll have answers afore nightfall."

"I hope so. I leave early tomorrow morning and need reassurance Lady Locke will remain safe while I'm gone."

"She will, m'lord. On m' life."

Locke paused and drew in a deep breath. He nodded and clapped Dimity on the shoulder. "And on mine. Let's hope it doesn't require that." Dimity handed him an object, and Bethany's heart lurched when she saw a flintlock pistol in the earl's hand. Locke stuffed it into his waistband and gathered the gelding's reins.

Bethany slipped around the side of the stable, hiding in its shadows as the door opened wide and the earl led Major to the yard and swung aboard. The stable master gave him a quick salute—a salute?—which Locke returned, and then the earl kicked the gelding and thundered down the road from which they'd just come.

CHAPTER 12

Fury all but consumed Locke. Lady Bethany was supposed to be safe at Moorewood, considering his men on the grounds and more in hiding that patrolled the estate's perimeter. But such a close call proved he was a fool to assume it.

Still, a rare form of admiration towards his lady filled him. The Whitton men had cherished their sister and daughter, had always said she was an exceptional girl. Lady Bethany was, truly, Lord Whitton's daughter. She'd shown no missishness during the entire fiasco, had obeyed Locke's orders and ridden as bravely as a soldier. Rather than having an attack of the vapors when they'd galloped into the stable yard, she'd flown from her stallion to check him for harm and then inquired after Locke's well-being.

He rounded a corner on the lane, a good two kilometers east of where the assault had happened, and exhilaration swept through him at coming upon more than a dozen men and horses gathered in a loose circle. Lady Bethany had seen three assailants beneath the tree; in the circle's center stood three blokes garbed in black, with their hands tied behind their backs.

Hugh, the tallest of his men, held one of the strangers at gunpoint and by his bright red hair, while Josh examined a bow and a quiver of arrows.

Locke dropped to the ground a few feet from the throng and pushed his way through, coming face to face with another of the other suspects, a man with near-black hair streaked with gray.

"Found the arrow, Lord Locke." Carter offered it to him. "The redhead was carryin' the bow and quiver."

Locke didn't miss the spark of recognition in the dark-haired man's eyes at mention of his name before he averted them. A chill grabbed hold of him. It did not bode well that this bloke may have met him some time in the past.

The redhead glared at him, and the third man, near bald and much older, growled in anger.

"They've admitted to nothing," Locke surmised.

"Not yet, sir," Devon admitted. "We'll have the information afore supper."

Locke turned angry eyes on his men. "How did this happen? How did they get past you?"

The dark-haired man snorted. With a French accent, he remarked, "They were good but not good enough. We navigated the narrow hollow to the north. Dangerous, but thick woods made good cover." His gaze flicked over Locke. "So *you* are the incomparable Lord Locke. I would never have guessed. Well, understand this, *monsieur*, our master wants what he wants, and the Whitton mademoiselle will give it up or die withholding it. Beyond that, we'll tell you naught, even on pain of death."

Locke pressed his lips together in a grim smile. In French, he replied, "I do believe you, *monsieur*. But having suffered the other side of what you'll soon endure, I'll tell you one thing and tell you true. There are worse things in life than death, and before my men finish with you, you'll pray for death."

The man spat on the ground at Locke's feet, and Locke gave him a disgusted look.

"Bring me word when you have it," he said. "And Devon, no matter what, these men do not get away, and they do not speak to each other or to anyone outside you lads, no matter what."

"If I have to cut out their tongues when we're done," Devon promised.

* * *

Bethany was too dazed to return to the house. Dark portent seemed to surround her. Or was it Lord Locke? The black gelding's stabbing on her wedding night. Today's incident. The cryptic conversations. Somewhat alarming before, they now felt dreadfully menacing. She couldn't ignore the most vexing thought of all. Her belief that this all had bearing on Locke's offer to marry her. For a brief moment she wanted to storm the house and face her twin cousins, but something ominous held her back. The fear she might learn more than she could bear?

Bethany found Dimity in the stable.

"Lady Locke," the stable master said with surprise. "Come to see your beast? Told ya he'd be fine. Seaworth walked him good and made sure he didn't drink too fast. Stud's in his stall downin' his breakfast now."

"Thank you, Dimity," Bethany replied. "But I can't rest until I see him for myself." She peeked into the stall, happy to find Raven enjoying the fresh hay and grain in his feed crib. "You were a champion, my love," she murmured. "May God in His Heaven bless you for protecting us."

The animal came to savor an ear-scratching and kisses on his muzzle before going back to his meal.

"Glad you're safe, m'lady," Dimity murmured. "Wouldn't wish ya any harm, and it would have gone hard on m'lord if you had."

Such words caught Bethany off guard. Would it have truly upset the earl had she been hurt? Why? Because it would inconvenience him? Embarrass him? Disrupt his sham with the *beau monde*? Certainly he'd dislike facing the ramifications with her mother and the Camerfields, especially Lord Matthew and Mr. Nicolas. But was there more?

What if they'd shot Lord Locke? She suspected Locke believed, as she did, that the arrow was meant for her, but what if not?

In her mind's eye, Bethany imagined the height and angle of the arrow embedded in the tree. Had Raven not shied, she surmised the bolt would have struck her somewhere in her right arm or possibly her side. Not necessarily a mortal shot. Anxiety had her heart pounding at the notion that if her stallion hadn't alerted them to the assault, there may have been a second arrow in store for Locke. And what would the assailants have done if they'd succeeded?

That terrifying thought drove the memory of yesterday's kiss into her mind, a kiss that had touched a place in her soul that would never be the same. It made her care what happened to Lord Locke, and to want to protect him as he was apparently protecting her.

Bethany had never imagined feeling this way about a man. A celibate life suddenly felt hollow and unfulfilling. Endless days and nights alone, never the tenderness that should pass between a man and a woman, no babes to shower with love.

It was hopeless to wish for something she couldn't have. But she did not doubt, seeing the alarm on Locke's face when he feared she'd taken harm, that he was concerned for her. Not likely more than as a friend, but she preferred that thought to indifference. In fact, she realized that at the least she truly desired her husband's friendship.

Bethany thanked Dimity and excused herself from the stable. Her guests would soon rise and she should be ready to greet them.

She'd no sooner rounded the stallion barn's back corner when she heard the clip-clop of horse's hooves on the road. Her heart stepped up its frightened cadence, and she hurried to sneak a look into the yard. Locke dropped to the ground outside the stable door.

Dimity was there in a heartbeat, taking Major's reins and the earl's pistol.

"Any luck, m'lord?" Dimity queried, brow furrowed in concern.

"Yes. We've caught them. They're tight-lipped, but Devon will do his best to wrest the information from them."

"Mmm." Dimity nodded. "Wouldn't want to feel the wrong side of that lad. Was it what you guessed? They was after m'lady?"

"Yes. Well, actually, they're after whatever it is they think she has."

Bethany froze, stunned by the revelation. "They" were after something she had? What in the world did that mean?

"Still no clue what that's about then?"

"No." Locke rubbed the back of his neck in thought. "Thus far I've gathered, through every channel we've sounded out, that it may be something her father gave her. Can't be obvious; she'd remember it. But why would Lord Whitton endanger his only daughter's life by giving her anything of import? He wouldn't purposely place an innocent at risk, particularly his own family. Perhaps he'd expected to return to England quickly enough he wasn't worried."

Shaking, Bethany all but collapsed into the wall. In that moment she saw everything about Lord Locke, their marriage—and her very life—in a completely different, more frightening light.

"It's stranger still, if'n ya ask me, that it's taken 'em this long t' come lookin' for 'er. Whittons have been dead more'n a year now."

"It is. But conspiracy's a strange creature, my friend, and people can only focus on so many goals or be in so many places at once. Perhaps this 'master' one of the scoundrels mentioned was held somewhere. In prison? Intent on some other endeavor? Who knows. Whatever the reason, I'm worried. This scoundrel recognized me."

"No!" Dimity stiffened. "Ya think he's made the connection to ya?"

"Yes. The lads have orders to keep the assailants isolated from each other and from other human contact outside of our people indefinitely. If they can't spread the word, I'm safe."

Sternly, Dimity replied, "Only safe word is the one can't be spoke. Nothin' but death guarantees that."

Locke nodded. "True words, but I haven't the authority to make that happen, even if I could justify it. Because I still suspect there's a traitor amongst us, I also can't send these rogues to London. Someone with greater authority than mine might set them free. I'm at least relieved to see Lady Bethany safe and the culprits apprehended. Send word when Devon and the others return."

"That I'll do, m'lord. Oh." He stopped Locke before he'd stepped away. "M'lady came t' the stable several minutes ago. Alone. Wanted t' see her stallion personal, be sure he was none the worse for the wear. Stayed but a few minutes. S'pose I shoulda escorted her to the house, but you rode in and I doubted she was at risk on so short a walk."

"I must speak to her, however. I cannot imagine how I'll break the news to her that she shouldn't go anywhere on the estate without an escort, not even to the stables. I suspect she's not the sort to tolerate restrictions well."

Dimity chuckled and shook his head. "Think you've the right of it there. She's a free spirit, likely likes t' grab the bit 'tween 'er teeth."

Sobering, Locke said, "And you should see her when she hurdles the fences, Dimity. Soars like an angel. Can't imagine putting fetters on that. No man should be so cruel."

Bethany pressed her brow to the wall, her head spinning even more. Did he really feel that way about her? What was she to do with all of this? It was more than she could digest at one time.

Silence held the men for a moment, and she looked up as Locke sighed and shrugged a shoulder. "Well, I must help Lady Bethany put this behind her while I do my best to play the part of a peer of the realm and at least appear to enjoy my friends' companionship while I can. I'll leave you to take care of Major...."

He was headed for the house! Bethany couldn't reach it before Locke would find her. Glancing around, she decided her safest course was to find him first. She scuttled behind a row of shrubs skirting the stable to a paddock fence on the east. She worked her way towards the manor following the fence. It was her plan to pretend she was innocently watching the horses, but her stomach was tied in so many knots, she felt sick.

Locke's exchange with Dimity had spawned a flume of questions with possible answers that terrified Bethany. Traitors? Conspiracy? Something Bethany possessed? And she couldn't ask the earl about it unless she wanted to admit she'd spied on him.

Not far from the courtyard, Bethany angled a path towards the house that would intercept Lord Locke's. She hoped it would seem coincidental.

When Locke saw her, he paused to frown at her. "Lady Bethany. You're alone." Then he took a second look. "Are you alright? You're frightfully pale."

"I was just nearly shot by an arrow," she reminded him. "I needed to walk and to think and couldn't bear being confined indoors."

Locke's visage softened. "I do understand. We caught them, my lady. I hope that reassures you. I do, however, need to ask another favor of you."

"I was hoping to ask one of you."

"Oh?"

"If it won't cause unreasonable inconvenience, I'd prefer someone with me, an armed bodyguard if you please, whenever I'm outdoors, even here on the grounds. Between Shadow's stabbing and men with arrows, well, I doubt anything so, er, *dramatic* will ever happen again, but I'd prefer not to take the chance."

The relief on Locke's face calmed the storm in Bethany's belly a bit. His lips turned upward in the barest smile and he nodded. "As my lady wishes. I considered the idea myself."

"Well, then it's good we're of like mind."

"It is. May I escort you to the house?"

"Please," Bethany replied, taking his offered arm. She truly wished she had the courage to ask about what she'd overheard, but she didn't.

Mr. Treadwell, in his usual post, opened the door at the earl's knock, his eyes flying wide at seeing Bethany with Locke.

"M'lord, M—M'lady."

Bethany could see he wanted to say more but couldn't find the words.

"It appears her ladyship preferred the company of the horse paddocks to the solitude of her room, Mr. Treadwell," Locke told him. "I assume she didn't warn you she was leaving the house."

"N—No, m'lord. I—"

"I'm sorry, Mr. Treadwell. I should have called for you." Bethany didn't want the earl's valet punished for her selfishness. To Locke, she said, "I was in a hurry. I shan't do it again."

"Thank you, Lady Bethany. We can keep you safer if we always know where you are. Inconvenient, no doubt, but wise."

"Your guests have risen early and are presently taking their meal in the dining room, my lord," Mr. Treadwell informed Locke. "Lady Locke asked me to apprise them of what happened."

The earl tipped his head in acknowledgement, and then Lord and Lady Locke repaired to their bedchambers to dress for the day. Afterward, together they journeyed to the dining room, where the men rose until Bethany was seated, and then sat down again.

"Lord Locke, Lady Bethany, are you alright?" Lady Camille asked, eyes wide with alarm.

Lord Locke related the details for them, the men muttering with anger, Lady Camille's cheeks losing what was left of their color.

"Poachers. Bet that's what they were," Scarbreigh said. "An unpredictable lot. Glad you caught them and glad you're both unharmed."

"Thank you, my lord." Bethany forced herself to smile. The bowmen were not poachers but let everyone think it. "I see Mrs. Ford put together a hearty breakfast. Please enjoy it. It's a beautiful day and a good meal will help us make the most of it." She, however, took nothing but a cup of tea. Her stomach upset still felt volcanic. She was grateful the others carried on civil conversation without her.

Finally, Lady Camille said, "Lord Locke, my rapscallion brothers must return to London tomorrow morning. Scarbreigh obviously must go with them, but how long do you plan to stay?"

A shadow darkened Locke's face as he admitted he would depart long before sunrise tomorrow.

"Then we must enjoy ourselves every possible moment we can," Scarbreigh encouraged. "Perhaps we should take a carriage ride somewhere. It would brighten the day, get Lady Bethany's mind off what happened."

"Canterbury!" Lady Camille cooed. "We could see the Cathedral, the ruins of the castle and St. Augustine's Abbey, and St. Martin's Church."

"Excellent. Or what about going north to the sea instead?" Scarbreigh suggested. "Whitstable is fabulous this time of year."

"Oh, yes!" Lady Camille said. "Wouldn't you idolize fresh oysters or clams, Lady Bethany? Or perhaps some fish chowder and fresh bread?"

Bethany caught another of those quick, meaningful looks the twins sent Locke before Lord Matthew intervened.

"Pull in your horses, Sister, Scarbreigh. Lady Bethany's not alone in needing rest. Lady Camille, you forget we four men just arrived here yesterday, and Mr. Nicolas, Scarbreigh and I stopped at Hannaford and Whitton on the way. We all leave again tomorrow. Scarbreigh may want to sightsee, but I'm afraid I, for one, don't."

A flash of irritation crossed the marquess's face. He rolled his eyes and shrugged.

"Just trying to be of help. Well, truth is, Lady Bethany does seem peaked. I suppose we should make the best of it here." His visage was grim but his remarks eased the mild tension in the room.

After abandoning the breakfast table, games and the inherent gossip carried them to midafternoon, when they undertook a picnic in the shade of the trees by the pond.

Bethany paid close heed to the brief visit Locke's stablehands Devon and Carter paid his lordship, and saw the quiet presence of the other two, Hugh and Josh, at opposite ends of the grounds. Armed guards, watching over them, she presumed. Men who reminded her that she wasn't safe, that someone thought she knew something that she was equally sure she didn't. She did, however, catch the disappointment on Locke's face at the information Devon whispered in his ear.

The sweet tranquility of the country—as well as Bethany's guards— served to calm her despite her qualms, and blankets spread under the shade trees offered a pleasant place to recline. Deciding to divest themselves of gloves and shoes, they made themselves comfortable. The others fell asleep, and Bethany herself dozed between Lady Camille and Lord Locke, to the sound of ducks and geese on the pond and the breeze ruffling the trees overhead.

Her eyes fluttered open when Locke stretched out beside her, the stress having slipped from his face and left it relaxed in slumber, dark lashes resting against the olive tones of his cheeks. He'd shaved that morning, but the stubble darkened his jaw again, and Bethany ached to touch it. He shifted, his left hand brushing her right one. She dared wrap her fingers around it, loving its masculine softness. A tingle skittered down Bethany's back and across her belly, reminding her that she found this man inordinately attractive. She loved the faint, woodsy scents of his shaving lather and whatever he'd washed his hair with that morning.

Perhaps sensing her gaze, Locke came awake, blinking his eyes. He laid perfectly still when she let go of his hand, his dark blue irises contracting and expanding as he took her in. She'd pulled the combs and pins from her hair and set it free before lying down. It was a wild mane around her shoulders, a thick strand draping itself over her right cheek. Locke's mouth rose in a soft smile as he gently stroked it from her face. His touch left heat trailing over her skin that made her shiver with pleasure.

* * *

Bethany's wide, emerald green eyes disarmed Locke, and the thought she'd been holding his hand. He'd never experienced such wonderment towards a woman. Her full lips, hovering on the edge of a smile, drew him. He wanted to taste them again, to know how it would feel to have her respond to him. To revel in her fragrance of honeyed lemon.

It seemed so natural to cup her cheek in his hand, to stroke her silky skin with his thumb. So easy to lift her chin and lean towards her. So breathtaking to have her moist, velvety lips parted to greet his. Locke's mind knew it was wrong to lead her on like this, to enjoy what he had no business taking from her and what he had no intentions of keeping.

His mind and heart warred with each other, but when he kissed her, her soft moan ignited a fire in his belly against which he had no defenses. He drew her close, intensifying the kiss, his hand exploring the roundness of her shoulder, the feminine planes of her back. Had she not slid her fingers up his chest to his shoulders, had she not threaded them into the hair at the nape of his neck, he could have pulled away.

But she did, and it welcomed him, and made him want more than anything to grab her and carry her to the manor, and make her his wife in more than name only. The fervor in her kiss persuaded him to believe she felt the same.

Hovering at the edge of control, he leaned over her, breathing her in, tasting her.

Then she stiffened and gasped softly, and he saw a flash of fear on her face. She pushed him, but with his weight trapping her beneath him began to panic. Her hands slammed into his chest and she shoved him hard, a tear dampening one cheek.

He wrenched himself away from her, whispering, "I'm so sorry, Lady Bethany. I had no right to do that."

She skittered back from him, pushing up against a near tree trunk and hugging her knees to her chin. Her stocking feet peeked out from beneath her skirts, and she looked like a frightened child, her eyes shimmering damply, her face pale beneath fevered cheeks. Panic and shame flashed through her eyes before she threw her hands to her face and sat mute and shaking.

Locke felt like a monster. In his youth, he'd upon occasion enjoyed the pleasures of a stolen kiss and found himself drawn to it enough to blind him to his duties. He'd ever after stayed as far from women as was humanly possible.

He was eight years Lady Bethany's senior. She was too young and inexperienced to understand such sentiments. She must think him an inconsiderate libertine, a monster who'd tried to take advantage of her, and that his agreement to demand nothing of her was just so much tripe. And this on the eve of his departure and after someone had shot an arrow at her.

He kept his distance, his heart breaking at the sound of sobs kept so silent, helpless to comfort her. Touching her, even kindly, might likely only make things worse.

Scarbreigh stirred and threw an arm across his eyes to ward off the late afternoon sunlight. Locke loathed the idea that his dear but sometimes frivolous friend would awaken and turn what had happened into a circus.

Rising carefully, Locke bent down and touched Lady Bethany's hand. She jerked it from him, but her expression bore no anger, merely surprise. He pleaded with her through his eyes, offering her his hand. She gulped, shook her head as if to clear it, and allowed him to bring her to her feet.

Silently they slipped from their comrades in the general direction of the manor. When they'd gone far enough Locke believed their voices wouldn't disturb the others, he paused and faced her. She could hardly meet his gaze.

"Please forgive me, Lady Bethany," he said in a voice barely above a whisper. "I have no excuse for my behavior except that you're a beautiful woman and we suffered a scare this morning. I want to protect you, and I suppose it's too easy for a man to let those feelings get out of hand."

Bethany grappled for words then wiped her cheeks, clasped her palms tight to her belly, and tossed that ravishing dark mane of hers back from her face.

CHAPTER 13

"There's nothing to forgive, my lord," Bethany said, her voice trembling, although to some degree there was. He knew things, important things, he kept from her. "I fear I suffered the same emotions. I shouldn't have let them get hold of me, either. But I—I have a fear of tight places or being held down, and I must insist, if our marriage is to accomplish its purpose, that our pact stand inviolate."

Locke remained quiet far too long and when she could look him in the eye, she saw a disappointment there she hadn't expected.

"Plain-spoken as always, my dear. I admire you for it. I pray we'll at least be good friends."

"I want that very much. We have a face to present to the world, but in private...." In private? She would want even more. Even now she hungered for his kiss. His ardor had crashed over her, tender but needful, and unbelievably tempting.

But his weight pressing her to the ground had triggered flashes of that distant, dark and dreadful place, of cruel faces and weak lantern light, and ghastly pain that pierced the soul far worse than the body. From those deepest recesses of her memory came images of doubled fists, deadly threats, and never-ending questions to which she had no answers.

Those memories mortified her. Having Locke know the whole truth would make it that much worse.

No, it was important to put a stop to things now. To remind both of them, once and for all, that their marriage was simply a business arrangement, one she'd treasure, but one that would keep them forever apart.

Locke nodded, his lips pressed together in solemn affirmation. Then he forced a lopsided smile and nodded towards their guests, who'd begun to rouse from their lazy afternoon nap. "I suppose we should join them."

Bethany watched him walk away, realizing the finality of it, fearing her heart would break into pieces. Despite the mystery Locke presented her, she knew no man in the world could have won that heart but Marcus Ashburn and couldn't imagine a lifetime of not being able to tell him so.

* * *

Bethany did her utmost to capture every minute of that day's shining memories. The company, the teasing and laughter, the camaraderie and well-wishing. She took part in it but not in entirety. What she'd overheard at the stable continued to trouble her, but so did what had happened between her and the Earl of Locke. She felt Locke's discomfiture, too, as if he could hardly wait to escape Moorewood.

Locke's farewell supper that night, so named by Mr. Treadwell on Mrs. Ford's behalf, was even more splendid than the night before and spread the length of the table: tureens of vegetables and potatoes, spiced beef and potted pork, *hindle wakes* and *caneton aux navets*, and beef and kidney pies.

"You'd think she was serving Prinny and half the grand dukes of Britain," Scarbreigh jested.

"They're all some of my favorite dishes," Locke mumbled. "Does she fear I'm never coming back?"

Mr. Nicolas laughed. "Be sure to leave an inch or two for dessert. Mr. Treadwell has a tray of glazed fruits in one hand and another of strawberry tarts in the other."

Everyone moaned and laughed, and moaned again with each bite of the wonderful meal. All but Bethany, who only nibbled at each dish and pretended to enjoy it, her worries turning the food to sawdust in her mouth.

"We need a piano," Scarbreigh said at last when, because of their brief time together, they again decided to forego the usual separation of the men to Locke's study. "Since we gentlemen all play the pianoforte, what do you think about each of us taking a turn at the piano while letting Lady Camille and Lady Bethany dance with the rest of us?"

Lady Camille applauded the suggestion; Bethany endured it.

Lord Matthew played first, Scarbreigh claimed Lady Camille's company, and Locke offered his hand to Bethany. Despite her reservations, his contact seemed magical as he whisked her around the parlor and took her, an average dancer, and made her feel elegant.

Or it would have if Mr. Nicolas, who waited his turn with the women, hadn't kept making faces at them to bedevil them.

"I think I should play," Lady Camille suggested after the men had all danced with both women, and her brothers had teased everyone mercilessly. "And you gentlemen should partner with each other."

They roared when Lord Scarbreigh and Lord Matthew effected a great show of joining the fingertips of their opposite hands and making a mockery of the minuet.

"Let's play whist," Mr. Nicolas said at last.

"I'll pass," Bethany said, Lady Camille seconding her.

"Why?" asked Lord Matthew.

"You cheat," Bethany said, grinning impertinently at them.

"I don't cheat!" Mr. Nicolas had the audacity to declare.

"Nor do I," Lord Matthew insisted.

Lord Locke intervened, admitting he would have to cry off as well. "I'm sorry, but I've had little sleep in the last few days and will leave before sunrise tomorrow. I must bid you all good night."

There were moans of disappointment all around, but Lord Matthew reminded everyone that the Hannaford coach would vacate Moorewood's doorstep in the morning, too. A decent night's rest was in order. Scarbreigh protested, reminding them all he wasn't an early riser, and Mr. Nicolas offered to allow him to walk home.

Bethany felt the regrets in the goodbyes they gave each other, but was eternally grateful Lady Camille would remain at Moorewood. She'd miss her guests, but mostly she dreaded being surrounded by nothing but strangers.

Before Bethany realized it, Lady Camille and the rest of their companions had gone off to bed, leaving her and Lord Locke to head upstairs together.

"There's no telling when I'll return, my lady," he said thoughtfully. "And my circumstances make writing difficult. I pray you won't hold it against me."

"Never. Just. Be safe."

"I'll do my best." His jaw set tight, that faint telling mannerism hinting at the risks of his exploits, whatever they were. "Please remember your promise to keep one of my servants with you when you ride out. Even Mr. Treadwell can go."

"Yes, m'lord. I've no desire to confront armed men, especially by myself. I'd like to be in one piece the next time you visit. Perhaps by then, you'll have the pleasure of seeing the refurbishment well under way."

Perhaps it would be done, depending on the length of his absence.

Locke smiled thinly, pausing outside her bedchamber door. The thought of his leaving had Bethany wishing to taste his lips again as much as she feared the thought; Locke seemed uncertain what to do. Then, for whatever reason, he bent and placed a hasty, chaste kiss on her cheek before nodding his good night.

That kiss branded Bethany's skin and sent its heat racing over every inch of her. She pressed her hand to it, as if to hold it fast.

Heart heavy, Bethany pulled the rope to summon Melissa and settled at her dressing table to wait. She was exhausted but feared sleep. Flying arrows and old memories would likely precipitate another onslaught of the recurring nightmares she'd suffered since that devilish night a year ago April.

Her thoughts turned to the discussion between Dimity and Locke. Her potential assassins had confessed they were looking for something her father had given her. An object? Information? What could it possibly be? Surely not her clothing, jewelry, shoes, or equipment for the horses. What of her books and perfumes? Toiletries and hair combs and other insignificant articles? She couldn't fathom it.

Bethany had brought all her valuables with her to Moorewood. She needed to scrutinize her belongings, to see whether she could solve the puzzle, but she doubted it.

* * *

"Is Polly ready?" Lord Locke murmured when Mr. Treadwell joined him in his room's flickering lamplight.

"Yes, m'lord. Seaworth kept him to his stall tonight. Don't want any of our guests seeing him the way he looks now."

Locke chuckled sourly. "This is a great deal easier when Moorewood is unoccupied, isn't it? We knew it would be."

"Indeed. Are you ready to dress?"

Locke nodded and began shedding the clothes of an earl and donning what Mr. Treadwell handed him. Threadbare but presently clean, the thin cotton shirt and trousers were cool against his skin. The ragged socks were thick, itchy woolen things that stiffened the old boots. When he sat at his dressing table and let Mr. Treadwell prepare his hair and face, he wondered, not for the first time, if this was how the pampered ladies of his class felt. Of course, it would horrify them that rather than powders and creams or hair tonics, his valet artfully applied dirt and grease to his hair and face, and added a streak of mud across one cheek. The subtlety of his skills made Locke appear genuinely impoverished. Time, travel and dismal circumstances, including hunger, would keep him looking that way, and that was what mattered.

Mr. Treadwell left briefly to ensure the manor's halls were clear. Confident everyone else was in bed, they slipped quickly to the ground floor, Treadwell shouldering the bedroll he'd prepared earlier for the earl. Locke found the food Mrs. Ford had packed for him sitting on the counter in the kitchen. Grabbing it, he stole out the rear door and to the stables with the butler on his heels.

"Evenin', m'lord." Dimity took Locke's provisions to Polly's stall. "Seaworth and I both checked your mount out careful and he took no harm from this mornin'. Seaworth put a new nail in a shoe, but otherwise, he not only appears fit as ever, he seems eager to play his part. Found a mud puddle to roll in tonight and all I needed to do was groom 'im enough his saddle won't rub."

Locke laughed lightly. Providence had an interesting sense of humor.

Devon materialized from the shadows, expression downcast.

"So you've still gotten nothing from them," Locke said.

"No, m'lord, sir." The young man's jaw set with frustration. "Tight as drums they were, and I did what I could without killin' 'em. Scars they'll have aplenty, but it didn't impress 'em. We'll keep 'em on rations that'll barely keep 'em alive. Hope that'll break 'em. We moved 'em to the secret post a couple hours ago, put 'em in the pits."

Locke shivered at the image. A horrible place to spend one's days. A necessary evil in surveillance and in war, he supposed, but he didn't like it. "You'll escalate as needed?"

"Of course. They may walk out someday, but if need be they'll do it without thumbs and most o' their toes, and once they've told us what we want, mayhap we really will relieve 'em of their tongues."

"Let's hope it doesn't require that, Devon. I hate such brutality."

"Aye. Don't like it m'self, but hands can write and tongues can wag, and her ladyship won't be safe lessen we stop 'em."

"Take it up with The Beau. His authority greatly surpasses mine."

Devon laughed. "The Duke of Wellington's authority surpasses everyone but His Majesty Himself, and I'm sure there's a whole host of powerful men 'twixt him and me. We won't step o'er the line without permission, m'lord. Promise ya that. But our mission's to see Lady Locke stays safe night and day."

"Thank you, friends," Locke said. Saluting them, he walked Polly, looking more like an old nag with his mussed mane and tail, mud-caked sides, and rickety saddle, out the back door of the stable. The animal no longer belonged to Locke, but to Locke's fictitious "master."

"No moon tonight," Dimity whispered. "Take care. No one will likely witness your leavin', but you know it makes the roads treacherous."

"And you know well how it works," Locke reassured the older man, who never ceased to worry. "I won't go far tonight. I leave late to avoid the curious eyes of neighbors, passersby, and in this case my visitors. I camp a couple of hours down the road and set off just before dawn. You also know how to send me word in an emergency. I'll come as soon as I can."

"Yessir, m'lord. And the same for you. May the Good Lord watch o'er ya."

"Likewise, for you and everyone here at Moorewood. Especially Lady Locke."

"'Specially her, sir."

* * *

"Can't imagine Locke set off hours ago," Scarbreigh grumbled, his back to the Hannaford carriage's open door. "How in the world can he stand the glare of such blue skies and green grass so early in the morning?"

The twins laughed and Lord Mathew pushed him hard enough he almost fell into the carriage. "He doesn't stay up until three o'clock in the morning," he said, and to the women added, "*Au revoir*, Ladies. We'll visit again before the end of summer."

"Sooner, if you can," Bethany urged, her unease mounting at being left to face the invisible threat that hung over her.

Lord Matthew took her hands, his face growing serious. "Locke's servants are on the alert, my lady. Believe it or not, you're safer here than almost anywhere else in England outside of Windsor Castle, with or without us."

"And I promise to visit you both again at my earliest convenience," Scarbreigh said. "But in future, I'll bring my own rig. Then I shan't be forced from my bed before I'm ready."

The twins snorted, slid inside the carriage after Scarbreigh, and slammed the door shut. Bethany and Lady Camille, chuckling, waved their good byes as the carriage pulled away.

Lady Camille sighed, her smile drooping. "I hate to see them go."

"Not half so much as I."

"Forgive me, dear. I'm thinking too much of myself, aren't I? You miss Lord Locke already, don't you?"

"I'll miss all of them and can't stand the idea of sitting around thinking about it. Will you ride with me?"

* * *

In short order they were off, with Hugh their day's armed escort. Unfortunately, the warm, muggy day was threatened by a storm. They returned to the manor sooner than they'd planned, only to find a carriage, two wagons, and dozens of men in the drive waiting for them.

"Oh, look, Lady Camille!" Bethany exclaimed. "Mr. Taylor-Ward has arrived."

The women hurried to greet the man, as spindly and mustached as ever, while Mr. Treadwell, Dimity and Seaworth inspected the workers' credentials. Reassured of their documents before they entered the manor, Bethany reviewed the plans and gave her final approval to the fabrics, paints, and trims she and Lady Camille had selected.

Bethany had little opportunity to miss her departed houseguests. Madness replaced their companionship. In a rush, the workers removed what was left of the old furnishings from the ground floor and transported their equipment and supplies inside before it rained. From that moment on, the air was rife with the racket of shouted orders and bellowed replies, rasping saws, creaking ladders, and the constant pounding of hammers.

Old, drafty windows, worn cabinetry and shelving, and chipped and outdated wainscoting and moulding would soon be replaced with new.

To lessen the inconvenience to Moorewood's residents, the work began with the top floor and the ground floor simultaneously, except for the kitchen. That left the cooking area and the middle floor for last, which included Lord Locke's, Lady Bethany's and Lady Camille's chambers, the bedchambers the twins and Lord Scarbreigh had used, the green and blue salons, the library, and a few other bedrooms still in serviceable condition—and several that weren't so serviceable.

The young women escaped the din at every opportunity. On this first day, they interred themselves in the green salon, with the door closed, and the sounds of raindrops drumming against the windows drowning out all else. They took turns with their needlework, happy conversation, and reading aloud from *Pride and Prejudice*.

Wednesday dawned with brilliant sunshine and a bedewed countryside, a perfect palette for strolling and later riding. Then on Thursday, Josh accompanied the women on a relaxing outing across the meadows.

* * *

Thankfully, as the work on the manor gained momentum, the demands of the tenants waned. Bethany responded quickly when needs arose but mostly trusted them to manage their own affairs.

Jason delivered Shadow to Moorewood one quiet afternoon. The gentle animal seemed fit enough, but the scar from his stabbing grieved Bethany. She'd decided beforehand that if he had so much as a hint of lameness, he'd spend the rest of his days at pasture.

The stately home began to take on a new face. Mullioned windows and both fashionable paints and wallpapers dispelled the dark corners and brightened the lackluster surroundings. Refurbished flooring, and new rugs, woodwork and draperies gave it fresh character; and, at last, the new furnishings and decor began to arrive, transforming it, piece by piece, into a new home. The kitchen's repair was troublesome, but both Bethany and Mrs. Ford deemed it worth the inconvenience when they set eyes on the new amenities.

Bethany loved the scent of the new carpentry and fabrics whenever she strolled through the manor to keep a watchful eye on the progress. Mostly it filled her with pride to see her and Lady Camille's creativity, and the many useful suggestions Mrs. Callen provided them, coming to life.

* * *

Lady Camille was often plagued with headaches in the hotter months and resorted to afternoon naps to relieve them, which brought Bethany an unexpected opportunity. She carried out a methodical search of her belongings, assessing every item with care. What, she begged Providence, could her father have possibly given her that lawless men were willing to hurt her to acquire?

Try as she might, she could unearth nothing.

So passed the month of July, marked by all of these things and the arrival of a number of new foals, lambs and calves. It was a warmer-than-normal year, temperatures rising to sweltering on too many days, yet afternoons spent in the shade near the pond, or riding to the river that ran through Locke's property to swim, made it pleasant enough.

Near the end of July, Lord Matthew and Mr. Nicolas visited for a week, and then Lord Scarbreigh followed them, brightening their days if only briefly. Bethany heard nothing from Lord Locke. She'd known he wouldn't write and wasn't supposed to care, but her heart wished he would.

With no further threat against Bethany, her fears faded. She wanted to believe she was safe. Nevertheless, Moorewood's staff remained nearby, Mr. Treadwell particularly attentive and conciliating, and Mrs. Callen as motherly as a hen. This affirmed Bethany's suspicions that despite the servants watching everyone who came and went from the property, they still feared an assailant could find his way past the safeguards.

At the end of the first week of August, Lady Camille admitted to a bout of homesickness. Bethany believed that more than anything, her cousin wanted to be closer to London and therefore Lord Scarbreigh. The marquess had sent at least three to four missives a week to Lady Camille since leaving Moorewood with the twins, and Lady Camille had dispatched that many or more to him and grown more starry-eyed with each one.

Thus, on the tenth of August, a month since Lord Locke's leaving, the Camerfield carriage transported Lady Camille home, leaving Bethany to manage without her.

CHAPTER 14

It wasn't so bad on her own, Bethany scolded herself, realizing that she could now do as she pleased. She could ride to her heart's content, all day if she wanted, and on as many of her horses as she liked. Or on her husband's horses, for that matter. Locke had welcomed her to them.

Motivated by the thought, she took a quick trip to her room and changed into her favorite riding clothes, a simple cotton blouse and thigh high boots tugged over riding breeches. She wanted to work Raven like she used to, and skirts were hot, in the way, and uncomfortable. They were also ridiculous when she straddled the saddle, and she refused to use a sidesaddle for serious work, regardless of whatever fashion dictated. She was in the country, at her own home, and riding alone, for heaven's sake.

Donning a skirt to hide the breeches for now, she intended to remove it before boarding Raven. Tying on her straw bonnet, she headed downstairs.

When she arrived, however, neither Mr. Treadwell nor the stablehand assigned to accompany her that day were present, and only two of the workers were working there. At first annoyed, she shrugged it off, tired of the whole affair. She wasn't even leaving the immediate grounds, for heaven's sake.

With no stablehands in the stallions' stable either, she groomed and saddled Raven herself. Lady Katherine would have scolded her, but Bethany didn't mind. It soothed her to care for her own mounts, and she swore they knew and performed better for her because of it.

In exploring Moorewood's grounds, Bethany had discovered a small stone paddock to the rear of the stables. Dimity used it for training and exercising the horses, a perfect place with few distractions and containment for the horse if it got loose from its handler. Bethany led Raven inside, latched the wooden gate behind them, removed her skirt, draped it over the top rail of the gate, and climbed aboard, pleased by the ease of doing so without the encumbrances of petticoats and yards of irksome fabric.

Raven's coat shown blue-black in the late morning sunlight, his dark eyes bright, his thick neck arched and tail held high. He could hardly wait to stretch his legs. He carried her briskly around the paddock in his warm-up paces. From a swift walk, Bethany sent him into a jog then finally a collected canter.

From her early childhood and despite being a girl, Bethany's father had taught her dressage, the maneuvers used on horses trained at the Imperial Spanish Riding School of Vienna. A cue to double-back had Raven repeating his actions in the opposite direction, executing figure eights with flawless changes of leads. His pirouettes, side-passes, and serpentines were near-perfect, and though Bethany considered some of her own cues clumsy, the stallion interpreted them correctly. He moved into the *piaffe* with a single prompt, and performed the *passage* as if he'd read her thoughts. Such incredible grace and power had Bethany feeling on top of the world.

It was difficult work, leaving both of them slick with sweat and breathing hard. Bethany praised Raven, patting his lathered shoulder and stroking his neck, and then cooled off both of them in a comfortable walk. She wished she could take the stallion into the meadows to ride, but dressed as she was and without an escort, she dared do no such thing. She already dreaded any repercussions of breaking her agreement with Lord Locke to this degree. Inhaling lungsful of Moorewood's clean, fresh air, she dismounted and gave the stallion a hug. Raven snorted and bobbed his head, leaning into Bethany with affection.

Suddenly the stallion started and huffed, nostrils flared and ears perked towards the stables. Then the paddock gate swung wide and Bethany's mouth fell open when Lord Locke stepped inside.

He did not look at all pleased.

"M—my lord," she stammered. "You're home."

Locke nodded, clasping his hands behind him and raising his brows. "And you're out riding. Alone." The way his eyes roamed over her, from head to toe, set her cheeks on fire.

Bethany gulped. "I couldn't find any of the servants when I came to the manor's entryway, just as no one was here to groom and tack Raven for me. I did it myself. I don't mind, really. In fact, I enjoy it."

"You understand why I'm not pleased with your decision, do you not?"

Her excuses died on her lips. If Lord Locke could surprise her, assassins or kidnappers could have done the same. Besides, she rued the disappointment she heard in his voice.

"I promise I won't take the risk again. I won't leave my room without a guardian at my side, if you wish." After all, blackguards and murderers would prefer she made a mistake.

"My goal is your safety not imprisonment, my lady, and only requires everyone's compliance. Just remember, if your full attention is on your mount, where it should be, you could get caught off-guard. I hear Lady Camille went home a couple of hours ago."

Bethany blinked at the change of topics. "She plans to return in a week or so. She was a bit homesick."

"She was a riding companion."

Bethany's heart fell and she bowed her head at this additional admonition.

Locke pointed at the window in the stallion barn at the loft level. "I was up there, in Dimity's work room, in conference with a homely lot of stablehands, when one of them gasped in shock. An audience gathered at the window, myself included.

"I didn't see your entire performance but observed enough to know you are a superb horsewoman. Skirts and sidesaddles must certainly get in your way." Another perusal of her figure made her wish to crawl under a rock. "But I imagined you exaggerated when you said you preferred riding barefoot and in breeches. It appears I was wrong. Not only was your performance breathtaking, but so was your wardrobe. I daresay you nearly gave old Seaworth a heart attack, but I cannot say the same about the estate's younger men."

He pulled her riding skirt from the gate and handed it to her. She quickly donned it and smoothed the folds into place. Bethany was hardly unaware of all the reasons she oughtn't to defy convention, but she never would have thought the possibility of disgracing her husband would matter so much.

"Josh!" Locke shouted, making her start. When the man came running from the stables, Lord Locke waved at the stallion.

"Who was supposed to escort Lady Locke this morning?"

"Oh, uh, Carter, I believe, m'lord."

"He wasn't at our meeting. I need to know where he was if not accompanying Lady Locke. Take the stallion and have someone groom him and put him away. Bring me word."

"Yes, m'lord," the young man replied, leading off Raven.

"Now, how goes the renovation?" Locke asked Bethany.

"You've not seen it yet?"

"All I saw and heard was bedlam, men and equipment everywhere."

Bethany dared offer a rueful smile. "As it has been since just after you left."

Bethany heard Josh before she saw him jog around the corner.

"Pardon, m'lord. Spoke to Carter m'self. He's dreadful sick, said he took a drink at the 'ouse, started feelin' bilious not much after. Told Mr. Treadwell he was hurryin' for the jacks, sure he was goin' t' lose his breakfast. Thought Mr. Treadwell would send for a replacement."

Locke's face creased with concern. He nodded and excused Josh to take word he would be out to see Carter shortly.

"What's wrong, my lord?" Bethany asked

"I spoke with Mr. Treadwell before coming to the stables, but he didn't mention Carter's taking ill." He ruminated a moment, then offered his arm and said, "I'd like to see the progress on the house."

They'd not gone more than a few feet, however, when Bethany realized Locke was limping.

"You're hurt! What happened?"

Locke shrugged. "Just took a spill and twisted an ankle. I'm fine."

"I trust you at least dodged mud puddles this time," she said, disconcerted. "Do you have accidents often?"

"More than I like," he admitted, looking away.

Lady Bethany wondered what secrets he harbored now. "Perhaps you shouldn't climb the stairs."

"It's a minor injury. I really am fine, Lady Bethany. Let's see the house."

* * *

Evading ladders, piles of equipment, and clusters of men, Lord and Lady Locke journeyed arm in arm through the manor. The changes in the place amazed the earl. He missed everything that reminded him of his boyhood, but his lady's inspiration was already giving his home a lovelier face. It plucked a cord inside him that made him truly sorry he could neither stay here longer nor come more often. As it was, he'd frequented Moorewood more this summer than he had in the last few years put together, and mostly because of Lady Bethany.

An interminable trip upstairs, on an ankle that reminded Locke of the close call he'd taken on his journey, revealed a work in various stages of progress. The ground floor and dozens of guest bedchambers on the top floor were now finished and decorated, while the work on the second level had begun days ago in the library—which was now completed—and the blue parlor. The green parlor was slated next.

They'd barely entered the library when a thundering of footsteps spun Lady Bethany around. Locke looked behind him, frowning when Melissa ran past the library's doorway towards the stairs. He heard her skidding to a stop and then she returned to stare at them with eyes rounded with shock and her face as white as bleached muslin.

"Lord Locke! My lady! Gore, ya won't believe it—I mean, pardon me, but somethin' terrible's happened. I went to tidy your room and lay out your day dress, my lady, and, oh, what I found! It's dreadful."

Feeling the rush of adrenaline, Locke pushed the girl towards the hallway. Lady Bethany ran alongside him—in his case he limped quickly—until Melissa stopped at his countess's open door, arms wrapped about herself as master and mistress walked into the room.

Lady Bethany gasped, and Locke stood dumbfounded at seeing the bedchamber turned upside down.

Bedding and the mattress, the latter slashed open, were tossed from the four-poster frame. The lined curtains were torn to shreds, the wardrobe doors thrown open and Lady Bethany's dresses flung to the floor like rubbish. Her dressing table and chest of drawers had been emptied and the drawers themselves pitched after their contents. Even the framed paintings were torn from the wall, and feathers bled onto the floor from gashes in her pillows.

"Why?" Lady Bethany emitted a strangled gasp. "Why would anyone do this?"

Locke grabbed for the pull-rope near her bed, repeatedly yanking it hard. Not a moment later, a number of footsteps thundered up the stairs. Mr. Treadwell was followed by the two footmen, Mrs. Callen, one of the housemaids, and finally Mrs. Ford.

"Good heavens!" Mrs. Callen screeched, clapping her hands to her mouth.

Locke whispered to Mr. Treadwell, who nodded and slipped away. The earl returned to Lady Bethany's side. Her face was chalk, her eyes brimming with unshed tears, but she stood resolute, taking it all in.

"Come, my lady. The servants can take care of this."

"No." She shook her head and stood firm. "This wasn't just hateful. They were looking for something." Her eyes met his, anguish written in them. He sensed she wanted to ask him questions but didn't know how.

"When Shadow was injured, at our wedding, I knew someone had done it either out of spite or as a warning of some sort, although I couldn't imagine why. The man who tried to shoot me wanted to hurt me, yet for some reason I don't think he wanted me dead. This." She waved at the room. "Isn't vindictive, it's methodical. Whatever the miscreant wanted, he began in the most obvious places, but he was in a hurry. When he couldn't find it." She paused, surveying everything again, and then stepped over one of the drawers to peer inside the wardrobe. "He resorted to tossing the lot on the floor after he'd examined it."

Too familiar with such things, Locke had surmised what she'd said the instant he laid eyes on the room. He would not, however, have imagined a young woman, a daughter of the peerage raised in self-imposed seclusion on her father's country estate, would interpret it so astutely.

The sounds of feet striding towards them again tugged their attention to the doorway. Mr. Treadwell arrived at the threshold and bowed to Lord Locke.

"They're assembled, my lord."

"Thank you, Mr. Treadwell. Bethany, I must run downstairs. Treadwell's had Taylor-Ward gather the workmen in the front entry for questioning."

"I'm coming—"

"But—"

"I'm coming," she insisted.

The workmen in the entryway appeared puzzled but not as concerned as Mr. Taylor-Ward, despite armed stablehands, fairly bristling with anger, standing behind them and guarding the exits from the house. Locke hurried down as best he could, while favoring his throbbing ankle, to greet Taylor-Ward and announce to the group what happened.

"Have any of your men left their posts in the last hour?" he demanded of Taylor-Ward, and to the workers added, "Have any of you seen someone leave his station for any reason?"

Lady Bethany tightened her hold on his arm. "My lord," she said. "Two of them are missing. They were working downstairs when I left for the stable."

Locke asked her to describe them, and Taylor-Ward swore under his breath.

"They're new, Lord Locke," he admitted. "Brought decent references from another overseer and applied for this job a week before we began. I had no reason to doubt them. What have they taken?"

"We don't know yet. See the damage for yourself."

Locke led the man upstairs, Lady Bethany clinging to his elbow as if he might get away from her. Taylor-Ward cursed when he saw the truth.

"I've never witnessed the likes of it. I promise you I'll see these men arrested."

Locke recognized the terror on the man's face, but not just fear for Lady Bethany; more likely fear that he might lose whatever profits—and reputation—he'd hoped to enjoy from this job.

"Lady Locke will give you a list of what's missing as soon as she's finished it. If you can recover the stolen goods, I'll hold only what was damaged against you. And Taylor-Ward, make drawings and written descriptions of these men, as detailed as you can make them. The constable needs to know for whom he's searching."

Eyes filled with worry, the supervisor gave his promise and returned to his crew.

Locke rested a careful hand on Bethany's shoulder. "Let the servants clean this up."

"No." Her lower lip trembled, more with anger than sorrow. "I want their help, but I must go through it myself. Otherwise, something might get overlooked."

Locke nodded and sighed. "You're right, of course."

Mrs. Callen and Melissa brought cleaning equipment and a dust bin for collecting the feathers, the damaged items, and the broken glass. The others returned to their duties.

Unable to tear himself away, Locke's heart tightened when Bethany struggled not to cry over a cracked bottle of a rare, fine French perfume. She explained that Mr. Collin gave it to her on her sixteenth birthday. It meant so much to her that she rarely used it, hoping it would last forever.

"I've an empty bottle, m'lady," Mrs. Callen said. "Could possibly save some of it for you."

"Thank you, Mrs. Callen. I'd love that."

Knowing the women would want to sort through Bethany's personal items in private, Locke finally withdrew. Mr. Treadwell joined him on the painstaking trip downstairs.

"I've failed you, my lord," Mr. Treadwell muttered, wise eyes couched in creases that more than six decades had etched there. "We've taken every precaution, checked every workman's identity daily, watched each room in which they've labored. Although I finished my rounds this morning as usual and Mrs. Callen locked every chamber not in use today, I was obviously not attentive enough."

"What more could you have done, Treadwell? These men knew what they were about. What happened with Carter this morning? I hear he wasn't feeling well, but Lady Bethany told me no one replaced him."

Mr. Treadwell came to a stop in shock. "Pardon? I expected he'd take care of it when he went to his quarters. My lord, do you think Carter's illness may have been orchestrated? To leave both the house and Lady Bethany vulnerable? I didn't consider it then, but before he became ill, Mrs. Ford put water out for the workers. What if he was poisoned?"

Alarmed, Locke called to one of the housemaids. "Run to Mrs. Ford, tell her I want to speak to her immediately. Then hurry to the stables. Carter may have been poisoned. Have Dimity check on him and send for my physician straightaway."

The girl ran off, while Locke took stock of the dining room. It glistened with a newness that should have cheered him but failed.

"Our truants were likely planted. And most likely one of them poisoned Carter. What if Lady Bethany had been in her chambers when they snuck up there? What would they have done to her? And have they found what they wanted? If they did, perhaps my lady is finally safe. But what will they do with what they found if they did find it?"

"My sentiments, exactly, my lord," said Mr. Treadwell. "We must be even more alert than before. Pardon me, but you should let the boys handle the matter for the time being. Your ankle needs attention."

The kitchen door opened and Mrs. Ford, cheeks sallow, hurried out, wiping her hands on her apron.

"My Lord." She dipped a curtsy. "You're really thinking Carter drank poison? I cannot fathom it. I filled half a dozen cups for some of the workers, and Carter joined them. Any one of them might have chosen his cup."

"Was there any confusion? Could one of the men have dropped something into Carter's drink?"

Mrs. Ford frowned in thought. "I couldn't say. There were too many of them."

"I see. Well, Dimity will keep us apprised of Carter's condition. For now, I need a cold compress for my ankle and some food to settle my stomach."

"Certainly, my lord," the cook said, bustling away.

Mr. Treadwell pulled Locke's chair out for him, dragged a second one close to rest his injured leg on, and then scurried off to fetch a pillow to cushion it.

Too long on the road and deprived of his ordinary comforts, Locke treasured his meal when it came, every wonderful dirt, bug, and mouse-dung-free morsel of it. With the worst of his hunger abated and his ankle feeling better, however, he found himself reflecting on the wreckage in Bethany's room and her reactions to it. As before, a timorous woman might have fainted when she saw what the thieves had done, but he'd come to expect Bethany Montgomery Ashburn to be anything but timorous.

And again it filled him with admiration. It also made him wonder about that place deep in his heart that ached when he imagined any harm coming to her. Protecting her was his assignment, and he would do it even if he disliked her. But that had nothing to do with the warmth that smoldered inside him and precipitated his fierce determination to defend her from an evil world.

CHAPTER 15

Cleaning Bethany's bedchamber carried on into early afternoon, one painstaking step at a time. Melissa and Mrs. Callen examined Bethany's clothing with care and rehung it or relegated it to the wash. Two vases and a crystal decanter, Bethany's laving bowl and pitcher, and several figurines were smashed to pieces and, along with the ruined mattress and pillows, were temporarily substituted by others from one of the guest rooms. Mr. Taylor-Ward would replace them with new as soon as possible.

The desk under the window had been divested of Bethany's writing implements, and the ink bottle had fallen to the floor and cracked, the ink seeping through the precious rug and staining the floor. One of the housemaids did her best to remove the stains, while Melissa and Mrs. Callen sorted Bethany's belongings into groups to allow her to examine each item quickly but thoroughly.

For all the wreckage, Bethany found only two things missing, a small music box of her grandmother's and her diary. Confusion plagued her. Why would they destroy a room and steal none of the priceless diamonds, or her favorite emerald earrings and matching pendant, or her rubies and sapphires and chains of silver and gold? Here in her engraved jewelry box were the pearls her grandmother had willed to her, and there, in the drawer of a larger music box, a handful of bracelets and rings bearing every imaginable jewel.

Not a single tear had fallen until she found the charm bracelet her father had sent her from Belgium, safe and unharmed. Then she wept with relief at knowing this last reminder of him had not been lost.

"Your ladyship needs to eat something," Mrs. Callen urged her.

Bethany nodded. She did, but in assessing the damage, she realized it would need Mr. Taylor-Ward's services after all, like it or not. She spoke to him again downstairs before joining Locke in the dining hall, famished. She'd not eaten since early that morning, before Lady Camille departed.

Finding Locke still at table, she paused at seeing his injured ankle raised on a chair, a cushion under it and a cold compress on top it. The moment he saw her, he made the effort to rise, but Bethany waved him back to his seat.

"Please take care of your sprain, my lord."

Locke gave her a wry smile. "I only twisted it. I'll be fit as a fiddle soon."

Bethany sighed. "And then you'll be off again?"

His silence acknowledged her question but the tipping of his head created a new one, making her heart skip a bit. Did she sound as disappointed as she felt? Would he care if she was?

"Have you received word about Carter?" she asked.

"My physician's with him now, and Dimity sent word he's greatly improved. What did the burglars take from your room?"

She told him about the music box and added, "I also cannot find my diary, but why would anyone take that? I'm sure it's just lost behind the furniture or something."

The guarded expression on her husband's face had her frowning.

"Sometimes we don't realize how important our deepest thoughts can be, my dear," he replied.

Bethany shrugged. "I grew up with brothers who enjoyed ferreting out the book and reading it aloud to their friends. I determined never to write down secrets. It's fun to record dates and special occasions, but I never put anything in it I wouldn't want others to read."

"Well, I hope you find it. How bad is the damage?"

"Bad enough. I spoke to Mr. Taylor-Ward about refurbishing the room after all."

"Excellent. You deserve a space as renewed and distinctive as the rest of the house."

"What of your room? Surely it could use a new face."

"No. Did it right after my father passed away. How do the tenants fare?"

Bethany resented the quick nudging of their conversation away from the earl's living quarters. Why did he seem so determined to keep his chambers and everything in it a mystery to her?

Locke expressed relief at hearing the continued progress, and about her work with the vicar and the area's blossoming benevolent society.

"I've grown tired of this chair, Bethany. Meet me in the gold salon. I've something I want to collect from my room, then I'll join you and we'll have a look at it."

"Can I help you upstairs?" She came to her feet.

He reassured her that he was capable and, after Mr. Treadwell applied his slippers, rose fluidly. He winced when he first put his weight on the injured ankle but plodded, with only a modest limp, for his room.

"Carter's truly alright, Mr. Treadwell?" Bethany asked.

"Yes, it seems so, my lady."

The servant's voice still sounded hesitant. She sighed with resignation and headed for the gold parlor, which had turned out beautifully. Locke soon joined her, carrying a worn leather attaché. He set it on the piano bench and rummaged through it. "I found my old case hiding under my bed right before leaving last time. Very unsociable of it. It holds the music I wrote."

"Oh!" Bethany exclaimed, thrilled. "Please, let me get a chair and sit beside you. I look forward to hearing it."

"I was hoping you'd play it for me. The ankle?"

"Oh, yes, of course. I suppose I can give it a try."

The handwriting on the yellowing pages of a few of the pieces was quite youthful, and there were mistakes in the music that made them both cringe. Locke laughed at some of it, said he ought to be embarrassed, but bowed when she complimented his work. Not many people could compose anything notable at so young an age, let alone so beautiful, and Bethany was, truly, impressed.

Locke considered her thoughtfully. "You do like music and dance, don't you? I wonder if you'd consider undertaking a brief adventure with me?"

"An adventure?" She frowned, seeing the curious—hesitant?—look on Locke's face. Hadn't he had enough adventuring of late?

"Yes. I have a few appointments in London on Saturday and must leave here on Friday. I think you could use a respite from the work. I'd like you to come with me; perhaps a two week holiday from the country? London is at a low point in August, you know, but a fair's on in Hyde Park this year. Many of the notables will surely attend."

Bethany cared little about who made appearances where, but she loved concerts and plays and liked to dance, and getting away from Moorewood actually appealed to her. But what about the renovations? And what about Carter?

"Carter will recover completely," Locke reassured her. "And Moorewood's servants can keep diligent track of the project for the short time you'd be gone.

"I've a proposition I think might sweeten the offer," he added. "How would you like to leave tomorrow morning instead of Friday, travel to Whitton and spend the day and tomorrow night with your mother? We could convince her and Lady Camille to join our trip. You mentioned your desire for additional decor for the manor. Why not choose it yourself in London? And I've no doubt many of the mini-season attendees would love to meet the woman who won my hand in marriage."

Bethany wanted to laugh outright. She imagined how some of London's elite would like to scratch her eyes out for it. Her devious smirk made Locke grin.

"But how would we get word to Mum and Lady Camille quickly enough? Mum doesn't tolerate last minute invitations well, and Lady Camille returned to Hannaford only this morning."

"In truth, I had the idea last night, on my ride home. I wasn't going to tell you until I received word, to avoid possibly disappointing you, but shortly after I arrived, I sent a rider with messages for both your cousin and the dowager countess, to feel them out. We should hear from them before supper. Considering the damage to your wardrobe, you'd probably enjoy the clothiers and milliners in London, too. With the season low, those businesses will dance attendance on you."

Bethany bit her lip against amusement. She had no desire for such attention, and there were particulars about London, especially in the heat of summer, that she detested. She had, however, selected her clothes frugally for the wedding and, before that, hadn't purchased a single dress or undergarment since her father had died. Some of her favorite gowns were growing earnestly shabby.

"May I take Raven?"

Locke threw his head back and chortled. "Only Lord Whitton's daughter would worry more about having a mount on which to canter round Rotten Row than she would about her wardrobe."

"How would I show off my wardrobe without a mount?"

Locke laughed again, calling for Mr. Treadwell. "Good point, Lady Locke. Alright, then, it's off to London we go, horses and all."

* * *

Bethany was amazed by the excitement Locke's invitation had inspired in her mother and cousin. The Dowager Lady Whitton received them with a broad grin when they rolled in late the next morning, and despite the earl's message having reached Hannaford right after Lady Camille arrived, Bethany's cousin was at Whitton when they appeared. So much, Bethany thought, for Lady Camille's case of homesickness.

Lady Katherine was thrilled to show off Whitton's restoration—which was excellent—to the threesome, but Bethany was more impressed by how the improvements had heartened her mother.

They retired to the parlor, where Mr. Drew—his thin but ceremonious self garbed in the finest clothes he'd worn in years—brought them tea, his faded hazel eyes twinkling at Bethany with unexpected vigor. Bethany couldn't help smiling at the man who had served them faithfully all her life and who seemed pleased that Whitton's plight, and his own, had been relieved.

Lady Katherine quizzed her guests regarding their goings-on. Leaving the harrowing confrontation with her attackers and her damaged room unmentioned, Bethany made a point of divulging the budding relationship between Lord Scarbreigh and Lady Camille.

"I'm excited for you, darling," Lady Katherine oozed. "He's a frightfully gorgeous man, quite the humorist, and I've believed for years he was sweet on you."

Lady Camille flushed and bowed her head in embarrassment.

"He'll be over the top when he learns you're coming to London, Cam," Bethany teased. "Rather than having to walk you around duck ponds or lift you over horse droppings in the meadows, he can drag you off to one rout after another."

Lady Camille rolled her eyes in repugnance but replied, "At least we'll have a great deal more fun this time, I'm sure."

Bethany's stomach dipped at the reminder of their season last year. Considering the break-in at Moorewood made it worse.

"Goodness, we'll have a veritable cavalcade headed for Towne," the dowager countess observed. "The four of us will ride in one carriage; we'll require a second vehicle for our ladies' maids, Mr. Treadwell, and the footmen; and we'll need a wagon for our trunks and for our purchases on our return trip."

"I shall ride my horse, my lady," Locke demurred, adding that the Ladies' horses would be tethered to the carriages, avoiding the need for riders.

"Well, we'll still make quite the spectacle. I do hope you've brought at least some of your good jewelry with you, Lady Bethany. We'll need to match your new wardrobe to it, you know," she said.

Bethany sighed, having agreed to Locke's request to add all her jewelry and baubles to her trunks to secure them in his strong box in his townhouse basement. She just couldn't imagine the tediousness of having to match dresses to all of them.

* * *

Mr. Drew came to announce the unexpected arrival of additional guests. Lord Matthew and Mr. Nicolas entered, grinning warmly at their welcomes and kissing the ladies' cheeks.

"What brings you here?" Mr. Nicolas inquired, laughing when Bethany turned the same question against him and his twin.

"Good fortune brings us," Lord Matthew replied, his gaze locking with the earl's. "We've just left London for home and thought we'd visit our beloved aunt."

"And we're staying the night with Aunt Kathrine before heading to Towne," Lady Camille commented.

"You must stay the night, too," Lady Katherine insisted. "It's been too long since we've all been together."

The twins accepted immediately, and a pleasant morning became a day full of enjoyment. Following supper, the women took their needlework to the sitting room while the men went to share a cozy chat and glasses of port in Whitton's drawing room.

* * *

The men relished the chance to share information not meant for the ladies' ears, but the twins were horrified to learn of the details of the vandalism of Lady Bethany's room.

"Thus your hasty note to meet you here," Mr. Nicolas noted. "This isn't good. Glad you're taking her to Towne for a bit. Maybe throw the dogs off the scent."

"It's my hope. Besides, she needs association with family, while giving you two more time to ferret out clues to her pursuers."

Nothing had been discovered since the last time they'd spoken.

Their discussion then turned to Locke's latest trip to France in his never-ending search for clues to the conspiracy surrounding Bonaparte.

"You're lucky you didn't break your ankle jumping out of that window," Lord Matthew said, his face puckered into a worried frown, when Locke was finished.

"Preferable to getting shot by a jealous husband," Locke replied, adjusting the routine cold compress Treadwell had delivered.

"Can't argue that point," Mr. Nicolas said, sipping his port. "Despite his not actually have anything to be jealous about. Ran this one too close, Locke. You're getting desperate for answers, but you mustn't toss more than a year's worth of hard work into the cesspit. You could have met with your French connection somewhere other than in her private rooms and spared yourself injury. We've done all we can in London. Let us help you with the rest, take some pressure off you."

Locke scoffed. "Identical twins draw curiosity like horse dung draws flies."

"Lovely image," Lord Matthew replied. "Need I remind you our cords were cut at birth? We're not only capable of working independently, we're most useful that way. We often dress alike, pretend to be one of us, and in essence visit two places at once. The sum of the intelligence we gather is often better than double, you see."

"It's true we're running out of time, Locke," Mr. Nicolas insisted. "But your hurried travels across the channel will eventually cause questions, if they haven't already, especially if you keep resorting to petty thievery or shameful scams with some of the Grand Ladies of Paris solely to garner information. How long can you keep it up? Particularly with individuals familiar with each other? In due course, you'll run across someone you recognize or who recognizes you."

"I did," Locke said, his expression growing serious. "I'd no idea my fine French Lady, from whom I was receiving this latest message, visits London upon occasion and recognized me. Doesn't matter she's on our side. Should she give me away accidentally, it could ruin everything." And could get him killed, he thought.

"It could. Give us leave; we'll do whatever you need."

"Lord Hannaford would burn me at the stake if anything happened to you because of me."

"Nonsense. Father's no stranger to the risks involved with foreign surveillance," Lord Matthew said dismissively. "You know as well as we do that he and Lord Whitton were into it thick as thieves until Mum became ill two years ago."

"How did he and Lord Whitton do this and keep their wives in the dark?" Locke muttered, more to himself than to the twins.

Lord Matthew's mouth curled into a commiserative smile. "We've often teased Lady Camille and Lady Bethany that they were switched at birth. Aunt Katherine stayed in Towne as much as possible, our sister's fondest wish since childhood. Left Uncle John to his own devices. But Mum was the provincial one like Lady Bethany and both curious as cats. Kept Father on his tiptoes. When we joined the Service, Father and Lord Whitton frequently sympathized with each other over it. Could have been caught out at any time but thankfully weren't."

Mr. Nicolas's brows knitted together with worry. "Locke, do I sense that you're regretting your alliance with our dear cousin?"

"It's been harder than I'd expected. I didn't worry about her finding me out; I travel late at night. With subordinates positioned as servants, I've better protection than most men could hope for, and that applies to Bethany as well. It never dawned on me she'd accomplish every task I gave her so well. The manor's coming along beautifully, my tenants praise her, she's an enviable horsewoman—I'm convinced my horses prefer her—and she keeps my books better than I."

"And she's uniquely charming." Mr. Nicolas grinned.

"We did try to warn you," Lord Matthew tossed in, growing more concerned.

"Answer me true. Did the two of you have ulterior motives in bringing us together?"

"No," Mr. Nicolas insisted.

"Exactly the opposite," Lord Matthew said. "Neither of you wanted emotional entanglements, seemed a perfect arrangement. Marc, we know your display for Scarbreigh was pretense, but it does seem you're rather … friendly."

Locke raised his brows in dispute. "On the surface perhaps, but something's wrong. Sometimes she's reacted strangely when I've touched her—and please refrain from making more of that than I mean. I'm not in the mood for your teasing. She's pushed me away, as if I've injured her. She understood her part in our arrangement. To keep the ladies of the *ton* distanced from me, she might have to pretend affection for me. She did help convince Scarbreigh, yet, despite knowing our agreement, she's panicked at things to which she oughtn't."

It wasn't his imagination that the twins' grew unusually quiet. They did know something, but their closed expressions meant they wouldn't admit it. He pressed his lips flat in annoyance.

"Bethany's a complicated creature," Lord Matthew finally conceded. "She makes friends easily, but not close friends. Has always been like that. Tends to keep people at a distance 'til she trusts them. It's been worse since her brothers and Uncle John died. She's afraid of losing the people she cares about."

"Can't say she cares about me, but it wouldn't serve well to have her suddenly slap me if I kiss her fingers at a dance at Almack's. Imagine what sort of contretemps that would create."

The twins' countenances darkened but they offered no further explanations. Locke sighed deeply and came to his feet. "The ladies will want to retire early to prepare for our trip tomorrow. Still don't understand why females find a day's drive so exhausting, but if I don't want feminine vapors or a world of complaint, we'd best let them retire soon."

* * *

Bethany had thought London actually sounded exciting when Lord Locke proposed the idea to her. But now, thankfully after arriving without incident, as they clattered along the cobblestone streets late Friday afternoon to the earl's townhouse, the edge of uneasiness clutched her in its vice-like grip. August sweltered, and she kept her perfumed kerchief pressed to her nose to ward off the stench of the streets. The carriages— Lord Locke's bearing the ladies and Whitton's taking the servants— inched their way through London's crowds, hawkers and beggars soliciting their coins, and horsemen and drays pushing alongside them.

Lord Locke rode Polly behind his vehicle, flanking Raven, who was tethered to the rear of it. Two geldings from Whitton, tied to the servants' carriage, were brought for Lady Katherine and Lady Camille.

Lady Camille leaned out the window, her face flushed with excitement, and Lady Katherine couldn't hide her smile of enthusiasm.

Would her mother seek old friends right away? No doubt Lady Camille would wait with bated breath for Scarbreigh's response to her missive, sent the moment she received Lord Locke's invitation.

Locke's townhouse stood in Kensington, not far from St. James Park—or anything else of import in London. Located in one the most enviable neighborhoods in the city, it lacked none of the prevailing comforts or charm, either. It seemed strange to Bethany, to imagine Locke probably spent more time here than at any of his other properties, close to Westminster and all of London's various offices, his gentlemen's clubs, and refined shops and entertainments. To her, Moorewood was Lord Locke, and encountering this prosperous and elegant place felt almost akin to meeting a mistress.

Bethany scolded herself at the inappropriate sentiment, but the privileges and responsibilities of her position overwhelmed Bethany as the butler, footmen, maids, cooks and various servants were brought to be inspected by Lord Locke and his guests. Despite Bethany's father having also been an earl, Lord Whitton's fortunes had been more modest, and Bethany had never experienced such opulence. Their own London townhouse had been a fraction the size of this one, positioned east of the Thames, and possessed a similarly modest staff.

"Follow me, my ladies," a cherubic young housemaid finally urged, directing the ladies and their maids up a grand spiral staircase. Those stairs surrounded a dazzling crystal chandelier and were flanked by elegantly carved and gilded railing, walls dressed in rare paintings, embellished with sconces, and rising to the third floor where the finest rooms were situated.

Lady Katherine's and Lady Camille's rooms sat opposite Lord Locke's and Lady Bethany's. Bethany was amazed by the elegant rugs and furnishings in her room, and the brocade and lace curtains that framed an amazing view of the city. Melissa stood gaping at the sculpted ceiling of the late Lady Locke's bedchamber and murmured that she was thrilled to have a small room of her own attached directly to Bethany's. She wouldn't have to hurry from the downstairs servants' quarters to see to her mistress.

"It's grand, Beth," Lady Camille murmured, her brow furrowed. "Mine is nearly as amazing. But if you and Lady Katherine don't mind, I'd like to take advantage of it. I've another headache and wish to lie down for a while."

"As would I," Lady Katherine said, her own face lined with exhaustion. "Never have liked traveling."

The cook wouldn't likely serve supper until the more fashionably later hours of evening, and none of them expected to receive guests or invitations yet. The trip had taken a toll even on Bethany, and she agreed the suggestion sounded wonderful.

She stretched out on her elaborate bed, grateful to abate the stiffness from hours bouncing over potholes in a cramped vehicle. She envied Locke's riding to town on horseback. She'd have preferred to have done the same.

She smiled, however, when she envisioned the thrill of riding Raven around town. What would some of those noble maidens who'd played impertinent with her since her coming-out think when they saw her on board such a fine animal? How would they react to her riding alongside the Earl of Locke? She supposed such spiteful conjecture was unworthy of her, but she couldn't help it, even if her relationship with her husband wasn't what others would be led to believe.

She drifted to sleep, drawn into a dream where her marriage was genuine, and where she danced with grace in her husband's arms, his dark blue eyes radiant with affection.

CHAPTER 16

"We should be grateful he at least gave us a few hours to settle in," Bethany murmured as she joined Lord Locke in journeying downstairs.

"That's one way to look at it," Locke said, chuckling. "Scarbreigh always seems to know how to walk to the edge of impropriety without stepping over it."

Bethany laughed in agreement. "Mum is a bit miffed at him, said we need our rest and to tell him she's indisposed for the remainder of the day."

Looking over her shoulder as footsteps hurried up behind her, she said, "Lady Camille. Your nap must have repaired your headache. You look lovely."

Cheeks flushed and eyes sparkling, Lady Camille said, "Thank you, Cousin. I do feel better."

"Especially with Lord Scarbreigh waiting for you downstairs?"

Camille grinned in response.

The marquess was strolling around the townhouse's atrium, examining the artwork and statuary that graced the walls and gleaming tables, when they arrived. Mr. Treadwell watched him with casual attentiveness.

"Ah, Locke. Lady Bethany. Welcome back to civilization. Please forgive my interruption without giving you warning." Scarbreigh took note of the earl's limp as he offered his hand. "Whatever happened to you?"

"A trifling bit of clumsiness. Nothing serious. To what do we owe the pleasure of your visit?"

Scarbreigh looked upward, his twinkling blue eyes watching Bethany's cousin make her way down the stairs. "Lady Camille," he said. "I apologize for not being able to wait to see you. It's been too long."

Bethany sighed as the couple went through the appropriate rituals of meeting each other, Lady Camille resplendent in her best day dress and glowing smile.

"I've a special invitation," Scarbreigh finally admitted. "To a recital tonight at the Carlton House."

Bethany was as dazed by the offer as Lady Camille. She'd set foot in that famous near-palace but twice in her life. A musical presentation held there would be suitable to the Prince Regent himself.

They were quick to agree, Scarbreigh insisting on bringing his barouche around at seven-thirty to collect them. "I've a new pair of silver grays I'd love you to see, Locke, and the carriage is near-new, should be perfect for the ladies' comfort."

"Sounds first-rate," Locke conceded. "Will you join us for a cup of tea and a visit?"

"No, no. I must return home to prepare myself, and I've already inconvenienced you by showing up uninvited."

A quick round of gratitude and farewells saw the marquess off.

Locke sent orders to the cook to prepare supper immediately. "I hope you don't mind, ladies. I hate eating late, despite what our London friends consider fashionable. The light refreshments at the recital will do nothing to appease a man's appetite."

Lady Camille was too dreamy-eyed to care, but Bethany agreed wholeheartedly. Sitting through a recital with a hungry stomach, snacking on sweetmeats and orgeat afterward, and then taking an elaborate supper at home near midnight was hardly her definition of sensibility.

Lady Camille suddenly soared out of her reverie to full awareness. "Excuse me, Lady Bethany, Lord Locke, I must run upstairs and have Melissa help me ready myself. I can't be late." She turned to barrel up the stairs, skirts in hand to keep from tripping, and Bethany couldn't help laughing at her.

"Are females always so giddy when they set their cap for a man?"

"Only if they're in love," Bethany replied then wished she hadn't. It drew Locke's dark blue eyes to hers, his gaze searching her face.

"My father once warned me love is hard to come by," he murmured. "Something to be treasured if once found. Wasn't sure I understood what he meant. Hard to imagine trifling with something so ... dangerous."

"Don't most men feel that way about romance?" she asked. "I assume that's why you've avoided it."

He laughed quietly. "I've often wondered if women experience love differently than men. Always thought it a practical thing, but women act as if it's magical."

Bethany's smile faded. "Perhaps it's a bit of both, depending on the objectives. Companionship, friendship, offspring. Someone with which to grow old." Her eyes felt glued to his handsome face as the magical side of it came to mind. Books often described love as an overwhelming fascination that brought an amazing color to life. Her acquaintances claimed a euphoria that elevated one above the clouds and overshadowed all other sensibilities. Bethany's married friends, however, who swore they'd fallen in love and who laughed and whispered behind their fans, claimed they were overwhelmed by the warmth of desire, the rush of heat at the touch of a man. Her heartbeat's cadence rose at realizing how close her own feelings about Locke reflected these descriptions.

"And I have no doubt," he murmured, "that the tenderness of affection has its own merits." His cheeks darkened and he blinked as if he couldn't believe he'd just said these words aloud. Bethany couldn't breathe after hearing them.

He straightened and smoothed his jacket into place. "Well, I suppose I should ready myself for tonight as well," he said, and then he called for Mr. Treadwell's assistance and headed upstairs.

* * *

Bethany echoed Lady Camille's sentiments that the recital was exceptional and the Carlton House breathtaking. The Prince Regent had, in fact, attended.

Despite her discomfiture at being examined narrowly by a number of notables, Bethany enjoyed herself. She wasn't sure Lady Camille could say the same. As soon as it was over and the prince and his acolytes escorted off, her cousin had been overwhelmed by a bevy of unattached ladies who'd heard the rumors about Lord Scarbreigh's interest in her. Good friends wanted to hear all the details; the rest seemed determined to carve her into pieces. If matters grew any more unpleasant, Bethany had determined she would intervene and drag her cousin away.

Soft laughter drew Bethany's gaze to her left, towards the group of gentlemen gathered around Locke, a few paces off. She had no doubt from the earl's expression that he was the butt of his own share of interrogation, probably because of his hasty and unannounced marriage. Her stomach twisted when she imagined the insinuations he might have to endure, everything from having soiled the dove and being forced to marry Bethany, to being tricked into matrimony. It did not surprise her, however, to see her husband handling it all with dignity. He was, after all, a consummate actor.

Under the circumstances, she didn't mind when Lord Scarbreigh brought them each a glass of punch. It not only quenched her thirst but his company kept her from feeling abandoned.

"Our songbird was most impressive tonight," Scarbreigh said, watching first Locke and then Lady Camille. "Haven't heard such a lovely contralto in a long time."

"She was superb," Bethany agreed.

"Must be nice to be so talented."

Bethany chuckled. "I can't imagine you offering a solo, my lord. You have other talents."

"I do? And what would those be?"

Bethany raised a brow in skepticism. "Surely you jest. You're death with a rapier, over the top in picking the fastest horse in a race, an exemplary strategist at chess, an excellent wordsmith, and far too handsome for your own good. I'd consider that more than your fair share of gifts."

Scarbreigh huffed quiet laughter. "Kind compliments, Love, but wagering is a fickle mistress, no one has ever won a war with a rapier or the chessboard, and I'm not likely to reap a fortune with my skills with a pen or my face."

"Then what talents do you think are your best?"

He pondered a moment, his eyes narrowing before he bowed to three older couples promenading past them. Bethany sank into a curtsy, recognizing among them Lord Robert Stewart and his wife, Lady Amelia Stewart, the Viscount and Viscountess of Castlereagh. Lord Castlereagh returned the nod, but Lady Castlereagh's cool appraisal unnerved her.

"Is there something wrong, my lord?" she asked Scarbreigh.

He chuckled. "No. I've just decided I believe my best talents are the grand designs of love and war."

Bethany tipped her head, wondering if this was a jest. Then she grinned, realizing he was certainly pulling her leg. "Then perhaps you should have rescued me from the men who tried to shoot me."

Scarbreigh's gaze softened. "I wish I had."

"I still wonder why they did it."

"They hoped for jewels? Ransom? Brigands and kidnappers abound in our day, you know."

"I wish it were not true."

"But it is. Dangerous world we live in."

Bethany agreed, thinking instead of the ransacking of her room.

"You look concerned, my lady. Is something else amiss?"

Bethany breathed deep to banish the memory and let slip about the burglary—if that was what it could be called.

"Good Law!" His eyebrows vaulted high. "What will happen next? Could it be a coincidence? What did they take?"

"A small, empty music box. And my diary's missing, but as I told Locke, the burglar is welcome to it. I never write anything important in it, only my list of the day's duties if I feel inclined to note them. What do thieves who don't steal go looking for?"

Scarbreigh pondered a moment then sighed in contemplation. "An odd conundrum. Normally I would think heirlooms, jewels, artwork, literature, various trinkets. Did the box have hidden drawers?"

Bethany paused. "Yes. One. But it was hard to find and even harder to open. The reason I didn't use it. And they didn't take any trinkets."

He gave her a teasing grin. "Well then, what about family secrets? Encrypted missives tucked away somewhere?"

"Certainly not that," she insisted, playing along.

"Did you leave anything of value at home they might have wanted? Boxes of important letters perhaps?"

"No. Some old clothes and shoes of which Mum will dispose, and I gave her a few books I outgrew years before my coming-out. We never kept letters around. Father always insisted we burn them. Couldn't stand the clutter." She paused, suddenly realizing the significance of this. "I do have a collection of Dresden dolls Father brought me over the years, and a host of figurines Lord Christian and Mr. Collin began giving me each Christmastide after my fifth birthday. I wasn't allowed to play with them, so they're still in their glass cases at Whitton, but I hope to move them to Moorewood one day soon."

"Well, I agree with you. Your intruders' intent was obviously not thievery. I suspect they were searching for a specific item. I'll ponder it, maybe give you some suggestions. Excuse me, my dear. I think Lady Camille needs rescuing."

Bethany was glad to see the marquess ready to liberate her harried cousin from the clutches of her jealous rivals. At almost the same moment he walked away, Lord Locke joined her, his eyes glittering with triumph. It seemed he'd had some success in managing his peers.

"Have you enjoyed our evening?"

"Believe it or not, I have."

He chuckled. "It's growing late, my lady, and I'm in need of another cold compress. Shall we repair home?"

"The sooner the better," she replied, fatigued from such a long day and their lovely but unexpected entertainment.

Scarbreigh and Lady Camille joined them, Lady Camille looking a bit wilted after such an unpleasant interrogation.

"I must beg your forgiveness, Lady Bethany," she said. "I believed you'd exaggerated the dangers of staking claim on a man of high esteem. It seems you're not mistaken. I'm grateful I still have my fingers and toes."

The other three laughed, but Lady Camille did not, until Lord Scarbreigh threaded her arm through his and bent to whisper something in her ear. Then she blushed and smile at him coyly.

To Locke, Scarbreigh said, "Your limp has worsened and I can only imagine how sore you are. And tired, all three of you, in fact. I'll have my barouche brought round, get you home right away."

Scarbreigh strolled off with Lady Camille but not out of sight of Lord and Lady Locke.

"You and Scarbreigh appeared intent on something of import," Locke said to Bethany. They stepped onto the front walkway, where carriages were rolling in and out of the drive, butlers and footmen scurrying to secure the waiting guests inside them. "Mind sharing?"

"We were discussing the break-in of my room. He gave me some ideas to contemplate as to the reason."

Locke was quiet a moment; then, when Scarbreigh's driver delivered the Scarbreigh barouche and the footman dropped the steps for Lady Camille and Scarbreigh to board, the earl turned to face her.

"Lady Bethany, I thought we'd agreed to keep what happened at Moorewood private."

Bethany froze, realizing Locke was right. "I shouldn't have said anything, should I? I haven't even told Lady Camille. I apologize. But I've known Scarbreigh a good part of my life. I've no reason to doubt him."

"No, no, of course not. Neither would I. Nevertheless, the man is friends with *everyone*, and he might spread details that we'd prefer remained contained."

"I wish I could undo it. I do know better. I promise to take care from here on, no matter the person or how innocent the conversation."

"Probably the best idea, especially considering how matters are progressing with your cousin and the marquess."

Bethany nodded, casting Lady Camille a patient smile as they boarded the barouche.

Camille asked about their plans for the morrow and it was quickly decided that the fair and trips to the shops were a requirement, but none so exciting to Bethany as a morning ride round Rotten Row.

"You're coming, Locke?" Scarbreigh asked.

"I'm on board for all of it 'til mid-afternoon. I've a meeting with my solicitor at three o'clock, another one at four-thirty with a knave at Tavistock Arms Pub who wants to fleece me for an absolutely delightful mare I want to add to my stable, and when I'm finished with that, if I survive it, I must make an appearance at White's."

"Ah, always the gentleman, Locke. You show up, what, half a dozen times a year?"

"Only if I have to," Locke replied, chuckling. "Hasn't ever been my forte to frequent the gentlemen's clubs, think it's mainly a waste of time, but I'd rather show up occasionally than become the talk of the town by snubbing them."

Scarbreigh laughed. "You're more the talk of the town when you do materialize. I think they lay odds on it."

Locke's cheeks darkened at his companions' laughter.

Set down at the earl's townhouse, the companions said good night, Scarbreigh nestling Lady Camille's gloved fingertips between his hands as their gazes intertwined.

Bethany inclined her head against laughter. She'd never seen either of them so besotted before. At last the marquess set Lady Camille free, and the three of them stepped inside to the sound of Scarbreigh's two-in-hand clopping up the street.

* * *

It seemed everyone looked forward to riding on Saturday's pristine morning as much as Bethany did. However, when the footman lifted her into the sidesaddle perched on Raven's back, Locke's warm gaze trailed from the feathered red cap on her head and down her new crimson riding habit—the only one she'd had made before they married—spilling over her legs, to her black riding boots.

"You and your stallion will stand out from every other mount and rider in England, Lady Bethany. I fear the envy of every man who sets eyes on you," he said.

"She's gorgeous, is she not?" Lady Camille said, and Lady Katherine offered her own stamp of approval.

"I recognize you hate sidesaddles, my daughter," the dowager countess remarked, perched on her own, "but you're as regal as a queen in one, especially wearing such a stunning gown. You should use both more often."

"Hear, hear," Locke agreed, giving Bethany one of those brilliant, toe-curling, dimpled grins of his and setting her to the blush.

The foursome rode through the streets to the Round Pond, where Scarbreigh waited for them. He greeted them warmly, his regard lingering on Bethany, and then he doffed his hat to Lady Camille and offered her another of his elaborate declarations of adoration.

Locke sighed, then nodded at Lady Bethany and set them forth down the Row, the others following, with Lady Whitton and Lady Camille riding on either side of Scarbreigh.

CHAPTER 17

Locke could hardly take his eyes off Lady Bethany. She was a vibrant ruby on a bed of black velvet. Passersby, of which there were many, stared at her in fascination, and more than one gentleman pulled up to admire both her and her stallion as their party jogged by. He heard Scarbreigh behind him, seated on his sorrel gelding, Jack, prattling on about how fair his "dear Lady Camille" appeared, a flower in the heart of Hyde Park's garden, but out of the corner of his eye caught his old friend gawking at Lady Bethany.

Just as at their wedding, it filled Locke with unreasonable enmity. His boyhood friend Kirk Bannister had had his chance to court Lord Whitton's extraordinary daughter, and Lady Bethany Montgomery had refused him. Now she was Locke's wife, his countess, his friend. He was no fool. He had no delusions regarding the ways of the world or the dalliances that occurred far too often among Britain's nobility. Yet deep in his gut he knew Lady Bethany was above such chicanery and the suggestion that the marquess—a person he had always trusted and admired—might have the nerve to seek such an alliance made him boil inside.

And what of Lady Camille? She seemed oblivious to Scarbreigh's wandering eye and blinded by his relentless compliments. Did the marquess have honest intentions towards Lady Bethany's cousin? Or was he trying to worm into Lady Bethany's graces by getting close to her through Lady Camille?

Apparently sensing his gaze, Lady Bethany turned to give him a most brilliant smile. Locke felt the dimples in his cheeks deepen in response. His wife was oblivious to Lord Scarbreigh. She was happy where she was, onboard Raven and riding beside Locke. He believed it, and it pleased him, whether or not it should.

* * *

The morning's riders were plentiful, as were the throngs of people patronizing the fair on the park's green. Locke's party stopped frequently to visit. Lady Katherine was thrilled at the pleasure of coming across old friends and exchanging *on dits* with them.

"The fair's delightful," Lady Piper, a plump matron, mentioned. "You shouldn't miss it, Lady Kate. Mimes and clowns, marionette shows, brief performances of everything from actors to fire-eaters to tightrope walkers. Wonderful booths full of fascinating items from all over Europe and even the Orient, and tents set up with a variety of delicacies you won't want to miss. Oh, we must get together. Just the two of us. I've missed you greatly, and Old Fuss-Budget." She waved at her obviously bored husband. "Doesn't like walking much."

Lady Katherine declared her excitement at the idea, reminding Bethany that it had been long since her mother had had opportunity to socialize. A year of mourning for her lost husband and sons, followed by her worries about Whitton's depleted fortune, had forced her to sell Lord Whitton's townhouse and retire from the extravagances of London.

Now, with Bethany's marriage to the Earl of Locke, Lady Whitton could rejoin the *haute ton* and renew her friendships.

When they finally separated briefly from Scarbreigh and retired the horses to the townhouse to change into day clothes for their visit to the fair, Bethany's mother offered her apologies and excused herself, deciding to accept Lady Piper's invitation. Melissa replaced her as chaperone to Lady Camille should she and Lord Scarbreigh, when they joined him again, choose to separate from Lord and Lady Locke.

Delivered to the fair at Hyde Park Corner in Lord Locke's carriage, they again met with Scarbreigh and found the park thick with clustered tents, booths, tables and people. Hawkers and vendors displayed wares, tumbling dwarves entertained children, and the scent of cooking fires and exotic foods wafted around them. Bethany had not seen its like since childhood. Locke bought her a lovely shawl of dark blue silk with fine golden threads woven into it, which looked exceptional with her cornflower blue walking dress, and later pulled a blood red rose from a vase full of them, nipped off half the stem, and tucked it behind her ear above the lovelock.

"A crimson rose for a woman who rides a black stallion in a crimson habit, a vision of loveliness that fair takes the breath away," he murmured, making her blush. She couldn't shake off his words as they wandered from entertainment to entertainment.

"Oh, look, Lady Bethany!" Lady Camille cried, pointing at a rack of finely tooled shoes. Melissa, at her shoulder, was "oohing" alongside her. Bethany and Lady Camille tried on several pairs before Lady Camille settled on slippers woven of camel hair, and Bethany chose new riding boots fashioned from the softest deerskin she'd ever felt. She also purchased a more practical pair of shoes that Melissa praised. The girl was stunned when Bethany gave them to her.

"Your own are worn out, Melissa," Bethany insisted. "And it's my responsibility to see my lady's maid dressed well. We'll get more for you later, as well as some material for dresses."

"Oh, thank you, m'lady," Melissa said, donning the shoes immediately.

"Good grief," Lady Camille said, looking around. "We've lost the men."

It was true. Neither Locke nor Scarbreigh were anywhere in sight.

"Where could they have gotten off to?" Then Bethany made a face. "I shouldn't ask such a silly question."

Lady Camille laughed. They were surrounded by stalls filled with bows and expertly quilled arrows; swords, knives and daggers; matched sets of dueling pistols—despite the illegality of duels in their day—and muskets, and all the trappings for carrying ammunition.

"How dreary," Lady Camille said before turning to admire a coat fashioned of silver fox hides. "Now this is marvelous. Oh, it's terribly soft and would be so warm in deepest winter."

Bethany lifted a brow in mock cynicism. "And would cause you heat prostration carrying it home in August.

"Nonsense. Scarbreigh will carry it for me."

Bethany laughed. "Scarbreigh would carry an elephant home for you if you wanted it."

Uncertainty lined Lady Camille's lovely face. "Do you think so? Does he care for me as much as I do for him? Is this what it feels like to fall in love? It's the most wonderful, most frightening feeling in the whole world, isn't it?"

Bethany's smile waned. "I've no idea, dearest. If you say so, then I'm convinced I want nothing to do with it."

It was Lady Camille's turn to raise a brow at Bethany. "Surely you jest. Even I can see that Lord Locke's admiration for you seems to grow day the day, and your cheeks turn red whenever he deigns to smile at you."

"Oh, they do not. Are those rugs Persian, my dear? They're elegant, are they not?"

Lady Camille smirked at her but came to admire the racks of rugs which were, indeed, from that far-flung place. Loving one for her bedchamber, Bethany indulged in bargaining with the swarthy man selling them but left off when he refused to take a more reasonable price.

"I'm getting hungry," Lady Camille fussed. "Where are those men?"

"I'm thirsty, too. You and Melissa stay put. Locke and Scarbreigh will search for us where they deserted us. I'll at least find us something to drink."

For the first time, Bethany comprehended the freedom of being a married woman. Locke had given her the privilege of crediting her purchases to his accounts, and propriety no longer demanded she take a chaperone. Weaving through the tents and tables, she finally saw some booths offering a variety of refreshments.

Movement to her left made her come up short. She caught a brief glimpse of a thin man, garbed in clean but simple light tan clothes and a shoddy forest green waistcoat. He changed directions and scurried away. Prickles danced down her spine. Pushing past customers to find a shorter line, she came around a corner and paused, only to catch sight of the thin man again. Abandoning her quest, she searched for a circuitous route back to Lady Camille, only to realize the man was following her.

Anger swept over her and she turned to face him. His eyes rounded at being caught and he turned to hurry away. Muttering, Bethany pursued him. If she found guards nearby she would complain.

Seeing her behind him, he hurried his pace to a jog and disappeared. Bethany's heart raced. Where had he gone? A flash of green caught her eye and she chased it, around one corner after another and past other patrons. She caught sight of the man just as he crashed into someone who looked like—Scarbreigh! It *was* Scarbreigh.

The marquess stumbled back and grabbed the man's arm, his face twisted in anger. They argued and struggled and then Scarbreigh pushed the man and he ran off.

Bethany ran to Scarbreigh, whose shock at seeing her swept away the anger.

"Scarbreigh! I'm desperately glad to find you. That man was following me, and when I dared walk towards him, he fled."

Scarbreigh glanced at the man and then back at Bethany, jaw dropped. "The wretch! Tried to pick my pocket. Gave him a piece of my mind."

"I wish you could have given him one for me as well."

"Did he hurt you?"

"No, I'm fine. But." She frowned at him in puzzlement. "Where have you been? You and Locke abandoned us."

"What? Locke's run off? How wicked of him. I plead guilty to getting enthralled by a pair of falconers. Followed them and a small crowd to a patch of grass over there." He pointed to some obscure place to the southeast, on the other side of another group of tents and tables. "When I turned around, I saw I'd gotten lost. I went looking for you ladies and finally arrived here. Seeing that lamppost over there not only gave me my bearings, it reminded me I've a brief meeting with an old acquaintance beside it. And then that bloke ran into me."

"Well, I'm glad he's gone and you're here. Scarbreigh, we waited until we were too thirsty to wait any longer."

"So sorry. Can't leave, though. Need to wait for my friend." Then his face lit up. "I'm glad we found each other, my dear. I've a, uh, a couple of gifts, for Lady Camille. I'd love your opinion on them."

The twinkle in the marquess's eyes eased Bethany's anxiety and she agreed. He slipped his hand into his jacket pocket and withdrew a small box. The lid fit tightly enough he struggled to pull it off, but when he did, a gasp escaped her, her hand flying to her throat.

"Oh, Scarbreigh, does this mean what I think?"

"That depends on what you think it means."

Bethany blinked several times, stunned by the beauty of the golden ring, studded with at least a dozen bright diamonds. "I think it rivals a queen's wedding ring."

"Truly? Then it would please our dearest Lady Camille?"

"If you mean to give it to her along with your offer of marriage."

"Ah." He grinned wide. "That was the idea." Again he searched to his left and to his right. "But I also have something else in mind for her, and the gentleman delivering it is truly late. I'd like to walk around, look for him. Come with me, will you?" He took her by the arm and drew her along the walkway, steering her past foot traffic going slower than he seemed to like.

"Lord Scarbreigh?" Bethany protested. "I can't. I mustn't."

"Of course you can. It won't take long."

Bethany jerked her arm from his grasp, miffed at his cavalier attitude. Scarbreigh had always been too good at treating her like a recalcitrant child. "I've left Lady Camille and Melissa hungry and thirsty, and they'll worry about me. I need to go back."

Scarbreigh glared at her, but passersby were frowning at him, and Bethany's dark look had caught the attention of a nearby guard. Scarbreigh sighed and brushed a hand through his hair.

"I apologize. I've no right to take my distress out on you." Producing his coin purse, he purchased a tall flagon of ale and tin cups from a nearby vendor. "I feel less than a gentleman, my lady, but this is important and if you can't wait with me, then this is the best I can do. Can you carry this with you? I promise if he doesn't turn up in the next five minutes, I'll follow you." He gave her hand a quick squeeze and pointed her the right way, northwest of the lamppost.

The idea rankled. He should be more concerned about her safety, but it certainly wasn't the first time in her life Scarbreigh had behaved this way and one of the many reasons she couldn't have married him.

Finding her bearings, she took the path she was fairly sure led to her cousin. Her progress was slow with the flagon, and nerves had her watching every corner along the way. Across a small patch of grass, she saw one of the booths near the rug vendor and headed in that direction.

No! She paused. The man in the waistcoat! He slipped out from behind another tent, staring fixedly at her, at least until he glanced to her left. Bethany's gaze followed his, her hands shaking when she saw two more men, one of medium height and with shoulder-length red hair, the other short and stocky and bald, both in the same costume. The redhead gave her a dark smile then a brief nod to her right. A fourth man, his long, dark hair pulled into a soldier's queue, not only wore the green waistcoat, he was walking towards her. She was trapped between them.

Flashes of old memories, of abuse and intimidation, and of a bowman with sharp-tipped arrows assailed her. Panic sent her dashing inside the closest tent behind her, a large one with its doors thrown back. Praying for a friendly face, she found herself inside a makeshift pub. A fiddler sat astride a tall stool, playing a mournful refrain, while men at small tables were engaged in quiet conversation and drinks.

The gentleman furthest from the door straightened. Elbowing the man sitting beside him, he pointed, his companion giving her a grin that turned her face hot.

"Help you, my lady?" someone offered, and Bethany turned towards a young man dressed in military uniform, rising from the closest table.

"Oh, yes, please," she replied, praying he was an honest sort. "I need an escort to my family."

"I'll accompany you, my lady. Where are they?"

The suspicious men were gone when she stepped outside, and Bethany led the way, forever grateful to have the soldier bear the heavy flagon for her. Nowhere on their trek was anyone wearing cheap green waistcoats. When she rounded the corner, Lady Camille reached for her and Bethany fought with tears as she threw herself into her cousin's arms.

"Dear Beth, you look petrified. What happened?"

Bethany found herself babbling her tale, including her annoyance with Scarbreigh, but just barely managed to hold back the part about the ring. Melissa thanked the soldier and Bethany offered him several coins for his service when the abigail accepted the ale from him. He refused payment, touching his cap and giving them a bow, then slipped away.

The three women were grateful to slake their thirst, but when Lady Camille cautioned that they should leave some for the men, Bethany scoffed at her.

"They left us to die of thirst. Let them find their own drinks."

Lady Camille laughed, knowing Bethany was only, at least in part, joking; and then Scarbreigh arrived quietly enough he startled them. He gave Bethany a sharp look, smiled at Lady Camille's gratitude for his return, then handed Melissa a small package, wrapped in brown paper. Bethany supposed it was the gift from his friend.

"I'll have your maid hold this so I can hunt for food, my sweet," Scarbreigh murmured, his scrutiny drawing Lady Camille like a hypnotized mouse. "None of you must open it or try to figure out what it is by groping through the paper. Hopefully some sustenance will grant me your forgiveness."

"There's nothing to forgive," Lady Camille replied, her face glowing.

"You're too kind, darling," he replied, blowing her a kiss and fading into the throng, like the soldier had done. Thankfully, he returned shortly with meat pies, pickles, and roasted vegetables to appease their hunger, and confections to cheer them.

"It *is* growing late," Scarbreigh commented, again pulling his watch from his waistcoat and checking the time. "Good heavens. What could be keeping Locke so long? Didn't he say he had a meeting with his solicitor this afternoon?"

"At three o'clock," Bethany supplied, worry now twisting her stomach into knots. Something was wrong.

"Let's go back the way we came," Scarbreigh suggested, "see if he's just gotten lost trying to find us."

They walked eastward towards Bond Street. Then, following that road, they pressed on to Hyde Park Corner, although without success.

"I'm baffled," Scarbreigh said. "He's simply, er, evaporated."

Bethany swallowed hard, fearful the earl may have become the victim of foul play. Lady Katherine had cautioned Bethany to watch out for pickpockets and troublemakers, but her mother constantly worried about such things, so Bethany had paid it little mind. Now, she knew there was more truth—and danger—to the idea than she'd given credence.

Scarbreigh finally hailed one of the officers patrolling the Fair and explained their predicament to him. The constable encouraged them to wait on a bench in the shade and sent several men to discover whether anyone had spotted trouble in the park that involved a peer.

What seemed ages later, two officers came towards them, one with his hand hooked under a gentleman's elbow. Bethany's eyes widened when she became aware the gentleman was Locke, and his disheveled hair and clothing and pale countenance had her running to him, her heart in her throat.

"My lord, you look awful," she hissed. "What happened?"

"We need to get him to our tent first." The officer raised a hand to stave her off. "He must sit down and catch his breath." He pointed at a stout tent to the right of the corner gate, bearing the flag of the guard.

The others tagged along, obviously shaken. A sergeant greeted the earl and listened to the constable's story, concern etched on his narrow, seamed face.

"Take a seat, my lord. Ladies, please take the other two."

They did so, Bethany impulsively clutching Locke's left hand in her own and silently praying for him. The sergeant and constable stepped outside to speak with the other two officers. Their quiet conversation did little to enlighten Bethany, although Scarbreigh looked at the earl in surprise when one of the officers stated Lord Locke didn't remember what happened or see who'd done it.

"Are you badly hurt?" Bethany whispered, leaning into Locke. He blinked and raised his free hand to touch the back of his head.

He murmured, "If you define 'hurt' as a goose egg-sized lump on my skull and a headache as wide as the Thames River, then, yes. Skin's not broken, or anything else for that matter, so I suppose I'll survive."

Bethany flicked a faint smile of relief but saw nothing amusing in the incident. Soon the sergeant returned with the constable, bearing a glass of water and a cold compress for Locke, to question the earl as well. Locke remembered nothing but seeing the women approach the display of shoes.

"They took your signet ring and your pocket watch and fob?"

Locke nodded, and self-consciously touched his right trouser pocket. "And the funds I had on my person. I'm glad your men found me. I might have rolled out from under the shrubbery and fallen unconscious into the river and drowned."

"Good fortune, yes. Well, it may come back to you later," the sergeant encouraged. "If you do remember, please send word. We need clues to have any chance of finding the culprits."

When Locke said he felt better, Scarbreigh insisted they take him home. "You need to lie down, my friend," he insisted, helping Locke to his feet and onto the walkway.

"I'm fine, Scarbreigh, but I must admit a soft pillow sounds good at the moment. Would you have my carriage brought round? I still have appointments this afternoon and won't feel up to them without rest."

Scarbreigh rushed off to do his bidding. Lady Camille joined him, Melissa at her heels.

"I'm so worried about you, my lord," Bethany whispered. More than worried. Terrified for him and—yes—terrified of losing him. "You're frightfully pale. You're sure you remember nothing?"

Locke peeked through the tent door at the officers who'd taken a seat at the small corner table, talking and scribbling notes. His grasp strengthened and he pulled Bethany out of earshot before leaning shoulder to shoulder with her and whispering, "They knocked me unconscious, as I said, but the rest I remember as clearly as I can see you."

"What? Then why—?"

"I don't want busybodies spreading the tale about this either. We'll talk at home."

Bethany nodded and when his coach arrived, she stepped aside to allow the footman and Scarbreigh to guide him to his seat.

CHAPTER 18

Locke forced his face into passivity during the ride. He wanted to ask a dozen questions about what happened after he'd been lured from his friends, and it took everything he had to play the invalid.

In truth, the knot wasn't that big, and the headache, while unpleasant, not unbearable. His clothes hadn't sustained much in the way of dirt or grass stains, and whoever had removed his signet ring had done it carefully. Not only having been the victim of pickpockets upon occasion, but being a rather good one himself, he knew the difference between thefts that could be done at leisure and those that would require brute force. It was as if the perpetrator had done the least harm possible, which made absolutely no sense. Being so careful would place the felon in greater danger of being caught.

This person—persons?—had a motive apart from stealing.

"May I accompany you to your appointments today?" Scarbreigh asked, his face wan. "I'd love to be of help."

"You'd be miserable, Scarbreigh. Gordon Davies is a considerably efficient solicitor but a terrible bore. Actually, I'm thinking I'll cancel the appointment at Tavistock Arms. The mare can wait. So can White's. Maybe I'll go on Monday. You can join me then, if you like."

"What if the shock caught up with you and you blacked out on Davies' doorstep?"

Locke donned a lopsided smile. "You're a good friend. Thank you."

"I've a few petty errands to address. I'll come for you afterward."

Lord Locke and Lady Bethany preceded Lady Camille and Melissa inside the house, while Locke's carriage conveyed Scarbreigh back to his barouche, still at the park.

"Would you indulge me, dear?" Locke said to Lady Bethany. "I'd feel safer climbing the stairs with you alongside me."

Lady Bethany frowned, probably wondering what he was about, especially when the townhouse's butler offered to help him instead.

"I'm fine, Mr. Williams, but send Mr. Treadwell up to me," Locke said. Then he grasped Lady Bethany's hand and allowed her to lead him up the spiral staircase. By the time they reached his quarters both his head and his ankle were in truth pounding. Locke handed Lady Bethany his key to let them inside his bedchamber.

At his request, Lady Bethany accompanied Locke inside. Her expression told him she felt strange here, but also that the elegance amazed her. For him, things were merely things, but he was nearly overcome by the feelings that assailed him at having his wife alone here, in his private rooms.

Visions of their shared kisses, of the delicious scent of her—and the mutual attacks that could have taken their lives—begged him to toss aside caution and wrap his arms around her and never let go. He had to work hard to temper the need for her burning in his gut. He mustn't let it override him. He couldn't. For her sake, he wouldn't.

"Your color is improving, my lord," Lady Bethany remarked, observing his flushed cheeks. "I'm relieved. Can we discuss what happened today?"

"Yes. We must. If you'll take a seat?" He cast a hand at two ornate armchairs that sat in a nook by the far window, flanked on either side with end tables and fronted by a low center table.

A knock came at the door and the earl called entrance. Mr. Treadwell hurried in, anxiety on his face followed by surprise at seeing Lady Bethany perched on her chair. He held a tea service set for one.

"Word has spread like wildfire throughout the neighborhood, my lord," Mr. Treadwell said, face pinched with worry. "How do you feel?"

"Not good, but better than I want anyone to know, including the rest of the staff. I don't want the tea. Would you care for it, Lady Bethany?" When Lady Bethany nodded, Mr. Treadwell set the service before her.

"Cold compresses for me, Treadwell," he added. "For both my ankle and my head. And one of Cook's amazing tisanes? My brain feels like it's going to explode from my skull."

"Immediately, my lord." Mr. Treadwell hurried off and returned quickly with the tisane and the compresses set in a bowl of iced water. He helped Locke remove his boot and apply the first compress to his ankle, and after Locke touched the other to his head, he excused his valet and insisted he lock the door on his way out.

Lady Bethany poured his tisane and added sugar to both their cups.

"I was so worried about you," she said. "I knew you wouldn't go off the way you did without good reason."

Locke weighed carefully what to tell her. He now worried less about his secrecy than about saying or doing something that might place Lady Bethany in greater jeopardy.

"Public gatherings draw the unsavory sort and I stood off a distance to keep a lookout. I'd hoped to allow you and Lady Camille to appraise the boots and shoes and enjoy your shopping.

"A few minutes later, someone bumped into me hard, and when I stumbled away from him, he grabbed me, apologized profusely, and then hurried on. That's when I realized he'd stolen my watch and fob and it infuriated me. Scarbreigh had drifted east, engrossed in watching a puppeteer entertaining a crowd of children. It would have taken too long to get his attention, but I was certain he wouldn't fail to watch over all of you. Probably my stupidest decision in a great while, I chased the pickpocket alone."

* * *

Bethany frowned in confusion. Hadn't Scarbreigh told her that he'd been drawn off by a falconer? Was Locke confused? He'd just been hit on the head, after all.

"The scoundrel saw me and stepped up his pace," Locke continued. "Had I hollered 'thief,' he'd have taken off running, so I hoped to follow him until I ran across a nearby watchman or policeman. Chap led me a merry chase, barely far enough ahead I couldn't catch him, yet not so far off I lost sight of him."

Despite her tea, Bethany's mouth went dry. This was too similar to her own experience. What a strange coincidence.

"When I least expected it, he dodged between two tents in a long row of them near the Serpentine River, and playing the fool even better, I followed him. I'd no sooner rounded the corner when I sensed someone behind me. The crack on my skull happened before I could turn around, and that's all I remember until I came to, at the water's edge, under some bushes and being shaken awake by the police."

"That's horrible. But you told the police you don't remember anything?"

"Because this particular thief was odd. He was too neat, too clean. Dressed in beggar's clothes too decent for a beggar's life. I wanted to think about it first."

"I don't understand."

"It wasn't the clothes that impressed me. It was their fit, not exactly new but in decent enough condition they seemed, well, tailored for him."

* * *

The more Locke reflected on it, the more it bothered him. It was almost as if the man had been issued some sort of uniform, perhaps designed to both hide and mark him simultaneously. The average person might not pay the slightest attention to him, but one who knew what to look for could spot him easily.

"That is odd." Lady Bethany said with anxiety. "He had no insignia or trappings that stood out?"

Locke shrugged. "Just a tan tunic and trousers and a rather tawdry forest green waistcoat."

Lady Bethany gasped and her cup dropped to the floor, shattering into a dozen pieces. Locke dropped his cold compress in surprise.

"Lady Bethany! Good Heavens. What's wrong?"

"Oh, dear, I'm so sorry," she cried, seeing the mess she'd made. Her hands were trembling when she added, "But I'm ... I'm shocked."

"By what?"

"Describe the man to me, will you? His height? His hair?"

"Tall, thin, shoulder-length red hair."

Lady Bethany shot to her feet, her face wan enough Locke feared she'd faint. His head and leg protested when he rose with her, but he ignored them. He reached for her shaking hands and held them tight, pulling her away from the broken glass and urging her to look at him.

"What does he mean to you?"

Although her story came out in disarray, like a handful of jackstraws, it filled him with anxiety. The man who'd lured Locke off sounded too similar to the four who'd followed Bethany—in fact was probably one of them.

Locke still didn't understand the way they'd treated him. If they'd wanted him dead, they'd have slit his throat. They could have stolen his clothes and left him to bear the shame of it in public. Instead, they'd carried him to the bushes, arranged him—so the police said—so as not to do him any further harm, and disappeared.

These ruminations took but a moment, but he was convinced it was connected to everything that had been happening to his wife. And as for Lady Bethany, if Scarbreigh hadn't wandered off, she wouldn't have gone looking for refreshments and made herself so easy a target.

Of course, he had to gently admonish Lady Bethany for going anywhere alone. Today proved she wasn't safe, not even in London.

"I was foolish," she admitted. "I convinced myself having so many people around protected me."

"I'm glad you found help, but it could have turned out differently. I'm furious with Scarbreigh for abandoning you as he did, not just once but twice, and I'll have a word with him about it today. His friend was already late. He should have escorted you straight to Lady Camille and Melissa. Nevertheless, we're both home safe. I ask your patience in allowing me to investigate all of this. In the meantime, please trust me and do not to discuss this with anyone, not even Lady Camille or your mother."

"Alright," Lady Bethany said, the faith—and remorse—in her eyes touching his heart.

"I'll ring for Mr. Treadwell to clean up the broken glass, but I insist you take some time for yourself, my dear. You're as distressed from the day as I am."

He guided her toward their adjoining door, his eyes pinned to hers. Tears glistened in her eyes, and she looked so terribly small and fragile, nothing like the headstrong, willful girl that he knew had once climbed trees and thrown rocks like her brothers. What had happened to her that robbed her of that part of her self-assuredness? Certainly today's events didn't just frighten her. They'd conjured up loathsome memories and left her trembling.

He'd done everything he could to distance himself from her, believing it was what was best for both of them. She'd resisted his marriage proposal at first, but after these months of acquaintance, she'd been frantic for him at the park. And now? She believed in him! He feared she shouldn't and he knew she deserved better, but heaven help him, she believed.

That moment of compassion got the better of him. He slipped his arms around her, amazed when she nestled against him, clenched hands tucked beneath her chin. So soft, sweet-scented, seemingly defenseless. Her tears had him pressing a kiss to the top of her head.

"It's alright, Lady Bethany. We'll sort this out soon enough."

"I was so frightened, more for you than for myself. I pictured you kidnapped and mortally wounded and couldn't stand not being able to find you. I'm so very grateful you weren't seriously wounded."

Her words plunged deep into his soul. This was no artifice. Her concern was real.

"I'm honored, my dear. But I'm most relieved that nothing happened to you." He said it as softly and tenderly as he felt it, his heart tripping when she raised her red-rimmed eyes to his. He saw the confusion there, the same confusion that he supposed marred his own face. Gently he wiped her tears, his pulse racing at the flutter of her eyelashes against his thumb tips. He couldn't resist the beckoning call of her barely parted lips.

He pressed his mouth to the soft pillow of hers, her sigh of pleasure shattering what was left of his resistance. Her fingers spread across his chest, warm and gentle. He caressed her back, her shoulders, struggled not to crush her against him. Her arms encircled his neck, deepening their kiss, and he reveled in the taste of her, the sweet lemony scent.

Desire had him smoothing the creases from her brow with his kisses, then her upturned nose and flushed cheeks. When he bent to taste the whiteness of her throat, she tipped her head back and gasped with pleasure, and welcomed him when he claimed her mouth again.

Breathless, he clutched her to him, afraid to let go even if he was terrified by the ramifications of this moment.

"What spell have you cast over me, my lady?"

Those stunning emerald green eyes, again sparkling with unshed tears, rose to meet his. "It's you that's worked your magic on me," she murmured.

"I never dreamed I could feel this way about anyone."

She gave a faint sob. "Nor I, but I've lived in fear for so long, I no longer know how to dream."

"In fear of what, my sweet wife? I've seen it in your eyes and it tears me apart. I'd never hurt you. You believe that, don't you?"

He ached inside when she took far too long to answer. At least her arms tightened around him as she buried her brow into his chest. "I trust you implicitly, but." Her ragged sobs dampened his shirt. "I cannot change the truth nor rid myself of the horrors."

"What horrors, Lady Bethany? Please tell me." He needed her to let him help, needed to comfort her, needed to do what he could to make her whole again.

"I've never made sense of most of it. Why would anyone do what they did to me? I don't remember my father giving me anything for which someone would want to kidnap me or shoot me. I can't tell people things I don't know."

Locke stiffened at her comments. From where had she gotten these ideas? Unless?

"I-I don't understand, Lady Bethany. Take your time. Who hurt you? When?" When she froze against him he worried that she would withdraw. "Please, my dear, let me help."

"I can't," she hissed, her voice filled with both terror and shame. "Some parts I don't remember. Others—" Her breath caught and he could feel the anguish radiating from her. "Heaven help me, sometimes I simply become unhinged, and I want to hit and bite—"

Locke shushed her and guided her to the settee near the fireplace. He sat down and pulled her into his lap and cradled her like a child. Her bones felt as delicate as a bird's, and he held her gingerly, as if squeezing her too tight would break them. As if pressing her too hard would shatter her soul.

Her cries softened and gradually faded away. Locke handed her his kerchief and she scrubbed her face dry the way no ordinary lady would. He smiled wryly, reminding himself that Lady Bethany Locke was, of course, no ordinary lady.

And, he realized, he loved her, not just the way she was, but because of who she was.

"Are you comfortable with staying in London? Or do you want to return to Moorewood?"

Guilt colored her face. "Have I embarrassed you too much, my lord? Please forgive me—"

"You haven't embarrassed me at all. You're a strong woman, and beautiful, and you have a mind of your own. I admire you for it."

Lady Bethany barked cynical laughter. "A description that could ruin a woman with the *beau monde*. Lady Camille would faint at such a characterization."

"And I wouldn't want Lady Camille for my wife. Now that I know the stuff of which you're made, I also comprehend why I haven't cared the slightest for courting my countrymen's daughters. I despise the simpering and giggling types, the pretense of empty heads solely for the purpose of landing a moneyed gentleman. I've no patience with vanity or greed, or infidelity, no matter the reason. I'm not sure you have any idea how you entice men, and I'm quite certain you haven't an arrogant bone in your body. Speaking your peace has no doubt ruffled some feathers, and I suppose that's part of why you prefer the quiet of the country, where you're allowed to think and behave as you wish with less fear of reprisal, but I appreciate that you're a sensible woman."

Lady Bethany's cheeks darkened in embarrassment with each of his comments. "Then I would shame you in town. Perhaps I should go back to Moorewood and never leave."

Locke lifted her chin to look deep into her eyes. "Do you remember what I told you this morning when you boarded Raven, and again later when I placed the crimson rose behind your ear? I meant every word I spoke. That you are a vision of loveliness that fair takes the breath away, and I truly fear I'll gain the envy of every man who sees you. I care most about you're happiness, my lady. I know you're not fond of London, but I'll have dealings here all the days of my life and would always welcome your company. I'd never be ashamed of you."

A small pendulum clock on the mantel chimed once, drawing their gazes. Locke sighed and pressed his lips to Lady Bethany's brow.

"Scarbreigh will arrive at any moment. Mr. Treadwell needs to clean up the broken teacup and ready me for my meeting, and I'm certain you could use some rest. Can we discuss this again tonight? Please?"

Lady Bethany seemed hesitant but nodded. She must dread facing the unpleasant things, but hopefully she trusted him enough to do so. She slid from his lap to her feet and let him gain his own footing. Then he bent and kissed her once again, rejoicing when she reciprocated that kiss.

* * *

Locke opened the door between their rooms, revealing Melissa perched in a chair under the window, a nook similar to the one in Locke's room, and busy embroidering. The abigail tossed aside her work and rose quickly when she saw Bethany's tear-stained face.

"My lady! Are you ill?"

"Just muddling through today's misadventure, Melissa." Bethany looked at Locke, amazed at how different he seemed to her right now, more than ever the man who'd proposed to her in Whitton's garden.

"We'll sup here tonight?" she asked.

"Please. Between my headache and today's upset, I'm of the opinion a quiet evening and an early bedtime would serve well."

Bethany was still stunned at everything that had happened today, from both the delights and the scares at the park, to shattering the tea cup, to the moment Locke had kissed her.

Had he just admitted he truly cared for her? Found her beautiful? Admired her independence? Her lips ached from the force of his kisses, evidence of what had surely taken place.

"Tonight, my dear," he murmured, his eyes memorizing her face as his mouth brushed her fingertips. "And an additional discussion, to see if we can lay some demons to rest."

Bethany nodded, missing everything about him when he departed, but realizing that nothing between them would ever be the same. Especially when he knew the whole truth.

"May I comb out your hair before you lie down?" Melissa offered.

"I don't care to lie down, Melissa, but it would relax me to have my hair combed."

"Yes, my lady," Melissa said, following her to her dressing table.

* * *

Lord Scarbreigh accompanied Locke to his solicitor's office and afterward—so Locke reported later—endured a tongue-lashing about abandoning Bethany and Lady Camille at the park. After a fervent apology to both women and an even more fervent plea for their forgiveness, the marquess joined them for their early supper. He remained quiet during the meal, signifying both his remorse and the shock they all shared regarding the day's events.

After the meal, the Dowager Lady Katherine volunteered to join her niece and the marquess on a walk in the neighborhood, leaving Bethany and Locke to breathe sighs of relief.

"I've never seen Scarbreigh so humbled," Bethany remarked.

"Nor I. He needed a good dose of humility. I dare say he won't ever repeat such a mistake. Will you feel like going to church in the morning, my dear?"

"I'm not the one who took a blow to the head, my lord. Will you?"

He smiled. "An opportunity for earnest prayer sounds comforting."

"It does," Bethany agreed.

She needed to collect the jewelry she wanted to wear tomorrow, and with the two lovebirds engaged elsewhere, this was as good a time as any to journey to the strongbox in the earl's basement. Bethany searched the several velvet-lined drawers for what she wanted.

"I cannot decide between the blue dress and the green one you provided for my trousseau," she mused. "After today, it seems more frivolous than ever to care about such things, but whichever one I wear, I must choose between my emeralds and my sapphires." She held an earring from each pair before her ears for his appraisal. "What do you think?"

Locke made a show of looking them over, mirth twinkling in his eyes. Because she often wore green, he said he'd enjoy seeing her wear the blue. Bethany returned the emeralds and sorted through the other jewelry, selecting the lovely string of pearls and sapphires that her grandmother had willed to her, and a silver ring for her right hand, crowned with a sapphire flanked by two pearls. Last of all, she decided upon the silver charm bracelet her father had given her. She secured all of it in her pocket while the earl put the lockbox and its contents back in the safe, and then he escorted Bethany upstairs to rejoin their guests.

"Thank you for the evening," Scarbreigh said, shaking Locke's hand in parting. "And my deepest regrets for offending you, Lady Bethany."

"You're always welcome, old friend," Locke reassured him. "Besides, I'd rue denying Lady Camille the happiness I see on her face right now."

Lady Camille pinked, and Bethany, smiling wryly, put an arm around her cousin's shoulders. "I fear we are fated to endure the roguishness of men, dear cousin. A thicker skin might serve us women well."

"We won't torture you," Scarbreigh insisted, flashing a winning smile. "But we will test and try you."

"Of that, I have no doubt," Bethany replied. "Just remember to go easy on Lady Camille. She isn't the eccentric I am and doesn't deserve ill treatment."

"I knew that long ago," Scarbreigh said, offering his farewells. Lady Camille's cheeks glowed with his now-familiar parting bow and kiss in the air above her gloved fingertips.

CHAPTER 19

After Lady Camille went upstairs, Lady Katherine intoned, "I'd forgotten how tiresome courting can be. In future, I'll let one of the maids follow them."

Bethany laughed. "Too much ogling going on, I suppose?"

"Indeed. And reams of questions, mostly directed at my niece, but some to me. Necessary when young people begin to learn about each other, I suppose, but I honestly don't remember Lord Scarbreigh being so serious a conversationalist. He's always been a mite on the jaunty side, as you've pointed out, my daughter. Perhaps it's the sign of a man ready for domestication."

Bethany narrowed her eyes in bemusement. "What was so serious it annoyed you?"

"Oh, nothing important. Whether Lady Camille's parents would welcome him as a visitor. How often and how long she plans to stay at Moorewood and what you and she like to do there. He also had questions for me about your father and Lord Christian and Mr. Collin, especially right before your father and eldest brother went to Belgium. He seemed to miss them far more than I would ever have dreamed. Said he was upset Mr. Collin had gone off to war, and that your father had placed himself and Lord Christian in danger by leaving England."

The countess turned to Locke. "For a man who's supposedly your friend, he doesn't seem to know as much about you as I'd have expected, either, although I can't say I blame him. I've had little beyond modest acquaintance with you and couldn't answer his questions myself."

Locke smiled and shrugged, although Bethany saw concern on the earl's face. "I'm a private man, Lady Whitton. In my opinion, the peerage often takes itself too seriously, sometimes not seriously enough, and I dislike being the butt of jokes or the center of frivolous gossip. Scarbreigh's nearer Mr. Collin's age and didn't spend as much time with me when we grew up. I suspect what happened today distressed him greatly. Maybe he's worried I'm up to some skullduggery and have gotten into trouble—or could cause Lady Bethany trouble. I assure you, my lady, I am not."

"Well, maybe he is," the countess retorted, chuckling at her own joke. "Mostly, I think he's simply a man in love and in a twitter. However, I must say I'm grateful you married my daughter, my lord. I'd have welcomed Scarbreigh for a son-in-law had Lady Bethany accepted his suit, but I fear we'd have endured a lifetime of fireworks."

"Most certainly," Bethany said with acrimony. "We're too alike, both strong willed and opinionated. Lady Camille merely wants to enjoy each day as it comes, and she's perfectly happy to let the love of her life manage the decisions." She paused to consider Locke. "You're getting wan again, my lord. You'd best retire. Sleep well, Mum. I hope you'll join us for church."

"With delight. Lady Camille said she will, too."

When they journeyed upstairs, Locke admitted Bethany to his chambers, pausing to examine her face intently.

"I understand your dread at facing unpleasant memories, Lady Bethany, but I hope you see the importance of it."

Apprehension dried Bethany's mouth. "I mightn't have appreciated it if not for the catastrophe at the park. Now, how can I refuse? I feel somehow responsible for what happened to you."

"You aren't. Don't even think it."

Mr. Treadwell served them tea again when they were seated, but Bethany ignored hers. Her hands again shook at the prospect of delving into the past, and she had no desire to break any more teacups.

When Treadwell departed, Locke set aside the cold compress the valet had brought for his head and collected her hands in his. He stroked them gently with his thumbs.

"I've pondered everything that happened at the park, and I'm certain the two attacks on us were connected."

Bethany nodded, adding, "As I'm convinced it has something to do with the attack on Shadow on our wedding night, the man who shot at us with the arrow, and the wreckage in my room."

Locke sighed. "Unfortunately, I agree, my dear. It would help me if you would answer some questions."

Bethany pressed her eyes shut and breathed deep to ease the dread. "I will do my best."

"I can ask no more. And if you can't bear it, we'll stop." She nodded, and he continued. "As o'erset as you were, I'm not sure I understood you earlier, but I believe you stated someone did something to you. That they asked questions you couldn't answer. You also said, 'I don't remember my father giving me anything for which someone would want to kidnap me or shoot me.' Can you explain any of this?"

The dread turned into shame. She hated having to admit she had eavesdropped on more than one of the earl's conversations at

Moorewood, but he would think even less of her if she didn't and he found out later.

"On the morning of the bowmen's attack, I overheard the exchange between you and Dimity. When you told him the assailants were after something my Father supposedly gave me or told me, I surmised it was important enough they were willing to either shoot me, to capture me and wrest it from me, or kill me and prevent my ever revealing it." Seeing his serious look, she added, "I have no such knowledge. If I did, I wouldn't tell them—but I would tell you."

Locke looked away, and Bethany was certain he must be disappointed in her. "I didn't intend to eavesdrop," she murmured. "It just happened."

"Like when you were in the dining room and heard my conversation between the twins and Mr. Treadwell, when I returned from the Continent?"

"Yes. I stumbled upon you at the wrong time."

"But you said someone *did* something to you," he urged. "Does that incident have anything to do with why you avoided marriage?"

Bethany felt as if a hand had tightened itself around her throat. How could she get through this? How could she not? Lord Locke deserved the answers, but it would without doubt change everything between them.

"Yes," she managed.

His fingers squeezed hers. "I can see that it troubles you greatly. When did it happen?"

She managed to answer, "April last year. That night we first met."

On an exceptional London night with uncommonly clear, dark skies and faint stars overhead. She'd not set foot there since that night. Music resonated in a faraway corner of her mind, laughter, figures dancing that cast shadows across fine draperies on the other side of a tall window. She stated the date and the hour. That her friend Lady Jessica Trent was ecstatic at receiving a dance number with the Earl of Locke. Bethany jealous at not being given the same privilege. Locke whisked off to the game tables by his bevy of admirers and Bethany never seeing him again.

Until he'd come to ask for her hand in marriage, of course.

"And what happened after I left you in the dance hall with Lady Trent?" Locke murmured.

"I went onto the veranda for fresh air; it was sweltering inside. But I think a man was with me. I can't remember him or his name, just his presence. I believe he invited me to walk with him, and I vaguely remember insisting we have a chaperone. He pointed to a couple on the walkway below us and told me that they were his friends and would join us."

Her eyes flew open as the all-too-familiar sense of terror ignited within her. She couldn't bear thinking about it. Rivulets of perspiration rolled down her brow. She could see it as if it had happened yesterday. Shadows in nearby shrubbery. Unyielding hands grabbing her, a gag in her mouth, being dragged somewhere. Fighting to get free; hot, angry tears. Wrists bound together, a carriage nearby. A burlap sack tossed over her head.

Locke's gentle touch, his curled finger stroking her cheek, gave her proof she'd spoken these things aloud. "That's enough, dear heart. You're too upset. It may take a number of tries to get through it. We'll try again tomorrow night, if you can stand it."

Numb enough to not realize he'd pulled her from her chair until he guided her to their connecting door, she felt relief flood her, grateful that the mishap was far enough past it could do her no tangible harm. Grateful when Locke kissed her a gentle good night.

Grateful to escape to her room and let Melissa prepare her for bed.

* * *

Bethany had always loved Westminster Abbey, its architecture and it religious and historical significances. Worshipping there as Locke's countess now gave it personal importance for her, and memories she'd forever cherish.

Thankfully, their day at home was equally as tranquil and lovely.

Evening brought messengers with written invitations to call on or to receive calls from a host of notables throughout the week. Scarbreigh also sent a missive for Lady Camille, the one Bethany had expected, an invitation to join him for a special evening at his townhouse on Thursday night. Lord and Lady Locke and the Dowager Lady Whitton were included, of course. Lady Camille was in transports over it.

On Monday, Locke and his guests found themselves tossed into the social whirl typical of the "little season." Several visitors arrived to meet Bethany; Bethany and Lord Locke made visits of their own. Lord and Lady Locke, and Lady Camille and Lady Katherine took walks along London's most legendary streets where they visited with a good number of the *beau monde* doing the same. Bethany submerged herself in shopping for Moorewood's final refurbishments, Lady Camille and Lady Katherine serving as her astute advisors.

Tuesday and Wednesday mirrored Monday, although the evenings differed: one night the theater, the other a concert.

Locke and Bethany collaborated briefly each night, but still she couldn't see her attackers' faces in her mental fog, let alone confess what they'd done to her.

Finally Thursday dawned. The morning began the same, with additional invitations, especially for the upcoming weekend's activities, but a tumultuous afternoon storm sent them hurrying home to escape the rain.

They were surprised to find the Hannaford coach at the curb when they arrived.

"My brothers are here?" Lady Camille wondered aloud. Then she gasped with excitement. "Perhaps it's my parents. What would bring them to town?"

They hurried inside and found the esteemed Lord and Lady Hannaford—Glen and Eva Camerfield—ensconced in the morning room. With them sat Lord Matthew and Mr. Nicolas, and Bethany's chest tightened at seeing the worry lining their faces.

"Dearest Kate," Lady Eva said, coming to buss her sister's cheek. The two women looked almost as alike as twins themselves, despite Eva being three years younger and frail from years of illness. "We've brought disturbing news."

Bethany caught the silent warning that passed from the twins and Lord Hannaford to Locke, and her stomach clenched in fear.

"Heavens, Eva, what's the matter?" Lady Katherine queried.

Lord Hannaford cleared his throat. "We received word from Mr. Drew that your manor was broken into early Monday morning."

"Whitton's manor?" Bethany and her mother cried in unison.

"Yes. We insisted on delivering the news ourselves, rather than sending you a post."

Lady Katherine's pallor frightened Bethany. She put out a hand to steady her mother.

"Unbelievable," the dowager countess said, her face twisted with fear. "How much damage did they do? What did they take?"

Lord Hannaford, a rather nondescript man with nondescript grey eyes, pinned Locke with a grim look. He glanced at Lord Matthew and Mr. Nicolas before responding. "It's a puzzle, my lady. And is disturbing in its senselessness. It appears little of value was taken. A silver teapot set, the one you've had in the library as a conversation piece for so many years I've lost count. And a handful of old books Mr. Drew said you left on John's desk—"

"Books?" Bethany protested. "The ones I gave to you, Mum?"

"I suppose." Lady Katherine seemed bewildered. "What would anyone do with a dozen old children's stories?"

"I've no idea," Hannaford interjected. "Unfortunately they did a lot of damage. John's desk drawers were pillaged, their contents thrown on the floor, furniture overturned, the rugs tossed aside, and the statuary and such were smashed."

Bethany froze in place. "What do you mean?"

"Your porcelains, my dear. All of them were broken."

Now it was Locke who braced Bethany as a quiet wail escaped her. They'd destroyed the figurines her brothers had brought her from Europe? Her Dresden dolls from her father? She couldn't conceive of such maliciousness. There was something more than met the eye about this villainy than just the act itself. Who hated her or the Montgomerys enough to carry it out?

"I'm sorry, dear," Lady Eva said, coming to stroke Bethany's arm. "We feared you'd take it hard. Messages of hatred or vindictiveness might have explained it, yet they left none. If damage was their goal, they'd have done much worse; if theft was the reason, they'd have taken more."

Bethany didn't realize her mother was crying until Lady Katherine buried her damp cheek against Bethany's neck and hugged her tight. Bethany hung on, trying to listen to that something that tickled the back of her mind, warning her that this should make sense if only she could remember why.

When they'd managed to collect themselves, Lady Katherine urged Bethany to pack quickly so that they could leave early in the morning.

"Hold tight, Lady Kate," Lord Hannaford interjected. "There's no need to rush home. Brought workmen in for you immediately. Might be better if you stay away for a while, let them—and the constable—do their jobs."

Lady Katherine breathed deep and pressed her kerchief to her eyes. "Thank you, Lord Glen. So kind of you."

"Come sit and talk, Sister," Lady Eva offered, leading the dowager countess to a nearby sofa.

Quietly, Lord Hannaford said to Bethany, "Think we'll head to the library, give you ladies a bit of privacy, my dear. You need time to make as much sense of this as you can."

She nodded, feeling numb inside but also feeling the hairs rise on the back of her neck at seeing those secretive looks darting between the four men. They had more to discuss than broken Dresden dolls and toppled furniture.

When they'd departed, she sniffed wetly and said, "Excuse me, Mum. It appears I've forgotten my kerchief."

It wasn't true, but it gave her opportunity to do what she ought not to do. She'd never been one to eavesdrop, even as a pesky little sister following her brothers around. On the other hand, she'd never faced so much misadventure in her life, either, and she wanted answers, even if she had an uneasy feeling she might hear things she didn't like.

Making sure no servants were nearby, Bethany tiptoed to the library, pressed her ear to the door and concentrated on the rumble of the men's voices beyond it.

* * *

"Excellent vintage, Locke," Lord Glen Camerfield, the Earl of Hannaford, said, inhaling the fragrance of his port. "Good for calming the nerves."

"Only finding a solution to this muck will calm mine," Locke grumbled.

"Mmm. Any progress with the men you arrested? You've a crack team of interrogators."

"No. Scoundrels may or may not be first-rate archers, but not even Devon has succeeded at finding out who ordered them to shoot Lady Bethany."

Hannaford sighed then jerked a nod at the twins. "They probably shouldn't have dragged me into this. You know I've been cheerfully out of the field for years. But they wanted my opinion at Whitton before calling the authorities, and after seeing it myself, I understand why. No one with half a brain would believe burglars did it. The swine were obviously searching for a specific article. Considering the attack on my niece, the ransacking of her room at Moorewood, and the stabbed gelding, there's no doubt this escapade is, as you surmised, connected."

Lord Matthew set down his glass and added, "There's something else. We followed the leads you gave us, Marc, but Nicolas went only as far as Calais. I never even left London."

"What? I expected both of them would land you somewhere near Paris or possibly into Belgium. I'm convinced these scum are followers of Bonaparte. They'll stop at nothing to return him to power."

"Wish we could prove it. Had you followed the clues, you'd have drawn the same conclusion. If there's a connection to Napoleon, it isn't direct. We're convinced something else is going on here, and whatever it is, isn't good."

"And Lady Bethany is somehow linked to it," Locke said, all but tasting the bitterness the thought spawned.

"Yes."

"What aren't you telling me, Matthew?" he insisted. "May I remind you that everything we've done up to now, from my marrying your cousin and sending her to Moorewood, to making sure she has the utmost protection England can offer without her knowing it, has been based on the premise that Bonaparte's supporters are after her. If not, then who?

There's no jilted lover, no offended patron, no overzealous devotee stalking her?"

"No." Mr. Nicolas replied, but added, "Our sleuthing, however, led us back to London and sealed records in underground vaults in the Offices. You can imagine our astonishment after getting them unsealed and upon discovering a connection between the three Whitton men's deaths."

"What?" Locke stared at the twin in shock.

"You knew that Mr. Collin's commission was a fraud," Mr. Nicolas said.

"Of course."

"Meant he could travel to and from various destinations with his 'detachment', move away from it or rejoin it as needed. In contrast, Lord Whitton's connection with the Service, as was his heir Lord Christian's involvement, was secretive investigating but not undercover spying, unlike yours, your father's or ours, and certainly not like Mr. Collin's."

"How does this connect with their deaths?" Locke asked with impatience.

"Humor us," Lord Matthew said. "Communications from all of us took a similar route, arriving in packages sent—at first—to Lady Katherine, to give them the look of family correspondence. Inside the packages were either smaller ones or letters addressed to each of us—you excepted, of course; would have raised too many questions—which we would collect when we visited. Your correspondence was sent in the same envelope with mine or Mr. Nicolas's and we routed it to you."

"Yes, but as to Lady Katherine, I remember her opening something she wasn't supposed to open and saying too much about it with a few friends," Locke noted.

"That's when we began funneling the parcels through Lady Bethany, of course. We knew she was trustworthy," Mr. Nicolas said. "But we all worried when Mr. Collin stopped writing."

"I didn't learn about it until later," Locke said. "I was busy sneaking around Spain and France. If I remember correctly, Lord Whitton was certain something was wrong and was livid it was taking too long to organize a rescue mission. Then he received a letter from Mr. Collin in mid-March, which set him at ease. That's when the proposal came from Belgium from the Leclerqcs, inviting Lord Whitton and Lord Christian to discuss a possible arrangement with Lady Elizabeth Leclercq. And where both met with fate in the carriage accident."

"Entirely fictitious," Lord Hannaford said, sighing. "London's sealed documents reported there was no such correspondence from Mr. Collin and that the accident happened in Portugal."

"What?" Locke said again. "What were they doing in...." He paused, considering the meaning. "There was never a parley with the Leclerqcs."

"No. Lord Leclercq verified that fact during the investigation after the 'accident.'"

"Which means Whitton and his heir had gone to find and rescue Mr. Collin themselves."

"Yes, well after a fashion," said Lord Matthew. "The supposed invitation had to be extended to Lord Christian, of course, a ruse that required his going to the Continent. Lord Whitton's joining him would be a mere formality our aunt wouldn't question. Uncle wasn't daft enough to risk his heir unnecessarily, especially when he was about to place himself in harm's way.

"According to the report in the file, during the inquiry after the accident, the investigators found an encrypted journal, stitched into Lord Whitton's jacket, which told the story better than anyone but Whitton himself could have. After secluding Lord Christian in an inn in Lisbon, he set out to the area from which we'd last received correspondence from Mr. Collin."

Mr. Nicolas chimed in. "Collin was supposed to have been positioned near Torres Vedras, Portugal, and although nothing *we* do is safe, the area was as safe from any actual military conflict in war as possible. Uncle, who was good at what he did, apparently located Collin near Tolosa, Spain, where the Allied army had preparations underway to drive the French out of Spain."

"The beginning of the War of the Sixth Coalition," said Locke.

"Yes. It appears Mr. Collin was tracking three French spies and collecting intelligence on their activities when *they* caught *him*."

Lord Matthew then added, "Whitton rescued Mr. Collin and returned with him to Lisbon. Mr. Collin revealed to him and Lord Christian what he'd discovered, the truth about a conspiracy of some sort and a secret code that went with it. It was apparently important enough he did not reveal that information in the journal. Whitton did admit that Mr. Collin had devised a most ingenious way to get the information to us—and to the prince. It appears they accomplished their task, but then—"

"An unexpected carriage accident happened and killed them all," Locke surmised. "Was it our agency that chose to continue the deception about the Leclercq's offer and to lie about where all three bodies were found, to avoid anyone here in England making the connection?"

"Yes. It also bought our agents time to locate the other two French spies and eradicate them, supposedly before any harm was done."

"But they were wrong," Locke said. "There was harm done. At least one of them sent word to his superior. Which is why someone is after

Lady Bethany." He scrubbed his face roughly in frustration. "What I don't understand is why Lord Whitton, who adored Lady Bethany, would risk her life by sending her something so terribly important someone would hunt her down for it. And if enemies suspected Whitton's wife and daughter knew anything, why didn't they pursue both women immediately? It's been near a year and a half, for heaven's sakes."

Dread drew deep lines in Lord Hannaford's cheeks and lowered his thick, graying brows. The twins stood stiff and pale. Locke glared at them, his lips pressed together in mounting anger.

"Out with it," he demanded. "You've kept it from me long enough."

Lord Matthew sighed his capitulation. "They didn't wait. It appears Lady Katherine never came into their sights—we've no idea why—but they sought Lady Bethany even before we knew Uncle and the boys had died."

"You're joking! *More than a year ago?* And you withheld this information because…?" He wanted to break Lord Matthew's jaw. Surely this had something to do with Lady Bethany's fears.

"Because they hurt our dear cousin. Badly enough she can't remember all of it. And she's forbidden us to discuss it with anyone, including *her*. Marc, you insisted without fail, like most of us in the Service, that you have neither time nor capacity for matters of the heart. We assumed she'd be safer with you than anywhere else on earth because you would never expect anything from her."

"I feared something like this might be at the root of it. I want the details."

"We *can't*. She *forbade* us," Lord Matthew insisted. "Besides, there are other matters afoot. We all agree that our deepest concern is of a leak, a traitor somewhere in our network."

"We do," Locke conceded. Then suddenly a light dawned. "Lady Bethany has information about who the real traitor is! That's what you suspect, isn't it? That she just doesn't remember it? But if they failed to get what they wanted from her before, why would these schemers think they can get it now?"

Hannaford shrugged. "Perhaps something's convinced them that she's finally remembered? Maybe they believed they were safe and now realize they're not? Perhaps they're running out of time, just as we are, and have returned to where they started?"

"We must keep in mind that a mastermind fuels his coterie," Lord Matthew interjected. "The zealots we've managed to intercept have spouted volumes of rubbish surrounding a new regime on the horizon and the failings of Britain. A few consider it a travesty to have Napoleon wasting away on his island kingdom of Elba; everything would resolve if he ruled the world. Not once, however, have we found any proof that *this* particular group is connected to a plan to free that madman. We're convinced they have a different agenda, but we may not discover what it is until we unveil the architect of the scheme himself."

"And Lady Bethany's life is in danger until then," Locke growled. "I sent a missive your way regarding the fiasco we endured over the weekend. Did you receive it?"

Lord Hannaford's brows rose high. "Didn't make it to us before we left home. What happened?"

Locke outlined the events at the Fair, subconsciously touching the knot on his head. It was better but still bruised and tender.

"This isn't good," said Lord Hannaford, alarmed.

Finally Lord Matthew said, "The major purpose of a uniform is to make a man stand out in a crowd. Why would men up to no good want to become obvious to others?"

"I think perhaps they didn't know each other," Locke suggested. "The uniform would help identify them. The outfits were quite subtle, and they expected to move quickly enough to not leave an impression."

Mr. Nicolas's expression softened. "Brilliant. Once they'd accomplished whatever they'd come to do and then separated, tossing aside the waistcoats would erase the uniform and allow them to blend into the crowd in a heartbeat."

"But their plans fell flat," Locke continued, sorting through his memories of that afternoon. The first man led him a merry chase and the other knocked him senseless. Lady Bethany had not only seen both of them but two others as well. Thankfully she'd managed to evade them. He still believed it was her they'd wanted, just as with the attempted shooting, which also convinced him they were merely trying to keep Locke out of the way. The idea chilled him to the core.

"We've left the ladies longer than we should," Lord Hannaford remarked, checking his pocket watch.

"A little forewarning before we join them," Locke told them. "Scarbreigh's invited us to supper at his place tonight. I'd cry off, but I'm afraid the marquess intends to bid for Lady Camille's hand at the gathering."

Lord Hannaford's brows rose high. "Without talking to me first? Cheeky boy, but he always has been. Perhaps you'd send a message to his place, Locke, to inform him we're in town. If he's half the man my daughter deserves, he'll want my permission."

Locke smiled wryly. "I doubt you'll have a problem there. Scarbreigh's an impulsive sort, but he won't defy convention if he doesn't have to."

"Mmm." Hannaford nodded. "I hope Lady Eva feels up to it. Her health is so delicate. We've tried everything, trips to the mainland, to Bath, to dozens of physicians. I wish I believed planning a wedding would perk her up, but it will assuredly exhaust her."

"Let Aunt Katherine take care of it, Father," Lord Matthew suggested. "She would have loved having longer to plan Lady Bethany's nuptials. Taking care of Lady Camille would make up for it, and as her sister, she understands Mum better than anyone."

Hannaford agreed. "And it would entertain my sister-in-law enough she won't realize what the four of us are about. Shall we join the women?"

"Yes." Mr. Nicolas discarded his glass. "And from now on, we mustn't leave Lady Bethany alone for long, no matter where she is, until we've put an end to this."

CHAPTER 20

Bethany's heart pounded at what she was hearing—and at the risk of being caught out. She scuttled back to the morning room, schooling her face against the emotions that nearly overwhelmed her. Followers of Napoleon might be after her? Mr. Collin's commission was a fraud, Lord Christian's trip to Belgium was a ruse, and everyone believed Lord Whitton had sent Bethany information that might reveal a traitor?

She didn't know whether to laugh or cry.

In her absence, the ladies' conversation had changed to Aunt Eva's health. Her aunt had pulled a throw around her shoulders, and Lady Camille now doted over her.

"It's a tiring drive," Lady Katherine scolded her sister. "You probably should have stayed home. You'd just removed from Bath."

"I'm not on death's door," Bethany's aunt scoffed. "I'll do well with my feet up and pleasant conversation. Oh, here you are, Beth. We'd begun to think you disliked our company."

"No, of course not, Aunt Eva," said Bethany, hating the lie she must now perpetuate. "Melissa's still on an errand I gave her earlier and I had to find my kerchief on my own. I'm so sorry you're not feeling well. Did your bevy of physicians not help you?"

Lady Eva rolled her eyes and sighed. "I'm convinced I'll die from smothering before I succumb to any known malady. Here, sit down and tell me every detail about your wedding. I was crestfallen at not being able to attend."

Bethany perched on the high-backed chair beside her aunt, and with the help of her mother and Lady Camille, began an accounting of the affair. They hadn't gotten far, however, before the men joined them.

They were completely changed when they walked into the room, still as subdued as they had been by the news delivered on this day, but not as if the four of them had so recently discussed matters that reeked of intrigue and peril.

Bethany ought to confront them, to demand they explain themselves. But they'd agreed her life was in danger and that she must know something that she was equally sure she didn't. She'd faced such accusations before. She couldn't do so now.

For better or worse, she was grateful to have her uncle guide the discussion towards Lord Scarbreigh and his intentions regarding Lady Camille. Her cousin flushed at the revelation, and Lady Eva seemed undaunted when faced with the excitement of the mini-fête at the marquess's townhouse that night.

* * *

Scarbreigh's invitation to Lady Camille's parents and brothers was extended almost immediately, and he greeted them all warmly when they arrived on his doorstep. Welcoming his guests alongside him was the Dowager Lady Scarbreigh. Her unexpected presence flustered Lady Camille and generated meaningful looks between her parents and brothers.

After settling his guests with refreshments, Lord Scarbreigh nervously requested Lord Hannaford's company in his study. The rest of them chattered while Lady Camille fussed about what was taking so long. When the men did return, Scarbreigh's blue eyes twinkled with pleasure, although he revealed nothing of what he and Hannaford had discussed.

Supper was excellent, but the entire evening transformed for Bethany when she caught Scarbreigh watching her, more than once. She might have thought it coincidental if not for the wistfulness she saw reflected in his eyes.

Enlightenment mingled with dismay when she overheard the Dowager Lady Scarbreigh discussing with Lady Katherine her continued amusement at how Lord and Lady Locke's unexpected marriage had taken the *ton* by storm. Scarbreigh heard it, too, and envy radiated from his eyes as he turned his gaze on Locke.

More troubling, Locke mirrored his expression, the rancor passing between the two men almost palpable.

Then Lord Hannaford cleared his throat and the atmosphere changed. Scarbreigh gave the earl a smile and a nod and rose to address his guests.

"Mum. Dearest friends," he said, "Thank you for coming tonight. I hope everyone will remember it fondly."

"Hear, hear," said Lord Hannaford, offering a belly laugh that made everyone chuckle.

Scarbreigh smiled down at Lady Camille and extended his hand to her. Cheeks aflame, she clutched that hand and came to her feet.

"You are a wonder, my darling," he murmured, pressing her fingers to his lips. "I'm still amazed that you can put up with me. I've told you often I love you, although I haven't spoken it in front of witnesses." He turned a cocky grin on the rest of them. "But I have now. And not one of you can say otherwise. I have two gifts for you, dearest Lady Camille. I hope you like them."

He pulled a wrapped gift from his jacket pocket and handed it to Lady Camille, who trembled when she opened it. She gasped at the sight of the diamond-studded necklace he withdrew from the box nestled within the wrapping. He fastened the chain around her neck and beamed at Lady Camille's obvious delight.

Scarbreigh's grin faded and his eyes darkened with affection. "I do love you, Lady Camille. And I have reason to imagine you feel the same."

Lady Camille granted him a nod, a tear glistening in her eye. Scarbreigh now removed the wooden box from his pocket Bethany had seen at the fair. This time he opened it easily, as if he'd practiced, and showed its contents to Lady Camille. Lady Camille gasped again and held still as Scarbreigh dropped to his knee, his face raised to hers.

"Then marry me, my love. Be my wife."

Lady Camille gasped, hands to her cheeks, and cried out, "Oh, dear Scarbreigh! Yes. Yes!"

The marquess surged to his feet and kissed Lady Camille with nothing less than the fervor anyone would expect of a man in love. After he set the ring on her finger, Lord Hannaford offered a toast.

Bethany gave little heed to the words of the toast. Seeing her cousin so happy drew the main part of her attention, despite Lady Camille draining her glass too quickly. But she did not mistake Scarbreigh's look in Bethany's direction or the feeling of sickness when the truth, and his disappointment, slammed into her.

Bethany loved Scarbreigh dearly, as a friend. True, he could ruffle her feathers and enjoyed doing so, often worse than her own brothers. But he'd provided the merriest entertainment all her life and she'd had no doubt he was fond of her.

But now Bethany knew the worst. The man loved her. He'd truly wanted to marry her. Now, seeing the truth so blatantly spread before her, she realized that the marquess had been subtly courting her for most of the last year, even during her mourning. Why had she not realized it before? She'd always seen him as a friend. She'd never considered he wanted more, not even when he proposed to her. He must have been devastated that she'd not only refused him but immediately afterward accepted Locke's proposal.

Scarbreigh had declared his love for Lady Camille, but Bethany feared his heart wasn't as true as it should be. Could he give Lady Camille everything she needed? Everything she deserved? Bethany wanted more than anything for her cousin's life as Scarbreigh's marchioness to be sweet for her.

She pushed the thought aside when the others jumped to their feet to cheer and to congratulate the couple and, afterwards, she joined the games and comfortable banter and the never-ending drinks and refreshments, even if her heart wasn't in it.

Near the end of the evening, Bethany tensed when Scarbreigh came to sit in a chair beside her. She offered him tentative congratulations.

"Mmm, thank you, cousin-in-law-to-be. Should have done it long ago. I'm enjoying making Lady Camille happy. Oh, my," he said glancing at the bracelet on Bethany's wrist. "Lovely piece," he commented, gently fingering it. "I don't think I've ever seen it before."

Bethany frowned in surprise. "I was wearing it the morning you—" She paused, uncomfortable with dredging up the past. When he raised a brow at her, she finished with "the morning you asked me to marry you."

"Really? I'm embarrassed. How obtuse of me. Didn't notice it. It's truly remarkable. How did you get it?"

"Father sent it to me from Belgium, right before he died."

"Ah." Scarbreigh's gravity deepened as he leaned over the circlet. "A European creation, then. You must treasure it. May I see it?"

Bethany chuckled and raised her wrist to allow him to examine each charm intently. Brows puckered, she said, "I'd be insulted if you've concocted a plan to memorize it so that you can have a copy made for Lady Camille."

Scarbreigh coughed, his cheeks reddening. "You've caught me out. I was contemplating exactly that, and you're correct. It wouldn't be at all respectful." Then he winked. "Something like it perhaps, but not a copy."

A shadow fell over Bethany's shoulder. She looked up to see Locke staring at Scarbreigh. The marquess set her hand free and produced a bland smile.

"Delightful piece, isn't it, Locke? Lord Whitton always did have good taste."

"He did."

Locke congratulated Scarbreigh on his betrothal, and the marquess thanked him before excusing himself to find his fiancée.

"Odd to have a man so entranced with a bracelet," Bethany murmured, turning the chain around on her wrist and examining the charms. "But Scarbreigh has always been a bit odd."

Locke laughed. "He has. I fear my ankle and skull need a reprieve, my lady, and Lady Hannaford wishes to go home. Shall we do likewise?"

"I'm beyond ready," Bethany replied, despite dreading their nightly talk tonight—if they talked—and what it might bring. And whether they did or not, she wondered if she'd be able to sleep, worried the way she was about Lady Camille and Scarbreigh.

* * *

Lord and Lady Hannaford and the twins retired to their own townhouse for the night, but Lady Camille was already established at Lord Locke's home and opted to remain, at least for the time being. She was in transports on the way home, giddy from the depth of her love and three glasses of wine. Bethany had no desire to criticize, although she had to stifle laughter when her cousin broke into song along the way. At least Lady Camille was sure of foot when they arrived, and bid them good night, sailing up the stairs to her room without a backward glance.

"What is wrong with the younger generation?" Lady Katherine murmured, shaking her head in disapproval. "My niece has always been the most refined of my and my sister's children. I would never have expected such a display from her."

"She's happy, Mum," Bethany said.

"She's lubricated," the countess replied, and then she barked laughter. "But I can't say I blame her. She has the exceptional prospect of marrying for love. Would that we all could make such a claim. Sleep well, daughter, and you too, my lord."

Locke's smile faded when Lady Katherine departed. "Would you like something to help you sleep tonight, my dear?"

Had he read her thoughts? Bethany agreed and requested an herbal draught, Locke sending Mr. Treadwell after it and his own tisanes. They mounted the stairs to his room and sat on the settee this time, comparing notes on the night's excitement until Mr. Treadwell arrived. The honeyed tea tasted good, and Bethany prayed the mixture of chamomile, valerian root, and mallow would truly help her sleep.

Locke bid Mr. Treadwell good evening and began their discussion by asking whether anyone at Almack's that long-ago night didn't seem to belong there. She denied it. Bethany and Lady Camille had danced with both Scarbreigh and the twins, followed by a dozen acolytes, including young Lord Jamison and a few of the Notables. She'd stepped onto the veranda to escape the heat with that elusive someone, or perhaps more than one someone, but she still had no idea who.

"What about the men who grabbed you up? Can you describe them?"

Tremors ensued that had the teacup clattering on its saucer. Locke set the dishes on the table for her and then sandwiched her hands between his own. "Keep it simple, my dear. One thought or feeling at a time."

She described Almack's veranda, and the ensuing walk on the grounds. The fetid breath of her kidnappers. The gag choking her; the burlap sack scratching her face. She heard river traffic in the background when they arrived, and the stench of fish and neglected horses and dogs. A location near the docks?

And one man, pulling off the sack, slamming her against the weathered slats of a wall, and in the near distance a voice, a cultured voice, demanding her attention. She was in a stall in a stable. The cultured man stood behind her, in the abandoned stable's aisle, where she couldn't see him. He warned her that resistance was useless, that there was more at stake here than she could ever imagine.

He then spoke to the man holding her against the wall by her throat, telling the monster that he and his two comrades could do whatever they needed to get the information from her they wanted—with three exceptions and a warning.

"Do *not* damage the girl's face, break no bones, and you dare not defile her. And whatever the outcome, return her to the Whitton townhouse stable within the next two hours."

Then he departed and left her to them.

On a makeshift table to the side of the room lie a horrendous row of gleaming tools, weapons she had no doubt were meant to exact torture. Not far from them was a fire in a small brazier, a poker submerged in its burning coals.

"Tell me what I want," the man said, yanking the poker from the coals and waving it too close to her left eye. "Or you'll wear burns that'll ruin ya' fer a lifetime."

But he'd been told not to mar her face! Did he not care?

Then came the multitude of senseless questions and demands for answers she couldn't give. Bethany wept her innocence, swearing she had no idea. Her father had given her nothing important. No letters, no books, no messages in any sort of code. Why would he use a code, she'd cried out? And to whom would it mean anything? The monsters had pushed her around between them, slapping her, tearing her skirts, ripping one shoulder of her dress, mocking her, yelling at her, demanding she tell them what her father had given her.

Their fists avoided her face, of course, but nothing else. The second torturer repeatedly nicked her shoulders and both arms with a small, singularly sharp knife with each unanswered question, leaving bloody trails down her appendages. The third man employed the poker, running it over her arms and legs, her back and feet, all of them laughing when she screamed.

Locke shushed Bethany's sobs, murmuring, "Oh, dear heart. I cannot believe they did this to you. Rest a moment. You needn't go on if it's too much."

"I have to say it now," she said, her voice breaking up, "before my courage fails."

The monsters suddenly stopped their torture.

"She don't know," the third man finally said. The leader nodded.

"Seems you're right," he'd replied. "We've not much more time before getting her home. I'd kill her, if'n I had my way, but you know how The One feels 'bout her."

"She's a pretty wench, she is. Doesn't seem fair 'e should have all 'e wants of 'er, while we be doin' all the work," said the second. They laughed in agreement.

Bethany cringed at what followed, desperate to forget it.

But her mind carried on, the memories pouring out in a flood.

Suggestive laughter and hands touching her, pulling her hair. "You're right 'bout that. She's a bruised apple already. Mayhap we should take a bite outta her, see how she tastes."

Bethany cried out in misery and Locke's groan sent the nightmare spinning away.

"Come, my dear, let me hold you." He stroked her head and rocked her, his own eyes moist, and let her cry into his chest.

What seemed eons later, with her sobs drifting into silence, Bethany was amazed to find her burden feeling lighter. If nothing else, sharing this much of the horrors had helped lessen their power over her.

Locke pressed his lips to her brow, and she looked up, winded at the warmth in his eyes. He lowered his head to press the tenderest of kisses to her mouth. She adored its sweetness, but remembering what those men had done to her made her pull away from him. She couldn't do this. She had no right to his affections.

His hands stilled and then he curled a finger and lifted her chin until her eyes met his.

"It's alright, my love," he said. "One step at a time. We shan't rush." He went round the room dousing the lanterns, leaving but one candle at the bedside burning. "Come, lie down beside me. Rest and feel safe. I won't let anything happen to you tonight."

Bethany opened her mouth to decline, but then he stretched his full height out on top of the coverlet and offered to hold her. Bethany hadn't realized trust was a tangible thing until that moment, when she found it waiting for her, disguised as her husband's warm and sinewy arms. They wrapped themselves around her and encouraged her to fall into a safe, dreamless sleep nestled against him.

* * *

"This is awfully sudden, Beth," Lady Katherine protested, her brows furrowed in apprehension. "Is something wrong?"

"No, Mum. You know I've no love for the city; it's hard enough for me to admit this week was a nice change of pace. But I want to go home."

"Well, if you must. Lady Camille and I are moving our belongings to the Hannaford townhouse. We'll go home next week, as we'd planned. I've loved spending time with you, darling, and I'll send you a note when I'm ready to visit Moorewood."

Bethany nodded and returned her hug, and then faced Lady Camille after her mother walked away.

"What's going on, Lady Bethany?" Lady Camille murmured.

"Nothing," Bethany replied, but she glanced towards Locke.

Lady Camille twitched a tentative smile, although she rubbed her right temple against a wine-induced headache. "You'll tell me when you're ready, but Melissa said you didn't come to your bedchamber last night. That you sneaked in from Locke's early this morning."

Bethany sighed in irritation. "Gossiping servants. It's not what you think. Yes, we spent the night together, talking and then sleeping, and I mean sleeping. Locke is, well, he's trying to help me work out ... what happened last April."

"Bethany, that's capital! That you've told him at least some of it and that he cares enough to get you through it is wonderful. Has it helped?"

"To some degree. He was best of friends with Lord Christian and Mr. Collin, and I dare say he knew my father better in some ways than did I. In a sense, my loss is his loss. But I still can't tell him everything, and I've no doubt how he'll feel when he knows the whole of it." Bethany ached to confess to her cousin what she'd witnessed over the summer, her eaves-droppings and her accidental discoveries, especially now, but something still held her back.

"He's truly in love with you, Beth."

"I've no idea what that means, Cam. Is falling in love enough? Besides, he'll be gone most of the time, and I fear he's involved in something ... dangerous. I'm convinced he's preferred his solitary life because he's safest without connections. I cannot elaborate now, but perhaps I'll understand it better by the time you come to Moorewood again."

Lady Camille nodded and squeezed Bethany's hands. "You're traveling without jewelry again, except for your wedding rings," she noted. "Locke's still worried about thieves?"

"Yes. I've a few pieces of lesser value in my trunks, but the rest will stay here in Locke's safe. I suppose it's best."

Lady Camille stepped back so that Mr. Treadwell could help Bethany and Melissa into the carriage. The trip home would be easier. Locke's carriage and one wagon would take them, Bethany's purchases, and Moorewood's servants home, while Locke rode Polly. The rest of it would remain with the dowager countess and Lady Camille.

Parting wishes said, they soon departed, and that evening, following an unremarkable ride, Bethany was grateful to unwind her stiff joints from the carriage and step inside the manor.

She was even more grateful to find her room undisturbed. Taylor-Ward's crew would finish the rest of the manor within the next week or so, but Bethany's paints, a new wallpaper she was eager to try, and the new furnishings had not yet arrived. The work on her bedchamber couldn't begin until then. Wanting her privacy and as close to familiar spaces as possible, Bethany did not mind.

Things, however, did not return to normal. Bethany felt smothered, watched every minute of the day by the staff, from the household servants to the gardeners to the groomsmen.

The next morning, Locke rode with Bethany and two burly stablemen Bethany had never met before—where had they come from?—to check on the tenants, expressing his pleasure at how vastly improved things were. Autumn was at their doorsteps and he was convinced all would be fit for the coming winter. His only concern was about the progress of the harvest. Mr. Matheson's damage to Moorewood had included demanding spring sowing without providing sufficient seed or replacing broken or aging tools and equipment. The tenants had worked hard after Locke provided them what they needed, but the estate hadn't produced what it had in past years. Bethany worried that a reduced yield could leave them, the tenants, and the surrounding villages short on provisions for the winter and fewer profits for Lord Locke.

Locke acknowledged her fears. "It was a good year, Lady Bethany, and my other holdings are doing exceedingly well. Please work with my solicitor if winter brings trouble. Davies will offset shortcomings at Moorewood with excesses from the others."

Such reassurance meant Bethany could visit the tenants with confidence. She was glad to see Elway's boy working hard alongside his father; and Hedley's girls and little Rob growing, not only in height, but also in health.

In parting, Laura and Beatrice offered Bethany handfuls of bright yellow dandelions, Mrs. Hedley blushing in embarrassment. Bethany winked at her and accepted the "flowers" with grace.

CHAPTER 21

When they arrived home, Locke excused himself to his study, claiming the need to review his and Bethany's ledgers. He sent his apologies for not joining her for their noon meal and was distracted at supper. It reminded her too much of her first night coming to Moorewood.

Melissa had not yet helped Bethany don her nightdress and robe when Locke knocked at their adjoining door. He stepped inside and sent Melissa away.

"Can you face this again tonight, my dear?"

Steeling herself, she gave a tight nod and joined the Earl of Locke on the comfortable sofa that fronted her bedchamber's empty fireplace, the butterflies in her stomach having mutated into angry hornets.

Locke slipped an arm around her and rested his cheek on her head. "I'm still hoping for clues, my dear, as to what your father may have given you. I also feel compelled to believe your kidnapping was connected to someone you knew."

"Why would you think that?" She looked up at him.

"You wouldn't have accompanied a man you didn't trust, so he was likely familiar. You can't remember the other person or persons on the veranda, either, which sometimes happens in the event of a great emotional shock—mostly because you'd never expect the person who betrayed you to do something so evil. Does that seem likely?"

All of it seemed as likely as it was evil. War. Conspiracy. Kidnapping. Duplicity. She let her thoughts drift to Almack's walkways and the scattered lamps that cast more shadows than light along the street. She had not wanted to go there, but someone on the veranda had done something to reassure her. She paused to reconsider. Yes! There'd been *two* men on that veranda, one keeping to the shadows and whispering to her escort. Then he walked away and the escort took her out for their walk.

She caught a "glimpse" of her escort's face at the corner of her mind. She turned to Locke, straining to say a name and still couldn't find it.

"Don't force it, Lady Bethany," he murmured. "Just let it happen. Describe what you see."

A tall man, dark hair, a soft, fluid voice, stately gestures, she said. She swallowed hard at the thought this was important information.

"Were you enjoying yourself? Frightened?"

"Irritated. I think I'd begun to suspect he wanted to take advantage of me. No. Of his station."

"And then?"

Bethany flinched and pressed her fist to her brow. "The men who were hiding in the nearby shrubbery grabbed me. I was so confused. I expected the gentleman to defend me, but instead he deserted me! Then the brutes were gagging and binding me and dragging me to the carriage that waited at the street."

"Did you notice any insignia on the carriage?"

"No, it was a hack. It was too dark to see the driver and they tossed the sack over my head and threw me to the floorboards. One sat inside with me and kicked me if I made any noise. I felt the others climb on top of the carriage."

Locke stroked her arm to calm her. With pauses between, he asked, "How long did they drive? Did they converse? Give directions to the driver? Ask questions? Were there familiar noises in the background? Scents?"

Bethany loathed the anxiety the questions drove inside of her. It might not have been more than fifteen minutes from Almack's to the sounds and smells near the piers, she told him. Her abductors said not a word. Then she was tumbled out of the carriage and dragged like a sack of grain inside the old stable.

"You know what I remember of the rest," Bethany said, fighting with those damnable, tormenting tears.

"But there was a man in the aisle, a man with a cultured voice?"

Bethany froze. Her lips parted in surprise. "Yes. Yes!" She met Locke's worried gaze, shock coursing through her at the revelation. "It was the man who convinced me to walk with him! I'd not connected him before. He left me to those ruffians but joined us later at the docks. He *helped* them kidnap me!"

"And he was familiar."

"I think he was someone ... important."

"Alright. Let's work on your kidnappers' questions. You've told me your impressions, but can you remember their exact words?"

She struggled but couldn't grasp it.

"Relax, Love," he entreated her. "Imagine you're standing there listening to what they're saying. Think only about their words."

Bethany bolted to her feet to pace back and forth while her thoughts roamed. Considering what she'd learned from Locke's conversation with Lord Hannaford and her cousins, it all made more sense than she liked. She paused when that terrible vision enveloped her, feeling nearly disembodied, as if she were hovering above the men and watching them do their wickedness. Slowly the finer details began to fall into place.

"They wanted me to admit my father and brothers were spies. I couldn't fathom such a thing." She hadn't known it was true then, even if she knew it now. "Father and Lord Christian were peers of the realm, and Mr. Collin had bought his commission and was with the army in Portugal. The monsters demanded I give them the information my father had sent from Europe for His Majesty. I'd received nothing from him beyond simple letters of love and encouragement. How could I tell them something I neither knew nor believed?"

She paused to inhale a shuddering breath. To listen to those faraway shadow-voices.

"One of the scoundrels sounded disenchanted, muttered to the gentleman that he believed I was telling the truth. The gentleman told them to go after my mother then; she must have the information if I didn't. The second scoundrel laughed, insisted there was no possibility 'a woman so inclined to gossip as Lady Whitton' would be trusted with such important matters as—" Bethany halted, the words clinging to the tip of her tongue.

Of a sudden, the words burned their way through her mind like flaming arrows. She remembered! And if what she'd heard was true, then—.

"A list! A list of men who were close to the Prince Regent ... but wanted him." She gasped. "They want him dead! Lord Locke, that list, wherever it is, unveils a plot against Prince George!"

Locke obviously hadn't expected this revelation. She knew from his conversation with the Camerfield men he'd thought the conspiracy involved Bonaparte.

"I don't understand," she said. "If the list was lost, weren't they free of discovery? It's been sixteen months since they kidnapped me. Why would they come after me again now?"

"I've no idea. However, one fact about subterfuge is true. Conspiracy only works if the conspirators remain anonymous and forever silent. Perhaps one of them threatened blackmail over the others. Mayhap new evidence arose that again endangered them or made them believe you had the information after all."

Bethany's mind still whirled. "I recall something else. Before the gentleman left me to them, he threatened the others, told them 'keep their traps shut,' reminded them that the people on that list were paying them and they dared not forget it. Then he added, 'The One'—and he emphasized it that way, as if he were referring to the man in charge—'The One has spent years building a reputation that will protect him and the plot from discovery. No one would ever suspect him and therefore the rest of us, unless you fools grow loose tongues. And if you do, you'll pay for it. Now, get it done.'"

"But they couldn't," Locke murmured, rising slowly to his feet, "because you didn't know what they thought you knew."

Locke's voice faded from Bethany's awareness, her thoughts pulled again into the past, hating that gentleman for walking off and leaving her to animals who'd done unspeakable things to her.

"What else is there, dear heart?" Locke searched her face, challenging her to let it all out.

Bethany swallowed hard. He would shun her if she told the truth. Society would expect it of him. They would do worse to him if he didn't. She turned her back to the man she had no right to love, the man she couldn't allow to love her.

Locke drew her back against him, wrapping his arms around her and whispering over her shoulder, "You can tell me anything, my love. If you are not strong enough to bear it, I will share the burden. Tell me what happened next."

"I—I fainted, after all they'd done to me. Lady Camille said the kidnappers took me to the Whitton townhouse stable afterwards, although I don't remember it, but I faintly recall her taking care of me in what I realized later was an inn. She and the twins were doing their best to protect my reputation—or at least to pretend that I had one to protect. I was delirious and needed a place to recover where others wouldn't overhear what they called 'my fevered rantings' and where I could heal enough to go home without having to admit the debacle to my mother. They say I healed, and I have scars to prove it. But in my heart...."

"You're courageous, my sweet. And nothing less. When I get the chance, I'll hunt down the swine and skin them alive."

A grim smile touched her lips.

"But I know that isn't what's troubling you the most. You've left some of the story untold. Infection festers inside of us, dearest, and only if we lay it open do we have a chance to heal. If you cannot say the words, then perhaps you can let me say them for you."

Bethany trembled and tears again burned her eyes. "I don't think I can stand it." She choked when flashes of grotesque images assailed her, the fear and anger roiling in her gut. She heard her own voice, floating through the distance from past to present, begging them to stop, to let her go.

"They hurt you in the worst way a man can hurt a woman, didn't they?" Locke said gruffly, and Bethany could hear tears in his voice. He knew that she was tainted, ruined.

"No man will ever want me," she whispered. "How can I blame them?"

His hands turned her around and she found his incredible dark blue eyes not only filled with tears, but also brimming with a wondrous blend of compassion and love.

"I cannot pretend it doesn't trouble me, Sweetheart, but these were evil men. Evil men do evil things and leave behind broken hearts and a broken world. The ones injured are not the guilty parties. I love you, you know, and want to share my life with you."

Her tears turned to quiet sobs, and he wrapped her in his arms and held her gently. When her cries calmed, he offered his kerchief and smiled as she dried her face.

"You're beautiful even when your nose is red," he said, chuckling with her.

"I love you so much it hurts, my lord, but I have no right—"

He stopped her with a kiss, at first gentle and then more insistent. Her heart swelled, glorying in the feel of it.

"You are my wife, my dearest Bethany," he murmured against her lips. "You have every right. I am your husband, and I want you, I need you, and if you will allow it, it is my right to love you back. It is *our* right, and no one else has the power to take it from us. Everything I have, everything I am, is yours forever if you will take it."

Could she believe it? Did she dare? She was hardly whole.

The hope in his eyes captivated her. There was nothing anyone else could do to take that away from her. It would take time for her heart to heal but she could. It would take patience, but nothing could mend her wounds better than the love of an understanding man. The love of this man.

Everything about him enticed her. His beautiful dark blue eyes, the dimples that framed his heartbreaking smile. The breadth of his shoulders, the strength of his arms, the faint masculine scent of his skin and his soap and his cologne.

She pressed her lips to his, glorying in the taste of his kiss, first tender, and then moving over hers with a hunger that set her every nerve ending on fire. His hands enchanted her body, sending heat racing over her skin and filling her with a passion that throbbed deep within her core and demanded satisfaction. His hope became hers, and it reassured her that tonight they would fill each other's needs, and it would be the most beautiful, most wonderful night of their lives.

* * *

The Countess of Locke spent two glorious nights and one day with her beloved husband before he again journeyed to London.

177

The nights that followed left Bethany alone and victim to her old nightmares. On the third night, she awoke with a start, having to light her lamp to chase away the demons. Catching her breath and wiping beads of perspiration from her brow, she propped herself against her pillows and pondered the dream. Unlike those night terrors that had tormented her before marrying Locke, these newer ones had teased her about the identity of the cultured man who'd given her over to her kidnappers.

Tonight, however, her imagination had riveted on the other man in the shadows of Almack's veranda. She wondered if he had more to do with her abduction than she'd realized. Despite the briefness of the tête-à-tête between the two men, she was beginning to question whether he'd masterminded the whole thing. Unfortunately, no matter how long she mulled over the details, she couldn't see the man's face.

Sighing, she threw aside the covers and paced the room. Praying for inspiration, she pondered what message her father could have given her— and how? She'd put all of her belongings away after the vandalism and couldn't see that searching through them again would make any difference. Besides, her jewelry box, the likeliest object she believed might contain some secret, had been left in London along with most of her more valuable jewelry or baubles.

She paused when she thought about everything she had brought home, most of which had come from her father. How could she figure out which one, if any, was the answer?

Wandering to her dressing table, she pulled the key from its hiding place behind the mirror and unlocked the drawer in which she'd placed the jewelry. She considered the few pairs of earrings and necklaces, a couple of pins and broaches lying there. Some she'd had for years. The most recent gift?

Her gaze settled on the charm bracelet her father had supposedly sent from Belgium. From Portugal, instead? She'd not had the courage to confess her eavesdropping on the conversation between her husband, cousins, and uncle in London, something she was determined to rectify when Locke returned, as well as asking questions of her own.

Most of the correspondence she and her mother had received from Mr. Collin in those last few months had come to Bethany, with individual sealed missives addressed to others tucked inside the main envelope. The bracelet Lady Katherine had handed to her after opening a missive from Lord Whitton, saying he'd wanted Bethany to enjoy the trinket. Bethany knew nothing about the piece. Her father normally gave her documents that signified the history, the designer, and the value of his gifts, and it was odd that he hadn't done so with this one.

She lifted it and toyed with the charms, remembering her amusement at the idioms her father had had inscribed on them. The pictures, simple sketches really, had never made sense to her. They were curious but had nothing to do with either the wording on the opposite side or anything related to Bethany's interests.

Taking it to her lamp, she painstakingly examined each charm. With no connection between picture and word, she grew even more puzzled.

She tried reading the words both forwards and backwards, or jumping every other word as Collin had taught her when they'd written secret messages to each other as children. Twice she had an odd feeling she was on to something but couldn't quite bring it together, which, of course, persuaded her to believe she must be grasping at straws.

"Alright then, what about the pictures?"

That made less sense, with no two of them having any similarity. Then she paused, leaning closer to the light. On the charm she was examining, she could see that each portion of the sketch of a crown was made up of a string of numbers. The number six.

Was there a message here after all? Her stomach clenched from both excitement and fear. But how to sort it out? She had no key to solve it, if it were.

Unfastening it, she laid the bracelet on her lamp table, directly under the lamp's yellow light. She faced all of the charms with the pictures upward. Her pulse sped up when she noticed that of the dozen charms, every other one had a string of numbers on it, like the crown, but they weren't in numerical order. The crown was in the center, the number one to the far right, the number two the second to the left of the crown. Still, on those charms, every tiny, engraved picture bore a string of numbers. She couldn't imagine what it would have taken to create any one of them, let alone twelve of them pleasing to the eye.

She yawned, fatigue dampening her curiosity. Flipping the charms over, she read the idioms, but again found no clue to what they meant beyond their obvious messages.

Still, something about the bracelet unsettled her. Considering all she had suffered, she wouldn't take chances. She would show it to Locke as soon as he returned from London.

Replacing it in the drawer, Bethany climbed into bed and doused the lamp, grateful to at last find peace in sleep.

* * *

Lord Locke arrived home the next day, and Bethany felt as if she could breathe again. When the servants were not about, the earl took advantage and kissed his wife until her toes curled. When they were nearby, he and his countess chattered enthusiastically about the estate's undertakings in his absence, Locke's activities in London, and about news of the outside world.

"I've something to share with you," she said at last, when she was sure Locke wouldn't mind humoring her. "Please come to my room."

"Most willingly," he grinned, laughing when she pushed his arm in censure.

"The servants might hear."

"Let them. I'm not concerned they might decide we like each other."

Bethany laughed and scurried upstairs, Locke trailing. When she turned back from her dressing table, she handed him the bracelet. Puzzled, he draped its featherweight over his fingers as if he wasn't sure what to do with it.

"Come to the window. You need to see this."

With the lighting better there, Bethany pointed out what she had discovered. Her smile faded as she saw the look of shock that passed over her husband's face.

* * *

Locke stared at the evidence before him, his heart taking leaping bounds in his chest. Why had he not paid better attention to this bracelet before? Careful perusal assured him he had neither the time nor the expertise to decipher the code, but it was, surely, a code.

"You said your father sent it from Belgium, did you not?" He suspected it was what Whitton had sent from Portugal, of course.

"That's what my mother told me. It puzzled me that *she* gave it to me. My father and brothers had been sending their packages to me for some time, to deliver to the rest of the family. But Father had just left for Belgium and I didn't understand why he would send something for me to my mother. For some reason, I'm persuaded that this may be what my kidnappers were looking for."

Locke laced his fingers into his forelock and pushed it back from his brow, his mind spinning with all the ramifications.

"I think you may be right, my dear. Might I borrow it? Not for long, but I'm acquainted with someone who could look it over for me."

Lady Bethany hesitated, and he knew that while she wanted the mystery solved as much as he did, she dreaded having to give up this last reminder of her father. Then she nodded.

"Of course. If it's the evidence they were looking for, I'd rather it serve its purpose—and that it not be on my person."

"Thank you, my darling," he said, dropping the bracelet into his jacket pocket. He would have Seaworth take it to his London connection as soon as he could saddle a horse.

Noting a troubled look on her face, he offered her his arms and hugged her gently. "Something else is on your mind," he said. And it had nothing to do with sweet kisses and words of endearment.

"Yes," she admitted. "I have … I have another confession to make."

His heart tripped over the meaning of those words. "Remember you can tell me anything."

"Yes, I know. But that doesn't mean you'll like it."

He chuckled. Put that way, he probably wouldn't. Then she began, painting a picture of her standing outside his London library door, listening to the discussion between her husband, her cousins and her uncle about how her father and brothers had died … and everything that went with it.

* * *

Warm kisses awakened Bethany, forcing her eyes to open and adore the sweet smile that greeted her.

"Wake up, sleepyhead. I'm shocked you've let the rooster beat you out of bed again."

Bethany giggled. "Not by much, and he didn't spend the last week sharing my bed with you."

"I hope not," Locke said. "I wouldn't have enjoyed that at all. I've some news, sweetheart. Are you awake enough to hear it?"

Bethany blinked at him warily. "What's wrong?"

"Nothing. Simply a message. The twins are bringing Lady Camille to spend the next couple of weeks with you."

Bethany's smile vanished. "You're leaving again."

"Not right off. I just thought you might prefer to greet our guests in something other than your nightdress."

Bethany grabbed her pillow and hit Locke hard with it, squealing when he chased her across the bed and out of it, following her around it until he caught her.

"They'll arrive in two hours," Locke said between toe-curling kisses. "Melissa has your bath ready for you."

"Thank heavens. I need a bath more than I need clothes."

He laughed and kissed her again but insisted she take advantage of both the bath and her wardrobe.

When Lady Camille arrived, it was a joyous reunion, although Bethany resented that irksome, silent request the twins sent Locke. They needed a personal audience with his lordship. Again. She was grateful her sweet husband insisted they all admire the nearly-completed manor first—which they did with alacrity—and afterward share tea.

They'd barely finished when the contractor's wagons arrived for their final day of work on the manor and to deliver the materials for Lady

Bethany's room. Locke and the twins headed off to Locke's study, while Bethany and Lady Camille retreated to the cool of the rear veranda. Lady Camille made a great show of leaning into Bethany's face and squinting at her.

"You seem different," she said. "What's happened?"

"Different? In what way?"

Lady Camille seated herself in the chair beside Bethany, her gaze intent. "You look ... happy!"

"Are you saying I've always looked unhappy?"

"No. I'd say you look terrific." She grinned, her bottom lip again caught between her teeth. "I think my closest friend and only cousin has found love at last."

Bethany opened her mouth to deny it but her flaming cheeks gave her away. "You're incorrigible, you know. Am I not allowed to keep anything private?"

"No. You must tell me all about it, Love."

Bethany's smile faded. She'd very much like sharing her deepest hopes and darkest secrets with Lady Camille, but there were some things she still really preferred to keep to herself.

CHAPTER 22

"We broke the rules coming to you first," Lord Matthew muttered, drawing something from his pocket and setting it on Locke's desk. "We should have taken it straight to the Iron Duke. We just thought we owed you first, considering."

The earl eyed Bethany's bracelet, inhaling deep against what he did not doubt was the worst of news. "You broke the code?"

"Yes," Mr. Nicolas replied. "It was one of the most convoluted we've seen in ages, combining a portion of the code you did recognize with a mixture of letters, symbols and a numbering system none of us did. It led from the front to the back of each charm, in a clockwise circle half a dozen times around the bracelet. Took our best men night and day for six days to unravel it. Lady Bethany certainly couldn't have made sense of it."

"Incredible," Locke said, taking his seat behind his desk. He opened the clasp on the charm bracelet, laid it out before him, and fingered the charms until they all lay with the pictures face up. Mr. Nicolas set a slip of paper on the desk, bearing the key to the code on the front, the answers on the back.

Locke toyed with the code until impatience got the best of him. Flipping the sheet over, he felt gut-punched when he read the message's details and the list of five names written in Lord Matthew's curling script. The sixth, couched within the inscribed crown, was that of the Prince Regent.

"Good law," he muttered, digging his knuckles into his throbbing temples. "I'd prayed this wasn't true."

"You suspected him, though?" Lord Matthew pressed his finger to the man whose name topped the list.

"Yes. I only prayed I was wrong. This is too hard to bear."

Lord Matthew and Mr. Nicolas shared one of their bookend looks, an exchange that went beyond words.

"In all due respect, it will come harder to some than to others," Lord Matthew murmured. "In truth, I'm not sure which is worse, having been played as fools, or having to ruin people's lives fixing it."

"I don't want to know the truth," Locke said, lifting the bracelet. "Not if it means this."

"A bit late for that," Mr. Nicolas said sadly. "And we still have to tell the higher powers what we've discovered, what we plan to do about it, and face whatever comes of it."

Locke saw the pain on his cousins-in-law's faces and sighed. "You must run our plan past Wellesley, of course, but I have a feeling, under the circumstances, he'll approve."

"In all likelihood," Lord Matthew said, returning the offending jewelry to his pocket. "We should leave immediately."

"Not so fast. I have some questions for you boys, and you're not leaving this time until you've given me the answers."

Apprehension marred their countenances, but they took a seat at his request and listened as the earl painted a picture for them of the night Lady Bethany had been kidnapped—not as they knew it, but as she had lived it.

"You have no idea how much I want to hurt you both for deceiving me the way you did," he warned them. "The least you owe me is your side of the story."

Abashed, they offered muttered apologies and then took turns revealing the whole tale and what the twins had now finally pieced together with the key to the bracelet's code.

Only three of the men on the list had been at Almack's that night. The other two, Baron Gladwell and Sir Shreeves, close friends, spent the night at White's. Locke was familiar with both of them and agreed with the twins that, without the acumen to orchestrate a conspiracy, they were a part of it but not in charge. Elderly Lord Perry died from a weak heart only two weeks following the assault on Lady Bethany. He certainly wasn't in charge now. The cultured gentleman whom they believed had taken Lady Bethany onto Almack's veranda was one Viscount Beckwood, a second cousin by marriage to one of the Grand Dukes. Naturally Lady Bethany would have trusted him. He was a powerful man and no one would suspect him. She was probably honored he invited her to walk with him.

Which meant, without question, that the first name on the list, the second gentleman at Almack's, the man Lady Bethany saw in the shadows, was most certainly their ringleader.

"We received an urgent message at Almack's near ten-thirty that night, just before Almack's patrons served supper," Lord Matthew explained, "from the groundskeeper at Lord Whitton's townhouse. He insisted one of us come posthaste but to not let on something terrible had happened. Nicolas pretended a headache and left."

"Seems the stable dog's barking led the groundskeeper to the stable," Mr. Nicolas said, "where he found Beth, injured and unconscious. He was quite fond of our cousin and thankfully forswore his silence in honor of her, otherwise her reputation would have been ruined. She was in a bad way, but I dared not trust anyone outside the family to care for her, not even either of our townhouse's servants. Thankfully, our parents were on another trip to meet with doctors and we had our townhouse to ourselves. So, I sent a note posthaste to Matthew hinting what was afoot."

"Supper had just been announced," Lord Matthew said, "but I hadn't yet gone inside when I received Nicolas's message. I pulled my sister aside and whispered what I could of the trouble at Whitton. Lady Camille was most dutiful, managed to keep her composure as she approached Lady Katherine and claimed not feeling well either, said I was taking her to our townhouse, and that Lady Bethany had agreed to accompany her and stay the night with her."

"While our aunt—who later told us she enjoyed herself 'til early morning—was kept busy, we rushed Lady Bethany to a favorite inn out of town, one we use on assignment, where we pretended we'd had too much to drink and needed lodgings for us and our 'lady friends'. The next morning we left Lady Bethany in Lady Camille's care, reporting to the innkeeper that my 'sweetheart' had taken ill—the only one of us who truly was ill. We hired a doctor for her whom we knew would keep his mouth shut, and then returned to London, to look for clues as to her assault. Later we learned the extent of her injuries and were bowled over by it. Broken ribs, multitudes of cuts and bruises, dozens of burns large and small, shallow knife wounds, and...." He left the rest unspoken.

"The next afternoon, while Nicolas was trying to find out anything he could, I reported to Aunt Katherine that Lady Bethany had tired of the *ton*, and on the spur of the moment she and Lady Camille had decided to head for our country estate—another deception, of course. Lady Katherine was miffed, but to our relief said she'd planned another week's stay in London in the company of friends and had no intentions of following Lady Bethany home so soon. It meant we could return Beth to health and get her home with no one the wiser."

"Then four days after Almack's, the news arrived of Mr. Collin's death, in Portugal, followed two days later by word of the accident that took Lord Whitton and Lord Christian's lives, supposedly in Belgium. We know this was fabricated now, but we didn't then. Our aunt took it so hard she was too distraught even to write and unable to travel for weeks after. As far as she knew, Lady Bethany was dealing with the loss at home, with Lady Camille as her comfort. They were still at the inn, of course, but Beth was recovered enough, we had to break the news to her."

"I think she reacted worse to the deaths than what happened to her," Mr. Nicolas took up the story. "Everything was in shambles for a while.

Her sorrow. Getting her home before Aunt Katherine arrived. Fending off visitors. Refusing them audience because she was too grief-stricken.

"For whatever reason, the blokes left our cousin's face untouched, which did make things easier for her on the surface. But her heart was wounded, and holding the atrocity so deep inside made it worse for her in some ways. We tried to find clues to her abduction, but when she forbade us telling anyone else about it, not even the authorities, our hands were tied.

"It was heartbreaking to see her coming unhinged anytime she found herself in tight spaces, or if someone touched her unexpectedly. Of course, her deepest fear was marrying. She couldn't hide the truth from her husband. If he rejected her or resorted to public humiliation, her reputation would be in shreds. She withdrew from the world of courtship and announced to the three of us she'd prefer to remain a spinster the rest of her life than take that risk."

"Do you blame her?" Locke muttered.

"Never," Lord Matthew replied. "But we did the best we could under the circumstances."

"It may be small consolation, but at least they did not get her with child," Mr. Nicolas murmured. "You have no idea how greatly she feared that, and how relieved she was when it didn't happen."

"You're sure no one else knows?"

"We told our father," Lord Matthew admitted. "Before Lady Bethany forbade us telling anyone. We needed his help to find the culprits—and to keep another eye on her in case they ever tried again. Neither Lady Katherine nor our mother knows the truth, and they mustn't ever. It's too late.

"Marc, mourning kept Lady Bethany's suitors at arm's length, but afterward, when the estate began to fail, Lady Katherine pushed her hard to marry. It's been a dark time for her. We suspect you two have feelings for each other. If so, we applaud it. But. You must be more cautious than ever around her. You know you're forbidden to tell her who you are."

"That presents a problem. I do need to warn you that my indomitable wife admitted to eavesdropping on more than one of our conversations."

"What?" The twins chimed together.

He related what she had confessed, watching a blend of guilt and shock mar their countenances.

"She still doesn't know everything, especially regarding the mastermind of the plot against the Prince Regent, but she knows enough. If we keep anything from her, it must be because it is better for her not to know.

"I've never loved anyone as much as I love Lady Bethany, and she returns my feelings, and that's all I'll say for now. But I'm not sure how long it will take me to forgive the two of you for the imbroglio you tossed me into with her. Knowing the truth would have changed everything."

"But you might not have—"

"I would have. I swore to protect her in her father's place—and in his memory. You sold me short in not allowing me to make the decision fully informed. It would have spared me confusion and protected her from my mistakes. Please believe me when I tell you that if either of you ever withholds important information like that from me again, you may or may not live to regret it."

The twins nodded, properly chastened and convinced of his sincerity.

* * *

Lady Camille hardly heeded her brothers' leaving, but Bethany sensed the edge of melancholy that went with them. One glance at Locke, whose mask had slipped, told her that something troublesome had passed between the three men, something he wouldn't—couldn't?—share. Locke gave her a tenuous smile when he again excused himself to his study to prepare for another trip he would soon need to make to London. He again took his noon meal locked up there.

Thus, Lady Camille's raptures over her wedding plans engulfed the bulk of Bethany's attention.

"Mum insists we take our time, wants the finest wedding imaginable next spring. I expected Scarbreigh to protest. He's old enough I'm sure he'd like to see the birth of his first child before he grows long in the tooth, but he agreed with her. Said he didn't want me to regret a single detail. You ought to hear what he says regarding the gossip around town, now that we've announced our engagement. I empathize even more with what you endured, Lady Bethany. Kind wishes and sage advice notwithstanding, the daggers and cat's claws could pierce the most stalwart heart."

Bethany chuckled her understanding. She still worried about Lord Scarbreigh's loyalty, but there was nothing to do except to pray for them and hope for the best, and that she did fervently.

The next day, Lady Camille received a note from her father, informing her that he'd learned of another physician in Harrogate whose excellence was all the rage. He was taking Lady Eva there immediately for another hopeful consultation. After that, a note came from Scarbreigh, stating he had pressing matters with a fishing fleet he owned near the Thames docks and from there would travel to Scotland to oversee his ancestral property's preparations for harvest. The twins and Lord Locke made a number of trips to and from London and exchanged several posts over the next two weeks, Bethany relieved when the earl came home to her quickly each time—unlike going to the Continent or who knew what other destinations he might have chosen.

With Scarbreigh and her family away, and having no particular plans for the remainder of August and into September, Lady Camille offered to remain at Moorewood indefinitely. Bethany happily accepted. Then, a post came from Lady Katherine, announcing her plans to come for a three day stay the second week of September.

Excited by the prospect, Bethany proposed arranging a small party to welcome her. Lady Camille suggested they make it a surprise. Locke teased Bethany that he'd been on the verge of planning some sort of route if she hadn't and gave his hearty stamp of approval, along with a handful of sealed invitations for Bethany to send off with her own.

* * *

The dowager countess arrived in complete awe of Moorewood and beyond delighted to greet a few old friends who insisted on dropping by during the day—although thankfully none of them let slip tomorrow night's surprise festivities. To Bethany, Lady Katherine seemed more herself than she had since the loss of the Lord Whitton and her sons. She pricked her ears at local rumors, gasped at scandals, and teased Lady Camille about her transports over Scarbreigh. The countess also cheerfully joined in their games, their walks, and a ride across the meadows.

The next day, the day of the surprise party, Mr. Treadwell delivered another missive to Bethany before Lady Katherine came down for breakfast.

"Just delivered by post, my lady," the butler said.

"Thank you, Mr. Treadwell. Oh, it's from Scarbreigh."

"What?" Lady Camille objected. "Why would he send you a post? He's aware I'm here. Why wouldn't he address me?"

Bethany chuckled. "You're wearing the wrong shade of green, cousin. I'm Moorewood's mistress. He's merely following convention and accepted my invitation to the party. He'll arrive this afternoon."

Lady Camille squealed with delight and began chattering—as if she'd lost her senses—about so many notions at once Bethany could make neither heads or nor tails of it, other than for understanding that her cousin was thrilled to be able to show off her fiancé to Moorewood's guests.

Locke joined the three women at luncheon, where Bethany informed him of Scarbreigh's visit.

"I'm glad he accepted the invitation. Will he stay the night?"

"The next two nights, unless you object."

"Of course not. He's always welcome. Please forgive me for not offering you the best of company today, ladies. I've got a lot on my mind. I promise not to carry a long face to our evening's entertainments."

Bethany nodded, concerned for him. That long face had grown even longer the last few days, his mask seemingly forgotten.

* * *

Locke returned upstairs, leaving the women to greet Scarbreigh when he arrived. The marquess was as animated and jovial as ever, his wit and good mood quickly putting the three women to the blush and entertaining them throughout the day.

Lady Katherine was astounded when her guests arrived at once that evening for the party. At first embarrassed and then thrilled, she quickly became the belle of her own party.

When Locke joined them, the scowls and brooding meditations had disappeared. He'd apparently found his mask again.

"Would you be wounded if I gave your mother the first dance?" Locke whispered in Bethany's ear, daring to nuzzle her shoulder and send a shiver trailing towards her toes.

She craned her neck back to look up at him. "It would mean a great deal to her for the first dance to be with her esteemed son-in-law."

Locke grinned and winked at her, ambling off to intercept the countess as the music began.

"Love becomes you, Lady Locke."

Bethany turned around to see Scarbreigh, whose smug grin was meant to annoy her, standing there. She smiled back, refusing to let him get under her skin. "Good evening, my lord. My cousin outshines me, you know."

He leveled his gaze on Lady Camille, dressed in a silk gown a shade darker than her fetching blonde curls, being whirled around the dance floor in the arms of a giddy youth with bright red cheeks.

"She's a lovely, gentle creature. A man couldn't ask for a truer woman." He then watched Locke, whose elegant dancing had the Dowager Lady Whitton's face all aglow. "Locke's natural magnetism puzzles me. He's never had to work at getting or keeping the ladies' interest as I have. And yet, he avoids his admirers. Rather like you, my lady. You get on so famously. Care to share the secret? I want only the best for Lady Camille. She deserves it."

"Scarbreigh, you sound so unsure of yourself. You've been one of the most sought after men within the peerage for years."

His smile faded. "Have I? Seems to me people want little more of me than my money or my title. I adore Lady Camille for loving me for myself. It's hard to find such a woman. You were her only rival, my dear.

I've been fond of you for a long time, even if I wasn't good enough for you."

Bethany's heart thundered in her chest, both at his admission and having her suspicions confirmed. Scarbreigh loved Lady Camille, but it was Bethany he'd wanted.

"That's not true, my lord. I was never the woman for you. We're too insufferably stubborn to get along with each other, and if you've found a way to see past that, then you're a better person than I."

Scarbreigh chuckled and shook his head. "Kind even in crushing a man's heart. You needn't fear, Cousin-to-be. I do adore our dear Lady Camille and will do all I can to make her happy. Ah, good, the number has ended. Excuse me. I'd like to claim my fiancée for the next dance since I was too slow for the first. I'm also determined to keep her away from the punch if I can."

Bethany laughed and bid him good luck in all his endeavors.

Locke bowed to Lady Whitton and handed her to an older gentleman with steel-gray hair just as Mr. Treadwell appeared at the blue salon's open doorway. Locke went to hear the butler's news and then left the room with him.

Curiosity, and more, had Bethany following. She hated that too-familiar gut feeling that something was wrong and resented it, tonight of all nights. She'd barely peaked into the hallway toward Locke's study when she caught sight of Lord Matthew and Mr. Nicolas in guarded conversation with Locke and Mr. Treadwell, their expressions far too serious for such an auspicious night. She shrank from their line of sight but when they'd slipped inside the study, she wrestled with the temptation to eavesdrop again.

Her conscience won. She didn't need another round of eavesdropping to confess. Locke would confide in her if or when he felt it was right. Until then, her responsibility lay with her mother and her guests.

The green salon boasted half a dozen tables for card games, and Bethany took the opportunity to visit with the several guests there. Eventually she joined a lone matron who needed three more people for the necessary foursome. Scarbreigh arrived and sat down opposite her, grinning impudently and challenging her to beat him.

At that moment, Locke ambled into the room, the twins on his heels. The earl rested one hand on Bethany's shoulder and winked at her, holding his other hand out to her in a bunched fist.

"My apologies for interrupting, Lady Locke. You said you wanted to wear this to tonight's festivities. It seems you forgot it." He slipped that object into her hands, cool and silvery, and she gasped when she realized what it was.

"My bracelet! Oh, thank you. I did forget about it." She paused when he offered to put it on for her, thinking it seemed different, but catching the odd look on his face she bit her tongue. She would ask later. "Will you play cards with us?" she said instead.

Locke shook his head in regret. "I'm afraid I promised Lady Reynolds a turn on the dance floor."

"I'm determined to entertain my aunt," Mr. Nicolas said, grinning at Scarbreigh, "and Lord Matthew insists he has to do his best to talk Lady Camille out of marrying Scarbreigh."

Scarbreigh laughed with them. When the others left, he said, "I really do idolize that bracelet. Are you sure you won't let me borrow it? My London jeweler actually had one similar. I almost purchased it for Lady Camille, with charms of my own for it. The links on this chain, however, are unique, and he'd have to see it to create anything half so delightful."

Bethany suffered a moment of weakness but realized she couldn't give in, especially if it was as important as Locke thought it might be. "I'm so sorry, my lord, but accidents—and highwaymen—can happen. Perhaps when Locke and I next visit London we could meet you at the shop and let your jeweler have a go at it."

Scarbreigh sighed and shrugged. "Well, you can't blame a man for asking, can you?"

Another gentleman joined their table, and the game began, Bethany enjoying besting the Marquess of Scarbreigh. Laughing afterward, the marquess congratulated her and excused himself, and Bethany did not see him again—or Locke or the twins, for that matter—for most of the evening as she turned to her duties as hostess.

When darkness of night crept into the dark of early morning, many of the guests began to leave, and Bethany joined Lady Camille, Lady Katherine, and Lord Locke at the front door to bid their guests farewell.

Scarbreigh and the twins joined them, just as the final guest departed, the marquess taking Camille's hand and smiling at her. Bethany couldn't help teasing the man by raising her wrist and saying, "If you'd like to examine this silly piece of jewelry in brightest daylight, I'll meet with you and Lady Camille on the veranda as soon as we arise this morning."

"Afternoon will suffice," Scarbreigh replied, grimacing. "Surely my brains would fry before two o'clock."

Camille giggled, her eyes sparkling and cheeks ruddy. Bethany feared she'd overindulged in the punch, despite everyone's efforts to thwart her. Lady Katherine, herself rosy-cheeked and exhilarated with pleasure, hugged the young women in delight.

"Thank you, my dears, for such a wonderful get-together. I'm exhausted but thrilled. We'll talk about it in detail tomorrow. Good night,

Lord Scarbreigh. I'll see Lady Camille to her room. She's had enough fun tonight."

Lady Camille laughed, blew Scarbreigh a kiss, and then mounted the stairs alongside the countess. The rest of them followed, Lord Matthew and Mr. Nicolas on either side of Scarbreigh, and then Bethany and Locke trailing behind them, arm in arm.

Bethany paused outside her room, puzzled by the concern written in Locke's eyes.

"I fear I must speak with your rapscallion cousins for a while in my study," he murmured, kissing her with something that felt like regret. "I've some trouble with a matter from London on which I need their opinions."

"Will you join me later?"

"Do you mind? I'll try not to wake you."

"I hope you do wake me," she whispered.

He laughed, kissed her quickly, and headed towards his study.

CHAPTER 23

Candlelight did little to dispel the shadows in Locke's study, or on the three men's grim faces while they talked over as many versions of their plan as they could imagine. Twenty minutes became an hour, then near an hour and a half, and Locke was exasperated by the time they'd come to the conclusion their first inclination was the best, even it was far from ideal.

"And I repeat," he said. "Lady Bethany knows too much to be left in the dark about *this*. She'll be safer if she knows what's coming."

Lord Matthew sighed and scratched his head roughly, like a boy fresh out of bed. "You'd be violating orders."

"But if she's hidden the bracelet so he can't steal it, he could go out of control. I won't chance it."

Mr. Nicolas grinned impudently. "If you're in bed with her, he's not likely to cause a ruckus."

"If he's thwarted, he could get desperate. I'd rather not get shot."

"Then you should take your lady into your bedchamber," Mr. Nicolas said with amusement. "If he sneaks into her empty room and finds the bracelet easily enough, he'll take what he wants and go."

"Lady Bethany would have too many questions if she saw my room, and then I'd have to tell her anyway."

Lord Matthew snorted quiet laughter. "He has a point, brother."

Mr. Nicolas sighed and shrugged. "I'm still disputing the idea that we need to trap our quarry with the bracelet. Haven't we enough evidence to arrest him without it?"

"In my opinion, yes, but Westminster doesn't agree. They consider the bracelet the linchpin," Locke said. "And my lady needs to know."

"It's your neck on the line, Locke. You'd best go now. Our 'friend' has been most dutiful tonight, a sign he's not worried. Might mean he's not planning to move tonight, but maybe not."

"My point exactly," Locke said, coming to his feet. "If he does act, my wife is in jeopardy."

"Let's pray for some sleep," Mr. Nicolas murmured. "Just a little of it. And for a private arrest when the sun rises."

"Mostly I want to avoid a ghastly scene," Lord Matthew said. "It would worsen matters exponentially."

Mr. Nicolas rose and stretched out some kinks. "The reason our boys from London arrived after the party was in full swing, to avoid anyone observing and making a scene. Their numbers will also strengthen the men Locke has had secretly patrolling his borders since Lady Bethany arrived. Oh, by the way, Locke, Seaworth decided to put the detachment up in your long-row bunk house. A bit more comfortable than the hayloft."

"Hmmm, yes, but I hope the watch keeps an eagle eye out. Men in the loft might hear something. Maybe not so easy from the bunk house. If anything goes wrong, we'll need help quickly."

The twins agreed, even while all three of them felt suitably confident. Locke doused the lantern, and the three men returned to their rooms.

* * *

Bethany left her candle burning when she climbed into bed. Exhausted, she quickly drifted off to sleep. Another nightmare assailed her, however, and she came awake shuddering. This time she'd caught the barest glimpse of the man in the shadows at Almack's. The fellow whispering to ... Viscount Beckwood.

Viscount Beckwood! She remembered his name! The monster who'd coaxed her onto the veranda, where the gentleman in the shadows had shared some private words with him. The gentleman departed and Beckwood persuaded her to walk with him. She flinched when the images transformed into the horrors of her kidnapping.

Glancing towards the candle on her night table, she saw from the taper's length she'd not slept more than an hour. The blanket snagged on her bracelet when she turned to her side, and she gently freed the jewelry from it, raising it to admire the metallic sparkle of candlelight on the links. Whatever it was that was different about it disturbed her, which in turn had made her want to wear it to bed tonight, so that she wouldn't forget to ask Locke about it.

She jumped when a soft knock came at her door. Locke? No. He'd enter through the door between their rooms, not the hall, and she doubted he'd bother with knocking. Only a moment later, the tap came again.

Rising and tossing on her robe, Bethany took her candle and went to crack the door open.

"Lady Bethany. I'm sorry to disturb you," a familiar voice whispered. Bethany opened the door a little more and saw Scarbreigh standing there, hair rumpled and face drawn. "I'm afraid I must beg your help."

"Scarbreigh! What's wrong?"

Scarbreigh shifted from one foot to the other, then admitted, "Nothing earth shattering, but embarrassing for Lady Camille."

"What?

"I was just awakened by the sound of an angel singing. Thought it was a dream, and then I roused enough to deduce that the noise was outside my window. It faces the stables, you know, and I got up to see someone serenading the stars in the middle of the night."

Bethany groaned. "Lady Camille had too much to drink after all, didn't she?" It wasn't like her cousin to indulge as much as she had lately. They would have to talk about it tomorrow.

"Yes, I fear so. I can't go after her alone. Wouldn't be proper, but I don't want anyone else to catch her. For her sake, of course."

"Of course," Bethany replied, thinking it edged indecency for her to go with Scarbreigh alone in the middle of the night. Should she? How fearful she'd grown this last year. Wonderful things had happened to her, but so had terrible ones, and they made her doubt even her old friend. But what about Lady Camille? Her cousin needed help.

Only these circumstances persuaded her. "I'll change my clothes."

Choosing haste over propriety, she donned her tunic, riding breeches and a thick sweater for the chilly night, clothes that didn't sport myriads of buttons and would require Melissa's help. London might be scandalized, but she just wanted to collect Lady Camille.

Scarbreigh's brows furrowed when Bethany joined him, but he made no comment about her wardrobe. He'd seen her this way many times in her childhood. Noting her bracelet, he said, "Must mean a lot to you if you sleep with it."

She smiled. "Proof I'm far too sentimental."

She glanced towards Locke's study and saw the faint gleam of lamplight under the door. Her husband and the twins must still be in conference. She was tempted to knock on his door, or at least leave him a note, but it would only slow her down and endanger Lady Camille's reputation.

Still, she questioned her decision all the way to the stallion barn, praying they would collect Lady Camille quickly. A mere sliver of moon was near setting, leaving faint starlight to light their way. Rather than wearing her boots, for the sake of haste she'd pulled on her slippers, and now the gravel stabbed her scarred feet and occasional rocks twisted her ankles. Thankfully Scarbreigh took her arm to steady her.

Bethany paused when they came in sight of the stable yard. "I don't see her. Or hear her. You said she was standing here?"

"Yes." He pointed towards the window that was his. "My room's up there."

"You're sure she was here?"

"Absolutely."

Foreboding crawled up Bethany's spine, cold and prickly. "My lord, I'm going back inside. I want to knock on Lady Camille's door. Perhaps she returned to bed when you weren't looking."

"No. I saw her out here," he insisted, gripping her arm too tight.

Bethany shook her head. "Scarbreigh? Please let go of me."

"I still need your help, Lady Bethany," he pleaded. "Look, maybe she's gone inside the barn. She might have gotten confused or maybe fallen asleep in one of the stalls. She'll scandalize anyone who finds her. Check it out with me, will you?"

The worry in his voice made Bethany fear for her cousin.

Scarbreigh unlatched the stable door and pushed it open, creaking softly. Her breath caught when lantern light eked out, buttery yellow against the shadows that hung from the rafters.

Scarbreigh nudged her inside, and then he closed the door behind them. Bethany blinked as her eyes adjusted. The long corridor stretched out before her, every stall door closed. Why? Hadn't Dimity said he left them open to allow for a breeze?

"Does Dimity usually burn a lantern all night?" Scarbreigh's near-whisper echoed her thoughts. "Not too safe, in my opinion, around hay and straw."

"I've never been here at night, but I can't imagine it." What's going on? she thought.

"Lady Camille?" She raised her voice enough to hope her cousin would hear her if she were awake. No answer.

The scent of hay and horses blended with a few equine snorts, grumbles and stomping hooves from behind the doors.

"Shall we begin the search?" Scarbreigh said. "I'll take the right hand stalls, you take the left?"

Bethany's stomach tied itself into knots. Anyone could hide behind closed doors. Anything could happen inside a darkened stall. Dear Lord, what if someone has kidnapped Lady Camille, as they had her, what seemed a lifetime ago? What if they were lying in wait for Bethany?

"I won't do it without a lantern," she insisted, although what she really wanted was a gun.

"Of course, my dear," he murmured, tip-toeing up the aisle. Bethany shuddered, seeing him pass door after fastened door. Waking nightmares taunted her, of Shadow's stabbing, of Locke's assault in London. Of flying arrows and overturned furniture and monsters in the dark.

Scarbreigh reached for the lantern and more images jumped into her mind: of men in forest green waistcoats; Locke, his head bruised and aching. Her aunt and uncle breaking the news of the attack on Whitton. Broken shelves. Shattered Dresden dolls.

Bethany telling Scarbreigh all about them at Carlton House. Locke troubled by her having done so.

Scarbreigh took the lantern and carried it to her, looking her over in too familiar a way. Then he glanced left and then right at the closed doors, and the ghosts of Bethany's past welled up like evil specters, cast in the profiles Scarbreigh presented her. The shadows that defined the distinctive planes of his face triggered those hateful memories like frightened bats.

She envisioned the man at Almack's, the silhouette that had leaned towards Viscount Beckwood, whispering to him, and nodding to what Beckwood whispered back. Then the form, tall and lean, had turned and walked away, and left her to ... *them*.

Horror welled up inside of her and it was all she could do to keep from crying out in shock.

Scarbreigh! It was Scarbreigh who'd given her to the kidnappers! The realization tore her world apart.

Scarbreigh raised a brow and twisted his mouth into a smirk. "Ah, I see my beautiful Beth has had an epiphany. I knew you'd realize it sooner or later."

"You mean, about what you did to me?"

"Me? I didn't do anything to you."

His amusement made her want to strike him. "You're an animal. No gentleman could do to a woman what you ordered done to me."

The marquess's gaze hardened. "We thought you withheld important information and did whatever we needed to get it. I made sure they avoided the obvious, like your face, but personally, I don't care about scars."

"I withheld nothing from them. I knew nothing."

He barked soft laughter. "But you *have* what I wanted; it simply took happenstance to find it." He leaned down and yanked the bracelet from her wrist, ignoring her outcry of pain, and stuffed it into his pocket.

"Where's Lady Camille. If you've hurt her—"

"I assume asleep in her bed, my dear."

"You lied."

"To get you here."

"You have the bracelet. Let me go."

"Never."

A hot rock of terror dropped into her stomach. Was he going to kill her? If he took the bracelet and rid himself of the only witness to his crimes ....

Angry tears burned her eyes, and her lips trembled as she bowed her head in fear. "Please, Kirk. Let me go."

"Wish you'd accepted my proposal, my love. Would have avoided all of the rest. You just didn't understand how much I wanted you."

Bethany's head shot up. "I thought I made it quite plain that I didn't want you."

His hand flew out and slapped her cheek, staggering her back a few steps. Stars spun in her head and she shook it to clear them.

"Your first lesson in showing respect, my sweet," Scarbreigh said, strangely calm. "Be glad it was the palm of my hand. My fist would hurt far worse."

Bethany wanted to curse him but didn't dare.

"You have a lot of lessons in store for you. Consider your wardrobe. Always were a bit of a hoyden, weren't you? It was cute when you were small, but there's a time when a lady must behave like a lady. Your brothers and your father indulged you, but I'm certain a good whipping would have sufficed."

Bethany, her hand pressed to her stinging cheek, stared at him in shock. She'd never dreamed he felt this way.

"Our time runs short. If Locke comes looking for you and finds your room empty, it wouldn't bode well for either of us. I'm not so fond of your cousins, think there's something queer about them, but Locke's a dear friend, and it's simply unfortunate that he stands between me and you. He's safe if you cooperate, but mark my words, if you don't, I'll kill him."

Bethany swallowed hard. She had no doubt the Marquess of Scarbreigh would do it.

"We're headed for Whitstable. I have a fleet of cargo ships waiting for us, loaded with everything I value, and bound for the Spice Islands. I've enviable Indigo plantations there, where you'll be considered one of the richest, most beautiful women on the Islands. It's a frightfully long journey and not the best time of year to go, but that also means we're less likely to be followed."

"Whitstable?" Hadn't Scarbreigh suggested they drive there, right after the archer had tried to shoot her?

"We've no time for redundancy, dear. It's where I would have had you taken had the arrow wounded you. I'd have taken Raven and Jack and met you there. The arrow missed, but if you'd all joined me on the trip I suggested, with your cousins and your husband, you and I would have just inexplicably disappeared. As the French say, *C'est le vie*. Such is life. Things go right; things go wrong, and here we are."

He grabbed her arm and dragged her down the aisle to the stall opposite Raven's. He threw the top door open, and the marquess's sorrel gelding, Jack, thrust his head into the corridor, grumbling a soft equine greeting. Bethany's chill grew glacial at seeing the horse saddled and bridled.

"You'll be riding him. I, on the other hand." He went to Raven's stall and tossed it wide, too. The stallion's dark eyes sought Bethany. He was also readied to go. She could even see a bedroll tied to the rear of the saddle. Who had done this? She'd seen nothing of Scarbreigh during the party. Had he sneaked out here and tacked up both horses?

"I'll ride Raven. And I'll kill *him* if you give me any trouble. Now let's get on our way. We can't waste another minute."

"No," Bethany said, more tearful than belligerent. "I'm married, Kirk. I can never be yours. What about your mother? Your holdings? Your life in England?"

"Mum is a cold, selfish harridan. I don't care if she starves. I've no desire to spend my life in Newgate if I'm caught, which I fear is on the horizon. And as for marriage? I'm not one to care about the legalities. I'll have you to warm my bed and bear my children, and that's enough for me."

The barbarity of it swallowed Bethany up, like another form of torture. She couldn't bear it, but how could she stop it? Dimity's workroom was upstairs, in the loft, but he and the stablehands slept in the long-row building to the west of the stables. They had no idea what was happening here. Would Locke come to her room, or play the gentleman and sleep in his own bed tonight? She couldn't count on his help, either.

Bethany heard a soft click and nearly fainted when Scarbreigh pulled a gun from his waistband and pointed it at her. If he fired it, someone would hear it, but if he merely wounded her, he could still get her on board his horse and make off with her.

"Mount now, or I'll set the stable on fire and let the horses burn to death." He reached towards Raven, leaping back an instant later when the stallion pinned back his ears and snapped at him.

A string of profanities escaped the marquess, and he turned the gun on Bethany again. "Bring him into the aisle. Hang onto him till I board. Then open the stable door and get on Jack. You'll go out before me and head for the main road. Brisk walk only. I want to travel as quickly but as safely and quietly as possible."

Bethany reached for Raven's reins, shushing the stallion and petting his nose and then his neck as she led him out. The stallion's nerves were so taught he trembled. *You know something's wrong, don't you, Love? I don't believe he'll shoot you. He needs you. But he will hurt me. How can you help me?*

Scarbreigh pulled Jack from his stall and tossed the reins over the animal's neck. The horses now stood side by side. Scarbreigh gave Raven wide birth when he passed in front of him, his eyes narrowed and his hand tight on the gun.

At the last second, Bethany dropped the reins and screamed, *"Mezair!"* Raven squealed, rose to his hind legs and struck at Scarbreigh with his forefeet. Scarbreigh lurched away a split second before the animal's hooves could strike him, but he tripped and stumbled back, dropping the gun.

Bethany spun around and ran, leaving Raven charging after the marquess. Thundering up the ladder to the loft, she begged her eyes to adjust to the inky blackness of the space. There were two spacious windows on either side of the loft and at the near end, a door. To Dimity's workroom? She ran for it, but it was locked. Could she get out a window? They were high, but the west side window had a large trunk nestled under it. She jumped atop it, flipped the lock on the sash and strained upward. It was stuck! She wrestled with it, sliding it a bit. How far down was the ground? Fearfully far, but she'd rather jump and end with a broken leg than let his lordship Kirkwood Bannister kidnap her. Again.

She opened the window wider but panicked when she heard Scarbreigh's boots hitting the rungs of the ladder, his lantern making monsters of the shadows overhead. She raised the window the rest of the way and leaned outside—then screamed when Scarbreigh grabbed her and tossed her from the trunk to the floor. A solid kick to her left leg curled her into a ball of pain and harsh cries.

"Get up! Now!" he hissed. His hair was tousled and a bruise marked his left cheek. Raven must have struck him.

Bethany struggled to her feet, throwing her hair back from her face and glaring at him. "You can't do this, Scarbreigh. I won't cooperate. Shoot me if you will, but I won't go with you."

Then she froze. Had she heard what she thought she had?

The ladder creaked again, the accompanying thump of boots on the rungs marking someone else's assent into the loft. Scarbreigh snarled fury at her and pulled her in front of him, the gun pressed against the small of her back.

"Scarbreigh? Lady Bethany?" called a voice.

No! It was Locke! Of all the people in the world who oughtn't to come up here it was Lord Locke.

"Scarbreigh, we must talk. I'm not armed. I mean you no harm."

Scarbreigh's hand that gripped Bethany's waist grew damp with sweat. "Go back to bed!" he shouted. "You'll get hurt if you don't."

"Hurt? Why would you want to hurt me?"

Locke's head and shoulders rose above the trap door and the earl came cautiously onto the loft's floorboards. Slowly he straightened, arms to the side, making it plain he had no weapons. His eyes met Bethany's, full of anguish.

"Go back down, Marc," Scarbreigh demanded. "Don't want to hurt you, but I will."

"No you won't, Kirk. We've been friends too long, but I heard Lady Bethany scream, and I can't allow you to hurt my wife. Put aside the weapon and let her come with me. Please."

Scarbreigh laughed, but only until additional footsteps tapped their way up the ladder. Lord Matthew joined Locke, more surely cutting off Scarbreigh's escape.

"What's going on, Scarbreigh? Lady Bethany, has he hurt you?" Lord Matthew's eyes were filled with worry.

"She's fine," Scarbreigh snapped at the same time Bethany shook her head.

She wasn't hurt. Scarbreigh had wounded her soul, and the cheek he'd slapped was bruised, but she was more herself than she'd been in a long while. Now she understood who her enemy was. And no matter what else happened, she would not let Scarbreigh hurt any of the people she loved, especially Lord Locke.

More footsteps followed the others, and Mr. Nicolas slipped into the loft with Locke and his brother.

Scarbreigh growled in Bethany's ear and his fingers dug into her skin, no doubt leaving fingernail marks and more bruises. She gritted her teeth as the marquess yanked her with him, towards the window.

"Scarbreigh," Mr. Nicolas said. "You can't get out of this. You've been found out. You can't rob justice, and it won't serve to hurt anyone, especially Lady Bethany. She doesn't deserve it."

"I'll kill her before I let anyone take her from me. She should have been mine long ago."

Shock turned Locke's face ashen. He'd figured out that Scarbreigh was the traitor, but he hadn't understood any more than Bethany had that the marquess had wanted *her* as much as he wanted the bracelet. If only she'd confessed her reservations about their old friend a long time ago, they might all have been prepared for this.

More footsteps announced more arrivals. They came like wraiths, men drifting into place behind Locke and the twins, along the opposite wall. More than a dozen of them. All strangers to Bethany.

And then Mr. Treadwell and Seaworth arrived. Dimity and the stableboys. Even Mrs. Callen and Mrs. Ford joined them. And last of all, came Lady Camille, her cheeks streaked with tears. Bethany's heart was crushed to see her so. There was no sign of dissipation about her, just devastation. Scarbreigh had truly lied.

At least Lady Katherine hadn't been awakened. Bethany wouldn't want her mother to witness any of this.

Scarbreigh ground his teeth in fury. His plans were ruined and he was cornered. He was now more dangerous than ever.

One of the strangers stepped forward, his gaze fastened on Scarbreigh. "Kirkwood Bannister, the Marquess of Scarbreigh, I'm Captain Garner, and I'm sorry to say I'm here, with a detail from London and in the name of the Crown, to place you under arrest for treason. You can make this easy or you can make it hard; either way you'll be in London by evening tomorrow. Now lay down your weapon and put your hands above your head."

Scarbreigh barked laughter, his grip around Bethany tightening. "Didn't you hear me? I'll kill her if you get in my way."

"And then what?" Locke coaxed. "You've only two bullets, my friend. You can do terrible damage with them, but these men will shoot you where you stand. How will that compensate for hurting Lady Bethany? How can you consider hurting her if you truly love her?"

Scarbreigh's heart pounded against Bethany's back. He was terrified, furious.

"Scarbreigh, please," Lady Camille cried. "You're throwing your life away."

"Not any worse than if I'd married you. I wouldn't have gone through with it, you know. I was waiting for the perfect opportunity to get to Bethany. That ring and the necklace I gave you were meant for *her*, not you. You can have them, but Bethany's mine. If those fools at the fair hadn't botched everything, we'd be long gone by now."

Lady Camille withered before Bethany's eyes, her sobs tearing Bethany apart. She was grateful when Mrs. Callen clutched her cousin to her ample bosom to comfort her.

"You can't have delusions about making Lady Bethany yours, Scarbreigh," Locke reasoned. "Even if you run off with her, you know she'll never love you. So what's the point of it?"

"She'll learn to love me. And you've no idea what's going on here, old friend. I've done my best to protect you, but I'll hurt you myself *if you don't get out of the way.*"

Lord Matthew said, "Mr. Collin discovered your network in Portugal, Scarbreigh, and in Spain unveiled your schemes. He was as brilliant at fashioning and deciphering codes as you are and managed to uncover enough of yours, he needed to send a sample of it home. What better way to expose and condemn you than to use your own code against you? He often sent Lady Bethany gifts from the Continent and found the bracelet in a shop in Lisbon. It seemed the most inconspicuous vehicle possible, and with Lord Whitton and Lord Matthew's input, they had it inscribed and sent to the Prince through Lady Bethany. It not only revealed your conspiracies but also the top five leaders of your band of traitors. Your name is at the head of the list. You know that, of course, because one of your French spies sent you word before he was caught and killed."

"Not sure what good it did anyone when Bethany had no way of deciphering it."

"She didn't need to," Mr. Nicolas said. "Misfortune strikes all of us, Lord Scarbreigh. I paid my aunt a visit last week, managed to secure a confession from her that the package arrived addressed to *Lady Bethany*." He emphasized the title to censure Scarbreigh's presumptuous use of her name. "It held ordinary missives from the Whitton men for both women, and a smaller package, containing the bracelet and a note for either Lord Matthew or myself. Our aunt admitted she was in a foul mood that day and opened the package meant for us. She couldn't make sense of the message, but she believed the bracelet was for Lady Bethany. She burned the letters and the code's cipher, and gave the jewelry to her daughter. If we'd gotten hold of all of it then, you'd have been in prison long ago."

CHAPTER 24

Bethany's head spun. If that had happened, mayhap what Scarbreigh and his cronies did to her *wouldn't* have happened. For a split second she was angry with her mother for her unwitting part in all of this. Nevertheless, the plot was Scarbreigh's doing. The realization mocked her from her memories, from the dark recesses of a dilapidated stable near the wharves of the Thames.

"Do you know what they did to me?" she spat, digging her own fingernails into Scarbreigh's arm. His grip tightened around her shoulders in response.

"Of course."

"And you allowed it. You gave them leave to beat and burn me, and—and—"

"Leave some bruises. They weren't to mark your face, break bones or take liberties, and that you have me to thank for."

Bethany barked caustic laughter. "But they did break bones, and they did take liberties. All the liberties they wanted, and I have *that* to thank *you* for."

He hissed in her ear, and she felt his grip weaken. "You're not suggesting—"

"There are some things you cannot fix, Scarbreigh. And one of them is the loss of virtue."

Bethany had never dreamed she could say these words aloud, let alone in front of spectators. She was convinced, however, that these people were sworn to silence and it felt good to confront her archenemy.

Body tense against hers, Scarbreigh was silent for a long while. Then "I don't believe you." His head swiveled towards the twins, his arm tightening again, the pistol gouging her right flank. "And you two are what I suspected. A couple of spies. Well, it doesn't matter. I've got the bracelet now. You've no proof. Move aside and let us out of here. I'm losing patience."

Lord Matthew said, "Actually, that bracelet's a copy and nothing but gibberish. Had it created to trap *you*. The original is at the Offices in London and anyone who matters knows all about it."

Locke added, "Forgive us, Lady Bethany, for not telling you our plan. I was on my way to do just that, and to urge you to let Scarbreigh have the bracelet. Instead I found you gone from your room. You weren't with Lady Camille and, considering Scarbreigh and his personal items were gone from his room, it wasn't hard to deduce he'd taken you with him."

"Scarbreigh, your crimes are known," Mr. Nicolas said. "You're the ringleader in a plot to assassinate Prince George. We've witnesses to your conspiracies, Lady Bethany not the least of them. The bowman and his cronies? We caught them, remember? Two days ago, they piped up like songbirds, rattled off a lengthy list of your lackeys, more than a hundred of them, including the two men who ransacked Lady Bethany's room and Whitton's library, looking for whatever might have Lord Whitton's message on it. Of course, they were looking for a hidden piece of paper or parchment, not a bracelet. Your accomplices were eager to reassure us that it was you who had Lord Whitton and his sons killed in Portugal, to stop them from revealing you. Unfortunately for you, the bracelet had already been sent."

"No!" Bethany cried, tears welling in her eyes. She twisted in Scarbreigh's arm enough to look him eye to eye. "It was an accident! Please tell me you didn't murder them."

Scarbreigh's top lip curled with animosity. "Ah, but I did, my sweet. They weren't ordinary men and needed to be gotten rid of."

"No!" Bethany sobbed.

Locke said gruffly, "Perhaps it was because we've been friends for so long I couldn't see the truth. It's taken us more than a year to hunt you down, old friend. You were one of our toughest assignments."

"Assignments?" Scarbreigh shrilled. *"Assignments?* You're one of them?"

The man's shock allowed Bethany to twist in Scarbreigh's arm a bit more, trying to work her way free. She bit her lip when he dug the pistol's nose even deeper into her flesh.

Locke nodded. "Yes. I'm Secret Service for the Crown; as are the twins; as were my father and all three of the Montgomery men. Lord Whitton finished training me as an agent after my father died. I loved him dearly, and Lord Christian and Mr. Collin truly were the best friends I've ever had." He swung his hand towards his servants. "My so-called retainers here at Moorewood work for the Service in a variety of capacities, except for Lady Bethany's abigail, Melissa. You've led us a merry chase, but your conspiracy has failed. It's time to surrender."

Bethany's head spun with what she was hearing. They were all part of the Secret Service? Locke? The twins? Even Mr. Treadwell? It made sense in a dubious way but it was hard to digest. Scarbreigh's trembling became volcanic and Bethany feared he'd lose control and fire his pistol.

Feared he'd kill her, either by accident or in retribution, and then shoot Locke.

"The renowned Lord Locke. My dear friend since my youth," the marquess spat, his face twisted with hatred. "I cannot believe I spared you. I insisted two of my men detain you *safely* at the fair, so that they and two others could get to Bethany. If everything had gone according to plan, we'd have left that night, rather than enduring this disgusting scene now. Had I known what you were, I'd have paid them extra to cut out your heart. You've always wanted whatever I've wanted or had, haven't you, Locke? Every woman for whom I've set my cap, you've lured from me. And you didn't even want them. That's why you married Lady Bethany, to undermine me. I meant what I said. I'll kill her before I let you have her."

"You're daft!" Locke snapped. "I never wanted any woman until I married Lady Bethany, which didn't happen until after she'd refused you. I wish I'd caught you out before that night at Almack's last April. I could have stopped you before you did what you did to her. Perhaps my lady will find a way to forgive you," he added, "but as for me, it will take a lifetime. You offered to marry her so that you wouldn't have to kidnap her, didn't you? And when that didn't work, you tried several ways to get to her. Even proposing to Lady Camille was part of the plan. You hoped your engagement would lower everyone's guard and give you access to Lady Bethany that you hadn't gotten any other way."

Bethany sagged under the weight of such ugliness. Scarbreigh stumbled as he held on to her.

"How could you, Scarbreigh?" she cried. "We all grew up with you, shared our homes and our lives with you. How could you treat our family so vilely? We all loved you."

"Liar. You're all liars. So is that pig-headed fop to whom our frivolous countrymen want to hand the crown when the king takes to his grave. George the Fourth? George the Fool, you mean. He'll ruin us. Mark my words. It won't matter, though. We've a second, more valuable objective. To see that Napoleon rises again. I may have failed at my part. The others will not."

"And we'll do our best to stop them, but your part is over," Locke replied. "Now you can only make things worse for yourself. Let's get you downstairs, get everything in order, and get some sleep before we head off to London when the sun rises."

Scarbreigh looked over his shoulder at the window and Bethany saw fear darken Locke's face.

"You can't seriously think about jumping. We're nearly three floors high, Scarbreigh, and the ground below is rock-hard and strewn with gravel. Doubt you'd survive it and certainly not without broken bones."

Ignoring all of them, Scarbreigh hauled Bethany with him as he stepped backward onto the trunk. Bethany stumbled and floundered, but the marquess dragged her up in front of him. She said a litany of prayers, unsure if any of them were heard.

"Shoot me if you must, but I can't let you do it, Scarbreigh," Locke shouted before he charged towards the marquess, his fists doubled.

"Locke! Don't!" Bethany screamed.

The pistol's weight left her and a loud crack had all of the observers ducking or leaping away, the women screeching. Lord Locke stopped in his tracks not two feet away, a cloud of dust, straw, and chipped wood bursting at his feet. Rage flashed in his eyes.

Scarbreigh leveled his aim more surely this time. Growling with fury, Bethany bucked her head against his chin, but he struck her hard in the shoulder with the pistol's grip and again pointed at Locke.

"Kirk, stop," Bethany begged. "I'll go with you. They won't hurt you as long as you hang on to me."

Locke shook his head in disagreement, but Scarbreigh's hold loosened a fraction.

"Please, Scarbreigh," Locke begged. "At least let us all go downstairs, where we can talk it out."

"You cannot tempt me, *old friend*. But as for you? She cannot love a man who is dead."

Time stood still for Bethany as Scarbreigh's body tightened, as the gun's muzzle lifted. Her breath left her at knowing the marquess intended to kill Locke. No! She couldn't allow it, whatever the consequences to her. The anguish on Locke's face told her that he knew what she would do.

"NO!" she roared, shoving backwards and throwing the marquess off-balance.

"No!" Locke cried.

Scarbreigh lost control and the gun fired overhead, then he dropped it as he stumbled into the open window, his right arm wind-milling. His feet tangled with Bethany's, tripping her, and she fell backward into him. Locke leaped toward her, hands outstretched. Their fingertips met, but Scarbreigh threw both arms around her waist and fell, taking Bethany with him.

* * *

Bethany shrieked, clawing the air, and in a moment of unbelievable providence, caught the window's frame with both hands. She cried out again as Scarbreigh's weight wrenched her back and shoulders and the window sill cut into her hands.

"Bethany!" Locke shouted, lunging forward and throwing his arms around her to hold her up. A rush of bodies followed, Lord Matthew grabbing Bethany's right wrist, Mr. Nicolas the left, Mr. Treadwell bringing the lantern to shed light on the scene, and far too many offering help they could not give.

She sobbed, agonized at having her body stretched to its breaking point, the men trying to lift her up and Scarbreigh dragging her down. She felt Scarbreigh slipping down her body, his grasp at her waist dropping to her hips and then to her knees. If he didn't let go, his weight could tear her arms from her shoulders or break her spine.

Gritting her teeth, she looked down to see Scarbreigh losing his battle and sliding to her ankles. The insane irony drifted into her mind that the man who'd ordered her kidnapping was now clinging to the legs and feet his men had tortured and defaced with scars. His gaze met hers, and even in the flickering lantern light, she saw the fear in his eyes. He didn't want to die; he was simply desperate enough to hope he could somehow pull off his escape. And in his delusion, he thought he could take Bethany with him.

Searing pain lanced through her. She could take no more. She knew he realized what she was about to do the instant the panic flamed across his face. Then she jerked her right foot free, her slipper fluttering to the ground, and left him to grapple for the other foot ... and fail.

* * *

The bile rose to Bethany's throat at Scarbreigh's shout of horror and the sickening crunch of bones as he hit the ground. Then hands drew her inside the loft, voices drowning out her every thought. People everywhere asked her questions as they laid her down on the floor. Boots thundered on the ladder as men scampered downstairs to the yard.

"Lady Bethany, look at me," Locke insisted, cupping her face between his hands. "Stay awake, darling."

Her head swam and agony lanced through her, every muscle aching, her left shoulder a river of pain.

"Mr. Treadwell, do your magic, please," Locke insisted, and the butler—was that what he was?—came to check her body, testing joints, moving muscles that screamed in agony.

"Only twists and strains, my lord, sir," Treadwell replied at last. "She'll be terribly sore a good while, but nothing's broken."

Bethany heard tears, not her own. Then Lady Camille pressed her cheek to Bethany's. Whispers fluttered against her ear, her cousin's pleas for forgiveness.

"I took care of you after they tortured you. How could Scarbreigh order them to do what they did to you?" Lady Camille sobbed. "I feel as if I betrayed you just caring for him."

"No, dearest," Bethany murmured weakly, resting a hand on her cousin's shoulder. "He made you love him, as he made everyone believe in him. It's he who betrayed all of us and I who am ashamed I never confessed my doubts to you or to anyone else."

Her vision faded as footsteps approached. Lady Camille moved aside as Lord Matthew and Mr. Nicolas came to stroke her arms and encourage her. Someone reported that Scarbreigh was dead.

"Landed on a rock and broke his neck," an unfamiliar voice said, and Bethany couldn't deny the additional irony. Scarbreigh would have been hanged as a traitor, and the hangman's noose would have done no less.

Then what seemed like hundreds of hands lifted her, carefully handing her from person to person down the ladder, and then Locke bore her, cradled in his arms, to the manor. He was as gentle as she imagined anyone could be, but the pain overwhelmed her and unconsciousness brought her blessed relief from the misery of both body and soul.

* * *

Dawn drew the nightmares of the early morning hours into vivid, undeniable focus. This had not been just one of Bethany's horrific nightmares. Lord Scarbreigh was dead.

The manor came alive with what seemed an army of people coming and going, making preparations for London, grabbing carriages and horses, and a wagon bearing Lord Scarbreigh's shrouded body. Lady Katherine and Lady Camille insisted on spending the day at Bethany's bedside. Their faces were gray with shock and grief. Bethany was grateful for the laudanum Mr. Treadwell gave her to manage both sorrow and pain.

Not long after full sunrise, Locke came to beg her forgiveness for having to leave. He and the twins must report to their superiors, in person, the outcome of their confrontation with Scarbreigh, and then he would be home as soon as he was given leave.

The twins pressed farewell kisses to the ladies' cheeks, while Mr. Treadwell, Mrs. Ford, Mrs. Callen and Melissa all pledged to watch over their mistress in their absence. Sleep took Bethany away again.

When late afternoon stretched its fingers through her window, Bethany came awake feeling the quiet of her surroundings blanketing her in unfamiliar and precious peace. The monster who'd killed her father and brothers and done unspeakable things to her was gone, his minions captured, and none of them could ever do anything to her again. It was as if Providence had opened a window and let in the sunlight.

The thought so liberated her that she dared rise from her bed and walk gingerly around her room. Lady Katherine protested, but Bethany said she was getting stiffer by the minute lying there. She was admittedly miserable, but she'd had worse injuries on horseback and refused to let them keep her bedridden.

Insisting on taking supper in the dining room, Bethany was grateful to have her cousin and mother to lean on when each step downstairs jarred muscles and vertebrae that had been cruelly abused.

Mrs. Ford's offering was as simple as Bethany had hoped, the cook's fluttering concern endearing. Mrs. Callen brought cold compresses and cushions, and Mr. Treadwell and Melissa fussed over her precisely enough to remind her she did not have to deal with all of this alone.

But mostly the three women chose to reminisce about better times and better memories, and shed the tears that needed release.

CHAPTER 25

Moorewood's carriage rounded a corner in the blush of late evening, bearing Locke and the twins back to Moorewood. Five and a half days they'd been gone, and the scrapes, bruises, and strained muscles from pulling Lady Bethany inside the loft did not enjoy the vehicle's bouncing. Locke could only imagine how Lady Bethany felt.

"Wish you weren't leaving us," Lord Matthew said at last. They'd spoken little during their trip from London, when Locke had announced the decision he'd made. "Can't imagine doing this job without you."

"I'll still be around, just in a different capacity."

"Not the same," Mr. Nicolas replied. "Scarbreigh wasn't your fault, Locke. You needn't feel guilty."

"I don't. It's a miserably ugly revelation to learn a man I believed was a cherished friend was a traitor and to have to return him to his mother with a broken neck. Never mind having to explain the particulars surrounding his death to our superiors." He sighed and shook his head. "But I didn't create the monster. It was his choice. Truthfully, it all centers on Lady Bethany. I was so worried about her, I didn't stay focused on the evidence, which put her in greater danger. The reason we're cautioned to abstain from emotional entanglements, after all. How our fathers did it, I don't know, but I can't."

"But—"

"I can't and I won't. Do you understand she was willing to die for me? Do you know how that makes me feel? Besides, she knows everything. I can't hide it from her now, and she'd worry too much about me when I'm gone. I want to spend the rest of my life with her, which would likely work best if I didn't get myself killed."

Sighing deeply, Mr. Nicolas shifted in his seat. "By now I'd think you know Lady Bethany's made of sturdier stuff than that. She might not like being your excuse for abandoning what you've done so admirably for so many years."

Locke sent him a cutting look that had his cheeks reddening. "And she might appreciate reassurance that what she suffered in this disaster won't ever happen again, at least not because of me. It was reprehensible. That you two didn't tell me the truth about her still infuriates me. If I'd dealt with her wrong, I might have lost her, and of that I couldn't have forgiven you."

Shamefaced, the twins focused on something outside opposite windows.

The carriage slowed as they passed the stables and rumbled into the yard.

"Ah, Lady Bethany and Lady Camille await us on the front porch," he said. "It appears your carriage is ready. Let's make this as uncomplicated as possible, shall we?"

The twins disembarked, pulling their jackets around them in the cool autumn evening. They greeted their sister and Lady Bethany, then went to oversee the movement of their baggage from one coach to the other. Lady Bethany came to gingerly clasp the hands Locke held out to her. He pressed a tender kiss to her cheek, and they whispered their greetings in each other's ears. Locke was glad to see that though Lady Bethany's smile was weary and touched with sadness, the light in her alluring green eyes shown as brightly as ever.

"Lady Whitton?" he queried.

"She went home as she'd planned, the day after you left for London."

"She knows everything that happened?"

"Everything but the worst of what happened to me. Still, she knows I was kidnapped and why, and she's understandably distraught by her unintentional part in it. I'm glad she wasn't there to see what happened with Scarbreigh. I imagine if witnessing his treason hadn't caused her heart to fail, she would have shot him herself."

Locke's chuckle was grim. He turned to examine Lady Camille, her pale face and reddened eyes attesting to the depth of her mourning, and yet improved from when they'd parted five days ago.

"My lord," she murmured, offering a courtly curtsy when he greeted her. "How fared the proceedings?"

He swallowed hard against the knot in his throat, certain Scarbreigh's betrayal of England was nothing compared to what he'd done to this gentle, lovely woman.

"As we expected, Lady Camille," he replied, adopting her formality because he sensed she needed to hide behind it to maintain her composure. "His mother's expectedly devastated, but she admitted that her son had changed through the years, had grown unsettled and secretive, criticizing the Prince Regent and bringing friends to his country estate who often extolled Napoleon's virtues. They'd fought over it more than once."

"He lost his titles, did he not?"

"Yes, I fear so. The Dowager Lady Scarbreigh must relinquish the family properties, and she'll suffer the consequences of Scarbreigh's offenses for the rest of her life. At least she has a sister who's offered her a place in her husband's dowager house. She's a tough old bird, if you'll pardon my language, my lady. I believe she'll manage. But how are you?"

Lady Camille cast him a thin smile. "Relieved to hear it's over, sad for Lady Scarbreigh but glad she has recourse, and determined to survive, even if at the moment it doesn't seem possible."

"My condolences for your loss in all its facets."

"Thank you, my lord. I only pray we can learn to forgive him."

Locke nodded his understanding and walked slowly towards the Hannaford coach. He pushed aside his darker feelings and offered his hand to the twins in conciliation. To be forgiven, one must forgive; and he loved these two men, also like brothers. He treasured their kinship and refused to let Lord Scarbreigh's memory take anything more from him than the man himself already had done.

* * *

"Please visit often, Cam," Bethany begged, sad to see her go but aware it was necessary. "Locke will leave again soon, and you know I don't relish the idea of living here alone."

Lady Camille nodded. "I promise, Beth, but for now I need some time to myself. Please don't fret for me. I've sensed forever something was wrong, and I confess I've had a bitter seed of jealousy inside me since the day Scarbreigh proposed to you. Not towards you. Towards him. There's something ignominious about being considered second best, and while I was willing to swallow my pride and do whatever I must to win his heart, I feared I'd never have all of him."

"Oh, Cam, I'm so sorry," Bethany said, grief and guilt aching inside her. "He didn't deserve you, you know. He didn't want me, not really, just the information he thought I had. And to prove he could dominate me. That was always our relationship. You must keep in mind that the man we all loved wouldn't have done what he did in his right mind. I care deepest about the implications the affair will have for you."

Lady Camille smiled with sadness. "It will be hard to face our peers when the trials begin and the truth comes out. Some will doubt me, no matter what I say. When I'm ready to reenter to society, I hope you'll go with me."

"Without hesitation."

"You're alright?"

Bethany nodded, gingerly flexing her arms and her tender hands and wrists. "They're healing well enough," she said, and they were, but she could not say the same about her heart. That would take much longer.

Lord Matthew called to Lady Camille, who hugged Bethany hard, murmured her farewells, and then hurried to Hannaford's carriage. Closed inside, she and the twins waved as the vehicle lumbered away.

Locke turned to examine Bethany. His fingertips lightly grazed the fading bruise on her cheek. "Truthfully. How do you feel?"

"I'm better now that you're home. What about you, my love?"

He smiled and nodded. "I feel the same. You received my message?"

"Yes. Mrs. Ford has our supper waiting for us in your bedchambers, and the, uh, *servants* are already gathered in the entryway waiting to hear your report."

He escorted her inside the manor and stood near the bottom of the staircase so that all could see and hear him.

"I have news to offer of a lesser importance before we discuss The Marquess of Scarbreigh. You all know Geoffrey Matheson and his accomplices were rounded up right after Lady Locke and I married. They were this week found guilty and imprisoned for their burglaries. They'll not likely see the sunlight beyond the bars of their cells until they're long in the tooth." He glanced at Bethany and saw relief on her face.

"Was Viscount Beckwood caught?" Mr. Treadwell asked.

"Yes, as were Sir Shreeves and Baron Gladwell," Locke replied.

Then followed a deeper recounting of the proceedings in London than Locke had given Lady Camille, including the three men who'd tried to shoot Lady Bethany with the arrow also being delivered for trial. One of them admitted he'd stabbed Shadow. The four who'd followed Lady Locke in the park and attacked Lord Locke had been arrested, as well as the two thugs who'd poisoned Carter and ransacked Lady Bethany's bedchambers at Moorewood, stolen her diary and music box, and then, finding nothing, burned them.

"The last pair also invaded Whitton and destroyed Lady Locke's Dresden dolls, never imagining the information was contained on something as elaborate as the bracelet. Beyond that, agents have already detained a good number of Scarbreigh's co-conspirators. The rest will follow soon."

"Then it all turned out proper," Mrs. Callen said.

"It did. Although I think we'll agree that while we're justified in our relief and can commend each other for jobs well done, the outcome doesn't exactly lend itself to celebration. Besides, we still have worries about Napoleon to face."

"It's been a good run, Lord Locke," Dimity commented. "What happens now?"

Locke sighed, sharing a meaningful look with Mr. Treadwell—the man he'd always presented as his valet-butler.

"I've resigned my position in the Service," he said. Gasps surrounded them while Bethany's eyes flew wide. She'd barely set her husband's work straight in her mind, and now it was all undone. Then he raised a hand to calm them. "Because I've taken another," he added. The murmurs quieted.

"All of you have performed admirably. Some of you were assigned here solely to protect Lady Bethany and expect to go elsewhere now that the matter's resolved. Others have worked here for years, a few under my father. Truthfully, all of you and Moorewood itself have served well as a sanctuary for my missions.

"Because of that, the Service wishes this estate to carry on as a place to exchange covert intelligence or as a refuge for agents on assignment. When needed, I'll serve as liaison between those agents and London but my only disguise will be secrecy, the same as yours.

"Of course, I still have other properties to manage, here and on the Continent, and the responsibilities of my title. I must spend a respectable amount of time away. Lady Locke may not always wish to join me, which means someone has to keep affairs running smoothly here and make sure she's safe." He offered a wry smile at the whispers and soft laughter that rippled through the gathering. "Any who wish to remain here must inform me by week's end."

"I, for one, sir, would rather serve under no one but you, as I did your father before you," Mr. Treadwell said in a tremulous voice. Mrs. Callen and Mrs. Ford agreed, as did others.

Locke smiled gratefully. "I couldn't do it without you, and I'm eternally grateful."

Bethany's eyes drifted over the crowd, people "disguised" as gardeners and stablemen; housekeepers, maids and footmen; cooks and kitchen maids. Her gaze landed on Melissa's solemn smile. As Bethany's personal maid and a witness to Scarbreigh's death, she'd needed to understand what Moorewood was about. After learning the truth, she could not remain here without swearing her loyalty. She'd done so without hesitation.

"Now, friends," Locke said, relief easing the look on his face. "If you'll all excuse me, it's been a difficult five days and I wish to retire. Please enjoy the evening off. You deserve it. My lady?"

Bethany was grateful to head upstairs but hardly able to fathom her husband's announcement. His resignation would change their lives in a way she could hardly imagine. She sensed he'd done it for her but wondered if he would someday resent her for it?

* * *

"Taylor-Ward was set to tackle your rooms this week, was he not?" Locke said as they climbed the stairs. When Lady Bethany nodded, he added, "Probably not convenient under the circumstances, but did he meet your expectations?"

The twinkle that sprang into her eye chased away the remaining melancholy. "He just finished yesterday and exceeded my hopes. Would you like to see it?"

"Of course. And afterward I shall shed myself of my travel clothes and the dust that came home with them." He gave her a tender look. "And then I very much need to spend some time with my wife."

Lady Bethany gave him a heart-warming smile. "I'll see she's sends for you when you're presentable."

He laughed but afterward drew in a breath of surprise when Lady Bethany opened her bedroom door to him. It was her, he concluded, the softer tones of rose and pale pink against light sea green and bronze. The bed was canopied in silk, the bedcovers a faint floral design, and the curtains that matched were a good deal lighter and airier than the old ones. They hung from ceiling to floor and were tied back from the window with cream colored cords. The floor had been expertly refinished, the beige rugs on top it luxurious.

"It's exquisite," he said. "I've no doubt my mother is standing on the other side of heaven's veil applauding you." His eyes radiated his love as he added, "She would have adored you. Come, my sweet. Keep me company."

Lady Bethany's cheeks reddened when Locke pulled his key from his trouser pocket and unlocked the door that joined their rooms. He kept hold of her hand when they drifted into the formerly forbidden realm of his bedchamber, which bore the inviting aroma of the food set on the table by the window. It was a handsome, tasteful room, and he could see Bethany approved. But how soon would she feel welcome here? He grasped her shoulders in his hands and met her gaze squarely.

"Tell me true, Sweetheart. Has it been too hard? I hated not being here for you."

"It's been painful. Especially." She bit her lip. "Most especially with trying to forgive myself," she murmured.

Locke frowned at her. This he hadn't expected. "Forgive yourself? Whatever for?"

* * *

Bethany hesitated, and then confessed her part in Scarbreigh's death. "I despised him," she admitted between gritted teeth. "Because he lied and simpered and connived his way into our confidence. He killed my father and brothers. He ordered his minions to do what they did to me. He

216

hurt you. He destroyed Lady Camille. And I knew that if I didn't fight back, he'd take me with him, even to death."

Locke sighed. "I was terrified for you. I couldn't reach him, but if I had, I'd have thrown him off you. There's no crime in self-defense, my dear Beth." He searched her face. "What you did made me glad. If I'm wrong to feel that way, then so be it. I hated everything he did to you and to England. At least this way, he brought about his own death."

"It's one more hideous memory to bear."

"I know. But we'll do it together. You did what you had to do, my love, and you were not wrong."

Locke hugged her gently and then led her to his dressing room where he settled on a stool and removed his boots. Afterward he doffed his shirt and rose to wash up in his laving bowl.

So caught in admiring Locke's broad shoulders and powerful form, she didn't at first realize her surroundings. When she did, her eyes rounded in surprise. Along one wall hung the suits, fine shirts, neck ties, boots, and riding clothes that belonged to the man Bethany knew as Marcus Ashburn, the Earl of Locke. On the other side, were clean and neatly mended but obviously worn peasant clothes, and over there were groups of shoes, hats, wigs, and trappings that had no place in an earl's wardrobe. It was an actor's haven, a place to don a persona and go on masquerade. No wonder Locke hadn't wanted her here. She'd have been shocked to see it and would have insisted on explanations.

Locke smiled at her and shrugged. "It maintained my anonymity. I'll have it all placed in storage tomorrow. The agents we'll entertain may have use for such things, but I will not."

"Are you sure you won't miss it? You've worked so hard for it." She panicked at the thought he might blame her for having to leave it behind.

"Honestly? I'm tired of it. Of living in the streets with murderers and thieves, of lying and, I confess, having to steal. Weary of pretending to be someone else, of passing notes and searching for clues; getting shot at and stabbed, and doing my best to avoid getting either poisoned or hanged. It was a charade, one which I am very good at and proud of for the right reasons, but I'm finished with it and ready for something else."

Bethany smiled tremulously. "Like what?"

"Like you," he said, his voice husky. He pulled her against him and pressed a kiss to her lips that spoke of love and desire and deeper promises.

Bethany admired his handsome eyes, his strong jaw, his smile. Her fingers brushed a pale scar on his chest, one of several. Scars that attested to what he'd just admitted, old wounds very much like her own. She paused to savor its significance in her heart. His damp skin felt cool against hers, the male scent of him delicious.

"My life will change in every way imaginable now, you realize," he murmured, kissing her ear.

"Both our lives," she agreed, humming in pleasure.

"As I said to the others, it is my duty to visit Westminster regularly. No longer in secret or in disguise, of course, but without fail. Please journey with me, darling. I need the world to know we're building a life together. That I want to face all of life's trials with you beside me. To love you, to have children with you, and to grow old with you."

Such tantalizing words burrowed deep into the core of Bethany's being, sparking the overpowering heat of desire. She threaded her fingers into his thick, dark hair and pulled his head down until their lips almost touched.

"I would follow you to the ends of the earth, my darling," she murmured. "Such is my heart's desire. For love, for our posterity, and for a lifetime, I belong to you."

Locke's dark blue eyes shone with pleasure, his heart-melting dimples framing his adorable smile. "Beyond a lifetime, Lady Locke. From this moment and into forever, I am your devoted servant."

Susan was born and raised a California girl but is grateful to have lived on the Oregon coast and in the Rocky Mountains of northern Utah. She's now enjoying living with her husband in the incomparable beauty of the Redwood forest, nestled against the rugged coast of Northern California.

Susan raised a tribe of children, making ends meet as a registered nurse and lactation consultant, and now her tribe members have tribes of their own and she just doesn't get to see enough of them. She loves to travel and is thrilled with a good movie or a great book, but writing is her passion. She writes almost anything, especially epic fantasy and romance. *Saving Lord Whitton's Daughter* is her first Regency Romance.

Susan would love to hear your comments. Please review her book at your favorite retailer and at Goodreads. Take a peek at her website, susantietjen.blogspot.com, and/ or drop her a note at: stietjen.author@gmail.com.